Selected Stories

Follies and Vices of the Modern Elizabethan Age

Selected Stories

Follies and Vices of the Modern Elizabethan Age

Selected by the author with end list of follies and vices, and quest themes

Nicholas Hagger

Winchester, UK
Washington, USA

First published by O-Books, 2015
O-Books is an imprint of John Hunt Publishing Ltd., Laurel House, Station Approach,
Alresford, Hants, SO24 9JH, UK
office1@jhpbooks.net
www.johnhuntpublishing.com

For distributor details and how to order please visit the 'Ordering' section on our website.

ISBN: 978 1 78099 753 7

A CIP catalogue record for this book is available from the British Library.

Design: Stuart Davies

Printed in the USA by Edwards Brothers Malloy

Books published by Nicholas Hagger

The Fire and the Stones
Selected Poems
The Universe and the Light
A White Radiance
A Mystic Way
Awakening to the Light
A Spade Fresh with Mud
The Warlords
Overlord
A Smell of Leaves and Summer
The Tragedy of Prince Tudor
The One and the Many
Wheeling Bats and a Harvest Moon
The Warm Glow of the Monastery Courtyard
The Syndicate
The Secret History of the West
The Light of Civilization
Classical Odes
Overlord, one-volume edition
Collected Poems 1958–2005
Collected Verse Plays
Collected Stories
The Secret Founding of America
The Last Tourist in Iran
The Rise and Fall of Civilizations
The New Philosophy of Universalism
The Libyan Revolution
Armageddon
The World Government
The Secret American Dream
A New Philosophy of Literature
A View of Epping Forest
My Double Life 1: This Dark Wood
My Double Life 2: A Rainbow over the Hills
Selected Poems: Quest for the One

"'Folly', 'foolishness, lack of good sense'; 'a foolish act, behaviour, idea'" (*Concise Oxford Dictionary*).

"'Vice', 'evil or grossly immoral conduct, a particular form of this'; 'depravity, an evil habit, a particular form of depravity'; 'a defect of character or behaviour'" (*Concise Oxford Dictionary*).

*

"Take care thou be not made a fool by flatterers, for even the wisest men are abused by these. Know therefore that flatterers are the worst kind of traitors, for they will strengthen thy imperfections, encourage thee in all evils, correct thee in nothing, but so shadow and paint thy follies and vices as thou shalt never, by their will, discover good from evil, or vice from virtue."

Sir Walter Raleigh,
'Instructions to His Son and to Posterity', 1603–1605

"The last of verbal injuries to our neighbour which I shall mention is flattery.... A great man's vices shall still be called virtues, his deformities beauty and his most absurd follies the height of ingenuity."

Richard Allestree,
The Government of the Tongue, 1674

"In dunce's dance I take the lead,
Books useless, numerous my creed,
Which I can't understand or read."

Sebastian Brant,
Stultifera Navis (*Ship of Fools*), 1494

The front cover shows a painting by Hieronymus Bosch, *The Stone Operation*, also known as *The Cure of Folly* (c.1488 or later), in which a patient is being treated for madness by having a stone removed from his brain. For a fee the 'surgeon' in a funnel hat, which at the time indicated a charlatan, is drilling into the patient's skull to remove a stone. The woman, probably the patient's wife, wears a book on her head, which at the time suggested folly. She is also being duped. This is Bosch's view of folly and vice c.1488.

Nicholas Hagger's volumes of stories from which this selection was made:

- *A Spade Fresh with Mud*: Collected Stories, Volume 1 (1995)
- *A Smell of Leaves and Summer*: Collected Stories, Volume 2 (1995)
- *Wheeling Bats and a Harvest Moon*: Collected Stories, Volume 3 (1999)
- *The Warm Glow of the Monastery Courtyard*: Collected Stories, Volume 4 (1999)
- *In the Brilliant Autumn Sunshine*: Collected Stories, Volume 5 (2007)

Collected Stories: A Thousand and One Mini-Stories or Verbal Paintings (2007) includes all the above five volumes.

Note to reader

The stories within Part One are by and large arranged in chronological order, as are the stories in Part Two. The two Parts are parallel rather than consecutive, and so the first story in each of the Parts is numbered 1. The stories are grouped under the titles of the volumes in which they first appeared. Follies and vices, and quest themes, are listed on pp.235–241.

CONTENTS

Preface to *Selected Stories*

The 86 stories of Parts One and Two were written during a period of 40 years between 1966 and 2006. They describe the fortunes of an Englishman, Philip Rawley, in the UK and other countries from late youth to early old age during five decades of the second Elizabethan Age. Most of these stories originally appeared within four separate volumes between 1995 and 1998: *A Spade Fresh with Mud*; *A Smell of Leaves and Summer*; *Wheeling Bats and a Harvest Moon*; and *The Warm Glow of the Monastery Courtyard*. Others appeared in a fifth volume, *In the Brilliant Autumn Sunshine*, which was in *Collected Stories* (2007). *Collected Stories* presented 1,001 stories, a tally that echoes *A Thousand and One Nights* (also known as *Arabian Nights' Entertainments*).

The fundamental theme of world literature

In *A New Philosophy of Literature* I identified the metaphysical and secular aspects of the fundamental theme of world literature: the quest for metaphysical Reality, and condemnation of social follies and vices in relation to an implied virtue. This selection reflects the fundamental theme. It presents stories exposing the follies and vices of our time (Part One), and stories on Philip Rawley's quest and his growing awareness of the unity of the universe (Part Two).

The quest for Reality

The quest for Reality and the promise of immortality go back 4,600 years to the Mesopotamian *Epic of Gilgamesh* and follow the Mystic Way which can be found in the literature of every culture and generation. Confronted with the seeming finality of death, the soul turns away from bodily attachment, is purged and illumined, and undergoes a transformation that enables it to perceive the unity of the universe and sense the possibility of its own survival. The stories in Part Two are in the 4,600-year-old tradition of the metaphysical aspect of the fundamental theme. *See* pp.238–241 for quest themes in Part Two, all of which involve intense experiences of the oneness of the universe, Nature and history and awareness of the One.

Follies and vices

In every decade from the 16th century to today literary works have also looked back to the classical world and reflected its condemnation of social follies and vices.

What is the difference between 'follies' and 'vices'? Folly is associated with foolish acts; vices are associated with immoral, depraved or evil behaviour. Folly exposes people to vice. Some foolish acts are due to poor decisions. Sometimes people are too trusting and are taken advantage of by unscrupulous people whose behaviour is immoral or evil. An example of such gullibility can be found in the painting by Hieronymus Bosch, *The Stone Operation,* which is also known as *The Cure of Folly* (c.1488 or later). The painting shows a man being treated for a mental disorder by having a stone removed from his brain. The 'surgeon' (shown wearing a funnel hat which at the time indicated a charlatan) drills into the man's skull to remove a stone. Both he and a woman who is probably his wife (who has a book on her head, suggesting folly) are being conned. They will pay the 'surgeon' an extortionate fee for the pointless operation. The folly of the couple has made them victims of the immoral, evil 'surgeon' whose unscrupulous money-seeking is a vice. Follies are different from, but inextricably linked to, vices. Many vices could not be indulged without compliant foolishness.

A comprehensive list of the follies and vices in world literature can be found in the index of *A New Philosophy of Literature*. The list includes (F indicating folly):

> abandonment; acquisitiveness; alcoholism; ambition; arrogance; asperity; betrayal; bigotry; blindness; boastfulness; bravado; brutality; bullying; capriciousness; concealment; confidence tricks; corruptibility; corrupting worldly power; corruption; credulousness (F); cruelty; cynicism; debauchery; deceit; defiance; denial of principles; destructiveness; dictatorial behaviour; discontent; dishonesty; being domineering; drunkenness; duplicity; eagerness to marry (F); egotism; egotistical sensuality; enmity; envy; excessive mourning; exploitation; fantasies; fortune-hunting; frivolity; greed; hatred; hedonism; hubristic contentment; hypocrisy; idleness; illusions (F); impudence; inconstancy;

infatuation; infidelity; inhumanity; insincerity; interference; jealousy; lack of truthfulness; lust; lust for power; massacres; meanness; mercenary motives; miserliness; misjudgement; mistreatment; money-seeking; moral blindness; murder; naïve beliefs (F); neglect; nihilism; obstinacy; overreaching (F); patricide; pedantry; persecution; petulance; pretension; pride; prodigality; rebelliousness; revenge; ruthlessness; seduction; self-centredness; self-conceit; self-deceit (F); self-interestedness; self-love; shadiness; shrewishness; snobbishness; social climbing; strictness; swindling; thieving/stealing; threatening behaviour; treachery; trickery; troublemaking; tyrannical ruthlessness; tyranny; unscrupulousness; usurpation; vanity; villainy; voluptuousness; war; warmongering; and pursuit of wealth.

These same follies and vices can all be found in the 1,001 stories in my *Collected Stories*. They can all be found in this selection (with the exception of 'patricide'). The list below replicates the one above, and each bracketed number indicates a numbered story in Part One of this selection in which each folly or vice can be found (Q before a number indicating a story in Part Two, 'Quest for the One'):

abandonment (39, 42); acquisitiveness (10, 24, 25); alcoholism (23, 42); ambition (18, Q29); arrogance (6, 29); asperity (38, Q28); betrayal (2); bigotry (Q1); blindness (22, Q32, Q34); boastfulness (12, 34); bravado (12, 15); brutality (16); bullying (17, 24); capriciousness (15); concealment (Q15); confidence tricks (3, 12, 23, Q19); corruptibility (13); corrupting worldly power (10, 16, 28); corruption (10); credulousness (F, 12, Q19); cruelty (16, 27); cynicism (20); debauchery (14); deceit (12); defiance (Q14); denial of principles (32); destructiveness (42); dictatorial behaviour (24, 36); discontent (14); dishonesty (12); being domineering (17); drunkenness (1); duplicity (10); eagerness to marry (32); egotism (3, 23); egotistical sensuality (12); enmity (4); envy (8); excessive mourning (14); exploitation (13, 23, 26, Q29); fantasies (23, 35); fortune-hunting (11); frivolity (Q32); greed (10, 24, 41); hatred (33); hedonism (11); hubristic contentment (4, 6, 11); hypocrisy (1, 36); idleness (Q20); illusions (F, 34, 35); impudence (43); inconstancy (1); infatuation (12, 14); infidelity (1, 13, 28); inhumanity (33, 36); insincerity (11, 12); interference

(7, Q26); jealousy (8); lack of truthfulness (39, 41); lust (12, 14); lust for power (28); massacres (33, 36); meanness (4); mercenary motives (41); miserliness (24); misjudgement (32); mistreatment (37); money-seeking (24, 41); moral blindness (33); murder (9, 20, 24); naïve beliefs (F, 5, 15, 25); neglect (42); nihilism (14, Q2); obstinacy (3, 32); overreaching (F, 37); pedantry (4); persecution (27); petulance (38); pretension (4); pride (6, Q5); prodigality (1); rebelliousness (10, 22, Q3); revenge (10, 27); ruthlessness (9, 36, 41); seduction (12, 14); self-centredness (12, 19, 43); self-conceit (6); self-deceit (F, 5, 35); self-interestedness (12, 19); self-love (18, 32); shadiness (24); shrewishness (4, 8, 19); snobbishness (8, 40); social climbing (8); strictness (17); swindling (23, 24); thieving/stealing (24); threatening behaviour (24); treachery (2); trickery (23); trouble-making (24); tyrannical ruthlessness (9); tyranny (36); unscrupulousness (11, 12); usurpation (8, Q3); vanity (3, 23, 32); villainy (24, 31); voluptuousness (32); war (9, 16, 27); warmongering (33); and pursuit of wealth (3, 41).

Additional follies and vices which are also exposed and condemned in the numbered stories in Part One of this selection are in the list below, which is also in alphabetical order (Q again indicating stories in Part Two):

absent-mindedness (F, 22, 30); aggressiveness (4); anger (20, Q14); bitterness (24, Q40); boredom (14); bribery (31); burglary (10, 24); childishness (25); covetousness (8); deception (12); desertion (12); egocentricity (25); egoism (19); extortion (11); false jokiness (21); falsely claiming knowledge (Q15); gluttony (excessive drinking and drugs) (39); gullibility (F, 31, 32); hero-worship (23); idealisation (2); imperiousness (19, 38); trying to impress (21); injury (9); intolerance (36); know-all superiority (8); lack of good sense (F, 2, 3, 14); long-windedness (30); manipulativeness (7); mendacity (12, 36); nuns' worldliness (22); overbearingness (37); peremptoriness (26, 29); phoniness (23, 40); pomposity (18); posing (15); not facing reality (Q25); rivalry (35); robbery (24); roguery (3); self-deception (F, 5, 12, 35); self-importance (18, 29, 40); self-righteousness (4); servitude (17); sloth (14); stinginess (23); suicide (42, Q2); terrorism (33); theft (10); and yobbishness (43).

These two lists correspond to the list of follies and vices in each story in Part One of this selection, which can be found on pp.235–237. They total 151 vices and 10 follies. In fact, follies can be found in most of the stories in Part One, particularly in 2, 4, 5, 7, 8, 11, 12, 13, 14, 15, 21, 26, 30, 32, 34, 35, 37, 38, 40, and in some stories in Part Two, for example 1.

All these follies and vices can also be found in *Selected Poems: Quest for the One*, a companion volume to this work. Its Preface sets out numbered groups of poems and excerpts in which each of these follies and vices can be found. Readers may like to compare the treatment of follies and vices in *Selected Stories* and *Selected Poems*.

These lists in fact cover the vices identified by Chaucer and Shakespeare in their works (as shown in *A New Philosophy of Literature*), and the stories in Part One of this selection are in the tradition of Chaucer's and Shakespeare's treatments of follies and vices as well as in the tradition of the secular aspect of the fundamental theme.

Universalist balance of fundamental theme's two aspects

At different times one of the two aspects of the fundamental theme of world literature dominates the other in contemporary works, depending on the metaphysical or secular outlook of the particular Age, civilization and time within which the works have been written. Universalism seeks to reconcile contradictions, and the Universalist ideal seeks a balance between the two aspects, between social virtue and the soul's perception of the One. This selection is deliberately balanced: both Part One and Part Two contain 43 stories. In the Epilogue I have included two hitherto unpublished 'communications from Giza' c.2600BC which encapsulate and balance the secular and metaphysical aspects of the fundamental theme from a time that predates its appearance in world literature.

This selection introduces Philip Rawley's reflections, his growth and development, the wide range of characters he encounters from all backgrounds, their follies and flaws, and his glimpses of the One in fleeting 'epiphanies' (revelations). Death lurks behind the social situations, and though social life is presented as a Dance of Death there is a growing sense that the universe has a higher order that reconciles the contradictions of life, death and eternity and offers the hope of immortality. These stories reflect the Age and the One Reality behind the many phenomena, and suggest an ordered universe in which glimpses of meaning and purpose can transcend nihilism and despair.

Inspiration from the 17th century

These mini-stories present a new literary form. They are prose-poems whose titles (such as 'An Important Star and a Fossil-Lady' or 'The Bride and a Forgotten Joint') effect, in the words of Johnson's description of the wit of Metaphysical poets in his 'Life of Cowley', "a combination of dissimilar images" in which "the most heterogeneous ideas are yoked by violence together". In so far as their connections adhere to (and carry forward) Johnson's description of Metaphysical wit they can be regarded as Metaphysical stories, stories in the 17th-century Metaphysical tradition. Besides conveying an image with a poet's eye for significant detail, concreteness and realism they make a statement and therefore represent a Universalist synthesising blend of image and statement. They are verbal paintings that present an image in action, as if on a canvas, and can startle the soul into a new mode of perception and enlightenment.

This said, I must emphasise that this selection and my *Selected Poems: Quest for the One* (also 2015) anthologise my treatment in my stories and poems of the fundamental theme of world literature set out in *A New Philosophy of Literature*. Many of the situations that inspired these stories – and the poems in my *Selected Poems* – can be found in my two-part autobiography, *My Double Life 1: This Dark Wood* and *My Double Life 2: A Rainbow over the Hills* (2015).

14–15, 21, 25 April 2011, 19 September 2012, 9 October 2012, 1 November 2012, 30 April 2014

Part One

Follies and Vices

from *A Spade Fresh with Mud* (1995)

1
Neck out to Sea

"When I go to bed I stay awake and talk with my wife until one," said Jack the publican in the sheltered bay, "and we discuss the clients. We call them all by their names and their drink. So I ask 'How was Bitter Bill?' and my wife asks 'What about Whisky MacHenry, did he come in?' We call Grimble 'Mixed-up John', and not just because he always mixes his drinks. He may be a painter, but he's also a responsible married man, and he doesn't go to Lodge meetings every night you know, and his wife knows it. I see trouble coming in that family. Whisky MacHenry's warned him – you know, the BBC producer. I was there, and do you know what Grimble said? 'BBC producers are men with draped coats and sewn-up sleeves.' What do you think he meant by that? Anyhow, it's a question of bust and personality. We all like a bit of bust – I've got two lovely models tucked away, if you're an artist – but you've got to keep things in proportion, haven't you, and your wife comes first. No, he's mixed up. I've told him myself. I told him when Whisky MacHenry was there, and do you know what he said? 'Jack,' he said, 'no man's an island but this one's a bloody peninsula – he's all neck out to sea and minding his own business.' Strange bloke, old Grimble. I mean, you can't live like that, can you. You can't turn away from society and live as you want, as if you're a bloody genius or something."

"No, you can't," I agreed, because I was expected to, and I drank up and said "Good night", and on my way home I walked out to the promontory. There was a causeway of moonlight across the water, and as I clambered down onto the rocks the lights of the sheltered bay slipped out of sight and the wind flapped my trousers and tugged my hair and I felt a great exhilaration, braving alone the pounding of the sea.

2
Angels in a Golden Light

One evening I went to the College to borrow a book. The Baghdad sun was setting through the palms, and there were still a few students wandering in groups on the hot sand. Then I saw the Head of Department. He was standing alone in his shirt-sleeves by the brick building ahead, and he was just looking. He was always the first to arrive in the morning and the last to leave in the afternoon, but no conscientious, public-spirited sense of duty could explain his presence on the campus this late. As I drew level with him I slowed down and said, "Good evening Maurice."

He turned and gave me a brief, sad smile on his tubercular skull of a face, a smile that showed his decayed teeth, and then he resumed his gaze across the sand. "It's so rewarding belonging to this University," he murmured after a moment. "It's wonderful to watch the students and feel you've given them what they're talking about. Look, they're like angels in the golden light."

He fell silent, and I was at a loss for words. "Yes," I said, making a pretence of sharing his mood and gazing towards the palms, "yes, they are." Then I said, "Well, I must go on to the library," and he nodded almost absent-mindedly. I had always thought of him as an emotional, rather melancholic man, but now I saw him as a man who lived for his job because he had nothing else to belong to, and who fended off solitude with a public-spirited dream.

I was in the library about five minutes. When I came out it was still light but I could not see him at first. Then I saw him among the students. He was standing in the centre of a group having his photograph taken, and he had his arms round the shoulders of two boys I knew to be Communists. In fact the entire group must have been composed of the devils, for no Nationalist or Nasserite or Westerniser would be seen dead in the company of a Communist. Just afterwards the group broke up, and the Head of Department raised an arm in the golden light, as if signalling his acceptance by his dream, and I waved back.

A year later, when the Communists were being purged, he was given twenty-four hours to leave the country, all the charges being related to "certain photographic evidence", and according to one person who saw him off at the airport, his eyes had a totally bleak look, as though he were being expelled from a Paradise of innocence.

3
People Like Masks

I had already met Buddy Harrow, so I knew who he was when he appeared towards the end of a Tokyo party and ironically shook hands with his wife. I didn't know much about him, though, so I asked the man I was talking to, "Who's that?"

"Oh, he's an American businessman turned ideas man," was the reply. "He left his company about a year ago, I think, and judging by what his wife says, he seems to be living off her money. At least, she once told me he wasn't selling very many ideas."

Later I was able to talk to him. At first he had a kind of hunted look: his thick black glasses did not go with his stocky, pugilistic figure and his crew-cut. But when I said "I hear you're peddling ideas" he immediately came out of his shell.

"Do you know anyone who wants to get in on fifteen million pounds a year?" he asked.

"I might do," I said guardedly. "Tell me more. What's going to make fifteen million pounds a year?"

"Life-masks," he said, "and people's vanity. I've got a new technique in portrait-sculpture, and if I don't get backing within two weeks the whole thing's dead."

He told me in detail about the "new technique". It involved a peripheral camera. This camera had already been developed by Shell, in 1961 to be exact, but Shell was not using it for portrait-sculpture. The subject would sit on a revolving drum for no more than three minutes. Using the technique of the floating point, an old device in making maps from film, the sculptor would be able to produce the final bust or life-mask within half an hour.

"Look, I've got some photos," he said, whipping some display cards from his pocket. "Isn't that better than Epstein – isn't it more real?" The deliberately roughened head was certainly realistic, though to put it mildly, I would have preferred to respond to an Epstein. "Mass produced sculpture," he boasted, "and the subject needn't sit for more than three minutes. And just think of the applications. We could have Halls of Fame for every sport, and every company president could have a cheap bust of himself in his office. If we sold at forty-five dollars we'd be making a hundred per cent profit. And I've got another technique for scaling down, so we could produce miniatures: masks on rings, Beatle masks on brooches." He was quivering with excitement. "And I've got the publicity worked out. What I do is get an interview on the Johnny Carson show and get two million dollars worth of free advertising, for the show goes over to millions of people throughout the States. I'd ask for applications from department stores, and I'd get a thousand agents and have a thousand centres. I've got their profits worked out, and it still leaves us fifteen million pounds a year. And later I'd bring it over here. The possibilities for expansion are world-wide."

There was just one drawback. There was a man in London called Macpherson who was already using the peripheral camera in a small way. To be exact, he produced half a dozen busts or life-masks a day, and had even done some members of the Royal Family. The point was, this Macpherson was not doing it as a business proposition. "He's a complete fool," Harrow said. "He just doesn't realise the potential of what he's doing." I wanted to say "Perhaps he's as stupid as Epstein", but I didn't. "I've got to tie in Macpherson," Harrow wound up. "And I've got to get an agreement with Shell that'll give me a monopoly on the cameras. And I need four thousand five hundred pounds to buy basic equipment. Look here's a letter from Macpherson. You see, he's willing to sell the basic equipment for four thousand five hundred. I can do all that in London, so I need my air fare to London. After that I go to the States to fix up the publicity, so I'll need my air fare from London to the States. I'm not doing it for nothing, and my salary's two hundred pounds a week. And I've got to get backing quick, because Hollywood's interested. I wrote to Frank Sinatra a couple of weeks ago," he explained in an agitated stutter. "I was desperate for backing. And if he doesn't look after me, if he goes ahead and uses the idea without including me in the rake-off, then it's dead. I've worked on this for nine years," he went on. "The peripheral camera was almost known about at the end of the war, and I first had the idea just before the end of the war. This is a life's work," he finished, "and if I haven't got backing within a few days then my life's work is dead."

"What about your wife?" I asked. "Hasn't she any money?"

Harrow was silent for a moment. When he spoke all he said was, "I can't get the money from my wife," and I thought I understood the distance in the ironical handshake.

I have always been in sympathy with a dream, no matter how big-sounding or vulgar it may be. In those days I was at war with society, and I must confess, I derived a cynical pleasure from the idea of making a fortune out of bourgeois vanity and egoism, and of thereby liberating myself once and for all from its stupidities and being free to take Epstein's path. So I promised to help and arrange a meeting of half a dozen potential backers, one of whom belonged to Shell. If they liked the idea, they would contribute towards six shares of £1,000 each, each share to have one-sixth of any profits the resultant syndicate company might make. Harrow was to have a free share.

When I telephoned Harrow's house to give him news of the meeting, his wife answered. "I wonder what you and Buddy are up to," she said, after I had told her that I would ring back later. "He's mentioned your name several times recently, and he won't tell me what it's all about. Anyhow, let me warn you. If he's asked you for money, I wouldn't give him any."

"Why not?" I asked, stiffening.

"I just wouldn't give him any if I were you," was all she would say, and I knew she had refused to back his life-masks.

The meeting was, of course, a complete failure. Everyone was very impressed by the energy and drive of Harrow, but why had he no contacts of his own? Had the plan already been turned down by hard-headed businessmen? Why had he no money of his own?

"It seems to me," said Peters, our puppyish young English host who belonged to Shell and who was not renowned for his feelings for other people, "that you've never made a success of anything, and I'm just not going to back an Eternal Loser," whereupon he went upstairs and ran himself a bath.

That night Harrow was a little subdued, but he had not lost hope. The next day I heard he had got the money from a rich American newspaper owner.

I did not see him again for six weeks. Then I walked into a cocktail party and saw him by the door. "Did you get to London?" I asked, as soon as I had been able to detach him.

"Yes," he said, "but it was too late. Someone had tipped Macpherson off, and he wanted twenty-five thousand dollars. And someone had tipped Shell off too, so I didn't get the monopoly. I think it was that Peters, but I haven't any proof."

"So you didn't get any basic equipment," I said.

"No," he said. "My backer made it a condition I was only to get the equipment if I got Macpherson's agreement and the monopoly. And I've quarrelled with my backer," he went on. "The bloody fool messed up my return flight so I was stuck in Bangkok for eight days, and then he wouldn't pay me any salary. Then he said, 'You can pay me back the fare when you see me,' so I walked out on him."

"So it's all over," I said.

"No," he said, "I'm looking for someone to put up three thousand five hundred dollars so that I can make the equipment over here. It's all over in the States but it's not over here. You see, while I was in London I got all the patent details, and I also had a chance to get a proper look at the two machines Macpherson uses. I can make them myself."

"Will you get another backer?" I asked.

"I'm meeting someone this evening," he said, looking at his watch, "in fact, I must go and meet him now," and he went without another word to anyone.

I walked away and found myself face to face with Harrow's wife. "He's been making excuses to you," she said. "Well, if you take my advice you won't believe him, because he's the one that's responsible, not Peters or his backer." She was slightly drunk. "He's trying to destroy himself," she went on. "All this big talk – he's nothing and he's even trying to ruin that. Life-masks," she said scornfully. "Ever since he got the idea he's been dead to everything except his squalid little dream. He even treats people like masks. He uses people, and just when they're becoming useful, he quarrels with them. He always manages to find some pretext. And if he hasn't quarrelled with you yet, I'm afraid it's because he can't have thought you very useful. Well I'm just about sick of it. It's been hard enough not having children – I've got fibroids and I have miscarriages. In future he can just get on and destroy himself without destroying me too. Next month I'm going back to London 'for a holiday'. If I've still got enough money for the air fare," she concluded, and as she turned away to put down her drink, her face a pale mask, I wondered whether in fact any guilt had driven this man who saw people as depersonalised masks to wreck his job, his marriage and his life's work, and I understood that he had involved the entire world, from me to Frank Sinatra, in an inner drama, in the systematic destruction of his dream.

4
The Need to Smash

"Oh," said Plastick over dinner, after I had been telling his wife about China, "you went to China with him. I suppose you carried the bags."

"No," I said, smouldering at this aggression but refusing to be drawn. "I did my share of the writing."

Later the conversation got on to ballet. "Jim only likes ballet because of the ballerinas," said his wife. She was vivacious and she had round, heavily made-up eyes. "They all dote on him and call him darling. I remember going round the back after one performance at Covent Garden, heavily pregnant, and never have I felt more like a tank on wheels."

I raised Nijinsky, and said I would like to have seen him hanging in the air. "I wouldn't especially," said Plastick. "There was nothing he could do that Nureyev can't."

"I would like to have seen him in 1916," I persisted, "when he was still able to make an audience hold its breath."

"There was nothing unusual about Nijinsky in 1916," Plastick asserted.

"He was a congenital neurosyphilitic," I said with ironic patience, "and he did sit in complete silence for thirty years before he died in 1950."

"Died in 1950 – Nijinsky? Nonsense," said Plastick.

"Of course he did," I said, "everyone knows that, and everyone knows he was a congenital."

"A congenital?" said Plastick. "What's a congenital? I don't think the word exists. I think you're making them both up, 'congenital' and 'neuro' – what was that other word?"

"Everyone knows that Nietzsche was a neurosyphilitic and that Lenin got neurosyphilis from a prostitute in Paddington and that the whole course of Soviet Marxism depended on a prostitute," I said heatedly. "And everyone knows that Churchill was probably a congenital who was lucky. Whereas Nijinsky wasn't. Everyone knows about the syphilitic's bald domed head and his rather foetal look."

"Is your husband always like this?" asked bald, domed Plastick, leaning across the dinner table and addressing my wife. "Does he always invent new words? Is he ever right?"

"He's always right," said my wife, "he reads a great deal and he's always right," and I felt elated. And, the ladies having retired upstairs, I stalked off to the downstairs lavatory in some dudgeon.

When I returned Plastick and the accountant were sitting opposite each other, cradling brandies. As our host served me *crème de menthe* Plastick said pointedly to the accountant, "You see, it's all a question of how much drink you can take. For example, I know how much I can take and when to stop. I know how many brandies to have." There was a silence while Plastick and the accountant exchanged glances.

"In what context?" I asked, picking up my *crème de menthe*, spoiling for a quarrel. Plastick and the accountant smiled, and at that moment the ladies returned and we all stood up.

When we sat down I turned away and talked to a guest from the Embassy. My wife talked to the accountant's wife on the other side of the room, and Plastick leaned forward to join in. "Have you seen it?" the accountant's wife asked Plastick, referring to a garden in Kyoto.

"Of course I have," Plastick replied. "I go to Kyoto two or three times a year." Later he asked my wife: "Are those black pearls or beads?"

"They're beads," my wife said. "There aren't such things as natural black pearls – they're dyed."

"Oh but there are," said Plastick.

"Excuse me," said my wife, "but I was told by an expert who has had a lot of experience in dealing with pearls that black pearls are dyed white pearls."

"Well, he's wrong, there are," said Plastick.

Later my wife was saying to the accountant's wife, "There's a very good print shop in Kanda."

"Oh," interrupted Plastick, "there are masses of good print shops in Tokyo."

"Well," said my wife, "I'm talking about one particular one in Kanda."

"I don't suppose it's Kanda at all in fact," said Plastick.

"It's in Jimbocho, between Sanseido and Tuttles," my wife said. Then, to the accountant's wife: "It's open on Sundays."

"Everything in Kanda's closed on Sundays," said Plastick, "so it can't be in Kanda."

"Everything in Kanda is not closed on Sundays," said my wife. "We often go book-hunting on Sundays, and there are always two or three bookshops open, and this print shop is always open too."

Turning back to the accountant's wife she talked on about prints and somehow the paintings at Hampton Court came up and the question arose as to the date of Hampton Court. "It dates back to 1514," said the accountant's wife.

"Oh, it's much later than that," said Plastick, who had been out of the conversation for a while. "It was built by Henry the Eighth."

"What about the Wolsey rooms?" asked the accountant's wife.

"They were too," said Plastick. "It's much later than you say it is."

"I am afraid I do know something about it," said the accountant's wife, whose maiden name was double-barrelled. "I have an aunt who's got an apartment there." At this, Plastick got up and crossed over to me.

I had been discussing women in bourgeois societies, and Plastick's first remark was, "In England it's all a question of class. There are ten classes, and each woman behaves differently," and even without knowing its context I knew he had got a chip on his shoulder.

An hour later, having half-listened to him about his job and his four million pounds capital and how he'd come as advisor and ended up as boss and how when he left Oxford he was courted by ten companies and how *he'd* interviewed *them* and how he was responsible for buying chemicals throughout Japan and fixing prices, I sat in the back of a taxi and asked my wife: "Why has he got that neurotic need to dominate and impress? I suppose it *is* because he feels inferior?"

"I think it's all to do with his wife," she said. "She's more cultured than he is. He's only a chemist, and he has to cover up his ignorance."

"Yes," I said, "and so there isn't such a thing as neurosyphilis and Nijinsky died in the 1920s," and imagining all the men who would talk to his wife in the next twenty years, and who would have to be smashed, I glimpsed the insecurity and terror he must live in, and I had to admit to feeling a little sorry for Plastick, and a trifle guilty at having placed the truth above his image of himself. For could one be absolutely sure there was no insecurity whatsoever in oneself?

5
Rainbow Trout

As we drank the autumn crickets tinkled like garden bells, and across the sea there was a glow on the dark horizon, as if the distant city were a submerged midnight sun.

"Fumikosan went to this Shinto shrine of hers again on Sunday," Brewer said out of the night. "It's in the hills about twenty miles west of Tokyo, and I must say I'm very impressed by the priestess. She seems to be a kind of medium. Fumikosan took along a shirt of mine, and just by fingering it the priestess 'got a message'. She said, 'Your friend doesn't want to live much longer, and the thing he wants most of all is to see his dead dogs.' It's true. I'd give anything to see some of my old dogs again."

"*Don't* you want to live much longer?" I asked quietly.

"The consolation for getting old," he replied after a pause, "is that one doesn't want to live in one's time," and, save for the tinkling of crickets, there was a silence. "Anyhow," he went on, "Fumikosan was very taken by this, and she brought back a portrait of my patron saint, an extremely beautiful girl. She's called Benten, and now every morning I have to sit in front of Benten and say a few words and just look at her. I don't mind doing that, for she really is very easy on the eye. I said to Fumikosan, 'I don't mind looking at anything religious if it's a beautiful girl.' Besides it doesn't cost me much. Fumikosan's quite uneducated – her mother died when she was born and her father was killed in a mining accident when she was four, and she never had a chance to get an education – and if it gives her pleasure, that's all right by me. And in a way it's really quite uplifting. It's really quite refreshing to be quiet for a few moments at the beginning of the day. And one of the best things about Fumikosan's visits to the hills is that she goes to a shop next to the shrine and brings back the most wonderful rainbow trout."

6
Fils Under the Palms

"Everyone suffers at some time or another," Father Fisher said as we stood on his roof and looked out over a settlement of mud-huts along the brown Tigris. "Everyone. Even people who avoid committing themselves to others. And although we mustn't be *blasé* about suffering or indifferent to the pain of those who suffer, it can't be denied that even the most terrible suffering has its beneficial side. I once knew a man who taught at the University here. He was a philosopher and an atheist, about forty I should have said. He was handsome – he had very distinguished long grey hair – and he had a beautiful, adoring wife. He was undoubtedly very brilliant. I remember him at cocktail parties. He stood apart and never talked to people unless they came and spoke to him, and then he talked down and debunked anything slightly illogical with a cutting remark. He had staked all on the intellect, and from the point of view of his intellect he was probably justified in looking down on everyone. But he was arrogant and proud and scornful, and I used to think, 'He is waiting to suffer.' Whenever I saw him I had that horrible kind of premonition: 'He is waiting to suffer.'

"He had two strapping children, a boy of seven and a girl of five. Every morning the maid took them to school, and you see that road to the left of the *sarifa*s[1], that road with the houses on the left? That was the road they went down. One spring day a coach swung round that corner too fast and smashed all three of them against that *sarifa* under the palms, and the maid and the boy were killed, and the girl was permanently paralysed. I heard the skid and the scream and the bump, I went down, I knelt by them. The boy coughed blood and died in my arms, and his face was a dark blue. It was I who called the hospital," Father Fisher continued after a silence, "it was I who called the house. Scranton was in alone: his wife had gone shopping in Rashid Street. I asked him to come to my place as quickly as possible. I shall never forget the disbelief and the agony on his face as the ring of Arabs parted and he stood over the blood. Perhaps the driver saw it too. He was standing by the coach door, and that night he cut his throat under one of the palms.

"Scranton and his wife were in total despair for a good week. I visited them, I drove them to the hospital to see the girl, and Scranton was very bitter. I remember him saying 'God can't exist', and secretly I shared his feeling, for that small blue face coughing blood had made me retch, and in comparison belief was just rather unreal. After that he brooded a lot and after a time the initial reaction wore off. He was the same of course, outwardly, yet in a way he was a new person. He had been deepened, the intellect wasn't so important to him any longer. He once said to me 'Everyone's been so kind, I don't know how to thank them,' and he felt acutely embarrassed about his former attitude to people. People he'd torn to ribbons were now offering to do things for him, and he just didn't know how to cope.

"One evening I was walking up here, and I saw him down there under the palms, and there was a crowd of children round him. They wore those ragged nightshirts and looked just as grubby as they do now, and they all had their hands out. He was giving them *fils,* and there seemed to be enough for everybody. I went down and joined him. He looked a bit sheepish and tried to make out he was on his way home. We walked a short way together, and after a few ordinary trivialities he said: 'You know, what happened to Peter could happen to any of those children there. What sentiment could be more ordinary, yet what more significant? I want you to know that although I can't believe in your Christianity, I can understand.' We parted and he went back to England about a week later and I never saw him again.

"He *had* understood," Father Fisher said quietly. "He had understood his responsibility for all men, he had won his humanity, and he couldn't have done either without suffering. Can we really say it would have been better for him if he hadn't had a family? What he and his wife went through was terrible, but would it really have been better for him to have remained a bachelor and not risked suffering? Ultimately, perhaps that's a question only he can answer, but I know that if you're going to live to the fullest and be fully human, you have to involve yourself in life, and if you involve yourself, you have to risk suffering, and if you shirk the suffering by shirking the involvement, then you don't live to the fullest, you're not fully human. To *live* is to risk suffering."

Father Fisher was silent and his gaze into the setting sun was troubled, and with his bald head he looked so bleakly celibate that I could not resist the temptation to ask: "Have you suffered, Father?"

"Not enough," Father Fisher said enigmatically, and he stood apart above the mud-huts in inscrutably superior silence.

[1]*sarifa*s (Arabic), mud-huts

7
A Kingdom and a Tear

It was an old woman in black, and she had a wart on her right cheek. "Sorry to disturb you," she said, "but this young boy said he came here yesterday and spoke to a nice young lady. She's not in I suppose?"

"No," I said.

"Oh, well never mind," she said, "but while you're here, say, have you heard of *Watchtower* – The Jehovah's Witnesses? You see we're a terrible lot – we come and disturb people and tell them about the Coming of the Kingdom because the world has been in a terrible state since 1914. Look, it's all in this pamphlet. See, there have been troop movements and famine and ruin and pestilence, just as Christ promised, for 1914 was the end of the Gentile Times. But the Lord didn't intend us to die in a great fire, he loves us, and there's going to be a great cleansing, his Kingdom will come. And a congress of Christians recognised that in 1914 – I was there. But they changed their minds in 1916 and now we're left alone proclaiming the news: the Gentile Times have ended, and the Kingdom will come."

I had listened mainly out of amusement, and it was to score off her that I asked: "But what do Jehovah's Witnesses *do* about bringing in the cleansing and the Kingdom?"

"Oh we don't do anything," she said, slightly taken aback. "We just proclaim the Coming of the Kingdom, because the Lord said it would be preceded by terrible times and the terrible times came in nineteen-fourteen. There has been war and famine and earthquakes and pestilence, and the Day of Judgement is coming –"

"But those conditions must have been present in the Anarchy and in the seventeenth century Civil War –"

"Ah, but 1914 was the first *world* war," she countered, "and Christ said 'Nation will rise against nation and kingdom against kingdom, and there will be food shortages and earthquakes in one place after another. All these things are a beginning of pangs of distress.' Matthew twenty-four seven, it's all in the pamphlet. And after the distress, the Kingdom. And the Kingdom must come, mustn't it? We couldn't be deceived when we repeat in the Lord's Prayer 'Thy Kingdom come' – we couldn't be fooled could we?"

I said, "I think it very probable that we are fooled," and a tear trickled down her left cheek.

I was about to say: "I don't believe in any Kingdom. I believe in Nothing, I believe man will pass away, I believe the universe will grow cold and dark." But I couldn't say it now.

"No," she said, "we're not fooled. I've been in this fifty years. Ever since 1916. I've been in it with my husband, and we spent fifteen years in Hawaii, and we've been in Japan eighteen years. We were the first to start this up in Japan – we had to learn the language to do it – and now we have hundreds of nice people, like this young boy here. And this year my husband died, and now I'm on my own. People have said,

'Why don't you go back to New York,' but I can't. I can't just walk out on fifty years. No, I have sold my house and my goods and my lands and I have profited one hundredfold. Here," she said, "you can have this *Watchtower*. It's the only copy I've got with me, and it belonged to my husband, but I've got another one at home."

And as I took it and she added, "I'll call on you later, if I may, to hear what you think of it, because you too can profit a hundredfold," I wished I had been cruel, I wished I hadn't underestimated this wily old woman who had outmanoeuvred me with a tear.

8
A Cuckoo in Casa Pupos

"But even if I got an Exit Visa and left Ghazi, there'd be nowhere for me to go in London," said Henrietta despondently. "You see, my mother's house isn't all that large and my brother and sister-in-law are living in it. And I won't go near them.

"It's a very complicated story, but when my father died his money went into the business, and under his will my mother was to get a high rate of interest from my brother. Well, this Sharon was Yorkshire working-class, and she wanted to do better for herself. So she persuaded Simon to get my mother to sell out and reinvest elsewhere. This saved Simon nine-per-cent interest, you see, and he could spend it on mink-coats. My mother gets a much lower rate of interest now, and consequently she's not independent of Simon, but she doesn't see it that way – she hasn't any business sense. She's actually grateful to Simon and Sharon, and now she's turned against me. *I'm* the one who was trying to get her nine per cent, now, not Sharon. Sharon planted that idea. I think she must study Communism in her spare time – I don't think anyone could naturally be such a twister or so vicious – but apparently I wanted the money left in the business so that I'd get it when mother dies. Isn't it sordid?

"And now, Sharon has taken my place, and she really is *maddening*. She was a schoolteacher before she married Simon and I've never met such a know-all. 'Oh no, Henwietta, Faisal was a Hashemite' – you know, assuming you don't know what anyone who's lived here has always known and taken for granted. But the most maddening thing about her is the way she's imitated all our tastes. Mother's got an account at Peter Jones, so *she* has to have an account at Peter Jones. I bought some rather nice goblets, so *she* has to buy the same. Mother sent me a velvet picture frame from Casa Pupos – you know, the Spanish antique shop in the Portobello Road – and the other day *she* wrote and told me she'd 'discovered a nice new antique shop in the Portobello Road that sells velvet picture frames', as though I'd never been there. The last time I was in London she even assumed that I don't know how mother lives. 'I think we'd better go out to somewhere like Chartwell this afternoon,' she said, 'because mother has a rest in the afternoons.' She really makes me sick. Of course, it's all inferiority – anyone can see that – but she's a cuckoo: she's pushed me out of my nest and she's taken the nest over for herself.

"Her *coup d'état* was complete when mother wrote last month and said she was excluding me from her will. That's what she said. 'You've always been after my money, you're not getting any.' I wrote to Simon to protest and do you know, he hasn't even replied? I've always got on reasonably well with him, but he's terribly weak, and he's completely under Sharon's thumb. No," she said, "after that I think it's better that I don't go anywhere near them. And what would I do living alone and incognito in London? No, my marriage may be in a mess, but I think it's better to stay here."

9
Lumps Under Snow

One evening the Mosul train dumped four hundred corpses on the Baghdad platform. The next night searchlights swept the Baghdad sky and all next week you could hear the rumble of Iraqi bombers trundling north.

"I am afraid I cannot attend your lecture for a week as I must return to my village in Kurdistan," Mohammed Peroz said one day as I was leaving the college. "There has been too much bombing near

Sulaimaniya, and I have no news of my village." In a composition he had described how a band of Iraqi soldiers had rounded up "rebels" and hanged his father from a fir-tree.

"Of course, I understand," I said, as sympathetically as I could. "But how will you get up there? I've heard the trains aren't getting through."

"I shall travel in that car," he said, pointing towards a battered *baz*[1] that was waiting outside the gate. "That car is a Kurdish car. We shall take roads where there are no Iraqi soldiers. Now I must go."

"I hope your village is all right," I said, and even as he turned his lean, swarthy face with its clear, Northern, rather melancholy eyes and said quietly "Thank you", I realised he knew it was not all right.

A couple of weeks later I met him by the gate and his face had the same look. "How was your village?" I asked.

He cocked his head and shook it. "There was a lot of snow," he said. "We drove in at night, and I thought 'There is snow on the roofs.'" He shook his head. "There was no village. Just lumps under snow. And just one boy. He told us, Iraqi planes come low, like this. Several times. My family...." He shook his head. "Just lumps under snow."

"Terrible," I muttered.

"Yes," he said. "I scooped the snow in my hands, like this, and then I pulled up the ruins. I found my mother and my brothers and my father's father and I buried them in the mountainside. Then I pulled up the others and I buried them in the mountainside. I got back to Baghdad yesterday, and I went to a night-club and I spent thirty-three *dinars*. Thirty-three. I drank too much whisky and I had a Spanish woman. She had a hot body and we laughed. And...." He shrugged. "I shall attend your lecture tomorrow," he said, and he wandered off, picking his way between groups of Iraqi students and soldiers across the warm sand.

[1]*baz,* long wooden-slatted vehicle with windows and square back used as a group taxi

10
Jewels of a Ruling Class

I once did a spell of debt-collecting for an agent called Jarvis. I didn't do it for very long: I got two shillings for every pound I collected, and, never having the heart to press the claims, I never got much of a commission. One evening Jarvis came too, and I did well. We stopped for tea in a café, and I wrote something in my notebook. "So you're a writer," Jarvis said with a Cockney's curiosity. "I ought to write a book about my life."

"People wouldn't want to read about a debt-collector," I said.

"I don't mean that," he said. "I haven't always been a debt-collector, you know. You heard of Twinkletoes? Twinkletoes, the man who escaped with Rubberbones – the master jewel thief?"

"Oh yes," I said, vaguely remembering a headline.

"That's me," he said calmly. "I was Twinkletoes." And I looked again at his tall, lean figure and his long ferrety head with its pinched ears and toothless smile. "I was called Twinkletoes," he said, "because I always left a footprint on a piece of white paper when I did a job. That was my trademark. It was a kind of challenge like, for the police.

"When I was a nipper," he went on, "I used to look at the ruling class – you know, men in bowler hats and women loaded with jewels – and I used to think: 'If they can have it, why can't I?' I began as a creeper. I used to creep into people's bedrooms and get their wallets from under their pillows while they were still asleep. You have to do that before you become a finger man – you know, a man who plans it all and fingers the money without actually doing it. You don't get respected otherwise. When I became a finger man I didn't stop being a creeper. I used to go to parties in Mayfair – you know, I crashed them – and I'd go up to the hostess and say 'Nice jewels you've got there, ma'am.' She'd say, 'Oh, do you like them?' and after a few words I'd say, 'Must be a bit of a risk, keeping those in the house.' You've no idea what narks people are. Ninety-nine times out of a hundred she'd say, 'Oh we've got a safe,' or 'Oh, I keep them in the bank.' You know she'd tell me if there were any more in the house. Sometimes she'd even take me upstairs and show me the safe, and sometimes she'd even explain the combination and let me have a good dekko at what she'd got inside. Occasionally she'd let me have a good dekko at something else she'd got inside," he added with a dirty laugh. Well, I'd say, 'Thank you very much, that was most interesting – most interesting'" (he gave a good imitation of an Oxford accent) "and the next night I'd go back with three of the boys and shin up the drainpipe and do my own creeping, because I was the one who knew where to look. I'll tell you, I was clocking up a regular hundred quid a week, over and above expenses, and I was mixing with Cabinet Ministers. I can name you at least three Tory Cabinet Ministers I spoke to on several occasions – in an ever so posh accent, of course.

"Well, by this time I had quite a gang, and that's when the trouble begins. It was a gypsy that split on me. He felt he had a grievance about something, he hadn't been paid his full share or something. A few nights after I was arrested the boys paid this gypsy a visit. They did him in. His caravan was found the next day, burnt to cinders, and his body was inside it. I didn't order them to do it, you understand, it was them being loyal. Even so, I'm sorry they did that, I didn't like that. Anyhow, I was found guilty on all counts and I was sent down for eighty-eight years. I stood there counting them all up – you know, four years on this count, four years on that – and I thought, 'Christ.' Then right at the end the judge said, 'And the sentences are to run concurrent.' I thought, 'Phew.' I didn't show any emotion. A professional doesn't: it's a risk you've taken, it's all part of the game. The two I was tried with broke down in the Black Maria on the way to prison. They were amateurs.

"I did four years altogether, in the end. I lost my good conduct remission because I escaped twice. The second time I was free eight weeks. That was a time, I'll tell you about that one day. Anyhow, it's a strange thing, but both times I was caught by the same sergeant as arrested me in the first place. In fact, he was the one who was on my case right from the beginning. He was the one who collected all the footprints. Well, when I came out, I vowed I'd get my revenge. Not do anything violent, not do him in like the gypsy, you understand, just get even, because it was a question of pride. I'd challenged society, and I was going to have the last word. So I made a few enquiries, and I found out that he'd been posted here, and I also found out that he was always behind on his H.P. payments. Well, I wrote to a certain H.P. firm and asked if they'd like an agent to collect their debts. I offered reasonable terms, and I was taken on. My first call was at the local police station, and I asked for this sergeant in the name of the law. They thought I was joking. When the sergeant came to the counter he said, 'What, you again.' I banged him for a dozen outstanding H.P. payments and for a coal bill for forty-five pounds ten and ninepence, and you should have seen his face. I insisted on payment within three days or else 'the – ahem – the creditors will be forced to begin proceedings,' and in the end he was grovelling and begging, right there in the police station. He was a Catholic and he had about ten children.

"But that wasn't all. Later I really did have the last word. After that first collection my business grew and I had to collect a debt from the Master of one of the colleges here. It was a big debt and he couldn't pay and I was kind to him. We got chatting and I told him a bit about my past, because he was a decent old boy. Turned out he was arranging a conference for Prison Governors in the Playhouse. He said, 'I'm so glad I've met you, I've been trying to find someone who could go on the stage and give an hour's lecture on the weaknesses of prison government in Britain. I want informal criticism from a former prisoner.'

"'Sir,' I said, 'you've got your man. I've been in every prison in Britain.' I'm not kidding, I went up on that stage – no notes, nothing – and there, sitting in the front two rows, was every Prison Governor in Britain. You should have seen their faces when they saw me. And you should have seen their faces an hour later. I gave them hell. 'Longshanks,' I said. 'Your prison, Wormwood Scrubs, is a disgrace. The prisoners don't get enough sugar, and it's so easy to escape they can't sleep for resisting the temptation.' No one could interrupt for an hour, no one could leave, and I really let each one have it, and I felt I was talking for every prisoner I'd ever known. In the end I said: 'You're the ruling class now, but one day things'll be changed, and if I have anything to do with it, you'll be the first of the old order to be sent down.'"

Jarvis's eyes were shining as he finished reliving the elation of his victory. "And *will* you have anything to do with it?" I asked. "Will you work to overthrow the ruling class?"

"Wouldn't be a bad idea," he said after a moment's thought. "But I don't want to do it so much now. I've found my place, I can collect the debt society owes me, and yesterday I gave my wife a lovely jewel brooch."

11
A Villa on Cap Ferrat

Carl Prout was a lean dilettante with frizzy hair and a jutting jaw, and like most men who have rejected the System he lived off his wits. He had a dream. "Man, one day I'll have a white villa on Cap Ferrat," he once told me, "and it'll be full of beautiful women and I'll spend the mornings writing poems and the afternoon painting pictures and in the evenings I'll just recline in my *hareem*." One May he found an heiress who'd run away with him. She was called Cynthia and she was coming into a million on her twenty-first birthday, and he got her to sign a cheque for a quarter of a million and write 26th August in the space for the date. All he had to do after that was keep her sweet. He needed funds, so he married another girl who was around and took her father aside at the reception and got him to write out a cheque for a thousand pounds. Then he cleared off and cashed the cheque and met Cynthia at a friend's place in London. Before she arrived he got philosophical. "Man," he said, swollen with *hubris*, "you gotta make a choice. You gotta say 'I'll have a villa on Cap Ferrat' and then you go ahead and get it. It's as easy as that. Believe me, because I've done it. Nothing can go wrong now."

Three weeks later they were looking at villas in the South of France and they took a bend too quickly and the car rammed a tree and they were taken to a white hospital. Carl Prout had critical head injuries and when he finally came round a week later his head was covered in bandages and there was a dull throb where his wits had been. Cynthia's parents and his wife's parents and his wife were standing round his bed, and a few blackened shreds in the ashtray were all that remained of his dream.

12
A Liar in Paris

Solly Goldman was a fat bachelor of fifty and he chucked up his job as an insurance clerk and went to Paris and hit the bars. The first night he met a Dutch girl and he told her he was a writer and a columnist and he said he was on his way to China. "You come back with me tonight," he said, "and I'll take you to China with me." She was sceptical at first but he swore he was getting two thousand pounds for the assignment because he was being syndicated all round the world, and it would be so nice if it were true, and so she suspended judgement and half-believed what she wanted to believe, and she went back with him to his hotel and shut her eyes in the dark and nearly forgot he was ugly. The next morning he made a telephone call to London about her visa, and when he came back he said everything could be arranged but it would take a week, and he copied out various items from her passport and went off to the China Travel Service agent, and it was ten days before she finally got wind and went back to Holland. She wasn't exactly a virgin, so all she had lost was a dream.

That night he met a Swedish girl and told her his pen-name was Priestley and she was very impressed. A couple of nights later he told her he had lots of money and lots of books to write, and he asked her to go back to London with him and marry him, and she didn't see a Priestley paperback until after the wedding. When she saw the Council house she would have to live in, she broke down and wept, and a week later there was a photo in the *South-East London Gazette*. He sat before an empty typewriter, a bald fat slob with a Jewish beak, a hollow braggart driven by loneliness and failure, and with a woman's irrationality she had an arm on his right shoulder.

13
A Screw-Manufacturer in Business

"Most Englishmen who come out here to do business are cold and superior," the elderly businessman said. "That's our trouble. I've got a friend who's high up in a Screw Manufacturing Company, and he's always saying, 'You can't get anything out of an Englishman until you've got him drunk and you've given him a temporary wife.' That's what he does – he takes them to the Café Thistle, which is the most expensive night club in town. A little while ago he had to negotiate an agreement with Nettlefolds, the Birmingham Screw Manufacturers that Chamberlain worked for. He was trying to get an agreement that the two companies wouldn't undersell each other in the U.S., so the first night he asked him to pick any girl he'd like to have for the fortnight he'd be in Tokyo. The Englishman thought he was joking – it was his first trip abroad. Nonetheless he picked a girl and Misawa paid two hundred quid on the spot. If a Japanese is giving you an obligation, he likes to let you know it.

"A couple of nights later I went drinking with them. We went to a night club and we all had girls. The Englishman was short and balding and not bad looking. He was rather detached and superior at first, but that was because he was a little unsure of himself, and he soon loosened up. After a few whiskies Misawa had to go, so he paid the bill for the evening and left us to it, and the Englishman told me he'd been completely bowled over by the way Yokosan undressed him and bathed him and drained him in bed. He said: 'It's as if I'm a child, it's unimaginable in Birmingham.' Then he said, 'I've got a very sweet wife and we have relations once a week and four days ago she was worrying in case the creases fall out of my trousers,' and I suddenly knew the wife and his own raw doubts and I felt sick of the night club, and Misawa was a corrupt and ruthless pimp."

14
Yawns Under a Sepulchral Sky

"Cholmondeley went to pieces because he was bored, that's my view," said Brewer. "Also he was very able and he knew he should have done better than he did. He went to Cheltenham, and he called himself a failed B.A. at Oxford, though whether he was or not I don't know. Then he joined the Army and he came out to Tokyo in nineteen-thirty as a language student and learnt Japanese. After a while he left the Army and started up some phoney company which failed. Around this time he had a 'liaison' with a Japanese woman and had a son. He once referred to her as his wife, and he may have gone through a Shinto ceremony with her, but I think she was probably just his regular. About 1935 he took up teaching, and he married the daughter of a foreign teacher who'd lived in Tokyo for years. When war broke out he returned to England with his wife and rejoined the Army, and he did very well. He ended up as advisor to Mountbatten. It was all through his knowledge of Japanese.

"He once said 'I should never have left the Army – if I'd stayed in the Army I'd have been all right.' He liked the Army, and he could have ended up as General, for he had the ability. As it was, his wife persuaded him to leave at the end of the war and he came back to Tokyo as number two in the Embassy's Information Section. His wife didn't come out until 1948, and he decided it would be better not to contact his Japanese 'wife' and his son, so from 1946 to 1948 he lived by himself in the Embassy compound, and that was when the rot set in. It was understandable, I suppose. He'd been Mountbatten's advisor and the war had given him a sense of purpose, while it lasted.

"Now the job he had to do was dull, and well beneath what he was capable of doing, so he just didn't try very hard. In fact, he spent most of his time getting hold of women. He once told me, 'There's nothing else to do.' He'd sit in the Embassy and make lists of potential mistresses. Then he'd go out 'to get information' and 'make his contacts'. His boss knew what these 'contacts' amounted to, of course. He once said to me, 'Old Cholmondeley's supposed to be Liaison Officer between me and the Japanese, and he doesn't tell me a thing. If he'd tell me what his women say when he's f— ing them, that'd be something, but he doesn't even tell me that.'

"When his wife arrived in 1948 she found the house full of women, and Cholmondeley was already beyond caring. He just carried on as though she wasn't there, he had no regard for anyone's feelings by then. She soon got hysterical. She took to trailing round the Embassy compound screaming and weeping and telling her woes to anyone who'd listen. It was understandable of course, but she was a bore, and in the end she was persuaded to go back to England.

"After that Cholmondeley just became more and more aimless and decadent. In 1952 he finally chucked up his job and moved out of the Embassy and took to teaching, and he did make an effort in the beginning, because he was terrified of having to go back to England. That was his greatest fear, going back to England. But the effort soon spent itself, and he used to cut classes so that he could go out and look for women.

"By this time he was so steeped in sensuality that anything normal was just a bore. So he used to tour Tokyo looking for twins or married sisters, and he always found them, though exactly how I've no idea. And he got them to do the most incredible things in these troilistic sessions. He used to draw diagrams of new positions and postures and speculate as to whether they would be possible. And so after a time the twins and married sisters had to be contortionists or acrobats – anything so long as 'the material was resistant', as artists say, anything so long as finding them was difficult and the whole operation would fill his bored mind.

"He kept the most incredible diary. He once showed it me. He had at least three couples visit him a day and he was more or less booked up a week in advance. And after a couple went he would go and write up what he'd done and make a few sketches and decide what variation he would use next time. Of course there came a time when he was bored by troilism, and then he moved onto orgies and the postures became spintrian. It was that that probably killed him, taking his blood pressure into account. For in the end he had fantastic blood pressure. It was 264, and the average is only 110.

"He was ill for a long time before he finally died, and in that last year he was so blown out that he couldn't even go out of doors. He made a show of holding his classes in his house, but he didn't do any teaching. He had a 'maid' to look after him, and it was as much as she could do to get him in and out of the bath. The last time I saw him he was lying in bed. It was a winter evening, and he spoke his own epitaph. I remember his words, for I was particularly struck by the past tense: 'My trouble was I could never find anything I wanted to throw myself into, not really. The Army and the Embassy and teaching, they weren't enough. So I wasted myself. Switch off the light and let me die.'

"He died that night. I was an usher at his funeral, and a Japanese woman came into the church with a grown-up son who was half-Western. She asked me to show her to a seat. She said she had once known 'Mr Cholmondeley', and I knew she was the first 'wife'.

"Later I talked to her outside the church, and I asked her, 'What do you remember most about him?'

"She looked embarrassed – she didn't want to say anything bad about him at his funeral – but in the end she said in Japanese: 'He used to sit and watch the sun set and brood about his life, and he once said, "The universe is a sepulchre and I belong to a dying order. Everything's pointless so why should I do anything, why should I even bother to live?"' She said she had argued with him, but it was no good, and quite clearly the boredom he felt in nineteen forty-six was already infecting him, like a germ, in those early evenings before 1935."

15
Pipe-Clay Breeches and Geese

"Jeffries was very nice but he had one foible," said Brewer. "He loved to pose as the perfect hunting, shooting and fishing Englishman. There used to be an annual Japan-British Society outing to the old Imperial Riding Stables, the ones that are being pulled down to make way for the new airport. One year he rolled up at the station dressed to the eyebrows. He wore a hunting-cap and a stock and a waistcoat and pipe-clay breeches and black leather boots, and he strutted around with his crop as if he knew it all, and when he eventually got within sight of a horse a small crowd gathered to watch. He put one boot in the stirrup and mounted, the horse bucked, and he went flying over the head and broke his collarbone. He had to be taken away in the Imperial ambulance, the Imperial Red Cross was only too pleased to justify its existence.

"When he recovered he went shooting by the sea. He saw dozens of birds sitting on some rocks and he thought they were wild geese, so he flushed them with a stone and shot six. He sent a brace to Bill Burnam and a brace to the Ambassador. Bill's cook opened the bag and wrinkled his nose and said, 'You can't eat these – they're cormorants and they're full of rotten fish.' And they went straight into the dustbin. Bill hadn't got the heart to tell old Jeffries, though. He wrote and thanked him very much for the wild geese, and I suppose the Ambassador did the same, for Jeffries often boasted afterwards about the time he bagged six wild geese in a minute. And to give him his due, he wasn't a bad shot.

"Something went wrong with his aim at the end though. He had this gorgeous wife and he was always as blind about her as he was about himself. She was always tumbling into bed. She once told me, 'I feel sorry for my husband but I can't resist variety.' I'm not sure how it happened, whether she told him when she left him or whether a friend told him, but when he found out that most of Tokyo had been to bed with her he lost his head and shot himself. He missed the temple and got an eyeball, and it took him three days to die."

16
Skewered Pheasants Under a Scarlet Knife

"Life is forgetting Hell," said Brewer. "And anyone who doubts that should have been in Trebizond when I was. There were wolves. They used to come down on winter nights and roam the streets and scavenge for offal, and there were jackals to follow them up. When the moon was out you could hear them howling in the hills.

"One Sunday morning there was a rebellion against Kemal's garrison. It was crushed within an hour and a half and a hundred and fifty ringleaders were rounded up and hanged all down the main street, the street where I was living. Soldiers put three long poles into a tripod and they put a ring over the top and a rope through the ring. Then they put the noose over the man's head and pulled on the rope until the man's feet were well off the ground and then they tied the end of the rope to one of the poles and left him to dance and they went on to the next one. By sunset they were all down the street on both sides and one or two still twitched like chickens with wrung necks. And there was no one around. The city was like a tomb.

"That evening I kept watch from my balcony window. There was a brilliant frosty moon and I saw an old man lurch down the gauntlet of the dead. He was drunk and he was muttering and he held a lantern, and he shuffled from one corpse to another looking for his son. Soon afterwards a pack of fifty wolves came down and they swept through the street, sniffing round the poles and leaping at the ankles, and when dawn broke you could see a torn up carcass and a lantern near a slack untrussed thing that had a large Orthodox cross tied round its waist.

"The sky was very clear that day. The sun was low and the light was sharp and the dead were as still as a row of skewered pheasants in a butcher's shop, and suddenly a choir of twittering sparrows rose up from the graveyard behind the rooftops and flew towards a jagged wisp of scarlet cloud like a bloodstained knife. And as I looked up at the detail on the azure vault I almost forgot the still, cold Hell in the shadow of the street, and a rush of joy flushed me through and left me new."

from *A Smell of Leaves and Summer* (1995)

17
Capitalism and Mr Bluett

"Excuse me," I said to a lean, balding man in a blue boiler suit who looked as if he had yellow jaundice. "I think you're expecting us –"

"That's Mr Bluett," he growled, and I thought as he padded into the factory hangar, 'You're too miserable to be happy.'

I returned to the enquiries, and Mr Bluett (the foreman) was waiting to greet me, a pinched, elderly man with red cheeks and perched glasses that reminded me of a postman, except that he didn't wear cycle-clips. "We're very busy," he said, "Mr Joe Gobbo, our Managing Director, says the condition you and your boys look around is that you keep together and don't affect production. He's very involved in his work, you know. I'll let you have a quick look round for ten minutes."

I had expected a tour of two hours, as you got at Fords of Dagenham and Mollins and Harveys and other metalwork places south of the river, but I did not say so. We all went onto the oily shop-floor where dirtily dressed dwarves hunched under towering clanking presses. We lingered near a pile of car bumpers and accelerators, and then Mr Bluett said, after a long hesitation, raising his voice for the noise: "Now I'll go over to the Managing Director and ask if he can spare time for you to thank him." He crept over the floor and loitered nervously by a bench where the balding man in the blue boiler suit bent over a metal rail. I could not hear what he said because of the clatter of the machines, but by the scowl on the boss's wizened, yellow face I knew he was sent off with a flea in his ear.

Mr Bluett returned slightly flushed, and said apologetically: "He says he's too busy. You must understand, he gets very involved in his work. He always wears a blue boiler suit like that, and works on the machines side by side with his men. He's the hardest-working man in England. He's in at six-thirty every morning and not off till six at night, including Sundays. He started here twenty-six years ago with one press and twelve men, and now he's got two hundred working for him, and there have to be two lorries a day loaded up with finished stuff to go out. I never speak to him normally – none of us do, he keeps himself to himself like a prisoner in solitary – I just let him get on with his work, and if he wants me he sends for me. So you understand the set-up, I hope? So long as you understand.... Oh," he added, "could you send him a letter of thanks? He gets a little, how shall I put it, testy about school visits, and I don't want him to blame me."

18
The Director is an Idiot

Christine got married very suddenly to Anthony. He was her boss at the Museum Foundation, and no one knew there was anything between them until they announced it. They had kept their relationship quiet ever since Christine gave a party at her Greenwich flat and invited Anthony, not expecting him to come.

They held a reception some weeks after their wedding. It was at the Old Kitchen, Kenwood, and it took place on a fine Saturday in October.

The great white house, the rolling green lawn, the lake shimmering among the golden-red leaves – all provided an ideal setting. I arrived three-quarters of an hour late with Pippa, having encountered a traffic jam near St John's Wood.

"Sorry," I said to Christine.

Seventy guests were sitting at separate tables eating melon with forks. Christine, smiling and in a long dress, showed us to a table in a corner.

"Hello," said Jean beside me, "how are you?"

She was a friend of Pippa's. She had shared Pippa's old flat. I had not seen her since her wedding. She had been living in Paris.

"Perhaps we'll have a speech from you about how Christine had to come through your room to get to the loo," I suggested.

"This is a family affair, remember," she laughed.

"Do you know Anthony? Which is another way of asking, which is Anthony?"

"Yes, that's him over there in the black shirt and red tie."

She pointed to a gaunt, long-haired, thin man and I immediately saw he was ill at ease.

"His Director's here," Jean said. "That wiry man over there. Honour Marchant. Comes from Cumberland, large country house, wrote the official book on the First World War. Anthony's smiling up to him, hoping for promotion, see?"

As I watched, Anthony fawned up to a silky, grey-haired man with a face that was distinguished and strangely gross at the same time.

"Have you met Delia?" Jean said of a girl near me.

I found myself talking to a squirrelly brown woman who sat next to her husband.

"Are you working?"

"I'm writing a thesis for a PhD."

"Oh? What on?"

"Hardy."

We discussed this briefly. She was interested in the relation between fictitious places in Hardy's work and the real places – in how Hardy put real social communities into his novels.

"Are you ready for your next course?" a waitress asked. "Will you go up and help yourself?"

On my way I came across Anthony, and introduced myself.

"I gather we share an interest in T. E. Lawrence," I said.

"Oh yes," he said, "Christine's told me about you. I've edited the photos we've got in the museum and I've–"

At that moment the Director accosted him, and he was all ears.

Then Delia was beside me.

"You remember Delia, don't you," Anthony said to the Director.

"You used to work in the museum," he said.

"Yes, that's right."

"And this is your husband?" he said of me.

"No," I said, and I introduced myself.

The Director did not want to talk to a man.

"And you're writing a thesis on Hardy," he said. "What on earth are you doing that for?"

Anthony told me more about his book on T. E. Lawrence, and the next time I listened to the Director he was saying:

"Yes, but only military subjects are worth writing about. It's like toy soldiers in front of you, you give your interpretation of what they have done. Whereas everyone who's intelligent knows what Hardy is on about."

"But there's the economic and social side," Delia said.

"Sounds very sinister to me," the Director said to Anthony. "Communist."

"Yes," Anthony fawned, simpering.

"Literature is a waste of time. You shouldn't write a thesis on a literary subject. You should write one on a military subject."

I was indignant. He stood for false values, pomposity, and the confidence of a large country house. Yet behind it all he was just a boy playing with toy soldiers. I wanted to put him right. But then I looked at Anthony and thought how desperately he wanted promotion, and how I would spoil the atmosphere. The Director was too old to change, I wouldn't achieve anything. And besides, I *had* been invited, and it was a bit off for a guest to make a scene. I went off to fetch my lunch.

When Delia had returned with her plate I said: "What do you think of the Director?"

"He's a twit," she said. "I used to work with him. He thinks women are there to smile at him."

"I think he's an idiot," I said. "He sees everything in simple black and white military terms and has no appreciation of subjectivity at all. He's at the level of toy soldiers. He needs one pound of air deflating from his self-importance."

She smiled appreciatively. "I'm surprised you saw that so quickly," she said.

I looked back to where Anthony was fawning on the Director. He would go on intriguing and in thirty years' time he would have a high position, and then others would do the same to him, and then he would die. That was his life. I felt sad, and suddenly the party lost its meaning. You came in and you went out, and what happened in between was a waste: me saying things I didn't want to say and learning things I didn't want to know. I thought of Omar Khayyam's lines, as translated by Fitzgerald:

Myself when young did eagerly frequent
Doctor and Saint, and had great Argument
About it and about: but evermore
Came out by the same Door as in I went.

I wished I hadn't given up drinking.

19
An Imperial Egoist and a Car Wallah

Mrs. Mahawal, our Indian tenant upstairs, had six academic degrees, including a diploma in Russian, and she ran the government newspaper in Delhi. She was in Britain for three months on a Central Office of Information course, and it was soon apparent that though she hoped to become an Indian Ambassadress, she lacked all sense of diplomacy.

"I am not a true Hindu," she told me on her first evening with us, putting her long black hair behind her head, "I am an admirer of Ayn Rand, I am an egoist, I believe in egoism."

And she wasted no time in putting her belief into practice. She left the girl she shared a room with (a beautiful young Bhutanese with the clear skin of the Himalayas who read *The Tibetan Book of the Dead* and worked for the government newspaper) and came downstairs and opened our door and announced, "I want to watch your television, our course director said we must watch the news on both channels every night so I will come down before nine and stay till half past ten or eleven every night, unless you have a visitor."

We were so taken aback that we could not think of the words to object, and we allowed her to park herself in front of the television for the next three hours, during which she talked non-stop and asked numerous questions about British life with barely a glance at the screen. At half past eleven she ordered my wife to teach her English "because I need to know about British etiquette and intonation", and she was put out at being deflected.

"I am used to having servants in India," she declared, "normally I do not have to cook or clean or empty bins." It was soon clear she had found servants in Britain. She ordered us to make available a pressure-cooker "so I can cook rice", to arrange for the milkman to deliver two pints every morning "as I do not want to go to the shop on my way back from the course", to empty her bin, to put 10p in her electricity meter, to change her sheets, to hot up her radiator (which on principle she never turned off), and to pass on our newspapers.

Mrs. Mahawal lived out her egoism. She chattered non-stop late at night, opened the door to let out the smell of her curries "because it's a bit stuffy in here", and woke the children who complained of the stink. She never wrapped her rubbish, and besides ventilating her room, I was forever scraping wet onion peel from the side of her bin. Her baths mysteriously lasted three hours, during which the hot water in the house ran cold and no one could get into the bathroom to clean their teeth, and when she emerged with a bowl of wet washing she said disarmingly, "I was doing my exercises, you know, my Yoga exercises. They should be done in quiet, and I cannot do them sharing with Nima." She got herself into the bathroom just when I was leaving for work, and said, "In India I spend all day in the bath. My servants do everything, I just lie in the bath."

Then the breakages began. She broke a sash-cord, and the electricity meter. Then she dropped the iron and broke the back shield so that all the wires were exposed. She said, "I will get it repaired," but after several forays into the local shops the repair proved to be a piece of sticking-plaster over the vacuum. "I have left it as I found it," she declared. "It was broken before I used it." When I pointed out the danger of electrocution, she said, "It was dangerous before I dropped it," and she refused to replace it. (I deducted the cost of a new iron from her deposit in the end.)

After that she took to staying *four* hours in the bathroom, and even had a shower in the middle of the night. A new word entered the English Language: I spoke of "being mahawalled" when I could not get into the bathroom, 'to mahawal' meaning "to occupy egoistically for an indefinite period of time", with a secondary sense of "to be plain bloody awkward". The word could be abbreviated to "MW", as in "I've been MW-ed".

Mrs. Mahawal now spent the nights pacing her room above our bedroom, talking loudly to the Bhutanese until 3 or 4 a.m., often with the door open, and her husband sometimes rang her from New Delhi at 5.30 a.m. He seemed very surprised when I said, "She's asleep, I'm the only one in this house who's awake, you woke me up." Sometimes in the morning she left the front door wide open. Once when we were at work the front door was wide open for half an hour, with the empty house gaping invitingly, until my wife had a hunch that she should look back; and was able to close it. She dropped her front door key outside the front door; luckily I found it before any of the local burglars. Mrs. Mahawal never paid for her milk until I asked her three or four times.

She demanded to read the daily and Sunday papers before I had looked at them "because my course director says I must read the editorials". Eventually she decided "we will be paying rent weekly from now on, not four-weekly in advance", and was sulky for a few days when she did not get her way. One Saturday she announced: "I will be needing your front room tomorrow. I have a visitor who is calling and we do not wish to receive him in our room, so you will please use another room at 11 a.m. tomorrow." She thought it very unreasonable that my mother was visiting us at exactly 11 a.m.

By this time I had had as much as I could take of Mrs. Mahawal, and I was relieved when it was time for her to go. "We must be off at six a.m. on Saturday to catch our flight," she announced. "We do not know how to get our luggage to Tooting Bec station." I suggested a taxi to Heathrow, and rang two firms for quotations. Both said £12, which was "too much". So I agreed to get up at 5.45 a.m. after a hard week and drive them to the local station. "Then I will return to bed and sleep," I said.

That Friday night I went up to weigh her luggage on the bathroom scales, and was aghast at the confusion: clothes were strewn everywhere, one of her hold-alls had a broken zip which she ordered me to repair ("Get pincers and a screwdriver and mend this zip"), and despite her six degrees she seemed incapable of distributing the weight so that the two cases to be weighed came to no more than 25 kilos.

Eventually I escaped, and I tapped punctually on their door at 5.45 a.m. the next morning. The two women had still not packed, and Mrs. Mahawal was fiddling with her cases, having talked all night. I humped up the heaviest and crept down the darkened stairs with them and put them in the car boot, and at six Mrs. Mahawal announced, sitting at her table, "Now we are going to have breakfast."

"No," I said, "I've got up early to drive you to the station and I'm going back to bed. You said 'Off at six', and it's now gone six."

Ten minutes later, and with great reluctance, Mrs. Mahawal clumped noisily down the stairs, waking the children of course, and got into the car. I drove to Tooting Bec station and unloaded the luggage.

"We have changed our minds," Mrs. Mahawal declared without any reference to Nima, who did not seem to have changed *her* mind at all. "We have too much luggage, we want a taxi to Heathrow. Never mind the twelve pounds, order us a taxi."

I explained again, as she well knew, that a taxi could not be ordered from the street in this part of London at 6 a.m. any morning. It had to be telephoned for, and the telephone numbers were all at home. (I was not getting involved in phoning directory enquiries for local taxi firms from one of the perennially vandalised local telephone kiosks.)

"Ah," said Mrs. Mahawal, "you have a car, *you* can drive us to Heathrow."

I saw now where all her muddle had been leading, and why she had got me up at 5.45 a.m. after a hard week at work to drive her to the local station. Her egoism had a calculating, premeditated look about it now. She had cast me in the role of her chauffeur-servant, her car wallah. The Raj may have been reversed on the Indian subcontinent, but I was not going to be any national's wallah, and certainly not at 5.45 a.m. when, under the circumstances, I had already done more than I was required to do.

"No," I said, "I haven't got the map book in the car, I don't know the way. It's an hour or more to get there, and I would need to study the route. I'm not prepared, it's unplanned – "

"You can go home for your map book and study the way," Mrs. Mahawal said. "If we go by car we do not need to leave until eight o'clock. Now it is only just after six o'clock. There is plenty of time. We only had to set off at six o'clock if we were going by tube."

That did it. "No," I said, "I don't know the way, I should be in bed now. You have arranged to go by tube, and to change now will just cause confusion. There will be plenty of people to help you with these cases."

She treated everybody as her servant, she would have little difficulty in turning a passenger or two into her luggage wallahs. And, imagining how the traditional British imperialists in *A Passage to India* must surely be turning in their graves at the British role in this example of Indian-British relations, I carried the two heaviest cases to the top of the escalator and waited while the Bhutanese bought two tickets and Mrs. Mahawal trailed slowly down with one shoulder-bag.

The Bhutanese and I went down the escalator with the heavy cases and at the bottom we stopped and turned round. Mrs. Mahawal stood protestingly at the top, her shoulder-bag on the ground. "Come on," I called, beckoning her down with my arm. Mrs. Mahawal did not move. A train came in and left, and trains were not frequent at 6 a.m. Then a passing West Indian picked up Mrs. Mahawal's shoulder-bag and put it on the escalator, and Mrs. Mahawal herself reluctantly stepped forward and was borne down.

On the platform Mrs. Mahawal chattered non-stop about how she would not be able to cope. "We must change at Kennington and then at

Ly-cester Square. We cannot manage. We need a taxi and there are no taxis. You have a car. You should take us to the airport." There were no thanks, there was no appreciation for the fact that I had left my Saturday lie-in to help them, and I half-wondered whether she would propose that I drove her all the way to New Delhi.

Another train trundled in, the doors opened. I put the luggage inside, waved the two women in, smiled goodbye to the Bhutanese girl and stepped back. Mrs. Mahawal stood inside the doors, protesting. The doors closed.

"By-ee", I waved.

The train jolted and pulled out of the station, and my last glimpse of Mrs. Mahawal suggested the affronted look of an Indian imperialist who had been cheeked by the local British wallah, or of an egoist who could not understand why her latest whim was not granted. She had given an order, and I had disobeyed her. No doubt she would be back as Indian Ambassadress to the Court of St James, and would have more of a chance to enforce some of the orders she had such a need to give, but I could not help feeling that if she did become Indian Ambassadress, despite her six degrees and her diploma in Russian, Indian-British relations were destined to enter a period of unprecedented muddle and confusion.

from *Wheeling Bats and a Harvest Moon* (1999)

20
Angry Old Man

I went down for the papers with Paul and saw Chirpy sitting on the seat at the crossroads with his red hat on. A lorry hooted and he gave a jovial wave.

"Hello," he said in his Cornish Liskeard accent when he saw me, "how are you and the boys, do you like my hat?"

I said I hadn't seen him recently.

"You see I get a touch of blood pressure when I get up in the mornings. I get blots in front of my eyes, and go a bit dizzy. I'm getting the doctor to look in later today. Sun's bad for me so I'm not down as much as I used to be – I wear my hat now. Still I'm eighty-five next month."

"Wonderful," I said.

"I was in the trenches in the First World War, and I'm eighty-five next month so I haven't done badly."

"Trenches," I said sitting down beside him and observing his hooked nose and the magnetism of his ancient mariner's eye. "You must have been very interested in the Falklands, what with the mud there."

He waved at another lorry driver whose arm was flapping at him out of the window. "Doe," he said scathingly, "this Falklands business makes us old-timers sick, all this flag-waving for them when they come home, you know it's all a lot of nonsense. I was in the trenches two years and four months, under shelling, and I saw thousands dead and when we came home there was nothing for us, nothing. No one ever knew I was home. And I was in the Second World War. I think it's all political. Margaret Thatcher is building it up to build herself up. Yes, we saw it all. Nineteen sixteen I was in the trenches – all over. The Somme, everywhere. Saw thousands of them lying around like dead ducks, people we knew, people from other regiments, we just passed them by, no one took any notice. We had to walk over duckboards and keep going under shelling and there were water-filled trenches on either side, and if anyone stumbled because the boards were slippery and he had a heavy machine-carbine on his back and fell into the water, no one stopped to help him, we had to keep going. Saw the man in front of me drown like that several times, no one thought anything of it. Saw General Haig once."

"Oh," I said spellbound, "the books say he sent thousands to their deaths – "

"No, we loved him," said Mr Roberts. "He kept behind us most of the time, we were in front of course, but he came up occasionally, and I saw him just the once. We all loved him. No, this lot make us old folk sick, because we never had anything done for us."

21
A Tie in his Tea

That lunchtime I sat down next to Cuth, the school secretary; Mr Street, my Second-of-Department; and Maisie, the typist. Immediately the conversation became hearty.

"I saw your article," I said to Mr Street, "it's good."

"Oh yes," Cuth said. "He's editor, he didn't tell you that."

The jokiness drew a laugh.

"I went to Rochester last night," Mr Street said to Cuth, "and I don't remember how I got home. But a bollard must have moved for I've got a scratch across my car."

I expressed sympathy.

"Perhaps it was that pink elephant you saw when you came out," Cuth said. He had smooth hair and spectacles.

"Ha ha ha."

"I know I got a bruise just there."

"Have you thought of visiting Mrs. Short in the medical room? She'll massage you," Cuth said.

"Ha ha ha."

"I don't know how I got it. Perhaps when I climbed into bed Daphne gave me a kick."

"Ha ha ha."

"Or perhaps you were so put off by that pink elephant that you went next door by mistake and climbed into bed there."

"Ha ha ha."

"Or perhaps it was the policeman I saw."

"Ha ha ha."

"No, he didn't move, you couldn't avoid him."

"Ha ha ha."

"That's what I said in court this morning."

"Ha ha ha."

"Did you go to court this morning?" Maisie asked, suddenly worried.

She was red and squirrelly and she blushed whenever she spoke and had attention drawn to her.

"No," said Mr Street, "I was only joking."

There was a silence, and I took a long look at Cuth and his anxious eagerness to joke and be one of the lads and dream up "perhaps" situations connected with drink and sex. What strange insecurity lay behind it? Or was it just that he had been in an office all his life?

Mr Street, I knew, was insecure. He desperately wanted to belong to something. He spent his weekends drinking in the Press Club, showing his NUJ card, which a friend had procured for him illegally – and trying to impress. He also talked about meeting his publisher, though he never talked about the book he was publishing.

Soon after I left for coffee in the staff room. Ten minutes later I caught sight of Mr Street. He was bending forward and his tie dipped in his tea. He was not aware of it and a stain spread slowly up the bottom of his tie. No one else had seen, and no one was joking about it.

Mr Street looked ridiculous. This was not a "perhaps" situation, it was for real. Like the clown that he was, Mr Street bent further forward and by now the bottom half of his tie was in his tea. I watched fascinated, wondering how he would react when he realised.

Suddenly Mr Street was spluttering with indignation and dabbing at his tie. He squeezed the bottom of his tie into his cup, muttering inaudible words. One of my Department produced a tissue, and nowhere among the concerned faces was to be found the nervous jokiness of the lunch-table. That was only triggered by the world of "perhaps".

22
The Bride and a Forgotten Joint

Sister Moore invited me to a Mass of Religious Profession at a Catholic church at Clapham. The yellow slip she gave me said that Sister Françoise Peguy and the sisters of La Retraite in community at Clapham Park were very happy to invite me to the Mass, at which Sister Eleanor McBride would make Final Vows.

I had never been to such an occasion. In *The Nun's Story* the nun lay on the floor, and though I expected things to have become more liberal since then, I was not sure what to expect. Mrs. Marsh said my wife should take a veil – a headscarf – to cover her head in case she was the only one without her head covered, and we only remembered near the church. I stopped the car and my wife was in the shop when Mrs. Phelps's car came by with Mrs. Marsh in it. Mrs. Phelps's son was driving, and Mrs. Phelps got out. She was our absent-minded classics teacher. She always forgot things; I was always retrieving her keys.

"We thought you might be lost," she smiled.

She got back into her car. She had had a disappointing week. First she had discovered that one of her five children had truanted from a nearby comprehensive for 112 days. Then, two days later she had tried to prevent a class of West Indian girls from rushing at the door when the pips went, and in the ensuing scuffle her arm was shut in the door and so badly bruised that she originally thought it broken. It had been enough to reduce her to tears. The next morning I had obtained a list of culprits by holding the class in the Drama Hall and telling them there would be no classes until the offenders were identified. The ringleader was absent so we sent a car round to her home and brought her in, and after half an hour's grilling we had a confession and were ready to sue for assault.

The rather bare church was crowded. Sister Moore was at the door to greet us, unveiled, her face showing the spiritual beauty of a fully unfolded rose. She showed us to a pew next to Mrs. Phelps and Mrs. Marsh. People were standing, for contrary to tradition the whole parish was in on this ceremony and had been prepared with talks for a month or more. Mrs. Phelps's son was robed in white by the altar. The sisters of La Retraite were dotted round the congregation, easily identifiable by their modern blue habits and their head-dress, which they wore well back and hanging down their necks. They had come from nine houses all round the Order's province of England and Wales, and the atmosphere was very much that of a large family wedding, in which distant cousins and aunts greet each other for the first time in the year, all different people held together by one common bond – membership of a family.

There was an expectant atmosphere as the Entrance procession made its way to the front, the Bishop in a splendid mitre, holding his crook. The Mass itself was like a wedding. Sister Eleanor vowed to be faithful to God to the end of her life, and after the Homily came the Rite of Profession. She said in a loud clear voice, standing (not lying face down) at the front of the church, her black hair in a bun, like a bride, "I ask for God's love and to serve him in the religious community of La Retraite for the whole of my life."

She was asked if she resolved to "undertake and persevere until death in the same life of obedience, chastity and poverty which Christ chose for himself" and to seek God in daily prayer. Then she was welcomed into the community. Then 22 saints were called upon, one by one, including St Julian of Norwich and St Ignatius Loyola.

After the Profession of Vows and the signing of the Document of Profession, and after the Prayer of the Consecration, the moment of the mystical marriage came. The Bishop blessed the ring and put it on Sister Eleanor's finger and said, "Receive this ring; may it be a sign of your union with Jesus Christ in love."

The gifts were brought, and after the incense – symbol of fragrant souls rising to God in happiness – there was a Communion Rite, which neither I nor my wife took part in. I saw Mrs. Phelps returning looking serene under her brown veil. Then after a funeral hymn the one-and-a-half-hour service came to an end. There was loud applause from the sisters in the gallery as Sister Eleanor walked back looking radiantly happy.

My wife and I joined the jostling crowed in the aisle and slowly we walked down towards the Hall. Sister Moore came up and we fell into conversation between her greetings to various elder members of the community.

"When was your Profession, Sister?"

"Oh goodness, it was in the war. Nineteen forty-one, no nineteen forty-two."

"This must have brought back memories."

"Well no, not really. It was so different. I took my Final Vows in France – in French. I still repeat them to myself in French. No, it's all so different. This could have happened in theory but it wouldn't have happened in practice until fifteen years ago. It was the Pope's encyclical. Yes, fifteen years ago. But it's nice like this, to have the whole parish present."

There was a crush to enter the Hall. Sister Eleanor loomed and said, "I wish to shake every hand." She looked divinely happy, like a radiant bride – live a lie as a truth and it becomes a truth – and then Sister Moore took over and introduced us to the Headmistress whom she taught in Bristol and the Headmistress who taught her, a wizened old Sister on a chair, and a dozen other sisters, and she looked after us zealously, finding me an orange juice and insisting we drank. She was almost showing us all off. We were very much her guests. The nuns were all chattering – they were making up for months of silence, talking animatedly – and I asked her what the Loyolan tradition was like today and she pulled a face and was regretful that the Vatican no longer laid everything down: "We have to find our own Way now. We had the answers but we lost confidence in ourselves and changed everything and found we'd thrown out some of the answers."

But there was all this support. I liked talking to sisters. They were removed from the world – Sister Eleanor had just accepted security for life with her vow; though she had surrendered and sacrificed much she would never be short of a bed – but they were deep and peaceful, and I liked being with deep and peaceful people.

It was time to be going. Mrs. Phelps had gone out to phone her husband for the car. She came back and said, "I've just heard that I put the joint in a casserole and lit the oven, but I forgot to put it in the oven. My husband's just off to East Grinstead to sing and he was rather cool about the situation."

Everybody smirked. She had acted in character.

"Oh dear," she said, "what a thing it is to be losing one's faculties."

"Like going through the sound barrier," I said, "only into superconsciousness." And she smiled.

On the way out a child thrust a card into my hand. It said: "Come to Me all who labour and are heavy laden And I will give you Rest." The letters in "Come to Me" and "Rest" were printed as if they were composed of matchsticks – units of 'I' – and the image haunted me all the way back.

During the journey we passed La Retraite. It was an institutional-looking building with a chapel and a couple of effigies, one of which said *"Ecce, Mater Tua"*, and I could imagine the parquet floors and polish inside. Here was the bride's new home. She would not have to think about joints in the oven.

But as I thought of Mrs. Phelps and of the dedication in her life, I could not say this was preferable. It was a rewritten version of the story of Mary and Martha who "was cumbered about much serving": the intellectual one and the over-practical. Both served in the Kingdom. I knew that Mrs. Phelps, for all her chronic lateness and absent-mindedness, had just as much a place in the Communion of Saints as did Sister Eleanor with her specialist Ignatian exercises.

After half-term I saw Sister Moore in the staff dining-room. She joined me for lunch and we chatted generally about mixed ability teaching, which I said was favoured by materialists who see people as equal human bodies and not as abilities. We talked about education, whose purpose, I said, was to help each child locate her ability or talent and "lead it out" (*"e-duco"* it) and she said, "And to accept themselves with what they can't do. That's very difficult."

I looked sharply at her, and we both stood up and scraped and stacked our plates and on the way to the staff room I said, "It depends which self we have to accept. People have static and dynamic parts, and they can be carried forward in a surprising way. If St Joan had accepted her peasant self we would never have heard of her, history would have been different, she would have died in bed."

"Yes," Sister said. "With a call it's different."

I got coffee and we sat apart from the centre of the staff room and she told me in detail about the Ignatian Exercises which went on for a month or so, and which Ignatians had to do three times in their lives. She told me how Ignatius believed that God was in every situation, in contact with people, and she recalled Gerard Manley Hopkins' ideas and realised how Ignatian they were in origin. She said that in the mornings and evenings "we have to find our own way, and be grateful for what we can get and bear what we can't get". She said she had written an article saying that it was wrong to receive in prayer and give in the apostolate, because all contact in the apostolate was a contact with God.

There had been a television programme about nuns and I mentioned this.

"Oh yes," she said. "Of course it was *unbalanced* but parts of it were true. The Reverend Mother in debt, hopelessly impractical. And the welcoming of death, and the woman who had become a nun – they were accurate. And the torture over a lost relationship. That was very true."

She looked down. Did she regret not having married? I thought so.

"I believe one should go out into the world and meet people. I am against the monastic life. It can become a prison that impedes the religious life," Sister said, "and which has to be broken out of. Here in Wandsworth, for instance...."

"You could do so much, Sister," I said. "We have discussed this before. The European Movement to bring people back to Mysticism."

"Yes," she said. "Since you first said it, I have been getting this back from different sources. It all fits together. I am going to talk to my Reverend Mother, and also my Provincial Superior about it. I have had a talk already. It's how to get it started that's difficult. That's what she said."

"On the radio," I said, "there was someone from a pressure group who said all you need is passion, a group of people and information, and then people will listen. We could do something here, as I have said before. Like St Joan. It is not a fantasy – someone has to do it. Ignatius, Mother Teresa could have said, 'It is a fantasy.' Something is growing here. There is a group of people here who could develop from passive to active. The time is not right yet. It will happen of its own accord if it is going to. It must not be forced. And then we will proceed slowly, step by step." There was criss-cross wire in the glass. "One rung at a time," I said. "But at the end we shall have climbed a ladder."

"Yes," she said. "I am sure you are right."

She stood up and with her white hair I saw her as someone who wanted to be involved in a movement. She was less of a bride than someone itching to cook a religious joint.

from *The Warm Glow of the Monastery Courtyard* (1999)

23
Feet on the Ground

I went for a walk with Simon, who was now fourteen. The stars were incredibly bright, the Milky Way was like dust over the sea. We walked on Smeaton's stone pier and I thought, 'What if gravity suddenly stopped?' and I imagined myself falling head first out into space, and I felt a nausea, a giddiness and I could hardly continue my step.

As we returned a voice said "Hello Philip" and it was Ray, one of the new owners of the harbour. He was packing a red Mercedes wearing a suit and red bow-tie. He said he was going back to Essex the next morning. "Would you like a lift?" he said.

Then he said he had to get in out of the damp air – he suffered from asthma – and I turned to leave him and at that moment a tousled-haired, moustached Sean Stevens stood in the doorway. I was amazed at the degeneration that had set in in two years. He had changed from a well-groomed, quiet man into a florid, flamboyant, loud and unkempt-looking, debauched-looking *roué*. He greeted me.

"I've just been talking to Ray," I said.

"Ray?" said Sean, who was boozed. "He's my partner. What are you doing, Fox? If you want to reverse your car under the lever I'll do it for you. He's such an arsehole," he said.

I expressed the hope that the car would not roll back into the water.

"Oh no, a Mercedes says 'I'm not supposed to be here. Hitler won't allow it.' It'll get itself out."

I laughed.

"How old's Simon. Fourteen? He's old enough for a woman. Send him over tomorrow night and I'll arrange it." Sean gave a coarse laugh. He had been to prison. "How's the new place? Sounds as though you should let me get some planning permission and sell it. I know you're a millionaire. You got that house cheap. Sure, cheap every day of the week. Are you happy over there? You did a lovely job. I played cricket today. Rescued St Austell, rescued the Cornish! I went in number three and made forty odd. It was nought for one, and when I left it was a hundred and twenty for five. We've got our six-a-side again this year.

"I'm bringing nine professionals down, they're on three hundred pounds a man. Martin Crowe, Broad, Carl Hooper, Gus Logie. I take my cricket very seriously. I play with them. I field cover point or square leg. I'm quite fast. We've got a tent. I'll tell you what, as you're a polite and courteous fellow, you can be in our tent. Along with the boy. We'll have a great day, there'll be two and a half thousand people there, and you'll see two and a half thousand runs scored, I wouldn't mind betting. It'll be a great day. We'll drink a bottle of champagne or twelve."

At that moment a blonde girl dressed as a waitress came out. He turned and mouthed a kiss at her. She took him by the arm and led him in.

"Good night," he called over his shoulder. The door banged.

He was doing it all on borrowed money. Nine professionals, I thought, at £300 each. That's £2,700 for starters. As I walked back the stars were a long way away. I was glad I had my feet firmly on the ground.

I went and watched the cricket as Sean had suggested. There was no hospitality tent. I sat on the grass above a slope among twenty or more professionals, many of them international stars, and watched Sean open the batting with Broad. He made a few runs and was then bowled. About forty spectators watched in the mild sunshine and some cheered, and I later heard that there was doubt whether any of the professionals was paid his appearance fee.

24
Aladdin's Cave and a Disgruntled Look

John Hammock was a villain. He lived at the bottom of the lane, and had once owned seventeen acres in the neighbourhood, having come into a lot of money suddenly some years before. He had a bungalow with twelve rooms. He was swarthy and thickset with a deep voice and ferrety eyes, and I just knew he had been in prison. He took me up the road to his Aladdin's Cave. It was in several wartime corrugated-iron hangars (he called them barns) which were filled with reproduction Spanish furniture.

"You could have a chandelier in the Hall," he said. "It would look a million dollars."

I expressed wonder at his haul of lights and boardroom tables.

He said, "Bankrupt stock's cheaper than buying stolen goods."

I pondered the matter-of-fact way he said that. The implication was that to him buying stolen goods was normal, and therefore it was to me.

His friend Lee Wise, speaking of John, said, "You can't talk to some people. Like Mad Axeman Mitchell. He hit you with an axe. He didn't want to talk. John's a bit like that."

It was from a councillor who serviced our boiler that I heard how John had held up an Ilford jewellers. The councillor had had a drink with the jeweller, and he swore the jeweller (whose name was Ship) had said, "I was robbed of a hundred thousand pounds. I never recovered as a shopkeeper. Johnny Hammock did it. He led in four of his boys with sawn-off shotguns."

John Hammock was much feared by all his neighbours. He had quarrelled with them all at one time or another. One set he drove out by running his tractor all night under their window. They were replaced by a young couple who promptly moved their fence onto Hammock's land. Hammock retaliated by installing a cattle-grid in the road for the sole purpose of waking their baby. "He can be very awkward," Lee Wise said, "but you can buy him off."

A neighbour called Fennel would not buy him off. Hammock said Fennel had violated the rights of his road by transferring a right to another farmer. Hammock swore he would blockade the offending house and he put a tractor across the exit so that nothing could go in or out. Like any armed robber he wanted a share of what money was going. "His god's money," Lee Wise said.

Like all villains of some standing, John Hammock had a place in Spain. He had a villa and a restaurant nearby, which other people ran for him while he was in England. He took his young girlfriend out for one of his visits, and she started an affair with a Spanish waiter. Hammock found out and the waiter was found kneecapped. No one messed with John Hammock, but like all who worship the god Money he had not found happiness and despite his Aladdin's Cave he had a sour, disgruntled look.

25
A Chunk of Rock with a Fossil in it

We went to the house of friends of our children. It was a Sunday afternoon only four days after my operation and I had an enormous bandage round my toe and foot.

I shook hands with the bearded, ruddy-faced David and was shown into an upstairs room of Thai Buddhas and glass-cases of rocks and precious stones. I sat and put my foot up and asked him about his business, which was dealing in diamonds and precious stones in Hatton Garden, while the children played in another room and our wives talked in the kitchen. He said it had begun as a hobby when he was ten and he had made a living at it for the last ten years, and he told me how dangerous it could be, and that European diamond-hunters in Africa and miners were frequently shot in the bush, and their jewels taken.

He said, "Business is done through approbations, like stamp approvals, and everyone is very trusting, but you only break their trust once. I frequently walk about with a hundred and fifty thousand pounds worth of stones in my special waistcoat." Perhaps it was no coincidence that he had pistols in his attic which he used at weekends.

He showed me some pieces from his collection: green malachite, jasper, an ammonite fossil of a mollusc that resembled a snail, one side of which was polished, and a limestone tile with a fossil of a fish in it. He had shaped them all, and some of the rocks were fluorescent and glowed when he turned on his ultra-violet light. He produced a rock with a long green emerald in it, and a flat piece of rough ruby from Tanzania. He said the recession had destroyed the market in small stones – everyone did without pendants and rings now – but the big stuff was still all right. He produced a small ruby from his trouser pocket, wrapped in greaseproof paper, and said, "That's about fifteen hundred pounds." It would take him five weeks to turn it over and he would make a profit of 20 per cent.

We concocted a plan to make a fortune. He would go to Tanzania and buy from miners he knew in one of the river valleys and would seal the packets, and I would go in independently at the invitation of the Foreign Minister to write newspaper articles, and would pay out £20,000 in dollar notes of $10 and $50 denominations, and I would then smuggle out the sealed packets of stones, which he would later sell for a quarter of a million. We could both retire on the proceeds.

Eventually it was time for high tea of shepherd's pie, carrots and beans, and we went through to the kitchen and were joined by the four children, a dog and two cats, and the jewel-dealer suddenly changed. He had no conversation outside stones, and he now regressed to the physical like a child of ten and continually addressed the dog and the cats – "dog, you are a vile dog" and "you twerp" – and uttered loud noises like "Orrrhh!" at the eating feats of the animals and the children. From being a shrewd jewel-dealer in a dangerous profession, he was like one of his own fossils, a child's personality preserved in an adult's strata, a fossilised father who seemed strangely jumpy and to have no depth to him, an embryonic personality that seemed incapable of further development.

His wife had dark hair and glasses, and she took up rather extreme positions out of nervousness, making herself out to be excessively women's lib, wanting a holiday away from her children, making him break off to do odd jobs in the kitchen and help with the cooking, telling him off. The children were demanding. "Me first," whined the youngster in his high chair, and the girl kept asking, "I want more."

I connected the egocentricity with their mother, and was not surprised to find out later that the nursery school teacher had come to the same conclusion. She said, "I was the last of three children and my mother always made me eat. You know mothers are always attached to the last child, because after that there is nothing; it's as it was before they married." She was Anglo-Indian, and her mother, a midwife, had delivered Indira Gandhi.

After tea, fudge was distributed to each of the children and the dog (but not to us), and then the jewel-dealer took the cat to be neutered by the vet while the rest of us drank Darjeeling tea in the front room. I lay with my bandaged foot up and when he returned he sat in the window and made physical noises again and talked of when he was a boy. He asked, "So when are we going to Africa?" We talked briefly again of making our fortune while he vigorously patted the big black dog and let out physical grunts, but it was his stones I feasted my eyes on. The malachite, jasper and fossils, they were raw material which he polished into beautiful objects.

I was struck by how close were our occupations: I took the raw material of experience and polished it into an image or symbol. These stones were images for images and symbols, and in our different ways we were both artists. And sitting with my foot up on his leather settee, and thinking of the embryonic child that was still within him, I resolved to take a chunk of rock with a fossil in it and shape it and polish it into a beautiful work of art.

26
Bacon, Eggs, Sausage and Tomato

On Anglesey we went to the silent dining-room and sat in the window which looked out across the calm straits of Menai to the range of Snowdonia. The place had been specially built for Queen Victoria in the 1830s. The architect was Joseph Hansom (of the Hansom Cabs) and the Bulkeley family had paid for it, clearing 400 houses.

At the next table to us sat the bald, wizened man with a vein on top of his head and a large hearing-aid round one ear. The previous day he had had difficulty in removing the top of the marmalade jar, and he had held it out for Simon, who had taken it off. He put down his paper and shouted an announcement to the four other breakfasters, "Senna's dead. The second racing-driver to be killed in two days. Senna's dead."

Everyone made a show of frowning and murmuring concern, and then returned to their breakfasts, retreated back into the silence from which they had been disturbed.

The old man sat on over his paper and an elderly waitress approached and asked, "How are you this morning?"

"Bacon, eggs, sausage and tomato," the old man shouted.

"Thank you," said the waitress and retreated, while Simon bit his lip and shook.

A younger waitress returned with his breakfast.

"I've forgotten my tablets," the old man shouted. "Can you go up to my room, turn left."

"Yes," said the waitress, who was freckled with long auburn hair.

"Go to the desk, top drawer."

"Yes."

"Under the box, at the back, under the letters."

"Yes."

"A small bottle with a white label."

And the young girl retreated and the room returned to silence and whispered conversation.

Later I saw him shuffle towards a seat near the revolving doors to enjoy the sea view in the warm May sun, wearing a coat and hat, and I looked at this old man who could not hear what was said to him, and who lived in a lonely solipsist dream, and I could understand that for him communication was getting people to do things for him, converting them into lid-turners and news-listeners and pill-fetchers – and any enquiry after his health could trigger an instruction for bacon, eggs, sausage and tomato.

27
A Browning in Belsen

"The grounds are under control," I said to Harry, as he swept the path.

"Yes," he said, balding and leaning on his broom. "And you're off to the D-Day beaches next week?"

"Yes," I said. "Were you involved?"

"No. I joined the army on the sixth of June, 1943."

"Where were you?" I asked.

"Germany, on the Danish border, in May 1945."

"Did you see any camps?"

"Yes. I went into Belsen three days after it was liberated, with Sir Alan Lascelles, the Queen's cousin. The stench....We set fire to the buildings. The Canadians.... There were piles of corpses. They took the women guards, and there were trees all round. They bent two down, tied one leg to one tree and one to another, and let them go, and they were torn apart, leg one way, body another. I thought, 'This is wrong.' I stood up with my Browning to stop them, but the Queen's cousin said, 'As you were.' It would have been dangerous to stop them.

"I shot the commandant of Lubeck Disabled Persons Prison Camp, you know. He was coming towards me in the dark, and he looked like Hitler and I felt he was going to shoot me, so when he got as near as you are now I shot him. He was a German Colonel. There was a Court of Inquiry, but I said he was going to shoot me, and they accepted that.

"I shot a British Colonel as well, just behind the ear. We were guarding a hut and a car went by and I said to the other guard, 'We're supposed to be sentries, if a car doesn't stop we're supposed to shoot. That's what sentries do. I'm going to shoot the next car that comes by that doesn't stop.' Then another car came by and I shouted 'Halt' and it ignored me so I opened up. The car skidded into a tree and a woman climbed out and shouted, 'You 'ave shot ze English Colonel.' He had been out with a German girl and was trying to smuggle her back into base undetected. The Court of Inquiry said he was fraternising with a German woman, which he wasn't supposed to do, and I got off." He laughed.

"I still shed tears for my friends. Micky Roberts lost a leg and he was so excited he didn't feel any pain. 'Who done this?' I remember them as they were, if they'd grown old I wouldn't recognise them now. I often think back to those days when I always carried my Browning."

28
Ry-bald Comments and a Lost Cheque

The attempt to de-throne the MP ran into difficulties. A motion by one of the Conservative members was put down on the agenda of the constituency Annual General Meeting, but it was leaked to the press and seen off by a visit from a Central Office official. No deselection motion was brought before the Annual General Meeting, but as the case had made headlines the hall was packed. Whereas the average attendance was 45 and the scandal of the previous year had seen an unprecedented 65 attend last years' Annual General Meeting, there were now over 200 and every seat was taken as we walked in at 8 o'clock on the dot. The printer's daughter said, "The front row, that's all there is," and we made a very public progress through rows of crusty buffers to the platform and sat beneath the Acting President, Chairman and Deputy Chairman, and the MP, who winked at me, completely relaxed to the casual eye that missed the tension in his rippling jaw.

The Acting President stood above us on the platform and asked if any press were present. No one owned up and he said, "Good. This meeting is confidential and we don't want any reports in the press." Satisfied at the security arrangements, for entry was strictly by membership card only, he spoke in a thin voice and expressed his contempt for the member who had leaked. We then stood in memory of the President, who had died.

The short, slightly unkempt Chairman Donald Wheatear, who was a professional currency speculator, read his report, the printed version of which we held in our hands. Eventually he said that the Member of Parliament had retained his ministerial position in the Cabinet reshuffle and though he continued to visit many social and official functions in the constituency "his high profile does occasionally lend to ribald" (he pronounced it "ry-bald") "comments in the press necessitating supporting action by officers of the Association. Frankly, from the letters I receive and conversations I have with people around the constituency, I know there is a certain feeling of discontent among a part of the electorate who are of the opinion that an MP's conduct as well as performance are legitimate matters of concern."

There was a loud chorus of "Hear, hear" from the deselectionists.

The Chairman Donald Wheatear went on, "It must be remembered that the way an MP behaves can negate countless hours of effort by Party activists. Obviously, the whole situation needs to be resolved at an early stage as the possibility of a General Election sooner rather than later appears increasingly likely."

And, sitting like Madam Defarge under the guillotine, knitting my brows, I caught the MP's eye. Jack Marney looked significantly at me, pulled a face and shook his head as if in disbelief.

The meeting continued. We had the Treasurer's report and a vote for President, which saw the Acting President defeated in favour of a rotund, bespectacled ex-barrister who said in his remarks about himself that he had worked for the Party in the area for over forty years.

The Acting President stepped down rather wanly and with a crest-fallen expression, and the new President took his place. We then confirmed the election of the new Chairman and proceeded to the election of two Vice-Chairmen.

"There are three names on your paper," said the new President, "but the third one is invalid and so the first two are elected."

"Why is he invalid?" someone called out from the back.

"He hasn't paid his subscription. This has been checked."

The councillor in question, a supporter of the MP, rose and said he had paid for the last twenty-six years without a problem and he read out the number and date of the cheque by which he had made his most recent payment. "It's never got lost before," he said, "and I wonder why it's got lost this year of all years."

There was subdued uproar, and members of the audience called out that he should be included in the vote. Grimly, the ex-Chairman agreed. In fact the councillor was well beaten into third place, a reprimand for the MP.

Then the MP was called on to speak. I sat under the guillotine, knitting my brows, and the officers sat at the table, eyes downcast, totally still as if they were inanimate waxworks caught in studied disapproval. Raising his eyebrows, without notes, Jack Marney, a handsome, personable man in a suit in his late forties, spoke about threats from Europe, about the danger of Scottish devolution, about Labour, about renationalisation and high taxation, anything in fact that kept the subject as far away as possible from himself and his own suitability, and by making constant eye-contact with the packed, disapproving audience, he succeeded in talking for a quarter of an hour without any heckling and earned a good few murmurs of agreement.

When he sat down there was loud applause, and it had been a superb performance. The officers on the platform looked glum and one shook her head.

There were questions. They were all about Europe or renationalisation; not one was about his suitability. And in those five minutes when his opponents funked a confrontation they lost the chance to appeal for support and deselect him.

I had already folded up my knitted expression when a working-class councillor stood and asked a question about immigration. He made a passionate statement about how the country was being swamped by immigrants. "And if we don't stop them we'll end up with a Yugoslav situation, shooting them."

There was a gasp, and nervous titters. Jack Marney said, "It's people like him who make me appear moderate," and there was laughter.

A Turkish Cypriot rose and spoke heatedly about the immorality of making jokes about killing people, and a West Indian woman behind me rose and said she had been in Bosnia and killing people was not funny. Neither had a sense of humour.

The MP said quietly, all things to all people, "I understand your feelings, but I see what he meant."

There was then a presentation of a shield to the branch that had recruited the most members, and coming forward to receive it was none other than the "shoot'em" councillor.

"I'm sorry if I caused offence," he said in his demotic accent, "but I am as I am and you'll have to put up with me, and I'd just like to urge Canadian sea captains to sink all Spanish trawlers."

There was laughter and some indignation, and the meeting broke up, and I went forward and congratulated Jack Marney on escaping beheading.

Later, the councillor whose cheque had not been received got his revenge by giving an interview to the local press. Under the heading "MP's opponents are wasting their time" he leaked a very full account of the meeting in which he claimed the MP's opponents had been routed.

I did not know this as I left, of course. Outside in the night air I wondered at how two hundred prominent local worthies had come to give up an evening, drawn by the spectacle of a Minister in difficulty, and I grasped that the gruesome streak in the British character had not been eradicated with Tyburn; it had merely been suppressed into a democratic framework of statements by officers about ribaldry and ballots and dubious manoeuvrings, like the ruse of the lost cheque. But there had been a shift in favour of the victim, and the MP had survived without any apology or, indeed, reference to what he had done, and the ghoulish audience had been too polite to call for the topping they all secretly wanted and had come to see.

29
An Important Star and a Fossil-Lady

Moll Flanders was being filmed and a convoy of lorries filled the car park and turned the harbour into a film set. Two tall-masted boats swarmed with men in period costume, some up in the rigging, and the quayside was strewn with barrels and coops of squawking geese and crowing cockerels, while a bullock lowed from a pen near wagons and the makeshift stall the special effects team had built. The quay was strewn with earth to suggest a mud-track and above the steeply sloping ramp to the quay a coach and four horses stood waiting, the horses stamping their feet and dropping smoking manure. A hundred people clad in warm jackets, technicians and curious locals hung around between cameras shielded by plastic from the light drizzle.

I heard my name called and one of the occupants of the coach removed her black cowl and I saw the wife of the harbour-owner. I went over to the coach and leaned on the door; there was no glass. She sat next to two women and opposite a man and a little girl and boy, all in eighteenth-century costume, and I said, "I hardly recognised you among these ringleted people. What are you doing?"

"I'm travelling to America with Moll Flanders."

"Who's Moll Flanders?"

The ringleted lady with a wide face and flat nose said in a rather superior voice, "I'm Moll Flanders."

"Yes," said the harbour-owner's wife, "I'm supposed to be travelling with her. I don't know this other lady."

"I'm just travelling with them," said the young man. "This is my first day."

The assistant first director came up to Moll on the far side of the coach, wearing a cowboy hat, and I heard part of their conversation. Moll said, "I wasn't going to leave the Hotel to get here at 8.30. That's far too early for me. Can you get me a cup of coffee."

She gave the order in a very peremptory, unsmiling tone, and as the assistant first director said "Sure" and headed for a lorry that had "Set Menu" on its side, she looked away, and then I heard her say to the bonneted girl next to her, "I'm committed until October, and I don't want to do the second series. I've said I'm not doing it." And I knew she was a star who could throw her weight about. She was above what was happening around her, and bored, though the centre of attention, and when the assistant first director called to the cameramen "Three em, three em in?" and then "Action", and fires in small braziers sent smoke up from the quay and the four horses stamped and, their reins held by a groom in a wide hat, ran down the ramp, Moll's expression did not change. She was a star who was important, above the action, her face expressionless, bored.

The coach and horses galloped back up for a retake, and I wandered down to the fossil shop. An array of large and expensive portions of rock surrounded the walls, and there were many small fossils and trilobites. All were labelled with the number of millions of years old they were, and the fossil-lady, who was dark-haired and fiftyish and plump, told me it was a wrench when she had to part with any of them. Someone had bought a skull she had had for three years, and she missed it. "I felt quite sad last night, thinking about it not being here."

We heard a shout and wandered outside to see the retake. A girl in a bonnet and elaborate brown dress stood opposite under an umbrella, and the fossil-lady called, "Where are you going to put it away? Up your skirts?" She laughed. "In the barrel?"

"A girl comes and takes it from me," the extra called. "This is very uncomfortable to wear. It's hard to breathe."

"You're always complaining," called the fossil-lady and laughed, and the extra, who was actually prettier than Moll, also laughed, and there was a bond between the extra and the fossil-lady, which contrasted with the distance between Moll and the assistant first director.

"Action," called the man in the cowboy hat, and grooms ran alongside the four horses and the iron rims of the coach rumbled slowly by before plunging down the ramp, and I saw Moll looking distantly out towards the green hills, while the extra hurried down the ramp, involved in what she was doing, heading for the bustle by the boat.

"They're all so self-important," the fossil-lady said. "One of the cameramen came into my shop earlier. He likes fossils but he was so important. 'Oh,' he said, 'I must come back later, we're so busy now.' It's only a game, what they're doing, a game in fancy dress," she said slightly scornfully, and she went off and sat back among her fossils.

Later, Moll walked along the quay with a fop in a feathered hat, and between takes she nursed a hot-water bottle beneath a duvet and a couple of attendants brought her a chair to sit on. She said disdainfully to the extras near her, "Can I have two cow-pats please, I want to give one to a friend," and they all laughed. I later found out that she had just heard her husband had left her for an older woman.

The extras had to stand and wait, and I thought of the fossil-lady, and I saw that her fossils of creatures millions of years old were a timeless standard that judged and reproached the self-importance in the moment of these dressed-up, disguised people for whom the moment, the next take, was all.

30
Twenty-Five Years Like a Banquet

I was invited to the retirement banquet of Arnold Jayman, a bachelor who had served his boys' school for twenty-five years. The school was about to go co-ed.

The banquet also marked the early retirement of an IT teacher who was leaving after nine years to travel abroad. In the school library over drinks he looked haunted and had stricken eyes and combed-forward hair. He told me he would look for a business in the Caribbean, where labour costs would be cheap, and settle there if he liked it.

Arnold Jayman stood alone, looking suave, his rimless spectacles on the end of his hooked nose, wearing a dark navy suit, and surveyed the eighty guests who mingled and talked noisily, and I thought of how I had attended his 50th-birthday party in London, which had been preceded by Mass.

We all went through to the dining-hall and I sat at the join of top table and the centre of three long tables. I leaned over and talked to Arnold Jayman, who was in the seat of honour, when he was not being spoken to intensely by the new Head's wife. The Head was sitting next to the IT teacher, ignored by his neighbours and not speaking.

Next to me was the former Head of the Junior School, who had written to the Bishop of London urging that Arnold Jayman should be accepted for the priesthood. I had been asked to write as well, but had had no reply. (That particular Bishop of London, it later transpired, had a chaotic system for replying to correspondence.) That was how I saw Arnold Jayman. He was a would-be priest. Something had happened to debar him, and despite several applications he had never become a priest, and now he was retiring from his substitute career.

Towards the end of the dinner, after the prawn starter and meat and strawberries in meringue, there were speeches. The Chairman of the Common Room Association spoke a eulogy on the IT teacher, who replied, saying in quiet tones, that this was Arnold Jayman's day. He spoke modestly and openly and there was considerable applause.

After a decent lull the Head of the Junior School spoke his eulogy on Arnold Jayman, introducing him as a "latter-day Mr Chips". With a twinkle in his eye and to general laughter he said, "It is no secret that Arnold Jayman loses things – reports, essays, books. His colleagues have spent many hours in looking for Arnold Jayman's work."

Eventually Arnold Jayman stood to reply. He was a character, and a sweepstake was being run on our table to guess the length of his speech. "Thirty-two minutes," my neighbour said, paying his pound.

I leaned across top table and asked Arnold Jayman for guidance as to the length of his speech, and he said, "I've simply no idea, I haven't prepared anything."

Arnold Jayman began by saying his career came out of the influence of two Colonels. The first had humiliated him at prep school. During a trigonometry class he had said, "If you don't understand anything, ask." Arnold Jayman had not understood anything, and he made the mistake of asking.

"Jayman doesn't understand," the Colonel had said. "Jayman, go and ask Mr Sykes, who is teaching next door. He has been to Oxford and his explanation is bound to be good. And then go and bring four javelins so we can construct a model that will help you understand."

Arnold Jayman had gone next door and been soundly rebuked for disturbing a test which was being conducted in silence. He had then walked half a mile to the pavilion where the javelins were padlocked, had gone in search of the key and had eventually located four javelins and carried them back up the stairs in time for the end of class. Pupils flowed down past the spiked points he carried up, and it was difficult not to impale them. "Ah," the Colonel had said. "You're too late for the model. Now take the javelins back." And Arnold Jayman had missed his lunch.

The other Colonel had given him a special sixteenth-century *Bible* and had invited Arnold Jayman to tea. Arnold Jayman had modelled himself on this second, kindly Colonel.

Yes, he said, it was true he lost things. He told of how all the staff had written comments on report sheets which had been passed to him to finish. They were in two bags and they went missing in the Gym. Arnold Jayman scoured the Gym during lunchtime, searching all the upstairs lockers. Smoke rose through the floor and he went downstairs and found some boys had lit a fire. He arranged for them to be expelled. There were gales of laughter as he continued the story of his quest for the missing reports. Unwilling to admit the loss to his colleagues and to cause them to have to rewrite their reports, he caught the 6.45 a.m. bus and went to the Praefects Room – and fell over a boy who was illegally sleeping on the floor in a sleeping-bag. Arnold Jayman rolled around on the floor trying to disentangle his legs from the sleeping-bag. Eventually someone removed a raincoat from a peg in the Gym and revealed the two bags hanging from a peg. By the time the story was finished the top table were helpless with laughter.

Now Arnold Jayman became emotional. He said that the things that had meant most to him were drama productions – he had only been allowed to put on one Shakespeare play – and the Common Room

Association; and the pupils. He was a "people person" and kept in touch with his pupils and their parents (as he had with my sons and with me), and at the end of his speech he was in tears. He sat down heavily.

After the extensive laughter there was prolonged applause. The Chairman of the Common Room Association patted Arnold Jayman on his back and he sat looking forlorn. The ex-Head of the Junior School whispered to me, "Thirty-two minutes exactly," and looked pleased.

Twenty-five years had slipped away and all the relationships he, as a bachelor, had lived for, and now was his moment of truth. He had retired. There was a family atmosphere in the dining-hall: former staff who were present had retired before him – one was seventy – and his retirement had already taken its place within the pattern of decades worked by older and younger colleagues, a pattern from which his own stark act derived support and strength.

The new Head attracted my attention, and I leaned across top table to listen. He was telling me how going co-ed would not affect the school's sport, for although it might be true that there was only one good footballer per hundred pupils, he had done a deal with West Ham to buy in young professionals who still had to do their GCSEs, who would play football for the school.

The new Head then left, ignored and unaccepted by his colleagues, uneasy among hidden past relationships and affections. It later transpired that he had dismissed the two guests of honour by sending them a sequence of three disciplinary letters, in Arnold Jayman's case citing his propensity for losing things, which was deemed inefficient.

Arnold Jayman sat on, his eyes no longer misty but still in profound sadness while the kitchen staff cleared plates. Twenty-five years had slipped away like the banquet, and now it was time for a bare table and washing-up.

31
Past for the Best

I arrived at the annual school reunion and entered the crowded room, scanning faces for friends from long ago. I shook a hand and responded to a cheery wave and got my drink and was flapped at by a former head boy who told me how he had returned as a guest of honour for a speech, disguised as the Niwaz of Tiswaz, wearing a turban. He had blacked his face and he threw half-crowns to the boys. There was a guard of honour and everyone called him "Your Highness". He was unmasked and in a disgraceful scene there was a protest from the Captain who had organised the guard of honour. The Head had been in on the prank and had nothing to do with the protest.

We ate at a small table with tablecloths in the dining-hall. There were 170 present, and there were eight on each table. I sat between my old Latin master and Derek Minstrel, who lamented his misfortunes during the smoked-fish starter and the chicken Morocco.

"We weren't taught to be cautious," he said, "we were taught to be decent and helpful and so I was taken for a ride by a villain. There must have been a villain in Greek history I could have learned about. I gave a guarantee for my partner to get my magazine out, and he went strategically bankrupt and the bank then enforced the guarantee. It's a good thing we have parents, otherwise I'd have been on the streets. You see this card? You see what it says under my name, '*Scriptor Antiquus*'?"

"Reverend and ancient writer," I said.

"It's meant to say 'Old Hack'. Well at the height of my problem with the bank the manager said, 'And what about your antiques business?' I said, 'I haven't got one.' 'We'll have your antiques business,' he said, rubbing his hands greedily. 'What's it called, "*Scriptus Antiquus*".'"

I laughed as the red wine fumed in my head and felt an Anglo-Saxon sense of belonging at the feast in the hall. I was with people who remembered me from long ago, I felt rooted.

"I had a big disaster in Italy," said Derek Minstrel. "Would you like to buy the house near Florence? It's structurally unsound, but I'd sell it to you for six thousand. It needs twenty thousand spent on it and then you could sell it for eighty thousand. It hasn't got a garden but there's a vineyard nearby. The Mayor threatened to fine me for having an unsound building. He said I could give him an '*oblazione*', an 'oblation', and I gave him two hundred and fifty pounds. He banked it and then said, 'It ees not enough.' I said, 'Can I have it back please?' He said, 'No, it ees not enough.' So I had to give him another '*oblazione*'. Two thousand pounds. For Christ's sake, don't tell Marie. And it's still not enough. He still wants more. He's had two backhanders, two bribes, and he's waiting for me to give him a third one. The magazine's not making any money, and I'm Clerk of the local Council now for one thousand five hundred a year, and it's pretty full time. I wish I could get out of it. It doesn't pay enough to make people offer '*oblaziones*'."

The bearded man opposite us, who was younger, produced a gold fob-watch from his pocket. As Derek Minstrel turned to talk to his neighbour the other side while Jamaican pancakes were served, he leaned across the table and said, "Excuse me, could you pass that to your neighbour."

I peered as I passed it on to my old Latin master and lifted the three-branched candelabrum and held it down near the tablecloth to inspect it by candlelight. On the curved circular back of the watch was engraved a dragon above a sword – I wondered if it held the sword of Damocles – and "*Optimum quod evenit*".

"I'd like to know what it means in Latin," the bearded man said.

The Latin master hesitated, unwilling to commit himself. To save his embarrassment I said, '"Whatever has happened is for the best.'"

"Yes," said the Latin master, "that's exactly right."

"Ah," said the bearded man, "but '*evenit*' – does it mean 'happens', 'will happen' or 'has happened'?"

"'Has happened'."

"So it's optimistic," said the bearded man. "The past has happened for the best?"

"Yes," said the Latin master.

And, peering at the inscription, still holding the three-branched candelabrum with my old Latin master beside me, peering at my elbow, I thought of Derek Minstrel's past as a "*scriptor antiquus*" and buyer of a dilapidated building, and I saw that it had all happened for the best. The events had shaped and polished his character as the sea shapes a breakwater, and had given him the hilarious, sunny disposition that made him such jolly company, with an optimal view of the world.

Everything happened for the best under the benign Providential eye. A disgraceful prank, a repossessing bank and a Mayor's extortion were all events within the Whole and had a place within its pattern and so were good. They were just a few of the unexplained oblations of humankind. All the billions of events behind the ticking of this fob-watch and indeed the entire past had to be accepted in their entirety as being for the best.

The candlelight flickered hope and optimism in the mortal faces around me.

from *In the Brilliant Autumn Sunshine* (2007)

32
A Russian Girl and a Credit Card

Jim Drummond was an accountant of about sixty who took his wife on a tour to Russia. In Moscow the group had dinner in a hotel and there was a band playing Western dance music, and he invited a Russian girl sitting alone at the next table to dance. Somehow she slipped him her phone number, and Jim Drummond struck up a relationship with her. He went back to Moscow without his wife, who was waiting for a hip-replacement, and met up with her. She was in her twenties and had a young son. He brought her back to England for a visit.

A friend of his was worried about him and asked me to have a chat. He came, white-haired and corpulent, quite red-faced and loud-voiced, and said: "I've met this Russian girl and I've discovered she loves me and wants to come and live in England as my wife. She'd bring her child, of course. And I want it to happen. I'd leave my wife for her. She's of a good class. She has a very large apartment in Moscow, incredibly large and in a prime position, just round the corner from the Kremlin. She's getting used to England. She's had the novel experience of using my credit card to buy herself clothes."

"What work does she do?" I asked.

"Oh, nothing. She just lives in her apartment with her child."

"So who pays for the apartment?"

"I've assumed that it was her former husband, by whom she had the child."

"And what did he do?"

"Something in the government. She's a bit evasive about that."

"Are you sure he exists?"

He looked at me.

"Are you sure she's not making up the fact that she had a husband? To have a large apartment near the Kremlin suggests she might be working for the government and have had a child by an earlier relationship."

"How do you mean, working for the government?"

"The KGB have girls who 'monitor' foreign visitors and report on them. A girl sitting at a table near a group of tourists in Moscow may belong to the KGB."

"I hadn't thought of that."

"If she does belong to it, the KGB might want her to be brought to England under the protection of a well-to-do English husband. If she doesn't, the allure of England is economic. In comparison with her Moscow wages (if any) it is a paradise, with free health service for her child and access to unlimited Western goods in the shops via your credit card."

"You mean, she's not interested in *me*? She wants to be a spy over here, or set up home with me for my money?"

"It's possible," I said. "Of course, a twenty-something Russian might have fallen in love with a sixtyish Englishman at first sight. But if she's got a child and a large apartment she's been around and it's possible that she sees you as a way forward for her and her child."

He looked shocked. "Now you put it like that," he said, "I suppose you could be right. She *has* over-used my credit card and she *has* made use of the NHS for her boy. He needs an operation. And now I come to think of it, she hasn't produced any evidence that she had a husband. There are no pictures of him at her flat. It's not impossible that she's in the KGB and has had a child in the course of her work. Thank you for raising these points. I'm going to go away and think about the situation. Perhaps I don't encourage her to leave Moscow and come here. Perhaps I've not seen the situation as it really is."

The next I heard was that Jim Drummond had turned his back on the Russian girl and was living with his wife. It had not occurred to him that a twenty-something Russian girl might have other motives than love at first sight for latching on to a married Westerner. It is sad that all over Eastern Europe there are young girls who would gladly shack up with elderly Western men whose vain egos are susceptible to flattery and who in consequence are open to self-deception, to be allowed to live in the Western paradise and take part in Western benefits. Vanity always looks for the interpretation that suits its self-interest best in affairs of the heart.

33
A Dead Pipistrelle and Blown-Up Skyscrapers

The Lord Lieutenant came to lunch at one of my schools, wearing a blue blazer and tie. I greeted him and took him to the Head's room and for half an hour we had coffee and I showed him pictures of how it was before I'd converted the building into a school. He was able to see how the approach road was a single lane with passing bays and how in a Herculean operation which I directed we had built a sloping earthwork above the stream so that the road could be doubled in width into what had earlier been thin air. We showed him pictures of when the building was a house, before the rooms were converted into classrooms, and talked about the old days, how they lived in the eighteenth and nineteenth centuries, showed him an old engraving of a gardener cutting the grass around 1776. He told me his family had ten earls of Suffolk and that he was very interested in all I had done to revive an interest in history down there.

For three-quarters of an hour we toured the school with the Head. We visited a science lesson where the teacher was showing a dead pipistrelle, which smelt. Then we went into a small private room with a frieze of grimacing Jacobean Green Men and Wild Men of the Woods and spent nearly two hours having a three-course lunch, just him and me. We talked about history, the loss of the American colonies, Bush and how the Queen had misgivings about her new Prime Minister, Blair. As regards Royal Visits to Essex and possibly the school he said, "The Queen's difficult. She's only been four times in the ten years I've been Lord Lieutenant. She spends a lot of time in Suffolk with her friend there." I knew he meant Lord W. "I like the Prince of Wales. Camilla's done him good."

We got on very well. I showed him to his car and shook hands, and he said he would be inviting me and my wife to lunch with him and his wife in his country house. We stood together in the car park unaware that we were standing at the end of an Age, when we still thought in terms of England and believed we were in charge of our national destiny.

He later told me, "After saying goodbye to you I sat in the car and turned on the radio and heard the news that two planes had flown into the Twin Towers, and I instantly knew nothing could ever be the same again. Whenever I hear nine-eleven mentioned, I think of you." I for my part returned to the front door and put my head round the Head's door and saw our Bursar sitting in front of her desk. He said, "I've just been rung by my wife, two planes have flown into the World Trade Center." It was September 11th, the end of the old world and the beginning of a new age of war against terror, of pre-emptive strikes on al-Qaeda in Afghanistan and (mistakenly) in Iraq, aggressive invasions which rallied support for the Iranian Shias and turned Iran into the dominant regional power. Western foreign policy had failed to identify Sunnis as our allies in opposing Shias, and the insurgency in Iraq and Iran's determination to possess a nuclear weapon under the guise of merely wanting peaceful nuclear energy followed from our misreading of the reaction of the fundamentalist Arab world and global network.

The old world had died like a pipistrelle that had flitted and wheeled and swooped throughout long summer evenings and was now passed round for inspection, and the new world had been born in falling towers and smoke, the smokestacking collapse of skyscrapers that seemed to be blown up from within in a threat that seemed to have little to do with remote and distant caves, and baffled and enraged and triggered a confrontation between Muslim and Christian and a conflict of Muslim and Christian civilizations, or rather of extremists within the two civilizations.

The new world had been born in horror and disbelief, and from now on the West, which in the past had defended the world against Communism with such integrity, was an embattled aggressor that had forfeited all its moral legitimacy in deceitfully defending itself by seizing oil, erecting missile shields and finding and destroying non-existent weapons of mass destruction.

34
A Spectre at the Old Boys' Feast

I peered through grey hair and wrinkled faces for my former school friends at the school Shrove Tuesday reunion (a tradition since at least 1868), and shook hands with one of the two ferocious Rivers twins who used to try and bash us up.

"Which one are you?" I asked. "The one in Switzerland?"

"No, he's my brother, he's over there. He's adviser to Qatar."

I encountered Derek Minstrel, full of joviality and mirth with Victorian side whiskers and an upright, forthright manner.

"I've had a terrible year," he said. "My mother-in-law's been ill, and I've had to cope with all that. My one respite was going to Switzerland, and staying with Lance Rivers. You'd have been proud of us, we climbed the mountain. We started at three thousand feet and got to the top, nine thousand feet. My heart was pounding from the exertion, but I did it."

"I must shake hands with Lance Rivers," I said, and seeing him I extended a hand.

"You've shaken hands with me once already. You want my brother, he's over there."

I gave up on the twins and fled into the hall. I was on top table, at the end. Why? Had they made a risk assessment on all present and decided that those who would die earliest would be on top table and extended top table? Next to me was a man of eighty-one I had not met before. He told me that Johnny Lawton's wife had died. She had Alzheimer's disease; she had not grasped that her husband had just died, and now she had followed him. There was a view that in a lucid moment she had grasped the truth and had refused food to join him. Opposite me sat a young solicitor.

I ate my way through roasted salmon, *sauté*d chicken, wilted spinach in honey and orange sauce, the traditional pancakes and then the cheeseboard.

Then it was time for the speeches. The President of the Old Boys' Club was unable to attend. His speech was read by a former President, a sallow rather wizened-looking lawyer with a grey, whey face which I remembered from years back.

He described a football match: Old Etonians 0, our Old Boys 3. There was applause. The Old Boys applauded an idea: the supremacy of the Old Boys' Club. The attendance was: Old Etonians 0, our Old Boys 7. He gave an account of how three of them had arrived at the ground. One old boy, a car-dealer, had provided a top-of-the-range BMW. The former Geography master was in charge of navigation; his task was to use the automated navigator of the new BMW. They had all got lost in a remote village, and had had to ask their way to Eton. They arrived at the match twenty minutes late. Then they had met up with the four other Old Boys, supporters who were on the touchline.

The Head spoke, a slight man in a suit. He gave an account of the school's first-eleven cricket match against Brentwood.

"We won the toss, and Oliver Edrich put Brentwood in. As he came off the field, with the score at 243 for none declared, he said '*Sic panis friarit*', which means 'Thus the cookie crumbles'. His vice-captain said, '*Aut viam inveniam aut faciam*' ('Either find a way or make a way'), and we knocked off the runs with ten overs to spare, Oliver Edrich ninety-eight not out."

There was applause as the Old Boys applauded an idea: the supremacy of their old school.

It was time for the Head Boy to speak, and as the Head turned to introduce him a gaunt, pale elderly man who looked like a spectre of death at our Feast, sitting next to the Deputy Head on the "extended top table" below the platform where I was sitting, rose and said, "Sorry to interrupt, Headmaster, but I would like to propose the toast of the Old Boys' Society, cruelly sidelined by the Club, *Floreat Antiqua Domus*."

He raised his glass and sipped.

There had been bad feeling when the older Society had been replaced by the Club, and the toast was received in silence by the Club members present. A couple of the Old Boys on top table murmured

"*Floreat*", but that was all.

"Thank you," said the Head, and waved the Head Boy forward.

There was a thud. I turned and was in time to see a wizened, bald, elderly Old Boy fall from his chair ten yards away. There was another thud as his head hit the parquet floor. He looked very dead as he lay on his back, his eyes closed, in the gangway the waitresses had been using.

The Head Boy was about to speak.

"Is there a doctor in the house?" someone called.

A round fellow in a blue shirt and red tie bustled towards the supine, prone body. Now half a dozen elderly Old Boys had risen and were kneeling round him. They lifted him and carried him outside into the fresh night air.

The speeches resumed but for me the proceedings were now overshadowed by what had happened to the Old Boy who had fainted. Presumably he was not drunk? The red wine had been flowing, but he had passed out too suddenly to be drunk.

Had he died? Was that how it happened? You retired and went back to your boyhood dining-hall and passed out and died?

We sang the school song, with less volume than usual, and then broke up into groups and I spoke to the pianist and to Arnold Jayman the priest, who told me he had been off ill for three weeks: "Ecclesiastically I'm well but litigiously I'm not, my employer dumped me and I rang the ATL and I'm taking her to Industrial Tribunal. It's affected me."

Now death lurked behind the conviviality. Reality had intruded, the spectre of Death was present at the Feast of Fools. On the way out I saw Derek Minstrel and joked, "You have to earn your place on top table, I'm not speaking to the rabble, the *hoi polloi*."

But my thoughts were with Johnny Lawton who was lying in the churchyard across the road, perhaps now with his wife and perhaps soon by the man who had fainted. That was where all this back-slapping bonhomie and jovial geniality would end for all of us.

35
A Sombre Cherry Tree and Sunflowers

We ate Sunday lunch in the dining-room. Bernette sat at one end, dark-haired and fifty-two, and her son by her first husband, who was born just after he died, was at the other end, tall and bespectacled, his young, quiet wife beside him. She had done the cooking. I sat opposite Ted, who looked slightly uneasy but spoke fluently in French.

After lunch Bernette packed a tray of coffee and cups in the car and we visited Pierre. He lived in a low, traditional bungalow-farmhouse that seemed to have once been cow-stalls and to have preceded the *château*. Roses grew up the doorposts. His plump, blonde German wife greeted us with a smile.

Pierre was sitting in a wheelchair inside the door: bald and blue-eyed, forty-something, sun-tanned and confident. He had his own wine label with "Viscount" before his name, and he looked every inch a Viscount.

"Philip," he said to shock, "have you brought me a present?"

We chatted, and his wife wheeled him outside into the garden. We sat at a table in the open air. His wife and his sister Bernette sat opposite him. Ted sat beside him and I noticed they did not look at each other or talk to each other.

"I have a sick," he said. "It is like sclerosis, but it is not."

His nine-year-old niece came with a friend. She presented her freckly cheek to be kissed and came to me, a natural, open little girl, and did the same. Then she ran to the huge sombre cherry tree before us and put up a short ladder, climbed and picked cherries which she brought and put on our table. Pierre took a handful, picked them off the stalk one by one, put a cherry in his mouth and spat out the cherrystone into his palm and lobbed it over his shoulder onto the hard ground.

Beyond the cherry tree was a flower-bed.

"What's that flower in English?" Pierre asked.

"Delphinium," I said. Ted, feeling ignored by Pierre who had eyes only for me, stood and joined the girl at the tree. He jumped and swung on a branch, clambered up the trunk so he was upside down and pulled himself up.

"*Non*," Bernette called. "*Dangereux*. He will break his arm if the branch snap."

"He's fit," I said. "He goes to a gym and lifts weights to strengthen his arm muscles. He's strong."

"And I am strong," said Pierre from his wheelchair. "Feel my grip."

He extended a sturdy hand and gripped my hand hard. I shook hands equally hard.

"There is a new pill, it cause the brain cells to regenerate. In one year I will be walking," he said. "Maybe. It is very expensive. Two hundred and forty euros each pill."

I nodded.

"I will be walking soon," Pierre said. "And I shall walk round my sunflowers. That field is bare now, but soon it will be full of sunflowers."

"All looking at the sun," I said.

"Yes," he said. "They turn to face the sun. I am waiting for my field to turn into sunflowers."

And suddenly I thought how Chekhovian was the scene: a family sitting, talking about their lives and their dreams near a cherry tree, and there was a latent sadness and wistfulness behind what was said or unsaid, and self-deception. He would not walk again, he had a degenerative disease that did not have remission; he would only get worse. But he had to dream and believe in a better future, and tacitly I had encouraged him in this view. Beneath the shadow of the sombre cherry tree we spoke of sunflowers we could not see.

36
A Tyrant and a Lie

The coach stopped in Beijing's Tien An Men square. Our guide said to me, "That's the queue for Mao's tomb." I saw a long queue snaking round outside a large stone building. "Meet us at the flag at the end of the square in fifty minutes' time, five to ten."

I hurried Pippa across the wide road and towards the front of the queue to find out how long we would have to wait. Two young men in mufti looked authoritative – one had been speaking to the crowd through a megaphone – and I headed towards them. But before I could ask my question –

"No, no you over there, security check."

A round lady in her fifties in a padded jacket bustled up.

"Who are you? Why are you here?"

I explained we were with a tour and wanted to see Mao.

"OK, security, you put one bag inside the other and follow me."

I said, "We've only got till five to ten."

"No problem."

She bustled to the wide road and across a pedestrian crossing to a low office with a window. She pushed in front of the queue, passed the bag inside and took a counterfoil. What was going on? Were we being arrested?

"You pay forty *yuan* each."

I gave her a hundred *yuan* and she pocketed the change. Then she rushed us back through the traffic – I recalled the tanks that had trundled here in 1989 and the bravery of the lone Chinese student who had stood in front of them to stop them – and she pushed into the front of the queue that was filing slowly into the tomb. She was escorting us. After several stops we were admitted to a room in the huge Mao Hall where the Chairman lay on his back in a floodlit glass coffin, a flag below his chin. He was very yellow and stern, and looked very old.

The line was supposed to keep moving but when I was level with his head I stopped. I thought, 'You were a tyrant. You executed 20 million in 1949 and were responsible for at least 45 million deaths in all, perhaps more. You were as bad as Hitler and Stalin. You launched the Cultural Revolution in 1966 to purge bourgeois reactionaries and re-communise China. I saw the chaos it caused. Later I attended a meeting to discuss liberating China – a sixth of mankind – from you. It's happened, they've been liberated from you, you've been dumped. Outside they pay lip-service to what you did, but they've gone capitalist and Western, they've moved away from Communism. You launched the Cultural Revolution to continue your ideology, and it has not continued. You tried to emulate Dostoevsky's Grand Inquisitor. But you've been dumped by the people who worshipped you a couple of decades ago. You lost.'

Mao had an ugly expression on his face. He was snarling and scowling at what had happened to China since he died. He had been a ruthless dictator, a dreadful tyrant. I thought of Hamlet's lines, "Imperious Caesar, dead and turn'd to clay, / Might stop a hole to keep the wind away."

Then I realised that two 8421 soldiers – the unit that looked after Mao was the 8421 unit – were glaring at me, indicating that I had stopped the moving line. The guide was waiting for me with Pippa, looking agitated. So with a start I came to and joined them. We returned outside and retrieved our bag and the security woman gave us two tasteless butterfly brooches. I tipped her 70 *yuan* (£5.50) and we set off towards the Tien An Men gate.

Over it I could see the rostrum where the Chairman had spoken to the Chinese people during his lifetime. Below it there was a huge poster of Mao. The slogan said, I was told by our guide when we met him at the flag, that the Chinese had their own brand of socialism, meaning that it includes capitalism. That was Liu Shao-chi's position in 1966, when the Cultural Revolution was launched against him. Mao had lost the argument. But the poster was a lie. The picture paid lip-service to Mao's Communism while, as the slogan hinted, China had turned rampantly capitalist.

Then I felt a deep disgust towards Mao. He had butchered his fellow men. He had lied to the Chinese during his lifetime, and now his lying-in-state suggested that Communism was still with us. The Party wanted to suggest that there had been continuity, itself a lie, and he was being used by the Party to lie in death.

37
A Coffin and a Ladybird

I arrived in good time for the funeral, but the church was already nearly full. A bell was tolling. I found a seat in the middle, and, seeing a man lean over and snatch up one of the three Orders of Service on the pew, I took possession of one of the remaining two and took in the elderly nature of the congregation and stared at the two front pews that were filled with black-clad relatives. Francis Soames had never married and the younger ones were probably nephews or great nephews. I looked up at the stars on the vaulted ceiling and recalled that outside, over a door, was an inscription: "Gateway to Heaven".

A man came and sat next to me and took the other Order of Service, and then a domineering woman said from the aisle, "Is that place free?" and I said, "Yes," and she pushed her way past, followed by a man, and helped herself to my Order of Service, which was on a low ledge. She sat and began writing hymn numbers on it.

"Look," I said to her, "you're welcome to share it, but that was mine. I'd like it back at the end."

"Oh," she said, "but I've written on it and I want to give it to someone."

"I'm sure there'll be some left," I said, "but I need it to show some friends of his."

Then the coffin was borne in to a swinging censer and the funeral got under way with a hymn.

The man on my other side, who was Chairman of the Trustees of a local Hall, held his Order of Service out so that I could follow the words of the hymn. On my other side the woman hogged my Order of Service, leaving the man beyond her to fend for himself in singing and responses.

Now there was an address from a Canon from the pulpit. He said that Francis was seventy-seven. He had been at Eton and Cambridge, had acted in the Footlights – that was how he had been interested in Shakespeare. He told how he had become a barrister and how he had spent his spare time in charity work, sharing of himself. He told how he and his companion Marion went to Tasmania together and he came back an Aussie – there was laughter – and how Marion had died earlier in the year.

"I think he felt his work had come to an end. He soldiered on, he was very self-contained. He didn't complain of loneliness, he carried on, but went through the motions a lot. Sometimes if you said a key word in the course of a remark, it was like pressing a button, and a stream of thoughts would come out. There did not seem to be an off-button."

And everyone laughed sympathetically.

Eventually there was a high solemn Mass. A shrill bell trilled. There was a delay while the servers took Mass and then a churchwarden invited the family to go up. To my surprise all declined, even though Francis had been a churchwarden here. Several more declined, and then my turn came.

As we queued for communion, a churchwarden whispered to me, "To the right of the coffin." I knelt at the rail where one of the three servers of bread gave me a thick round wafer that crunched as I bit to dissolve it on my tongue. A priest came and thrust the chalice under my chin and said, "The blood of Christ." I thought of Mithras and Eleusis as I sipped, and then I stood and walked back past Edith Small who was queuing for her turn back in the aisle.

An hour and a quarter after the start we were singing the last hymn. A ladybird crawled from the Chairman of the Trustees' sleeve on to our Order of Service. We ignored it, and it reached the top edge and toppled onto the pew in front. A lady in front of us of considerable girth would sit on it, so I bent forward and pushed it two or three times so it skidded out of harm's way. But it crawled back into the danger zone and the Chairman of the Trustees turned his Order of Service on end and scraped it, like a card, onto the rush matting that covered the floor of the aisle.

I watched fascinated, forgetting to sing, and looked up and saw the four pallbearers turn with the coffin on their shoulders and, to a swinging censer, begin their slow walk down the aisle towards us.

The Chairman had seen too, and now he was bending in the aisle squatting on his haunches, carding the ladybird, making little scooping movements to get the creature out of danger from the approaching feet. The eyes of the two front men said, "Get out of our way," as, with one final scoop, the Chairman succeeded in scraping the ladybird back under our pew. He got up from his haunches and returned and stood to attention beside me and we bowed our heads as Francis passed, feet first, and was borne round the corner and (as I looked back) out of the church door where he was removed for private cremation.

We stood around outside and greeted those we knew and went to the church hall for a buffet spread Francis had thoughtfully paid for.

There was much conviviality among many familiar faces and there were not many mentions of Francis. It was as though everyone wanted to forget the coffin and catch the moment, like preserving an intricately beautiful red-and-black-spotted ladybird from being trampled on by grim pallbearers.

38
A Shrill "Shut Up" and Shambles

The celebration dinner was held in a large marquee at the foot of a sloping field adjoining a Hall. We arrived in heavy rain and parked on grass and picked our way in dinner jackets under umbrellas to the marquee, took champagne and stood amid a throng and worked out from lists which table we were on.

Then the new Leader of the Opposition came in. I was near the marquee entrance and suddenly Edith Small, now a Shadow Minister, was standing beside me, waving a hand in my direction, and he came and shook my hand, tall and looking around for new hands to shake, doing his duty rather than looking into people's eyes, saying "Oh, really?" in an offhand way that revealed his lack of interest in what he was being told, and I could tell he was not really interested in individual people.

We were asked to go to our tables and we stood for half an hour while he progressed from table to table, having his photo taken with all present.

"I might vote New Labour at the next election," I whispered to Pippa, "they'd do things more slickly and not keep us standing around for half an hour, getting deep-vein thrombosis waiting for the Leader to come."

Our table was the last to be photographed and the Leader's entire attention was given to positioning himself and concentrating on the camera. He had no questions for anyone on our table.

Then we were told over a loudspeaker to be seated, and he went to a low stage and was reintroduced by a local councillor and made a speech. He said that he had been called a lot of names but that there were a lot of seats to win from other parties, and the course he was on was the right one.

Edith Small said a few sycophantic words about what a "wonderful" speech we had heard. After that he left.

I had seen them come and go, hopeful would-be leaders – a procession of them, seen off by Blair. Was this one going to be any different? New Labour were imploding in scandals and incompetence, and it was a good time to be Leader of the Opposition, but five million voters had defected and who knew whether they would return. This Leader didn't stand for anything at all. And what a life he had, going from region to region, shaking hands, pressing flesh, making charismatic speeches, not staying to dinner, restlessly moving on elsewhere.

The meal comprised smoked salmon, roast beef and pavlova. Between courses I spotted an Essex MP whose parents I knew, and spoke to him. He was wearing a white jacket and said, "Your mother used to teach me the violin."

I was sitting next to the wife of someone who had been at school with me. She told me about her husband's illness. He had spent much of December and January in hospital. "It's a blood disease. Wegener's granulomatosis. It's a disease of the respiratory tract – nose and lungs – and kidneys. It first manifests itself as nosebleeds and chronic inflammation of the sinuses. It's quite rare. He broke his nose playing fives at school, a ball came back from the pepper-pot. He didn't realise it was broken, and it made the air passages more narrow and he had lung problems. He was diagnosed after a blood test to do with his lungs. The disease has made him deaf."

"And now," cut in a voice on a hand-held microphone, "we are going to play a game. Everyone must put a five-pound note on the table and stand with your hand on your head or your tail. I will toss a coin. If its heads and you have your hand on your head you stay in. Otherwise you sit down. And so on." There followed five minutes of shambolic embarrassment as all the men stood with their hands on their heads or their backsides and were relieved when eliminated, while helpers scurried round the tables scooping five-pound notes into tubs.

"And now," said the disembodied voice, "we come to the auction."

There were several bottles of champagne signed by one, two – in one case, five – former leaders of the Party. A caricature of Churchill signed by the great man went for £6,000, and all the other items raised as much again.

In the middle the lights suddenly went out and the microphone ceased to work. We were lit by the candles on the table and the auctioneer attempted to reach us with his own voice. Some were chattering, and Edith Small banged her spoons on her table to try and obtain silence. She was ignored.

After a few minutes the lights came back on and the microphone worked. Edith Small stood up from her table.

"And now," announced Edith Small in a shrill overloud voice, "we're going to draw the raffle. I'm going to draw, it's so exciting, we've got so many prizes. Number one is table 1 and on table 1 it's...." She said a name. "Number two...." Half an hour later she was deafening. "Number thirty-seven is this ladies' handbag. It's going to, isn't this exciting, Rodney Laird." And so it ground on. "Number forty-one, the penultimate, is this larger-than-life-size kangaroo." She had an enormous kangaroo toy round her neck. "Number forty-one's been won by, oh, isn't it exciting, by...." And finally with everyone deafened, each item having taken getting on for a minute, we reached number 42.

There was a hubbub of relief at not having to listen to her shrill voice any more.

Then Edith Small went straight into her speech.

It was a huge miscalculation to run the auction and the raffle together and leave no time for people to talk at the tables. The hubbub became a loud and animated chatter and her attempt to thank individuals for hosting the dinner, and to fawn about the new Leader, was drowned by an audience of 200 chattering, calling, laughing constituents relieved at being freed from having to listen to the raffle and preparing to leave. Some were actually on their feet, having collected raffle prizes. She was too shrill to listen to all over again without a break.

"Shut up," she yelled in exasperation.

I could not believe what I was hearing. Coriolanus had gone to the *plebs* wearing a gown of humility to be elected. Was this female

Coriolanus in her gown of humility really telling her voters to shut up? It sounded like autocracy rather than democracy.

The auctioneer intervened on the hand-held microphone.

"This is your MP addressing you. Please listen attentively," he said in a reproachful tone.

But it was no use. Edith Small was like a teacher who had lost control of her class. They had no respect for her, she had been too familiar during the forty minutes of the raffle and too shrill. The constituents had had enough. People were on their feet and moving towards the door. Accepting reality, Edith Small cut her speech short. The MEP took over and wisely confined his remark to two points, each of which only took a sentence.

"That was a classic example of how not to do it," Pippa said as we made our way to the exit. "You always have the speeches *before* the raffle, never after. The auctioneer should have done the raffle, not her. She was showing off and she lost it."

Edith Small was standing between us at the exit. Her shrill voice still ringing in my ears, I detoured round her to avoid hearing another word. I had seen through her. She was ordinary and survived by trying to be one of the lads. The MP had no clothes. I knew I would not be able to bring myself to vote for her in future elections.

"I'm going to vote New Labour at the next election," I said. "They organise things more slickly, that was a shambles."

"Oh," Simon said, "and you know I corrected the spelling mistake in your Christian name? There's another one, a new one. They've still managed to get your name wrong in the programme."

"Shambolic lot," I said.

And then I grasped that the reason this Party had been so long in opposition was that they were a shambles. It needed a fresh approach at every level to sweep away the resentment caused by weak candidates who took their constituents for granted and told them to "shut up".

As a writer, I reflected I was like Chekhov, who had been part-doctor and part-author. A writer has to have one foot in society and one foot outside it, at a distance, watching, observing the shambles created by the inept, being truthful. I had taken part in a shambles – and on my birthday, at that – but I was not a part of it, or of any Party. I would not shut up for anyone. I had an opinion. I would not vote for anyone who told me to shut up.

Representational democracy is a wonderful gift for those who have never had it, but we lived under an elective dictatorship which did not reflect our views. I was already disenfranchised, I was an observer, and looked in on the awfulness of organised society and defined its shallowness and inept pretensions with a scathing and cleansing indignation.

39
Horror After the Rave

Tina Cotteridge was a flame-haired, high-spirited young girl who was given an assistant's job in the Council Offices under a governmental trainee scheme. I knew her boss and met her on one occasion at this time. Her job involved meeting the public, and eyebrows were raised when she became pregnant by a lorry driver and flaunted the fact, and eventually she left.

Years later, her daughter, a hairdresser's assistant aged seventeen, was walking back from a "rave" in a local pub, a Kiss 100 FM music event. She was with a friend who was sixteen, and just before midnight they were on a narrow, winding dark road that dropped down through the forest. It must have been pitch black. They walked in the road, laughing and talking, and a van came round the corner and hit them from behind, stopped briefly further on and then drove on.

Both lay face down in the road with serious head injuries. The driver of the next car to approach spotted them, and stopped and called an ambulance. Both girls were taken to hospital and Tina Cotteridge's daughter died next day. Her friend was so badly injured that at first she had been left for dead; she could not be told of the death for two months.

The van was found abandoned a mile away, with a smashed windscreen and broken headlamps. The driver was arrested. Two witnesses who had been higher up the road claimed he had stopped, run round to the back to see what he had done and then driven off. He said he thought he had hit a tree, that he had stopped, confused and in a panic, and then driven on unaware that he had hit two young girls. The witnesses told the police that he had been driving without lights, which was why he was unaware he had hit people. He denied driving without lights, and the police said there was no evidence to suggest he had been responsible for driving into the girls. Drugs were found in the van: a supply of alcohol, Ecstasy, cocaine and cannabis. These were found in his blood, but he said he had only drunk a can of lager and taken some cannabis and an Ecstasy pill *after* driving home. The police said there was no evidence that he had taken these before driving without sidelights through the forest, and drew no conclusion from the abandoning of the van a mile away.

The case came to court. The van driver pleaded guilty to dangerous driving, failing to stop and report an accident, driving with no headlights and possession of Ecstasy and cannabis. The judge banned him from driving for twelve months and imposed a hundred-hour community service order. The judge said, "I make it absolutely clear, because I want everyone to understand, that you are not charged with causing death or injuries to the two girls by dangerous driving."

Thirty relatives of the girls called out, "No, this is a disgrace" and "Murderer". Tina Cotteridge rushed towards the van driver in the dock, screaming, "You murdered my daughter," and threw water at his barrister.

Outside the court her husband said that the judgement had sent out a message that hitting a girl was no different from hitting a tree or a lamppost, and that it was all right not to report an accident. Everyone was shocked that the van driver had not been sent to prison.

I read an account of the incident in the national press, and sighed and shook my head. I thought back to the flame-haired girl who had flaunted her pregnancy to the public, and I wondered at life's way of bringing in a new person and handing her to a mother who was not ready, and then so cruelly taking her away before she had started her adult life and inflicting such horror on her family.

Why had it happened? Had the rave left the two girls in an undisciplined frame of mind, and had they walked riskily in the dark and invited being knocked over? Had the van driver been on drugs and, driving without lights, would he have failed to see anyone walking in the dark road? And why had the girls' chaotic lives crossed the path of the chaotic van driver? Is there a law that a chaotic frame of mind attracts a chaotic event? Were the girls and the van somehow drawn to each other? Does a rave attract horror?

40
An Awesome Queen and Umbrella-ed Flunkeys

We were invited to attend a Garden Party at Buckingham Palace. It was in honour of the Duke of Edinburgh's Award. We arrived before 2.30 and walked to the Grand Entrance in front of the Mall and queued at a gate, showed our ticket, passport and driving-licence to verify our identities, then walked past two guards in busbies through an arch into the quadrangle, the three-sided Buckinghams' House behind the Victorian balcony *façade*. We walked to the door on the far side and entered the palace. I warmed to the red carpets and gold in the ceiling of the Grand Hall. We followed the moving queue into a corridor of statues and to the Bow Room and emerged by the balustrade overlooking the gardens.

There was a long tent in green and white on the left and, in the distance on the right, the Royal Tea Tent and VIP tent. The lawn was filled with placards on which were numbers held by young forces' personnel. These denoted groups where Council employees had gathered. In between them thronged suited men and ladies in hats and tight summer dresses, who stood or strolled.

It was a muggy afternoon. We went for a slow wander round the gardens. The sun went in and high cloud cooled, and there was a breeze. We ambled to the lake and then back to the small rose-garden of Elizabeth roses, all orange-pink and very scented. Then we crossed the lawn and sat in front of the main tea room until three, when tea was served. We went to one of the many tea-points inside the tent and took a plate with a depressed ring for a cup, chose sandwiches and cakes – one with a chocolate drop on top stamped with a gold crown – and received a cup of weak tea. We returned to our table, sipped our tea and ate our food, listened to two bands – and then went to another tea-point in the long tent and returned with second helpings.

Certificates were being presented in front of us on the lawn. In each group someone was speaking and there were regular rounds of applause when presentations were made. For the next hour there were regular claps. Before four the volunteers disbanded their Council groups, the placards were marched away and four lanes were formed, which the rest of us joined. They met in a radial point near the Royal Tea Tent. We sauntered and stood near where they met.

Young Sea Cadets were standing every ten yards, and Pippa asked one, "What's happening?" and the cadet said, "The Queen's coming along this lane and the Duke of Edinburgh that one, I don't know about the other two."

We stayed where we were. At four the Blues and Royals band struck up the national anthem. Some eight thousand five hundred people stood to attention. Far away I could see the Queen in a blue hat and the Duke of Edinburgh in a white hat and the Count and Countess of Wessex. They were standing on the steps of the balustrade, not far from the door to the palace.

We waited for the Royals to come into view. Important suited flunkeys strode round in the centre of the lanes, at least half a dozen of them. Each carried a furled umbrella, his badge of office. If it rained – and there was no likelihood of that today – they could put their umbrellas up and shelter the Royals. Some had yellow, bony handles with four knobbles on their umbrellas. Some had smooth orange handles. Did they signify a higher level and status? Their umbrellas were like the symbolic wooden staff of leadership under Elizabeth I. The flunkeys looked at their watches and stood and conferred in the middle of the lanes, conveying the impression that they were making it all happen. Yet if they had not been there, would the ceremony not have gone on just the same?

Other assistants without umbrellas arranged those selected to be presented to the Queen in groups of four or five that jutted out into her lane. These were Council volunteers with thirty or forty years' service in the Duke of Edinburgh's Awards drawn from all over the country.

It was cool with the sun in, and there was a pleasant breeze. We waited about forty-five minutes, and then the Queen came into view in our lane as the Sea Cadet said she would. She was talking to one of the small groups. Beefeaters had appeared and they took up positions with their backs to the crowd. They were reinforced by young ATC soldiers who stood on both sides of our lane.

Now the Queen was talking to the group nearest us. I looked at her face, so familiar from the stamps and coins on which she reigned. It was white. It was covered with a layer of foundation cream that made it look white. I noticed that each of those presented did the talking, and the Queen said virtually nothing, but listened. I looked at her blue silk dress, which was embroidered with very detailed branches and minimal blossom, and thought that her clothes were in the tradition of Elizabeth I – simpler, but never-the-less similar.

I looked around her. She had Beefeaters, or Yeomen of the Guard, like the Tudor monarchs. Sometimes – not now – she had heralds like them, too. There was no fanfare today but the Beefeaters carried pikes with pointed iron heads on long wooden shafts. She had a royal tent just as Henry VIII had a tent in the Field of the Cloth of Gold. She walked slowly in finery, and in theory all men bowed their heads and women curtseyed as she passed, though as I bowed my head when she went by, giving me a long look, I did not see many others follow suit. She walked on and entered the Royal Tea Tent enclosure.

I thought she was good for eighty, and I thought the Duke of Edinburgh even better, at eighty-five. He stayed out longer and seemed to be talking to more people. He left his lane and stood about ten yards from where we were, and walked off into the Royal Tea Tent enclosure. Five minutes later the Count and Countess of Wessex emerged from other lanes, chatting more to the crowd than the Queen.

Then I thought, this is odious. They're Germans, and he's a Greek. They're not English. It's all a fraud. She's descended from George I who couldn't speak a word of English. She's a Saxe-Coburg-Gotha, Windsor's a phoney name.

But then I thought, this is one of several garden parties which cover every aspect of charity life in England. It's good, what they're doing. It's good to invite leaders of charitable enterprises to be presented.

We strolled back to the chairs in the main enclosure and I found some iced coffees and carried them to our table. We sat and sipped iced coffee as warm sun came out.

"It's good that a family's the centre of our country," I said, "and not a corrupt politician."

"Yes," Pippa said.

"Does this make you feel English?"

"Oh, yes."

"British?"

"No."

"So you don't include Wales, Scotland and Northern Ireland?"

"No."

"And you want an English parliament?"

"Yes."

"And to stop subsidising Scotland?"

"Yes. This makes me feel English. I belong to England."

At a quarter to six, five minutes before the Royal Party were scheduled to leave, we crossed the lawn and stood on the side of another lane that had just formed. The warm sun scorched my cheeks. More naval Sea Cadets and ATC soldiers, spaced out, stood on each side of the lane. And the Count and Countess of Wessex came.

"Hello," the Countess of Wessex said to a lady on the far side of the lane. And she seemed pleased to be spoken to, and her face burst into a smile. A conversation took place that looked staged, artificial, not real. I was glad it was not me.

There was no sign of the Queen or Duke of Edinburgh. They had somehow been spirited away, perhaps in a buggy, from the Royal Tea Tent. There was no trace of them.

We walked back to the balustrade and leant on it, waiting for the national anthem to signal the close of the Garden party. The warm sun beat on our cheeks. The lawn was full of elegant, sedately-moving people.

I reflected that this was my sort of place. I felt relaxed inside the palace, among the statues and the gold. Perhaps I had been a monarch in a former life. I would not mind reigning. You didn't have to do anything, just be the same face that's on the stamps and coins, the face in your photo, and put yourself about, let people see you. You needed to have several flunkeys with furled umbrellas clearing the way. You had to be a still centre for the turning wheel. You had to say as little as possible, listen, keep yourself apart from your subjects, encourage them to bow and genuflect. Your house had to be substantial, like Buckingham Palace. It had to look as if it had been built to last, and to inspire awe.

Yes, I thought, the Queen had got the knack of reigning. She was a wise woman and very good for eighty, and for all my earlier doubts I had been privileged to see a historical figure who had survived the Blitz in this palace, talked with Churchill (her first Prime Minister) and received all the great men of our time. She too had greatness, I was sure of that, she was an awesome reigner. But I felt I had seen through the mystique and had worked out how she inspired such awe: by incessant devotion to duty and the fussing of her strutting flunkeys which kept her subjects in their place. Or was there a system which her flunkeys served, and was she a cipher-monarch, their puppet whose strings they pulled?

41
Notice and a Wheel

The sun was setting and it would soon be dusk. A male choir was singing to a small crowd the other side of the harbour. As I sat on a seat outside George, the antiques dealer, approached with his wife.

"Have you heard our news?" he asked. "We were given notice by Don Cushing at the beginning of July."

Don Cushing was a builder who had had a heart attack and retired. "He's sold an option on the whole of that complex to a property developer with planning permission to build four houses. We've been renting there for ten years. I've said to him every year, 'When you go, will you give us first refusal?' Each year he's said, 'Oh, yes.' But he hasn't. I've had it in my mind, I'd open a *café*, perhaps a small restaurant, above where we are at present. It's terrible. I don't know what we'll do. We've got a lot of stock. We have to be out by the end of

September. October and November are good months down here by the sea, people buying before Christmas. There's nowhere to put it. We've got to be out in a few weeks. We've got a house near here, as you know. We had planned to sell it and buy the Postmaster's house up the road and use it as a shop, for it has always been a shop downstairs. But our buyer's pulled out, breaking the chain, and we can't proceed. I don't want to retire yet, we're not ready to retire to France. We bought a plot in France, as you know, but we've got to build on it before we can retire there. I always thought Don Cushing was trustworthy, a man of his word, as we are. But he's not. We've learnt to our cost he's not. I don't know what we'll do. The stock I've bought is stored in a barn, but it's not suitable for people to go and see it there. Where are we going to go? Our world's been turned upside down." His wife nodded miserably in assent.

Later I reflected that one should arrange one's life, in so far as one could, so there were no shocks. That meant ideally being self-employed and owning one's own home to escape the unpredictable vagaries of employers and landlords. Where possible one should plan to live one's own life without being dependent on the goodwill of others. Noble self-sufficiency, that was the ideal. And one should order one's affairs so that if this day were one's last, one would depart life leaving everything tidy, no mess for someone else to clear up. One should retire and sift and sort one's own papers and place oneself in a state of readiness to be taken though still living positively with projects and tasks.

But then I thought, the television screens are full of war, Israel is invading South Lebanon, the self-employed and home-owners of Israel and Lebanon have not been insulated from war. War can suddenly overtake and lay waste the best-laid plans to live in a state of retirement and readiness. There is no guaranteed protection against the vicissitudes of life.

George was a home-owner but he rented his workplace, that was his flaw. No matter how well we prepare, the Wheel of Fortune can turn and we can be plunged down from whatever height to which we have been raised. And one can live in a state of readiness as easily at the bottom as at a height, though at the bottom there is the distraction of worrying about whether one can make ends meet.

All that can be said is that one should live one's last months and years in a state of calm and prepared readiness as if saying to the Lord, as in the Song of Simeon, "*Nunc dimittis*": "I have completed my projects and tasks, now let your servant depart."

42
Exhausted

I sat in the afterglow of going to the Light and thought of those for whom I had had responsibility during my life as if I were giving an account at the Last Judgement which takes place after dying, when one's life runs past the soul's eye in a succession of rapid images, and I thought of Alison Harmon.

Alison Harmon came to work on my staff. She had milk-white coiffeured curved hair. She was a good conductor of the choir, holding out her hands with her knuckles clenched between her thumbs and little fingers and fixing the girls' shining eyes with her own so that they all looked at her as she conducted. But one day the Head told me her breath smelt of alcohol and that she kept a small flask in her handbag. She was sometimes on duty in the playground, and in all conscience we could not turn a blind eye to the possibility that an inebriated teacher was watching over young children in a position of responsibility.

The Head challenged her, and she made light of her flask. But one of the staff who knew her better than the rest said she lived alone and had talked to her of suicide.

At exam time in the summer term she was absent and her exam papers were sent to her home to be marked. She was not on the phone but she rang from a call-box and reported that she had not been able to mark them as she had been too unwell.

"It's strange," the Head said to me. "She doesn't seem aware of the inconvenience she's causing by not handing in her marks for us to consider when we award prizes to her class. I'll have to get them back and we'll have to mark them here. Someone will have to go round to her house."

I said I would collect the exam papers as everyone else had a timetable to operate.

I drove to her small house, which was just round the corner from where I am living now. I rang the bell. There was a long delay, and then she came to the door in a long white dressing-gown. She had a pasty, unhealthily pale, unmade-up face and looked exhausted, drugged.

"Come in," she said.

She led me into a large sitting-room with two sofas and a piano. Otherwise it was barely furnished. I sat on one of the sofas.

"I hope you're feeling better," I said. "I've come to collect the exam papers. They need the marks to do their statistics before Prize Day."

"Oh," she said, "yes."

She walked unsteadily out of the room, and a long time elapsed before she returned with a large envelope and handed over the unmarked papers.

I chatted about the house. "It's a quiet road," I said.

"Oh, yes. It's near the Forest."

"Will we see you at Prize Day?"

"I'm not sure."

Something in her eyes told me she would not be there.

She came to the door with me and let me out.

"Goodbye," she said, more finally than I expected.

I drove back to the Head and handed over the envelope of exam papers.

"Any indications of alcohol?"

"No."

"How did you find her?"

"Strange," I said. "She didn't connect to the situation, somehow. She's not concerned about us. We don't impinge on her consciousness. I don't like it. I can't explain why, but I feel she may be about to commit suicide. I'm going to ring the police."

Then I felt slightly foolish. I had been going by my sixth sense, I had no evidence.

When I returned to my desk, I rang the police and explained the situation to the station sergeant.

"Could someone call on her?" I asked. "I'm afraid she might be about to commit suicide."

So the sergeant visited her himself and then rang me back. "She's all right," he said reassuringly. "I rang the bell and she came to the door in her dressing-gown. She said she had been unwell but was recovering."

There was no more I could do.

The next morning I had a phone call from the police sergeant.

"I'm sorry to have to tell you," he said, his voice squirming in embarrassment, "but last night she was found dead in her car in a side road by Knighton Woods. About two a.m. She must have driven there after midnight, it's a few minutes from her address. She killed herself with a hosepipe attached to her exhaust. I'm very conscious that you foresaw it and asked me to forestall it, and somehow she hoodwinked me into thinking you were wrong. I have since been back to her house. She had a large number of tablets lying beside a glass of water in the kitchen off the sitting-room, which she had piled up but didn't use. Looking back, I think it likely that she had planned it before your visit and was trying to commit suicide when you went round – you may have disturbed her. For some reason she decided not to go through with the tablets and to use the exhaust later on instead. You were right."

Exhausted. I was not surprised or shocked as I had somehow known deep-down that she would be slipping away.

It later transpired that she had attempted suicide several times before, and had written a letter at the beginning of the year to a friend in which she had said: "This is the year I intend to do it." Now, looking back on all those I had tutelage over, I am conscious that I was ahead of most of the situations but that this one slipped through my fingers like a dropped catch. Yet there was nothing more I could have done. I had done my best, my conscience was clear on that.

Now, musing on the Last Judgement that awaits my soul in the style of the Egyptian *Book of the Dead,* I think of all the things I should not have done in my life. I tried to be benevolent and to make things work but I can think of several things I could, and should, have done differently. But as an existentialist, I stand by what I did. Right or wrong, I did what I did and am defined by my deeds when my soul comes to be weighed against a feather.

I closed my eyes and went back to the Light. A watery pattern, like a dull, distant moon reflected in wind-stirred water, moved slowly and in the centre there was a brighter circle, a soul encircled in faint Light. I was not sure whose it was, but concluded that it was probably mine.

43
Fossilised Chivalry and Unknightly Yobbery

I admired the two giant stone fossilised ammonites Pippa had found, which were Jurassic (about 170 million years old). Each was almost too large to lift in one hand with fingers spread out, and one had a curling *nautilus* that resembled a tiny ammonite parasitically lodged on its end. Then we slipped out of the side gate into the wide green ride of the Forest, Pippa stabbing the ground with her stick. We walked down in windy sunshine to the Ching and crossed the road and walked to Chingford Plain, a clearing behind Queen Elizabeth's Hunting Lodge where a Forest Festival was being held.

Round a central rectangular enclosure of lists or palisades – crowd-control barriers with bales of hay on which people sat and watched skirling bagpipers – were small tents, all thronged. We sauntered among the exhibits while there was a display of dog agility and took in posters on Forest wildlife: birds, badgers, and plants from which butterflies take nectar.

Medieval crafts were well represented. A weaver dressed as a medieval peasant with a curled white hat, long dress and apron wove by twisting threads by hand, just as in the Middle Ages. A chandler dressed as a medieval peasant was dabbing tallow with animal fat. The tallow had a long wick. There was a display of medieval arrows, and archers held bows and demonstrated shooting. And – what joy! – there was a stall about jousting, beside which stood two sweating knights in armour. A child was saying to one who was dressed in black, "What are you?" He said, "I'm a knight."

I gathered there was to be a tournament so we had tea and cake at a tea tent and then found an unclaimed bale of hay and sat by the barriers or palisades in the warm sun until it was time for jousting, soaking in the atmosphere of the old world – a medieval crowd on foot in an ancient clearing in the Forest with the Hunting Lodge in the background. A central barrier was draped with cloths or capes in different colours, each of which bore a coat of arms.

Two Oriental boys pushed in front of me, treading on my toes and on Pippa's stick, singing out of tune and talking loudly to each other, unaware that they were blocking our view or disturbing our peace, and clambering on the barrier by our feet. When they moved away slightly we both stood up and tugged our bale of hay forward and sat with our noses to the barrier so that 21st-century globalised indiscipline could not prevent us from watching the spectacle.

The tournament began with a flourish of medieval music. A white knight wearing a white tunic over his armour with a red cross on it rode on a white charger. He galloped round the enclosure holding a flag on a pole. It fluttered in the high wind, which was just getting up. He told us through a microphone by his mouth that we were in 1348. I reflected that the Black Death reached England in the second half of that year, and was south of London but north of Bristol by December 1348 and spreading northwards. This crowd was just out of reach of the advancing Black Death.

He introduced four knights who, with great pageantry, rode on horseback side by side in livery, wearing armour with pointed headpieces and holding flags decorated with their own coat of arms. One was from the Continent, one from elsewhere in England, he said. One, he said, was the Earl of Chingford, who raised a cheer. The fourth one was the Black Knight. He said, "He always cheats. I suggest you give him a loud boo."

The Black Knight – the fellow I had heard say "I'm a knight" – ran round the enclosure in his armour waving his arms to drum up support but was met with a barrage of booing. Disgracefully he held a glass of beer. The commentator said it was unprecedented for such bad manners to be displayed in the lists. A jester with a coxcomb (a cap that had three floppy pointed bits with bells sewn on their ends) used his trumpet as a horse and "galloped", waving his free hand to the crowd. At that point the wind reached gale force and blew a round Henry-the-Eighth-style tent onto its side and rolled it across the enclosure until the knights gallantly intercepted it and stopped it.

The warm-up over, the knights swiftly began the contest. Two, galloping towards each other with their lances before them, each struck a wooden dummy holding a shield and ducked as it swivelled a ball and chain at the back of their heads. All four thundered up on horseback several times, and no one was hit by the ball and chain.

Now the knights galloped and speared a block from the ground with their lances. After that they galloped and tried to thrust their lances through yellow metal rings. Not many rings were successfully scooped, and at one point the gale blew down the central barrier.

Then ladies were asked to donate a favour to the knight of their choice, and chiffon scarves were collected from volunteers in the crowd and presented to different knights, who wore them as sashes. Each scarf was in the same set, suggesting that all the ladies were in collaboration with the organisers.

There was then, at last, a full jousting contest. Two knights charged at each other, tilted with levelled lances and tried to score a hit on the other's shield and unhorse him. The four knights had several goes and there were a few (expertly executed) clattering falls in armour. Eventually the contest was declared to have been won by the Earl of Chingford, to whom the commentator was very deferential, calling him "My Lord" and calling on his squire to take his lance.

The Black Knight disputed the Earl of Chingford's victory – his behaviour was unknightly and yobbish – and there was a *mêlée*, a mock battle between armed horsemen. There were disgraceful scenes which ended in a well-choreographed sword fight in which both men ducked as swords scythed over their heads. The duel ended with all the knights setting on the Black Knight and giving him a good kicking on the ground. After that the four knights left the enclosure on horseback to applause.

We stood up from our bales, back in the 21st century, and began our walk back through the Forest, edging our way through jostling crowds heading in the opposite direction for the car park, chattering, sprawling, not looking where they were going, adopting the manners of the Black Knight – who had reflected a modern coarseness and indiscipline.

And I thought of the old-world code of medieval chivalry and its gracious style, flattery of ladies who gave favours or love tokens, the code of courtly love, the values of courage, honour, courtesy, justice and readiness to help the weak, loyalty and Arthurian obedience until death, the combination of qualities expected of an ideal knight. And I thought of today's new-world debased behaviour, me-first selfishness and indifference to others, coarseness, loudness and indisciplined lack of awareness and refinement, which had pervaded our society. This new order looked on Pippa with her stick and me with my creased face as stone fossils, once-living creatures now as moribund as ammonites frozen in stone, but our old-world code of politeness, courtesy, self-restraint and awareness of others was preferable to the cackling laughter and pushy, flaunting yobbery of our democratic, liberal, no-holds-barred, amoral, ugly post-chivalric age.

Part Two

Quest for the One

from *A Spade Fresh with Mud* (1995)

1
A Spade Fresh with Mud

I had arrived at Khabarovsk airport and after waiting about two hours I was told to go to the restaurant for lunch. I walked through the rain and sat in a glass building that looked like the Chichester theatre. There was a long delay before all four courses were brought together, and I fell into conversation with the only other person at my table, a young, balding Baptist missionary who had sat behind me on the Aeroflot.

He was going to Japan on his first assignment, and his *fiancée* was going to follow him after a year. She was training to be a missionary. He had qualified as a physicist, and, wanting no part in the production of nuclear weapons or industrial smoke, had worked for ICI.

"People say I'm crazy to give it all up," he said. "But I should have done it years ago because of my debt to Christ. I literally owe my life to Christ."

"In what way?" I asked.

"My father took two years to die," he said. "It was cerebral cancer, and he ate his own *faeces*. I spent the last five days in the hospital. I was only sixteen at the time, and my brain cracked under the strain. I was put in an asylum, and in despair I prayed. I cried out to God: 'If you are there and I'm not talking in a vacuum, help me. If you cure me, I promise to give my life to you.' A few days later I was better. I went back to school and took my exams, and I had a new life because I had let Christ live through me. Yes, a new life. And I've seen it happen again and again. In North Scotland, recently, I saw a whole village come to Christ. That was truly the Word of God. One girl, a hunchback, was completely transformed into an open, cheerful soul, and when I went to see her mother she said, 'Can Christ help me?' I said, 'Why not?' And we prayed then and there, and she said 'He's here' – you know, in the room, a presence – and I felt it too. It was the moment one dreams about. Oh, my work is so rewarding. I'm completely involved in it. Before I came on this journey I spoke to a missionary I worked with for six weeks. She has a beautiful serenity, and it was a privilege to work with her. She was in Japan. One day a deformed Japanese girl with a twisted soul saw her at the chemist's, and she asked the chemist, 'Where can I find that woman – she has such a beautiful face.' She found her and came to Christ and was transformed. Anyhow, this woman advised me: 'Keep a journal of your impressions, keep it every day. A lot of what you write will be rubbish, but after a time your real task will emerge, that which is peculiarly you, what you have to contribute. Don't fritter your impressions away.' It struck me as good advice, but I think I know my real task. I want to tell people about Christ, and about my debt to him – I want them to see how important he is to me. I want to give them all his serenity and peace of mind."

"You'll have a difficult time," I said, "cutting through centuries of introspection and contractual relationships."

"It's a Gordian Knot," he replied after a few moments. "Christ can slash through anything. Through Christ, even the most introspective man can reach serenity and peace of mind."

The train for Nakhodka was not due to leave until 6.30, and a coach outing had been arranged to pass the wet afternoon. At his suggestion I sat next to him. There was an English woman in the seat in front of us, together with a child, the other half dozen passengers being Japanese, and as the coach approached Khabarovsk the missionary mimicked, for her benefit: "This is our Sewage Farm, replete with proletarian odours. And now we can see out of the window to the right the new Friendship Flats, entitled 'Glory to the Communist Party.'" Then, without any warning from the guide, who anyway had not said a word and could not speak English, the coach swung left into a cemetery. "Ladies and gentlemen," announced the missionary triumphantly, "we have arrived at the Khabarovsk cemetery."

While the English woman tittered, I looked out of the window. It was an impressive cemetery: on either side of the track, among bushes and knee-deep undergrowth, were tombs and obelisks surrounded by railings. Then the coach stopped. A lorry was crawling along in front of us, and there was a funeral procession of peasants behind it. The driver hooted several times and overtook. The missionary laughed.

"It's shameful," I said, "that their ceremony should be interfered with by a coachload of tourists."

"Some ceremony," he said, "when the obelisks have stars on them and there's nothing ahead."

"There's a cross there," I said.

"But doesn't the bar nullify it?" he objected.

"That's Russian Orthodox," I said, "and the bar is Christ's foot-rest." Then the coach stopped again, and the Japanese got out, and holding their jackets over their heads, ran off into the rain. I deduced they were visiting some graves from the Russo-Japanese war of 1904. I was not certain that there had been any fighting in this area then, but I could think of no other explanation. They belonged to a party, and the leader probably wished to report back to Tokyo that he had done his duty, with typically Japanese punctilious regard for the dead. I said nothing while the missionary and the English woman giggled at the idea of sightseeing in a cemetery, and I thought my conjecture was confirmed when the younger Japanese returned early, soaked to the skin, and laughed rather frivolously. Probably they had had to go out of obedience to their leader, but were rather embarrassed at having the idea of war dragged up before their 'host', the Russian guide. When the last Japanese had returned bedraggled from the rain, the coach reversed and turned, and we headed back for the road.

"Well," said the missionary to the English woman, "we have certainly seen the dead centre of Khabarovsk." And again: "This is a dead-and-alive hole."

At that moment the coach slowed and stopped. Another funeral party was emerging from the bushes, and the leaders were crossing the road to return to their lorry. Interment was over, and the atheists' brows were furrowed.

I said to hurt the missionary: "This ceremony is very moving. There's a genuine pain – look at their faces. And it's close to the earth, much closer than our bourgeois ceremonies in the West. Look, there's the gravedigger, with the mud fresh on his spade."

When I turned I thought the missionary was asleep. Then I realised he was praying, and a tear on his left cheek told me why he joked about death and valued serenity and peace of mind.

2
A Crown of Thorns

On my last meeting with the Reverend Luke Hodges I bared my heart. I was desperate. I had seen all Western civilisation ten foot under the earth, I had seen one tombstone turn the lives of all polite citizens with respectable jobs into grinning skeletons in a meaningless farce, and what I had seen had made me sick. I spoke in pain, I told him I had no future. "I have seen through everything," I said, "and I don't want to do anything, for nothing's worth doing."

As usual he heard me out in what I took to be sympathetic silence. I was sick from trying to think my way through a wall, and perhaps it had all made me a little blind to the despair of others – perhaps I should have noticed that there was something unusual about the sympathy in his silence. Anyhow I didn't, until he said slowly: "I'm going to tell you something I want you to keep to yourself. Will you promise? I wouldn't tell you if I weren't going back to Pennsylvania next week," he went on slowly, "and I'm only telling you now because I feel I owe it to you, in view of the talks we've had. I've been recommending Christ as the answer to your nihilism. I want you to know I feel a bit of a fraud. You see," he said quietly, "I don't believe in Christ any longer, and church services have become a meaningless ritual."

I was surprised, not angry. A balding Methodist Minister with a simian face and pale white glasses and a sallow skin seems, to a seventeen-year-old, too intellectually stable to have doubts. Then, in spite of my despair, which I would have given anything to escape provided it were not at the expense of the truth, I suddenly felt elated: I was right. "What will you do?" I asked.

"I don't know," he said after a pause. "I shall leave the Ministry, but after that...." He shook his head. "I'm not trained for anything else. There's nothing I can do. More immediately though, I shall go into hospital, that is, as soon as I get back to Pennsylvania. I've found out that I'm diabetic. Well," he murmured, after I had expressed my sympathy, "we may not meet again, and I'd like you to have something to remember me by," and he got up and went to his desk and picked up a carefully wrapped paper-bag, and I wondered whether he had planned his confession with the same care. "Open it outside," he said as he handed it to me. "It's a postcard. The picture always meant a great deal to me, and I hope it may help you overcome your despair," and he added: "Where it failed to help me."

Shortly after, I left. In the street I opened the paper-bag and was confronted with a postcard of Guido Reni's painting, *Ecce Homo*.

A month later I heard he had died of undiagnosed diabetes in Pennsylvania. And now that I am the age he was then, now I have accepted the wall and wear a crown of thorns and have sweated out a meaning and purpose, of sorts, I cannot help feeling that he was wrong to choose that way out rather than chuck Christ and start all over again.

3
A Gun-Runner in Danger

At dawn I duly walked in the Turkish Quarter and asked for the Agent. A beggar took me to the waterside and pointed to a motorised *caique* that was already chugging. The Agent was a big, fat Turk in a seaman's cap, and he took me on board with a nod and barely looked at the *drachmas* he stuffed into his pocket.

We left immediately. Neither of his crew spoke English, so I lay in the prow with my feet on the tarpaulin that covered the cargo and stared deep into the satin sea and watched the sun climb, and at noon we moored at the smallest of harbour walls. It jutted out from a long sandy beach that was completely wild save for the one small customs shed.

One of the inspectors spoke a little English. He said there was no road within ten kilometres, and no bank where I could change my *drachmas* within a hundred and eighty kilometres. "You better go back Rhodes," he advised and I had to agree. He went out and told the Agent and the crew, who were still unloading the *caique*.

After that he and his mate boiled me an egg on a small charcoal stove, and when I emerged an hour or two later I saw a man lead a laden mule over the top of a dune. When I pointed, the Agent laughed, and the crew laughed, and then the two inspectors came out and they laughed.

"Menderes no good," said the one who spoke English, and everyone laughed and turned to checking the cargo.

On the way back the sky clouded over and a wind got up and the sea became choppy. At dusk it began to rain, and soon it was pelting and the *caique* was rolling in a mountainous sea and shipping a lot of water, and after dark the Agent loomed up and thrust a bailer in my hands and staggered off. For the next few minutes I was only aware of hanging on in a driving rain while black waves crashed over the sides and receded into gigantic troughs.

When I next looked round a brilliant fork of lightning clutched at the mast. The Agent was clinging to it, as to the foot of a cross, and under his peaked cap his big face was split in what looked like agonised compassion. He was singing, with the rain running down his cheeks he was roaring and laughing and singing in sheer exultation.

4
A Thousand Feet and a Cage

"Most of all I loved the physical things," said Brewer. "Before the war I used to go gliding at Dunstable in Bedfordshire. The gliders were single-seaters, and there was a sort of cliff in the downs. I think it was originally a sea-cliff because they found some shells there once. Anyhow I often remember circling round this cliff, because you get a lift over a cliff. The wind beats against it and sends up a number of swirling currents. You get a lift over rocky ground, too, if the sun's out, and you get a lift if a hot front of air collides with a cold one.

"But best of all for a lift is a purple thundercloud. There's an upward suction, and it can be quite dangerous. I knew a man who disappeared under one. His glider got sucked up and it was struck by lightning and disintegrated. That was unusual though. Normally you sometimes broke a leg or something when you came down, but otherwise it wasn't dangerous. And you felt wonderfully fresh and free. I used to feel a thousand feet above routine, I was just sun and cloud and cliff and rock and lift. Sometimes you came down as much as fifteen miles away – that was a bore because it cost ten pounds or so to return the glider – and once I landed among the wolves in Whipsnade Zoo, and I found myself in an open-air cage. The wolves were far more scared than I was, and I was quite all right, but after that I always felt that coming down was returning to a kind of cage."

5
A Crag and Bursting Stars

I caught up with the Fiesta in Malaga. There was dancing in the floodlit streets, and I got drinking with a large bull of an American. "You want somewhere to sleep?" he said. "Go to Coin. CO-IN. It's a village about thirty kilometres up in the hills from here. You go there and ask for Señor Galway Rich. They'll take you to him. Say Bill Merwood sent you, and he'll put you up."

That night I slept on Malaga beach near a disused railway line, and the rats were as large as tom-cats. You could see their silhouettes prowling across the skyline above the sea, their great bellies hanging down. Never again, I vowed as a white dawn glowed, and late next afternoon I left the baking Fiesta and hitched up into the hills and towards sunset I stood in the spare rectangular plaza that was Coin.

"Señor Galway Rich?" I asked the local barber. He was sitting in the shade on his front steps, and he sprang up and pointed towards the frowning crag that overhung the far end of the plaza. I asked three more people as I headed for the crag, and their reaction was the same. The third man spoke a little English. "Señor Galway Rich – he big man, he not come down here," he said, and I began to understand that Señor Galway Rich had isolated himself high above the village, like a scornful god.

The ascent was steep and the sun had almost gone by the time I reached Señor Galway Rich's modern villa under the crag. It stood in a wrought-iron compound and when I opened the gate a couple of dogs started snarling. I dumped my bag outside the gate and went up the path and rang the bell, and the Señora came to the door, an elderly American woman with fuzzy hair.

"Who are you?" she asked under the hall light, and feeling the menacing stranger she took me for, I recited my bit about Bill Merwood. "Bill Merwood," she said, "I don't know anyone called Bill Merwood," and she backed away nervously while I looked on her like a judgement. "Galway," she called, and the Señor himself appeared, a balding man of about 70 with a long, American face and ridiculously long and baggy khaki shorts.

"What's up?" he asked, and I repeated my bit about Bill Merwood. "I don't know anyone called Bill Merwood," the Señor said. "I'm afraid you've been the victim of a grudge or something. I was the former Ambassador in Spain. Would you mind leaving now."

But having come all the way from Malaga I wasn't going to be thrown out so easily. "Can you recommend somewhere where I can sleep?" I asked.

"There's always the hillside," the Señor said indifferently.

The Señora added "He was Ambassador – you can't stay here," and I wanted to say: What difference does that make, isn't he a human being?

"Now would you mind leaving," the Señor said, raising his voice, and he went inside and shouted an order and as the dogs started baying I took to my heels and just made it before they tore out of the door and flung themselves at the wrought-iron gate, and as they barked I realised that in my escape I had lost my dark glasses from my breast pocket.

It was dark now and the lights of Coin looked a long way below. I was footsore so I forfeited dinner and unrolled my sleeping-bag near the wrought-iron compound. There was a tremendous silence and I became aware of the Milky Way, and I realised the sky was full of shooting stars. They were moving and squirting like a tray of live winkles – the whole universe was alive. From behind me, under the crag, I heard voices raised in a quarrel, perhaps over Bill Merwood, and I knew I did not envy the successful Ambassador the security of his villa, I was happy in my universe of jumping, bursting stars, I was happy and free on my hillside beneath the exploding night.

6
Mosquitoes in a Bamboo-Grove

Illuminations come when you're waiting for them, but when they come they surprise you. Like revolutions. I once went to a Zen temple to wait on an illumination. I went to Engakuji in Kita-Kamakura. It is just above the railway, and I took a writer-friend called Jesperson. We were hoping we'd be taught by Master Asahina, but he was away, and we were put in the charge of a priest with a shaven head, and I wouldn't like to have been interned under him during the war. That evening we sat in on the end of a meditation, and like the others we took our socks off. The mosquitoes whined past our ears every ten seconds, and after twenty minutes we were covered in bites. At the end of the sitting we went into another room for a discussion with the priest, and I asked if we might keep our socks on, as foreigners were more prone to being bitten than Japanese.

The priest grinned and told a story. Once upon a time a certain famous Master wanted to strive for *satori*. That was before he was a Master, and he went to another Master and asked how he should do it and he was told to go and sit in the nude in a nearby bamboo-grove. He went and sat in the bamboo-grove, and within five minutes he was bitten all over by mosquitoes, and he went back and complained. "Every time you are bitten you must laugh," the Master said, so he went back and for two days there was perpetual laughter in the bamboo-grove. Then there was silence, and the Master went up to the bamboo-grove and found him lying unconscious in a pool of blood, but he had achieved *satori*. "So you should not ask to put clothes on," the priest concluded, "you should ask to take them off," and the girls giggled and we went back sockless to the final sitting of the day and were badly bitten while the priest hovered with his rod. And when we finally got into our *futon*s in the hall we were forbidden mosquito-coils, though the priest had one, and all night we tossed and groaned and sighed and I remember Jesperson muttering: "Three hours more and then labouring? Oh God."

We got up at three for the dawn meditation, and I was in no mood for an illumination. I hadn't slept a wink, I had a throbbing headache, and so far from teaching me selflessness the priest's prohibition on mosquito-coils had made my self itch from scalp to toe. I went through with the trot round the meditation-hall merely because there was no way of getting out of it, and when we sat I wasn't really concentrating, and I was fully aware of Jesperson's horror when a deadly centipede with legs like rose-thorns crawled out of a log-pile and crossed the *tatami* floor. I even sniggered when the priest loomed up behind us and prodded Jesperson in the back, and he collapsed in a heap on the floor. But slowly the rhythm of my breathing controlled my thoughts and I sank into a mindless concentration on the pool of dawn shadow in the polished floor before me, and then all was silence, and a creaking floor-board, a whirring cicada were intruding distractions, like the labouring in my lungs, and all was a unity as the shadows moved, and for ten seconds – ten minutes, I do not know exactly for how long – my soul knew reality, and it did not matter that an hour later I was hoeing weeds outside the temple latrine.

7
A Scarlet-Robed Bedouin and a Colossus

On the way in we saw a scarlet-robed Bedouin. He was a tiny figure miles off on the red-brown desert horizon, surrounded by a vast expanse of sea and sand and twilit sky, alone under the fierce sun. I was struck by the smallness of man, the hugeness of Nature, and all the themes that obsessed me came hauntingly down to that lone figure on the humped sands. I wondered: why does he exist? What meaning has his life? What importance has his black tent? What is his smallness to the huge stars? And suddenly I imagined a huge heroic figure, of the stature of the Colossus of Rhodes, who knew the meaning of life.

Then I realized that ten years of searching through books and history and religion and philosophy and society and God knows what had led me to a dead-end, like Faust's, and that a little paring down might turn my hero into a figure of the proportion of *Pilgrim's Progress* or *Paradise Lost*. This was the image inside me that I carried through the outer world of my marriage and my job, of the noisy bustling Tripoli's waterfront, past palms and a silver sea, turning into the Italian streets round Istiqlal, and on past the rocks and sports clubs to the white American villas of Giorgimpopoli, I made notes in my pocketbook to carry my image forward, I jotted fragments as they came to me, utterly removed from the world around me. And my life had a wonderful meaning.

8
The Portmellon Water Splash

I chose to become an exile one stormy afternoon before I got married when William Carlyle (now a legend as an optimistic philosopher) was driving me along the Cornish coast. It was winter, and the sea was high. At Portmellon it washed over the road, and the water surged on either side of the car as if it were a boat. I said, with all the restlessness of the young, "I shall become a wanderer for ten years and see the world and find the meaning of life. When my search is finished I shall return."

I did go abroad for ten years. I searched among different religions and cultures in different parts of the world, I found. I returned stiller, with a great sorrow and knowledge on my weathered face and, revisiting Cornwall the next summer, drove to Portmellon to complete my vow at the water splash.

The sea was calm, it was nowhere near the road. Fishing boats bobbed gently, gulls hung over the new chalets. I stopped at the Rising Sun and had a beer while the sun set. Thinking of all the hardships and dangers and sufferings I had been through, I felt a fisherman's peace, but I wished the wind could have whipped the water into the boiling, threshing turbulence that washed across the road that winter afternoon when I was so ignorant of life – and alive.

*

Two moments at the Portmellon water splash, separated by twelve years. They are significant to me as psychological memories, but they are more than that. When we are able to perceive the world with true awareness, we feel we belong to a unity that includes what we perceive.

We see ourselves as part of a great Whole Being, that includes all moments and all things, we experience what it is to Be. We experience: "*percipere est esse*" – to perceive is to be. These moments of heightened perception put our souls in touch with a reality which we could experience every day, and we never forget those moments. They become images that are always remembered, that are always valid, for they are images of reality: of unity, of freedom out of time.

9
Freedom Over the Canal

At Oxford Rupert dared me to cross over and speak to a fantastic girl who was drinking coffee in the Playhouse bar. I went over and asked her if she knew anyone who could put me up in Paris – and it turned out she lived there. For me, the incident was just another demonstration of human freedom: we can do anything if we set our minds to it. But Rupert was not convinced. Walking back from where we had been drinking that evening he objected, "*I'm* not free."

He was an inveterate pessimist and self-despiser, and I told him, "Nonsense, it's all an attitude of mind. You can change your attitude now, this very instant." We were crossing the bridge over the canal by Worcester College. "You're free to jump in that water," I told him. "Jump in, and then you'll understand. Go on, jump."

It was shock treatment of course, and at first he objected that it would not do any good. I insisted: "There's no one about, jump in."

Rather doubtfully Rupert climbed onto the metal bridge. He sat, crouched on his heels, contemplating the yellow flecks of moonlight that glanced off the black water.

"Jump," I repeated.

Suddenly he was gone. There was a splash, and I peered down. In the dark blackness the water was still. I began to fear he had drowned, but then there was a whoosh near the rung ladder and Rupert staggered up, dripping moonlight. He waded with a curious loping side-to-side action to the ladder and climbed the wall hand over hand until he stood in the road. I ran round and joined him.

"This is a great day. You've broken the chains in your mind."

"Mmm," he said glumly, "I wonder." A puddle formed round his feet, under the nearby street-lamp I could see the scum on his hair.

It was two minutes to midnight when we stepped through the tiny barn-door into the College. Rupert left a trail of filthy water and Evans the porter stared in disbelief. "Good night Evans," Rupert said in his commandingly authoritative tone, and Evans called back gravely, "Good night sir."

"Now," said Rupert, well pleased with himself, "I shall have a hot bath," and I knew his revolution against himself had worked.

10
Chinese Flies on a Mountain

I had to write a newspaper article about the 1,150-mile-long railway the Chinese were building between Dar es Salaam harbour and the Zambian town of Kapiri Mposha. The railway was then going through its most difficult 98-mile stage in the Kilombero valley, Tanzania. Broken escarpments rose from the plain to mountains as high as 6,000 feet, and the railway had to cross precipitous valleys and quagmires and pass through eighteen tunnels.

I arrived from Dar by Land Rover, and lunched at a Chinese camp. We drank a lot of beer and the Chinese chinked glasses round the table at every sip. Then I visited the Ruaha bridge and the place where the Chinese had moved the middle of a mountain. Chinese and Africans swarmed over the earthwork sides like flies, cementing the hill against the coming rainy season, and as I thought of all the discomforts of camp life, the doing without women, the gruelling work in the hot sun, I felt a great sadness. It was a pioneering work, yes, like the Canadian Pacific or trans-Siberian railways, or our own London-to-Birmingham line, but pioneering seemed so remote beside the daily grind and human hardship of an operation which might be nationalised as soon as it was finished and therefore, for them, the Chinese, prove ultimately futile.

I spent that night in another Chinese camp at Mkera. During dinner the camp leader spat pieces of chicken and vegetable onto the floor. I drank beer until eleven and then went off to the mud-hut guest-room, where my bed was two wooden planks under a regal bell-shaped mosquito-net. The next few hours I tossed and turned, and when I finally dozed I dreamt I had my ex-wife in my arms; we were together again, and I was tucking my daughter up in bed.

I woke to the cold reality of a bush dawn: to the sound of hawking and spitting. Outside Chinese squatted near a runnel, elaborately cleaning their teeth. I went to the communal urinal – a lake in the earth that stank of urine – and when I saw that a culvert led to the vegetable garden and watered the camp-grown cabbage and beans I had eaten the previous night, I was nearly sick. How *can* they endure? I asked myself, watching a few Chinese start the slow motion early morning combat exercises I remembered from the Shanghai Bund.

That morning I visited tunnel 13. I walked through it, squashing against the wall as the train trundled through, and stepping from sleeper to sleeper, I trudged a mile between two mountains. I passed groups of African workers and came to bridge 25, which balances on two columns over 150 foot high. There a Chinese with a Chairman Mao badge on his lapel, a Mr Pan, introduced me to the man who was both architect and engineer of the bridge. Politely I asked if he would stand on the bridge so that I could photograph him, and to my horror he casually walked out to the middle, stepping from sleeper to sleeper, between each of which was a 150 foot drop. That was getting on for the height of the London Monument or Nelson's Column.

"He won't fall, I hope?" I ventured to Mr Pan. The interpreter translated.

Mr Pan said something in Mandarin and abruptly walked away, and the interpreter said, "He says you must see this operation from the point of view of the mountain." That was all.

His reply was totally unexpected. I did not know what he meant, but suddenly I felt as if I had had a revelation and changed my way of looking. I no longer saw with Western man-centred eyes. There were the hills and there were the men, and the two opposites were held together in a unity, like the valley and the engineer of bridge 25. One sought to dominate the other, and perhaps did for a time, but from the point of view of the mountain above us, all the hardship and suffering came down to a few moments in the history of the earth, and this pioneering endeavour would go the way of Greek roads and the Appian Way. Bound by emotion and self, we thought the present important, but the men swarming on this mountain were like flies on the Great Pyramid. The death of one was of no particular importance, there would be others, and the process would continue for another four thousand years, during which time the railway might disappear and be uncovered and disappear again. What I felt was probably very different from what the work-centred Chinese had meant, but because of the unity between man and mountain, it strangely did not matter if the engineer lost his footing and fell.

11
Saké and the Meaning of Life

"You must visit our Professor Emeritus, Professor," said Mr Gengo in Tokyo. And so one afternoon at three I duly made the journey by taxi to the luxurious house in the suburbs where the famous poet's aging wife received me. I was shown into a spacious sitting-room, and there, silky-haired and looking utterly incompetent, sat the old Professor. He waved me into an armchair, and we had the usual talk about literature: a series of questions on his part about post-war British authors, a feast of name-dropping.

Japanese make up their minds about you within fifteen seconds. If they like you by then, fine; if they don't there is nothing you can do to dissuade them from disliking you. The Professor evidently approved, for whisky was produced, and warm *saké*, and soon I was being told, "You're going to be famous, your ideas on writing are all new ones. But remember you must create your readership, make the public come to you. Never go to them." I stayed and stayed and stayed, and at midnight I staggered out. I remember the Professor Emeritus nearly fell over near the door, but I have no recollection of anything else he said.

I met him by chance at my University a few months later. He was wearing a tatty raincoat. "Come," he said. "I am going to a little *saké* bar

I know, we will drink some *saké*." He took me round the corner to a tiny place with sawdust on the floor and advised me to master Zen. I was carrying a copy of the latest *Encounter*, and he took a renewal card from inside the cover and took out an ancient fountain-pen and said solemnly, "I will tell you the meaning of life. You won't understand it now, but one day you will understand it. When you understand it you will become very famous." And he wrote: "(+A) + (–A) = 0." "Zero," he said, "Great Nothing." He would not elaborate, he stood up and pulled his raincoat collar up and ambled off.

He was right. I have discovered the meaning of life, how all opposites, including life and death, are contained within a unity that is reality; and I cannot express it more succinctly than his formula. Now I have framed that *Encounter* renewal card, and *saké* has philosophical associations. Who in the West could pass on so fundamental a truth as such a casual aside?

from *A Smell of Leaves and Summer* (1995)

12
A Smell of Leaves and Summer

One Thursday in June I took the backward boys I taught to St Nicholas's Hospital, Deptford, so they could see what it was like to work there. We were shown round the kitchens and the boiler-house, and then I ushered the dozen of them up to the Head Porter, who gave us a talk on wheeling porters' trolleys. He was a giant of a man, a full six foot seven inches tall and huge across the shoulders with a jutting jaw, and he wore a suit. He looked like someone out of a James Bond film, I could imagine whacking him in the solar plexus with an iron knuckleduster and he would not flinch.

He stepped aside as a trolley came out of the operating theatre, and I marshalled the boys against the wall so they wouldn't touch the pale unconscious patient who lay restlessly on it. "Anywhere else you'd like to go, sir?" he asked me, and Trevor Varnalls said, "Mortuary, sir. Go on, ask for the mortuary."

"Do you want to go to the mortuary?" the giant asked.

"Yeah," chorused the boys.

"Have you any objection, sir?"

I had to make a quick decision. "I hadn't thought we'd be going," I said, surprised at the words that came out, "but if it's offered I think it might be a good thing. These boys have to be introduced to the idea of death some time, and I think it's good to do it in a controlled humane way. It's all part of education. They can't be sheltered indefinitely."

"Wait here a moment then."

The giant strode off. A few strides and he was round the end of the corridor. While we waited the boys asked me one after another, "Are we going?"

"I don't know," I said, wondering if I would get letters from their parents. I thought of my responsibility. I wandered away from them and looked into my heart, and I felt my heart telling me to go ahead.

The giant returned. "Follow me," he said, and we all piled into the lift.

The mortuary was in the hospital grounds. It was an old yellow brick building with wired glass windows. It could have been a Gents.

"Burke'll be sick," Trevor Varnalls said. "What do you want to bring a wally like that for? Show us up."

"No he won't. You will more likely."

"Go out, I ain't squeamish."

"Yes you are, you're a bottler."

"Go out."

The mortician came to the mortuary door. He was a beady-eyed man with rimless glasses, and he wore a white coat. For a moment he conferred with the giant. "If you're sure it's all right," I overheard him saying. While I waited I lectured the boys on respect for the dead. I told them they must keep silent – and no arguing. Then I realised Trevor was missing. He was bending head down at a nearby wall.

"Come on Trevor."

"I ain't going in there, what do you take me for."

Inside the door there was a unit of fridge doors with long handles. The giant peered at the names, which were stuck on the doors, and then opened a door to reveal the ends of three drawers. The giant pulled a drawer, and out slid – a man of around seventy. He was still in his clothes, there was no sheet over him. He had grey hair and a small clotted cut on his head. As the giant pulled the drawer right out the old man's elbow caught on the side, and it looked as though he moved his arm.

The shock ran through me. It was a shock of recognition, a strange disgust at his absence from his limp body. Then I smelt the sickly sweet smell of death.

There was a stunned silence. The boys stood in a semi-circle, absolutely still, every eye fascinated by the thing.

"Sir, is he dead sir?" Burke asked in an undertone next to me.

"Yes," I said, disapprovingly final.

"Sir, is he dead sir?"

"Yes."

Burke thought about it, his eyes darting madly from side to side.

"See," said the giant. "He died this morning. Fell. See the cut on his head? He's just asleep. Touch him."

My palms felt damp. My awe, like that of the boys, was a mixture of reverence and repulsion.

"Go on, touch him. He's only asleep."

The boys cowered back.

That *thing* was living that morning, I thought, what would he have thought if he'd known when he got out of bed that a dozen backward boys would be staring as if he were a gorilla at the zoo?

"What the Head Porter says is true," I said, to impose some sort of control on myself. "He's just asleep. He's asleep. There's nothing frightening in death." That last sentence was what my mother said when she showed me my father.

But *I* would not have touched him.

"He's looking at you," said the giant. "Let's close his eyes." And he put his finger and thumb over the old man's eyelids.

"Sir, is he dead sir?" Burke asked again.

"Yes," I said, more matter-of-fact now that the silence had been broken.

"You're a wally, Burke. Course he's bloody dead."

"Shhh."

"Sir, he *is* dead sir. Is he?"

"Yes," I said.

The giant slid the drawer back in. He pulled out the one beneath it.

This one had a sheet over it. The giant pulled it back to reveal a woman of about fifty-five, her skull bound with a bandage. She looked like a nun in a wimple, and her face was a waxy yellow-white.

The giant pushed her back and closed the fridge door. He opened another door and pulled out a frail woman in her seventies. She looked very peaceful, and all her wrinkles were gone.

"She was alive this morning," the giant said.

Burke had a weird smile on his lips. His eyes were darting madly. This was obviously the experience of his lifetime. These people were dead – you could see he was sure of it now. As the giant pulled out another drawer he clenched his fists and shook them up and down, as he always did when he got excited.

When I came out into the sunlight and walked back to the main hospital entrance and smelt the green leaves, I felt faintly sick. Yet what I remembered was not the repulsion so much as the peace. I had not been consciously aware of it, but I had felt a deep peace towards the end. The dead were – still; in another place. They had shocked my heart into discarding all its rubbish, they had purified my heart of all the wants and desires that enslaved it most of the time, and as a result I had felt a peace that now revelled in the smell of summer.

I was fully alive, I felt the blue sky and the blinding sun to be wonderfully good, and full of a rich meaning. I loved life, for I saw it through my heart. I could not think of those dead bodies as useless material, as rubbish waiting to be burned – all that mattered was to live intensely, to enjoy life to the full. I noticed things out of the coach window, and when I got back to school I lunched alone and watched the cricket on television. It was the first day of the first Test between England and New Zealand, and I concentrated on every ball that was bowled. It was important.

Then I turned off the television and just sat quietly. I just sat and felt the meaning of life outside the window; which the reason makes us forget.

13
A Ladder and Quarrels at Church

Vincent Mullright was the local solicitor. He was stout with enormous jowls and he wore a black pinstripe suit and a bowler hat. He had lived a most conventional life as one of the most respected members of the community. He was a JP and he was on all the local boards and committees, he had climbed to the top of the social ladder before he moved out of the district. He threw himself into property – he had a dozen firms connected with it – and he was massively remote from anything personal. I once spent a week in his office room, to see if I liked the idea of being an articled clerk, and the only personal remark he made was, "What's that book you've got with you?" It was Chester Wilmot's *Struggle for Europe*, and he nodded gravely and said, "Not bad. You won't get much time for reading in the Law. Or for anything that has much meaning." It struck me as a curiously bitter remark for a man of his standing.

He was enormously good at making money, and after he left our town he lived on a rural Essex village green. One day he went to his son's cottage. His son was also a solicitor, but they did not get on, and he worked outside the family firms. Vincent Mullright did some restoration. He propped a ladder against a beam and climbed to the top. The beam broke, he crashed to the ground and broke his arm.

The consequences of that fall were not apparent till some while later. He took to sitting morosely in his study at home. "The Law has been a waste of time," he would mutter to his uncomprehending wife. "I've wasted my life on things I didn't want to do: cases, documents, work for other people, inessential things. Dinners and committees. Skeletons, that's all they are. Skeletons." He was on all the church committees, and it was disgraceful but this man of blameless reputation began quarrelling with everyone, from members of the congregation to the churchwardens and the vicar. The quarrels were over footling, trivial things. It was all totally unworthy. In addition he stopped answering letters. The following winter he had a nervous breakdown.

"The Church should have meaning but hasn't," he said as he was taken to hospital. "The Law should have meaning but hasn't. My home should have meaning but hasn't. Where has all the meaning gone?"

He lived in silence after that. He was always so solid in the old days, and I still sometimes imagine that I can see his portly frame turning the corner in our town, dressed in a pinstripe suit and a bowler hat.

14
The Clear, Shining Sunlight of Eternity

In the car I changed into my black tie and drove to the Catholic Chapel of Rest, the Holy Ghost, in Nightingale Square. Girls waited in the porch, there was scaffolding in the main part of the church. I lingered until I saw the mourners sitting quietly in the Lady Chapel. Among them sat my old Head, black-haired and upright in a dark overcoat, and aloof from the rest against a wall.

The coffin stood to the front of the aisle. It was on a stand, of yellow wood with gold handles, and six candles stood round it. There was a mauve cusp on top. I found a pew and sat next to a handsome, dark-haired, Bohemian young man with hair over his collar, and thought of how the train had hit James and blasted him to bits at Clapham Junction the previous Friday afternoon and closed the lines for three hours, and how my own son's breathing had stopped twenty-four hours later. Simon had been given back, but James had been taken. There was a silent wait while the Lady Chapel filled. Soon it was packed; many of the local people had read about the tragedy in the local papers, and had come to give quiet support. A bell rang, and the bereaved came in, Italian Mrs. Burns wearing black, her black hair hidden beneath a black head veil. She was supported by a group of relatives and friends and clutching white roses, and I thought how nearly it was me that was led in.

The local junior school trooped in. This was the choir, and it was led by a bald man with insincere eyes. Mass commenced, and for the next three-quarters of an hour I kneeled, sat, stood, sat and kneeled through a threnody of singing and praying. The priest wore a surplice with a Y-shaped cross on the front. He spoke of James as "having been baptised in this chapel". At one stage he spoke of James as "joining the saints" and the Bohemian man next to me pulled a face. I thought of the pinched, black-haired boy I brandished my cane at – he had bent down at the back of the class, inviting me to swish him – and of all the terrible things he had done after he ran away from home and before the remand home, and I avoided my old Head's eye. James was out of harmony with the universe, he was in opposition to it rather than in harmony with it, there was self-assertion, he hit policemen in the face – and I thought of a line from the *Tao Te Ching*, "He who is against *Tao* perishes young."

The Eucharist was served in a white goblet that glowed in the light like the Holy Grail. At the end of the Mass the priest walked round the coffin, shaking incense over it in a way that would have made James bristle with indignation. Then, standing by the coffin, he gave a short address. He said: "James died at the age of sixteen. This is young to die, but in the clear, shining sunlight of eternity a few years do not matter very much. Children die at one or two, and we will all die one day, and in fifty years' time a few years will not matter very much." I thought of the truant James as a Shining One, standing before the Clear Light of the *Tibetan Book of the Dead*.

At last it was time for the coffin to be carried out. The pallbearers came down the aisle, dressed in black. They all looked over sixty, and one had a patch on his shoulder. They hoisted the coffin up and turned it round, and as they advanced down the aisle Mrs. Burns leaned out and touched it, and the two women next to her did the same.

Then suddenly the aisle was full of jostling women in black. Mrs. Burns passed me, her cheeks soaked with tears beneath her black veil, and then out they all went, blubbing and sobbing, and I found myself walking beside my old hunched Head, his well-parted black hair greased flat.

"Didn't expect to see you here," he said.

I explained about the letter Mrs. Burns had sent me through a girlfriend of James's who went to my school. I said I had often seen him up and down the road, and that apparently, he had always liked me. "A miserable business," I said.

"I suspended him," my old Head said, "and now I'm attending his funeral." He added: "A myth is already growing up about him."

"The murder story," I said. "The suggestion that he was chased onto the railway line by a gang of coloured thieves."

"Yes. He was playing on the lines. He was in trouble as recently as last week."

I stood with the Head and watched the coffin in the flowered hearse. Mrs. Burns sat in the Austin Princess behind. She looked distraught. I gathered that she did not believe her son was dead. They would not let her see the remains as there was nothing to see, only a few bits of flesh, and she still hoped against hope that it was not James who had been killed, even though pieces of his clothes had been retrieved. She had a lot of suffering ahead of her. Once again I thought of James travelling unknowing towards this. He had been taken, my own son had been given back after the screaming ambulance-drive to hospital. There, but for the grace of God....

"Cigarette?" the Head asked, offering me a packet as he fumbled, and I said, "I don't," and we walked up the road towards our cars to return to our respective schools and normal living. Life went on. Those who died were losers, and besides, in the clear, shining sunlight of eternity – in the sunlight – what did a few years matter?

15
Frothy Weirs and a Rising Sun

I went to Winchester to attend a conference for mystics and scientists. I drove down the M3 and booked in at the Rising Sun in Bridge Street around six, then drove out of town to King Alfred's College, and, having been given a yellow non-resident's badge, ate a vile vegetarian dinner overlooking wooded hills whose peace reminded me of Kita-Kamakura. The elderly woman next to me said, "I've been told that this is my last life if I do well."

Sir Thomas Roper, the organiser, held my hand in a gentle healer's grasp. He looked like Albert Schweitzer with his now white hair and bushy white moustache, and he went into a trance while he tried to remember who I was. I said I was looking forward to hearing the biochemist, and he said, "Oh, he's in the Galapagos Islands, we've had to replace him." He strangely did not know who was doing the replacing, and hazarded the wrong name.

Sir Thomas Roper gave the first lecture. Typically he began, "This is a mo-MENtous occasion." The elderly woman whispered, "Sir Thomas is a bit like Moses, he's always looking for the Promised Land, but won't do anything to find it." We watched him in the yellow-badge hall on closed circuit television, for the main (white-badge) hall was full. I sat in a room darkened by curtains and looked at a curved screen which had yellow daffodils and white narcissi at the base.

A tousled-haired young physicist spoke next, about how subatomic physics had debunked materialism – he followed his book, which I had read – and then the leader of the Sufi sect spoke. He was disappointing; he looked like everyone's idea of a guru, with white swept-back Indian hair and a grey-white beard and swarthy skin, and his brown monk's cloak fastened at the front with a pin, but he did not so much as mention mysticism. He got lost in long words and in long analogies, and everything was "dynamic".

The physicist had said that scientific theories were "models"; so all language was an approximation to Reality that had no objective validity. There were too many words, and the mystic side was not presented and the conference was unbalanced. I went back to the Rising Sun and had a cider until closing time, and slept in a freezing room upstairs.

Next morning I had breakfast in the Pool Room near a log fire. Then I went out for the papers. I walked across the bridge and passed the old City Mill, 1744, in the sunshine. Two weirs converged under the Mill and frothed dynamically under the bridge, like the words in King Alfred's College.

That Saturday morning began with lectures by a psychic researcher, a Professor of Chemistry, and a biologist. There was a distinction between the mystic and the psychic, but there were no definitions. Again the words bubbled and foamed, but there was nothing about mysticism or the Light.

After a wretched vegetarian lunch I drove into Winchester, for we had the afternoon free. I saw the fourteenth-century Round Table of King Arthur, and then went to the Cathedral. I looked up at the mortuary chests which contain the bones of the Saxon kings, and of

Canute, and I was bossed round the Cathedral Library by an elderly woman. I lingered in the Guardian Angels' Chapel and gazed at the eight round murals of winged angels on the medieval roof. I wandered off to the City Cross – where William the Conqueror's Royal Palace stood, and where children pulled strings from toy hens and made loud squawking noises – and I walked back through the churchyard, where two lovers embraced on a grave, and saw the house where Jane Austen died.

I returned for the 5 o'clock lecture. The author of a well-known book on parapsychology spoke against scepticism. He made one point, which might as well have been a clucking hen's squawk, and there was still nothing about the Light.

I could bear it no longer. I sought out the subatomic physicist and said we were still awaiting something on mysticism. He agreed and said he was very disappointed in the guru. We discussed how physics saw the cosmic rays that shower our atmosphere and what happens to the body in enlightenment while women came up and smiled and said, "Thank you for your lecture yesterday," as if to say, 'I'm yours if you want to take me.'

"Is the enlightened brain a mirror or a bulb?" I asked him. "What model do you opt for?"

"I incline to the mirror view," he said in his Viennese voice, leaning back in his brown velvet suit and flowered shirt, "bulbs are an aspect of materialism, of outmoded Newtonian physics. We polish our mirrors to reflect the Light. But I think you are taking enlightenment too literally. It is understanding, not light."

Then I knew that he was one who did not know. The *guru* had said, "There are four categories of people: those who do not know they do not know; those who know they do not know; those who do not know they know; and those who know they know." This physicist was one who did not know he did not know. "No," I corrected him, "the mystic sees the Light as actual Light."

"I know strange things happen," he said, "once I looked out of a window at midnight, and everything was lit up as bright as day."

Again I knew he did not know. I extricated myself from the conversation by saying, "In your terms, human beings are particles."

"Yes," he said, "maybe photons cause the Light, but…. I do not know what causes the Light."

I saw he was speculating, and after another wretched vegetarian meal he gave a doctrinaire near-Marxist lecture at the end of which he said, "The whole cosmos is divine, and we relate personally to it, but there is no personal God in it. This is a Taoist or Buddhist view, and it is scientific."

I drove back over the bridge to the Rising Sun and thought of Omar Khayyam's words. In his youth he "did eagerly frequent/Doctor and Saint, and heard great argument/About it and about: but evermore/Came out by the same door as in I went". I had heard the subatomic Doctor and the *guru*-Saint, and all that had changed was that I had come out of the door in which I went.

That night the Rising Sun was filled with a drunken football team talking about the afternoon's game. Next morning I was up early as Sir Thomas Roper was leading a meditation in the white-badge hall. I jokingly said to the elderly woman whose last life this was, "The organisers know that the conference is unbalanced, so they're putting us all in a trance to outmanoeuvre our criticisms."

Some hundred people sat in the plush theatre seats. Soon I was feeling my breathing ("the ebb and flow of life" Sir Thomas Roper intoned), and the Light rose and kept threatening to send shafts up the sky of my dark being. I saw a revolving spiral in Light – a *chakra*? and then POW! Zam! There was an explosion of Light and shock waves of Light radiated outwards like ripples as if an atom had been split in my head ("see the Light that casts no shadow," Sir Thomas Roper intoned, behind where I was on the space-time continuum). I was held down by gravity, but my spirit felt buoyant and wanted to soar into the upper reaches of the air, and then up I went, I was flying on air currents, the explosion had been the firing of my rocket engines, and then I was out in space and hurtling into the Light ("fall upwards into the Light," intoned Sir Thomas Roper), and I felt clean inside, washed through with Light. I basked in the risen sun until it was time to leave Eternity and change my observer's position and fall back into time and return to my body back on earth ("pull the cloak of Light around you," intoned Sir Thomas Roper).

When I came to, blinking for the electric light, back in the illusory world of phenomena, I looked at Sir Thomas Roper. He sat, pale and gaunt and sallow, his white hair and white moustache like Albert Schweitzer's or Einstein's, a strangely disembodied spirit, an ethereal Guardian Angel with yellow wings, and I marvelled that he had appeared not to know about the Light at the conference about the Essenes.

I tottered out of the white-badge hall and walked unsteadily back to my car. The sun shone, spring birds were twittering in clean fir-trees, there were daisies in the field. Reality was what I had just experienced, and this peace at being one with the cosmos, at sharing its electrons and photons, and somehow I had gone beyond language, with its scaffoldings, its approximations that could be dismantled when their work was done; I had gone beyond works of art, which were only models for interpreting our experience. I had existentially made contact with Reality, and the words could be dispensed with; unless they served to record the thing-ness for future reference.

Soon I was walking back over the bridge to the Rising Sun for a lone breakfast in the Pool Room. I felt light inside, buoyant, exhilarated. One ray of my rising sun was worth all the words that frothed like water under the Mill of the lectern.

from *Wheeling Bats and a Harvest Moon* (1999)

16
Wheeling Bats and a Harvest Moon

There was gloom in the house. First a relative in Carlisle rang to say her husband was in hospital with angina, then a letter came saying another relative (a dead husband's aunt) was in hospital in the Isle of Man, and finally there was news that Uncle Hector was in hospital in Wales. "They always say trouble comes in threes," Pippa's mother said.

That evening I took Pippa to Golant. We went to St Sampson's, a thirteenth-century church, at dusk. It has a square tower and a long white roof and narrow diamond-shaped windows overlooking the

River Fowey, and as we went into the porch a bat flew out and wheeled around our heads, causing us to duck. Like a dead soul it flitted off among the graves, one of which (dated 1776) said "In Memmory of..." and we went into the porch.

There were two more of the pipistrelles hanging from the roof above our heads, their folded umbrella-like wings hanging on either side of their mouse-like bodies, and as we struggled to lift the latch on the heavy church door, the first bat wheeled back and darted round and round the porch.

We entered the church hastily, shutting the door, but the bat had got inside, and as we looked at the pulpit and the pews in the half-light it wheeled about, threatening to collide with our heads and sending a shudder of primitive dislike down our spines.

We beat a hasty retreat, and it pursued us out into the porch, and all three bats were flying about the churchyard. And somehow I connected them with the souls of the three sick relatives. They were messengers of death, waiting to escort us to our last rest.

We walked across the water splash where a parked car was wheel-deep under the tide and had a drink at the Fisherman's Arms, and then we drove home. On the brow of a hill we saw the orange lights of St Austell spread beneath us, and there was a beautiful orange round harvest moon. It was somehow clean and elusive, and I told Pippa: "I am a painter in words, I see bats and whereas a painter paints them I make vivid verbal images out of them. I have a painter's eye. One day, you see, there will be a collection of one thousand of my verbal paintings. People will be able to read them in bed, just dip into two or three and then sleep." I was full of belief as I drove towards the harvest moon, which was really quite high in the sky.

We stopped at Charlestown and walked along the jetty. The sea was very calm, and there was a glow over the hill. The stars were slightly hazy but I could see the W of Cassiopeia very clearly.

I looked for my harvest moon, but it was nowhere to be seen. No matter how far along the jetty I walked or which direction I looked, it had totally vanished, and I did not see it again and was rather sad that my moment of belief had passed. For somehow life was about that: a clear image of direction which hung high above the bats which waited to take us to our grave.

17
The Sweet, Fresh Mountain Air

That afternoon we packed up tea and put hooks on two rods and found worms under a stone near the back door – the children sang "No one loves me, everybody hates me, for I eat worms all day" – and then drove up through the Forestry Commission's padlocked gate (we had a key) to Laddie Wood, where ptarmigans can be found and golden eagles swoop. We left the cars and went down a path of bracken to the second waterfall, where Angus had said we might find some trout. There were boulders and there was a rushing sound from the two waterfalls, and we cut a worm in half and hooked the pieces on our rods – I loathed the taking of its life, but Henry, being a surgeon, was not squeamish – and we cast and probed the depths and waited.

There had been a drought in the Highlands for two months, and the burns were all dried up, and this one was low, and there were few hiding-places. We waited and watched a dragonfly go by, and, sitting over my line, I thought how fishing was like being a poet, who probes a seemingly transparent unconscious for a swish of a tail, a gleaming fin-like image he hopes to hook.

The afternoon lengthened. The youngest child fell in a pool, and then fell in again, and another one slipped and wet her bottom. It was clearly time to think of tea.

Further upstream Simon shouted, "A trout," and unenthusiastically we trod from boulder to boulder above the rushing water and cast. "I saw a tail swish," Simon shouted, peering, and I was relieved when there was nothing. I released the remaining worms and we headed back through the undergrowth.

It was an ignominious tally we returned with in our net bag: nil. But we would have defied the greatest trout-fishers on earth to find any trout in that bit of stream.

Then two deer ran across the track in front of our car, and then yellow wagtails dipped and flew, and the sun shone among the mountains, and it did not matter that we had not caught anything. All that mattered was that we were in harmony with Nature in the sweet, fresh mountain air, and I felt glad that the trout were hiding under the boulders in the large pools, and I felt sorry that we had severed a worm, and I wished we had not disturbed its peaceful existence under the stone by the back door.

18
Coughing and an Accepted Calvary

Denise Howe was forty-eight. She was a superb organiser. When she was with us she organised the gardening and then the kitchen. She made the cooks scrub the cellar stairs. Later she left us to organise private nurses. She organised the church cleaning rota.

That March I was choosing a card for my sister in the card shop, and Denise and her husband stood together, and she was coughing.

"Hello," I said, "you've got a bad cough."

"Yes," she said in a matter-of-fact tone, "I've got a secondary in each lung and I was in the terminal ward in the London Hospital – I'm not supposed to know that – and I'm starting chemotherapy on Tuesday. Yes, I've got a bad cough."

Appalled, I spoke to her about her future prospects, and said she could sit in the school grounds she used to keep weeded any time.

Denise called in that July. She sat in the window overlooking the gardens where she tilled, and coughed and coughed and coughed her way through a social chat. She looked white and thin, and her eyes were intense. She was clearly much worse, but she talked optimistically about beating lung cancer.

In August she died. She could not breathe one Friday night and was admitted to Whipps Cross hospital. She organised the nurses. She said, "I want heroin twice a day to kill the pain, and my drip's not working properly. Where's the nurse who sees to this?"

"She's having a tea-break."

"And how long is her tea-break?"

Her condition deteriorated on the Saturday. She told a consultant I know, "I'm dying."

"She's not, as a matter of fact," he told his wife, but sure enough on the Sunday morning at about 8 a.m. she died.

I attended the funeral. It was at Christ Church, Wanstead, and the vicar wore a square black hat with a tassel. The church was pretty full, and many were in tears, including her two children and doctor husband, who looked gaunt and sombre. After the eulogy, in the course of which the vicar said, "We must accept; if we accept suffering it ennobles us," the *cortège* got ready.

Pippa said, "It's not fair."

"But it must be accepted," I said.

We followed the hearse to City of London cemetery and watched the committal standing round the open grave, the relatives nearest to the pit. Later we all filed past, knelt and threw in a handful of earth. As I did so, glimpsing the flower-bedecked coffin at the bottom of the hole, I thought of her Calvary and I thought of Tennyson's lines in 'Tithonus':

> The woods decay, the woods decay and fall,
> The vapours weep their burthen to the ground,
> Man comes and tills the fields and lies beneath,
> And after many a summer dies the swan.

She had tilled our soil, and now she lay beneath and the whole thing was meaningful. But she had been a mainstay of the church and had lived a blameless and healthy life – she had never smoked – and it may not have been fair but she had died whereas her aged aunt was still alive, and it all had to be accepted. The meaning was in her next life, perhaps. So her Calvary had to be welcomed.

from *The Warm Glow of the Monastery Courtyard* (1999)

19
The Warm Glow of the Monastery Courtyard

In Ithaca I found a taxi-driver near the bust of Lord Byron (who visited the British-ruled island on his way to Messolonghi) and he drove us round the island. Both ends claimed Odysseus as theirs. The Vathy end claimed he waded ashore at Phorcys bay and hid Alcinous's treasure in the Cave of the Nymphs, which has a slit for men to squeeze through and a hole in the top for nymphs and gods, as Homer wrote in *The Odyssey* book 13, lines 107–108. According to the Vathy end, Odysseus's castle was on Mount Aetos. There are walls below which the Greeks have excavated and dated as 7th century BC, too late to be of the time of Odysseus (12th century BC).

The Stavros end claimed he landed at Polis bay and hid his treasure in a cave there that has since been destroyed by earthquakes but where archaeologists found the 12th-century-BC drinking vessel with a fingered stem which is now in the small museum. The Stavros end, in the person of the curator of the museum, said that excavators are finding Mycenaean relics in Pitikali, the Hill of Hermes, where Odysseus's palace stood and from which you could see three seas. We drove to the spot, and you can indeed see three seas, all still and deep blue and paradisal, as Homer said.

We returned to Phorcys bay for a swim. The stones were sharp, a line of olive trees gave shade, and little had changed in 3,200 years, I thought, up to my neck in warm clear water where shoals of small fish wriggled. Polis bay contained a sunken Byzantine city, Jerusalem, which had been destroyed by an earthquake, and while Tennyson's aged Ulysses could have seen the horizon beyond Cephalonia from a mole at the mouth of the cave, I thought Odysseus would have been too crafty to land under the noses of the suitors and then walk the entire length of the island to seek out Eumaeus on the Raven's Crag above me, near the Fountain of Arethusa. No, I thought, Odysseus landed at Phorcys, went up to the Cave of the Nymphs, from which a small tunnel led down to Phorcys, and from there he went on to Eumaeus. Only later did he storm the royal palace at Pitikali, near Stavros.

We caught the 4 o'clock ferry back to Cephalonia. I sat on the deck, my legs through the railings, and watched as deserted craggy Ithaca with its little sandy coves slid away into a heat haze on an indigo sea so calm that I occasionally glimpsed the bottom, and pondered my reconciliation of the conflicting views and Homer's evident detailed knowledge of Ithaca.

We were met by our Cephalonian taxi-driver, John Daphnos, a grandfatherly chain-smoking man with a bushy moustache, who drove us home the opposite way. We had come via Argostoli and the British monument by the sea causeway, and the island of Assos, and we returned via Sami and mount Enos and Frangata. He showed us where the Germans had massacred "many Italians" in 1943. He had taken part as a boy partisan. He rolled up his trousers and showed me two bullet wounds on his knees. "Germans, big problem," he said.

Suddenly he pointed at a long yellow wall and said, "Agios Gerassimos, famous monastery. One five seven zero. You want to go in?" And he pulled through an opening in a bell tower into the courtyard near an open door.

It was nearly half past six after a long day, and the boys showed reluctance. More out of duty than interest I got out, still in shorts, and Pippa followed.

"Come," said John Daphnos, beckoning.

He went in to a smallish room and lit a candle, the ex-partisan identifying with his Orthodox religion. A service seemed to be in progress. Just out of sight behind a screen to the left a Greek Orthodox priest was chanting. Over to the right a black-clad woman was leading responses from a dozen lay members of the public. A few more people were milling round, writing names in Greek near the candles. A nun approached with a shawl and put it over Pippa's shoulders. I saw a note in English: "Please enter properly dressed."

At the Cave of the Apocalypse in Patmos, where St John had the visions of *Revelation*, I had also been in shorts, and had had to hang a towel round my waist to get in. I felt as if I had just come out of a shower, or as if I were playing alongside Tony Curtis in *Some Like it Hot*.

Instinctively I took a step back.

"No, it's all right. Come," said John Daphnos with the authority of a man who had lit a candle and been a partisan and therefore had influence. "Over there, sarcophagus. Pure silver."

"Very good," I said.

"Come."

He propelled me across the room. Indignant stares and glares greeted my bare legs. No attempt was made to cover me, as if men were beyond saving. I stood by the rail feeling very self-conscious, and at that moment the priest appeared from behind the screen, still chanting, black-bearded and middle-aged. He unlocked the casket, opened the doors and pulled down a flap to reveal, in the bottom half of the casket, a brownish figure on his back with a reddish tapestry from waist to feet.

The black-clad nun had lined up a few of the laity, mostly women, and the first stood before the figure, knelt and crossed herself three times, and then kissed the tapestry, which looked like a piece of carpet.

"Is it a statue or is it dead?" I whispered to Pippa.

"Dead," she said. "I overheard a guide talking about it on the boat. There's no embalming, the flesh hasn't decayed. I'll tell you later."

With fascination and awe I watched as to incessant chanting from the priest and nun four more women in the queue stood, knelt, crossed themselves three times and kissed the relic.

The chanting black-clad nun was waving with her hand.

John Daphnos stood beside me, and I thought she was waving to him. Or was she indicating that I should go forward? In shorts? Surely not. Besides, I was not Orthodox, it was not my place to go.

I stood my ground. I was not going to kneel and kiss a dead thing that had somehow not decayed. I peered into the gloom of the casket from behind the rail, perhaps three feet away, and tried to discern the face, but could only make out a dark brown, fried-looking shape with beads round its neck, in clothes.

John Daphnos said, "We go now?"

We came out into the blinding sunlight, and I said to John Daphnos: "That was St Gerassimos?"

"Yes. He died one five seven nine. Flesh no decay. No odour."

"A miracle?" I said.

He looked doubtful and said nothing.

I felt the hot sun on my cheeks and was glad to be alive, having been confronted with an image of mortality when I least expected it, caught with my guard down. I had distanced death into conflicting views on Odysseus's landing and his chalice-like drinking-cup, and this saint had burst through my historical judgements with a dramatic immediacy that had taken me by surprise.

When we returned to Agia Pelagia and I had paid off John Daphnos and tipped him handsomely, and we were on our own, Pippa told me what she had overheard and we fleshed out the details from our guide-books. Although the books all called it a monastery, we had in fact been in a nunnery. Saint Gerassimos, the patron saint of the island, had been born in 1507, of a wealthy Greek Peloponnesian family with roots in Byzantium; they had been refugees from Constantinople in 1453. He became a monk when very young, and spent time in Jerusalem, Crete and Zakynthos before coming to Cephalonia in 1560. He established a monastery and nearby a nunnery which he called New Jerusalem (a phrase of St John's in *Revelation*) and planted two big plane-trees near the nunnery, saying it was God's job to look after them. He dug many wells to irrigate the fields round the monastery (or nunnery), and taught the children from the nearby villages. He lived down a hole in the small nunnery church I had been in. A passage led four or five metres down to an underground chamber and thence to another room, his home.

After he died miracles began to happen, demons were mysteriously exorcised following prayers at his tomb. An orange glow was soon seen coming from the ground where he was buried. Villagers were astonished, and after two years they disinterred his body to investigate and found it to be in near-perfect condition. It exuded a pleasant smell and was completely intact. It was reburied and re-exhumed eight months later, and was still found to be in perfect condition with a pleasant smell. The Patriarch of Constantinople was petitioned, and Gerassimos Notaras was declared an Orthodox saint in 1622, and to this day his body has miraculously defied decomposition – without any embalming, we are assured.

The nuns kept him dressed and changed his clothes, and each year a new pair of sandals was sent for his feet, and at the end of each year his sandals were worn out as his soul goes for a walk. He has been observed walking about the village in the evenings. Once a year, every October 20th, they carry him in an upright position in a procession from the church to the well and plane-trees. He was impervious to the process and odours of corruption, as was untarnished silver.

We ate by the blue Irinna Hotel pool in Agia Pelagia and drank local

Robola wine (Calliga). I was haunted by what had happened. I just could not get it out of my mind. The monk was a contradiction, or rather a unity. He lived down a hole in contemplation, yet he planted trees, dug wells and taught children, led a very active life. Had his perfection of the contemplative-active life resulted in some control of mind over matter through illumination, that prevented his body from decaying and gave it an orange glow? Had his mastery caused a natural process we do not understand to be at work and prevented his body from decaying? In which case I should have kissed his legs in admiration for what he had pioneered.

Or, on the other hand, had there been some skullduggery? All through history rulers had used gods to induce recalcitrant people to obey them. I was reminded of a carpet-seller who had accosted me at Ephesus: "Hello, how are you? I very honest. I show you very good carpet." Had the Orthodox hierarchy said to the people of Cephalonia "Hello, how are you? We very honest, we show you proof that if you are Orthodox Christians you will escape decomposition"? Even Lenin's treated body would decompose when exposed to air.

I wondered if I, along with the others in that church, had been exposed to a con: "Hello, how are you? I very honest, I open this sarcophagus to the air and you see there is no decomposition." I had seen this with my own eyes, but I could not vouch for there having been a lack of any treatment. His brownness reminded me of Ramesses II in Cairo. Had he been treated with a radioactive substance that glowed from under the earth? I recalled an image from an Indiana Jones film, in which an old body becomes dust. Now I was glad I had not kissed the relic, for to have done so would have been to accept the con, to have been proved gullible.

I thought of how I had reconciled the Vathy and Stavros schools of thought about Odysseus's homecoming. Perhaps in the same way Gerassimos's perfect balance of the active and contemplative lives had bound the flesh with spirit, and perhaps the subtlising of dense flesh had enabled some 16th-century pickling process to work more effectively than most. He looked fried, and perhaps some heat had been used.

I finished my meal and went up to my room and sat on the balcony and looked at the stars and faint line of mountain in the hot dark twilight. Cicadas were still chirping. I had to separate experience from all "Hello, how are you?" interpretations of it. I had to separate my experience of the carpet from what the carpet-sellers wanted me to believe. I honoured Gerassimos for what he had done for Cephalonia during his life, and I was wary of the "Hello, how are you?" display of his body, which served to keep some of the people of Cephalonia in the Orthodox Church's thrall.

Looking at the stars, I knew I had to stick by what I experienced, and be mistrustful of all carpet-sellers who sought to interpret my experience to suit their own purposes. I would observe and evaluate, but not kiss unless my deepest inclinations urged me to. I would not kiss when invited to by a black-clad nun. I would live in the harsh, glaring sunlight, in the warm orange glow of the monastery courtyard, not the still, chanting gloom round a silver sarcophagus in a convent church. I would live where Odysseus lived, among people in the open air, in the midst of life, in the courtyard, not through the doorway and removed from life and close to death.

20
A Gardener Goes into the Fire

Our gardener, Dave Ford, was a mournful fellow who was woefully short of energy. He picked a few weeds, hoed thistles and elder and sorrel, and then sat, and I soon discovered he had hidden cans of beer among the plants. He took to sitting on the school front doorstep with his flask at tea-time, and was oblivious to the efforts of parents to clamber round him as they entered or left the school.

He talked about his son. "He's doing so well," he said proudly, "he's got a forty-seven-thousand-five-hundred car."

He was not satisfactory but there was no one else, and after a while the flower-beds did look better so we continued to have him.

He had an ulcer, he said. Soon he would ring me up and say, "Mr Rawley, I'm afraid I can't manage it today. Today's not a good day." Or: "I'll be along at four today. Today's a good day."

Even on a good day he was not up to more than light hoeing, and after the leaves fell he knocked off for the winter.

In the late winter I had a phone call. "This is Mrs. Ford. My husband Dave won't be coming to you any more. He died yesterday morning." She dissolved into tears while I gave the ritual reaction about being shocked and surprised.

"He thought he had an ulcer," she said. "It was a cancerous tumour. He was told five weeks ago. He just deteriorated, and he died yesterday morning. I was with him. The funeral's on Friday."

I went to the funeral. The *cortège*, the hearse with "Dad" in flowers on the front, assembled outside his son's bungalow. I parked nearby and handed over my wreath to an undertaker and then went in and shook hands with the son: a pinched, stooping grey-haired man with Dave's looks and a taciturn manner. I shook hands with the son's forward wife, and with Dave's white-haired wife who said how pleased Dave would be to think I had come: "He often spoke of you."

We drove, or rather crawled, in convoy. An undertaker led the way, walking, and it took us half an hour to reach Corbet's Tey crematorium, Upminster. We stood in the cold, fourteen of us, all in dark suits, Dave's relatives; and as we followed the coffin into the chapel the bearded vicar shouted words of hope: '"I am the resurrection and the life.... Believe in me...."'

The service was short. We recited the twenty-third psalm, and the vicar spoke about the special relationship each had with Dave. He said nothing about his life, there was no mention of what he had done, and I thought of the memorial service I had been to for H. J. L. Somersby, which wafted the deceased to the after-life with madrigals and Byrd: there is one after-life for the rich and another for the poor.

Everything the vicar said could be repeated at the next service; it was all typical, generic, and nothing was individual to Dave. At the end he said, "All of us here – all of you – have to face death one day. There is no escape from it for any of us."

An uncomfortable shudder went through some of the tiny congregation as if they were confronted with their existential reality. As the curtain drew a lofty organ played and from the roof doves cooed, and Dave's widow burst into uncontrolled sobbing.

Outside I looked at the chimney for the smoke, aware that Dave had gone into the fire. As we all stood and looked at the wreaths a tremendous snowstorm started. Huge flakes of snow drifted and sailed and settled from a blizzard sky. It was as if Nature had heaved a groan.

But Heaven had gained, for in its gardens, somewhere, a new employee was sitting by his flask, having his first tea-break on St Peter's front doorstep, oblivious of the souls that filed past him, and soon he would be hoeing thistles, elder and sorrel with a mournful intentness that was mercifully now pain-free.

21
A Lion and Clacking Sticks

We went to Waltham Abbey to see the flower festival. First I showed the boys Harold's tomb, and explained how he had an arrow in his eye and how his body was found by Edith Swan's Neck. The inside of the Abbey was decked with floral arrangements that illustrated themes, spanning 800 years, and I paused in particular at the Denny tomb. Sir Edward Denny lay on his side, an Elizabethan knight, one hand on his sword, the other cupping his head, and his wife lay beneath him, while all round the tomb, like choirboys with their hands in prayer, clustered his ten children.

Outside this place of death I heard a banging and crossed the market to a side-street where eight morris dancers cavorted, leaning back in white shirts and black breeches. To two violins they nimbly moved their feet in a jig and, wearing red and yellow braces and holding batons, they knock-knocked while a tall lion with a red felt tongue ran amok, terrifying the crowd with its gaping teeth and threats to devour everyone and pausing once to wee at a lamppost. The morris dancers had ribbons on their elbows and bells on their knees, and they let out whoops of joy as the dance progressed, and the exuberance and exhilaration of their clacking sticks earned them great applause from the standing shoppers. And when some produced cameras between dances they all rushed to pose and then demanded 50p, to the merriment of all. There was a great joy in life.

I came away and, passing the weir by the Abbey, and walking along by the still stream, I looked back towards Harold's grave thinking of the contrast between the lion of Death and the life-affirming morris dancers, and I knew that I would remember what I had seen. It was as if I had been bombarded by events. It was not so much what I had heard, rather what experience had fired at me. I felt I had an arrow in my eye.

22
A Headless Statue in Nettles

I went to visit Copped Hall, an eighteenth-century ruin that has been a shell since a fire gutted it in 1917. From the Epping road it looks very imposing, standing on the top of a hill in the middle of green fields, but as I approached it past pine woods I was filled with the sadness of the roofless overgrown wilderness inside. The conservatory was blown up and unsafe, and lay in bits and pieces among stinging-nettles, and the beautiful Italian garden of fountains and marble balustrades and *parterre*s and follies that in photographs of 1908 led down to large ornate iron gates was under turf and brambles, and barely distinguishable between overgrown trees. I stood at the back and looked at the triangular pediments and Ionian columns and long windows and high chimneys and felt the contrast between the order that rises out against the dark, and the nettles which overtake it when it returns.

Later I found where the earlier Elizabethan Hall used to be. It had been razed to the ground as unsafe in the eighteenth century, and archaeologists had revealed the red brick foundations and wall bases and I could trace the rooms at the south end. Here Elizabeth I had stayed for the marriage of its owner, Sir Thomas Heneage.

Shakespeare was reputed to have come for the first performance of *A Midsummer Night's Dream* which had taken place in the Long Gallery. Theseus was based on Heneage and Hippolyta on his bride, the Earl of Southampton's mother. I followed the line of foundations into thick undergrowth and walked in an overgrown yew walk through the ha-ha to a brick folly at the bottom of which, on her back in an attitude of love, quite naked and with rounded breasts, lay the headless statue of an Elizabethan woman.

Nettles engulfed her, and I thought of woods with bluebells and violets in them, and saw the stone steps that Elizabeth I and Southampton and doubtless Shakespeare had trodden, I thought of the beauty of the Renaissance – a Venus with Pheidian curves – and mourned its warm sensuality which had "copped it" and which lay discarded and neglected now in this dark tangle of undergrowth and nettles.

23
Love Like a Cheek-Warming Log-Burner

For Valentine's Night we went to St Benet's restaurant in Cornwall. It was very foggy and we crawled into Lanivet and swung off the road and parked and walked to the low granite blocks of the Abbey gatehouse and through the studded Victorian door where a gentleman in a short-sleeved shirt and tie who had an open face and hair sleeked either side of his parting greeted us and led us to the lounge. He brought drinks – a slim-line tonic for Pippa and a red wine for me – and we sat in front of a log-burner with glass doors and felt the heat warm our cheeks and watched the logs and the gold-vermilion furnace through glass that reminded me of the soul. The gentleman brought a rose in transparent paper for Pippa and the menus, and I asked how old the granite blocks were.

"Fourteen eleven," he said. "And the fireplace and wood are Victorian." He told me that the building had been derelict and that the Reverend Arudell restored it from 1817 to 1850. I thought the Maltese cross on the fireplace and ceiling and in the Victorian windows had been put there by him.

We ate in a Victorian room with other diners. They all wore open-necked shirts, and the ladies each had a rose beside them. I had smoked-duck salad, mint-and-pea soup, steak and then peach and apple ice-cream in a chocolate cup. We had half a bottle of good champagne and talked in whispers like the other guests.

Soon we were in the lounge again, but this time far away from the log-burner, where another couple sat. The girl sat erect and awkwardly while the man talked. From time to time she nodded.

I sat and drank in the peace of the fifteenth-century atmosphere and marvelled that granite walls could seem so warm.

We drove home through fog so thick that visibility was no more than ten yards in places. There were no cats' eyes in the road and I crawled to avoid veering off at a bend. We got back to our house by the sea, and later I thought of the thick fog and the warm log-burner, and I knew that love is like a roaring burner with glass doors that throws out an intense, cheek-warming heat, and that one carries the memory away on one's journey through the thick fogs of arduous, social living.

24
A Soul Like Ripe Grain

A friend of Paul's died playing football. He had been in *Treasure Island* with Paul and had broken through into television and had left school two years before his 'A' levels to attend drama school with a view to acting professionally. He still liked playing football, and had been to Hawaii on tour with his team. He had chest pains and went to see a Harley Street specialist. After tests the specialist said, "If he were my son, I'd have him out playing football."

He died on a Wednesday. His side won 3–2. He scored the second goal and was breathless. He was substituted and joined his parents on the touchline. He said to his father, whom he called by his Christian name – they were a close Jewish family: "I can't breathe."

It was like an asthma attack but seemed to involve his heart. He collapsed on the touchline, was revived briefly but lost consciousness again. The game had continued. The ambulancemen arrived but he had died, aged sixteen with the world at his feet.

Paul went to the funeral the following Sunday. He told me about it. "It was in a Jewish cemetery in East Ham," he said. "I was taken by another friend's father who is Jewish. He gave me a skull-cap – a *kappel* – to wear. We went into a building with columns, which stood in the cemetery. No women or children were allowed as his dad didn't have his wife there. She's distraught. There were about three hundred men. An old Rabbi with a long beard spoke. He said he was kind. He won a race but ran back to help a bird with a broken wing he'd passed rather than collect his medal. He gave half his *EastEnders* money to his older brother, who couldn't stop crying. The Rabbi said sometimes those who are kinder than anyone else do die young, they're too kind for this earth. He said he had achieved more in his short life than many have by the time they're seventy. There was chanting.

"We went outside. The hole in the ground was twenty yards from the entrance gate. We watched as the coffin was lowered and then people took it in turns to shovel in earth. The Head and several of the masters at school were there, some in tears. The master who taught him drama shovelled in earth. His hands were shaking with grief.

"We had to go back to the building and wash our hands, that's a Jewish custom. Then we went back inside. There was more chanting, and a commemoration, more about his family. Then his father and brother sat on a bench outside and we all lined up to shake their hands while they sat. His father was grey-haired and lined but not crying. I said, 'I hope you have a long life,' for that is the Jewish custom. I was told to say that on the way there. I said to the brother, 'I'm sorry.' He smiled and said, 'Thank you.' That was it."

I said, "You will remember this for the rest of your life, you will still be talking about this at reunions in thirty-five years' time. All that youthful promise. It's hard to interpret why it ended so abruptly. You've been born into an age where the adults haven't got clear answers. Many would say, 'That's life, it's tough.' But I think of Hopkins' 'Wreck of the Deutschland': the soul is like an ear of corn, and when it is ripe with grain it is time for it to be harvested. He was kind, he ripened in June and was harvested. Many don't ripen until late August or September, but their souls have the same ripeness. 'Those whom the gods love die young.' Think of him as an ear of grain, and it all becomes – if not understandable, then at least acceptable."

25
Morphine and Tears

I picked up a pink begonia and a dozen orange gerberas, and drove to a village under the Downs. Sheila was waiting for me outside the large modern redbrick house. She had short bubbly blonde hair and looked much younger than sixty. She said, "You're punctual, it's bang on half-past two. He's not had such a good day today. He's slept all morning. He's been feeling a bit sick."

I followed her upstairs to the bedroom where James sat wanly in bed. He had aged thirty years, was thin with very grey hair and he now had piercing eyes.

"Look," she said of the begonia as he extended a feeble hand, "the same colour as your pyjamas."

I sat at the edge of the double bed in the large light room and looked through the glass of the sliding door to the terrace over the garage and a field where a dozen cows munched. Sheila said, "I'll make a cup of tea," and I sat while his two small terriers jumped onto the end of the bed and looked at me.

"How have you been?" I asked.

"A bit weak, Philip," he said. He stared at me with a stare that came from beyond the grave to the land of the living. I had brought him a book and a brochure of our new house, and he looked through the brochure.

I said, "I come with the best wishes of so many on our side of the family. Are you in any discomfort?"

"A bit, Philip."

"You've got some tablets there."

"Yes, they're morphine. I take a tablet at nine and then at nine at night. It's self-regulatory."

"When's the worst time?"

"Early morning. I wake at six and it hurts, just here, on the right side, my liver." He opened his pink pyjama jacket. "I take a painkiller. It takes an hour to work."

"Six to seven is the worst time?" I asked.

"Yes."

I said, "It's a wretched, wretched business."

"Yes, Philip," he said, "it's a wretched, wretched business."

I said, "As I remarked to you over the phone, there is a tradition that regards us as having an invisible body within a visible body. The real you may be an invisible body."

Sheila came in with tea and biscuits on a tray. The two dogs sat up at the end of the bed, staring at me but obediently not sniffing at the biscuits.

Sheila chattered about how she had to go down the road to the chemist for more tablets and for a commode, and James lit a cigarette.

"I've smoked for forty-five years," he said, "and it's unjust, this isn't tobacco-related in any way."

Sheila's eyes were flirtatiously attentive. She asked questions about my life. Then James got out of bed slowly and shuffled to the loo and I followed Sheila downstairs.

I asked her, "Will you be financially well provided for?"

She hesitated and said, "I'll have to be careful. I've got fifteen thousand pounds tucked away."

"Will you continue to live here in this house?"

Very quietly she began to sniff and her eyes filled with tears.

"I'm sorry to make you cry," I said gently, "but you must face it."

She sobbed, "I know. I haven't talked to him about it. I've been practical. I haven't really had a talk with him about the future. It would be upsetting. I don't really know what he's thinking. A lady from the hospice came and had a talk with him and told me, 'He's terrified. He's saying "I need a gun."'"

"I'll speak to him about that," I said.

When I returned to his bedroom he was flopped back on his pillows. I sat at the end of the bed and said, "If I were where you're lying, I'd be somewhat frightened – apprehensive – about what's ahead. But think about it. If you were going to be executed – shot against a wall or beheaded with an axe – there would be a question of 'will it hurt?' But you haven't got that. You'll be drowsy and you'll drift and come to and drift and come to and drift – and not come to. You'll be asleep. Then the question will be, 'Is there nothing or something?' If there's nothing, you're a winner because it's like being asleep, in a dreamless sleep. But if there's something it'll be part of a pattern for everyone and your parents and your brother will have been through it, and it'll be copable with, part of a plan, like going from a chrysalis to a butterfly. You'll be without your unreliable body."

James nodded. He said, "What I really miss is the pool. Each year it's open from April the first. This'll be the first year I can't swim in it. My arms are strong, if I could just get down to the pool down there, I'd swim in it. It's American, lined not tiled."

I said quietly, "I'll help you swim in that pool. Wait until the weather's warmer and the temperature in the pool's, what, eighty-two, and you're feeling up to it and it's a Wednesday, and I'll come and borrow a folding wheelchair from a hospital and get you down there, even if I have to carry you on a stretcher, and I'll swim with you. I'll make a bargain with you. I'll swim with you, and when my turn comes you can wait for me at the ticket-barrier. It'll be like waiting for the passengers to come off a train at Waterloo and hand their tickets in."

He smiled.

"I hope you don't mind me talking frankly like this."

"No. You've broken the ice."

I said, "I took our eldest boy to see a consultant. I knew the consultant had a terminal illness and had elected to carry on working. At the end of the interview I sent my son outside and said, 'I'd like you to know that one parent of one patient is grateful to you for continuing to work under the circumstances and hats off to you.' He said, 'I have dozens of patients each month here in Harley Street, but you're the only one who's said that. People don't realise the loneliness of the terminally ill. Everyone comes and talks about things other than what you really want to talk about, out of politeness and embarrassment. I'm grateful to you for talking about reality.'"

"Yes," James said. "I'm grateful to you for talking about these things."

I stood and said, "I'm going now, or I'll tire you. Remember, a hot day in three weeks' time and we'll go swimming together."

James sat up from his pillows and shook my hand. There were tears in his eyes.

"Goodbye, James."

"Goodbye, Philip."

He shook my hand a second time and I turned and walked down the passage. The last glimpse I had of him was of him sitting in bed in tears.

Downstairs I sat briefly with Sheila and told her what I had said to him.

"Did he say we haven't talked?" she asked.

"No, we didn't talk about you."

She looked relieved.

"You *should* talk," I said. "If you like, I'll take you back up now and get you talking."

"No, no, no, no," she said in panic, and I realised she did not want to face reality. "It's all right. I'll talk with him later. This began eighteen months ago," she said. "He's had no one to talk with. I can't thank you enough for coming and talking to him. You know, the first time I met him I knew he'd ask me to marry him and I thought, 'It'll last until he's sixty-five.' I knew he'd die at sixty-five, then, on that first day. I just knew. It's strange, isn't it? The hospice said he'd have a heart attack or stroke before he reaches the drowsy stage. I haven't told him that. Why did they tell him he's only got weeks to live? Why didn't they just not tell him? They could have kept it from him. I'm going to take the dogs for a walk now. Then I'll go and have a chat with him."

But I knew she would not. She was in flight from reality, and she would continue to act as if everything was normal and bottle up her feelings just below the surface so that they easily overflowed into tears. It was as if she, too, were on painkillers. And he would sit stoically, stiff-upper-lipped as the cancer in his liver throttled him, and not volunteer things his own feelings were crying out to express, holding down his own tears with self-regulated morphine.

After my visit he deteriorated rapidly, as if he had accepted his end and was almost willing it to happen, and a week later, to the day, that next Wednesday, he died.

The Lord Lieutenant of the county attended his funeral in uniform, and though people were standing at the back of the chapel took up a whole pew. His grandeur was asserted very arrestingly, and, thinking of James's simplicity before death and of the monarch's tribute to his work as senior magistrate, I was glad I had seen him as he was rather than as his society wished him to be.

from *In the Brilliant Autumn Sunshine* (2007)

26
In the Brilliant Autumn Sunshine, Among a Thousand Islands

The blue boat hove off in the sun till a much larger boat left the quay at New Grimsby. I could see the captain in his enclosed cabin, and had a closer look as he came alongside and pottered out to the open part at the back as the boat swayed from side to side. He had a ruddy face with a reddish beard down to his chest, and he wore an open-necked grey shirt and blue jeans. We descended the stone steps of the quay and stepped aboard and I explained to him where I would like him to take us: a tour round the outside of all the Scilly Isles (locally called "The Fortunate Isles", a title also claimed by the Canary Isles).

The captain said, "There are spring tides, and that'll take four and a half hours. Most people who hire me say they want three hours and they're fed up after an hour and a half and want to go back. I suggest you don't do St Agnes and the Western Rocks. You can do the rest in three hours, given the tides."

I told him I was interested in history, in whether the islands had all been connected at one time, in any buried walls and evidence of old houses under the sea.

"You can't see them," he said. "I've never seen any. I'll tell you what, though. I've been on Bryher all my life, I've got things from my grandfather, the family can trace its roots on Bryher back five hundred years, and I know there's no old stone walls on Bryher. But this lady came down and said she'd found a Bronze-Age wall. I told her, 'There isn't any.' But she insisted, so I went with her to see what she'd found. Ten years back I was clearing seaweed off a beach with a digger, and I piled all the stones up to clear the beach. That's what she'd found. I said, '*I* built that wall. Not the Bronze Age, me.'

"Another time I was knocking posts into ground up on Bryher. Some of it's soft ground, but sometimes it's hard, and I'd pick up a stone and bang it on top of the post like a hammer, and the post made a mark, a kind of round depression, in the stone. Of course, I threw the stone away and went on to the next post. We had a lady come down and she found one of those stones. She said it was Bronze Age and tried to make us stop what we were doing in the field – burning off the roots of a crop – as it was a 'prehistoric site'. We've only just got rid of her. I told her, 'I made the mark in that stone.'

"No, I don't go in for Bronze-Age walls and stones in these parts. It's like my family. My four sons say I should pay more attention to the past, but I say, 'It's dead and gone, and when I'm like that I won't want someone trowelling me up to have a look at *my* skeleton.'"

"What's your family's name?" I asked.

"Jameson."

"And your first name?"

"Dick."

We put out and threaded our way between moored yachts and launches. I said gently, "A book says that the Scilly Isles were all one around AD 500, called Ennor, and that the land subsided gradually until Tresco formed a single island with Bryher and Samson known as Rentemen. This was separated from St Martin's, St Mary's and St Agnes. So what's left are the high parts, and it's all connected under the sea. Another book says that Samson was connected to Bryher till just before 1016, but was separate by then. And of course, there's the story of Lyonesse. According to the *Anglo-Saxon Chronicle* on 11 November 1099 the land between here and Cornwall sank, and near the Seven Stones Reef – and off Newlyn and Mousehole – you can hear a hundred and forty church bells tolling beneath the waves from the lost land of Lyonesse that stretched from the Scillies to Land's End."

He said, "All I've heard from the Seven Stones Reef, which is about nine miles out from the Daymark, is that motor. You go to that Reef, there are just rocks, like any you see round here. There's no ruins on them. There's an engineless lightship there. And as for whether the islands were all connected, I don't know. If it was all one, why's the channel getting deeper? But a lot of people write books and make claims I know aren't true.

"Take Ronald Austin. He wrote in a book that he found a wreck about ten years ago. Well, I know that isn't true. I was with someone who found it on a Saturday evening, and rang him. He authenticated it and said he'd honour the site and no divers would go near it. But on Sunday morning two of his divers came and went down and took things away. *He* never found that wreck. People make claims in books about the islands being connected up, but I don't believe the books."

My profession of letters put in its place, I sat back and watched as we progressed north up the west coast of Tresco. From the wheel he pointed out two steps just above the sea-line.

"Oh," I said, "the ones used by the Special Operations Executive in the war."

"They were there long before the war," he said. "The Abbey made those steps. The books are wrong about those steps. They say the agents made them in the war. The agents used them, maybe, but they were there before. Anyway, most of the agents lived in boats."

"Fifteen hundred of them?" I asked, ignoring the fact that I had never said that SOE "made" the steps.

"Yes. They lived in the boats."

"And slipped off to France when they had a mission?"

"That's right."

We came to the ruined mound that was once King Charles's castle and the almost perfect sand-pie of Cromwell's castle below it.

"You see," he called from the wheel above the chugging engine, "Cromwell's castle's got no lintels. When Charles's castle was pulled down they rolled the stones down the hill to build Cromwell's castle, but the lintels went to the Abbey."

The previous day we had walked to the Abbey Gardens from the Island Hotel – no cars are allowed on Tresco – and had wandered in the frondy gardens laid out by Augustus Smith after his arrival as Lord Proprietor of the Scillies in 1834.

"So there was a building before Augustus Smith built what he built in 1834?"

"Yes, that's right."

We progressed to a rock where he stopped the engine and we drifted.

"You see, at the top of that curved rock," he said, "Latin numbers, nineteen. My grandfather told me that was a mooring for old yachts. There are iron rings, there and in three other places. There, over there and there. The old yachts came in and moored at one of the iron rings. That's the nineteen-foot mark. I don't know if it is true but that's what my grandfather said, and he got it from his grandfather."

"His grandfather may have known Augustus Smith," I said.

"I don't know, I haven't been into it."

We chugged on between many islands, and passed Men-a-vaur and St Helen's, and came to the Round Island lighthouse. We stopped.

"It's automatic now, but before that there were two keepers. They did shifts of two months in pairs. They climbed up that ladder to the top. They needed two because the light was on a three-hour pulley and it needed winding. One man was on watch while the other slept. Now maintenance is done by a man who comes down in a helicopter."

We passed a cormorant and a crested shag.

"Look," he said, "that big bird with a white front is a Great Northern Diver."

We made progress past White Island.

"Why is it called White Island?"

"Dunno. Why's that rock called the Brewer and that one the Baker, and that one John Martin's Ledge? It just is. They just are. I don't ask why."

He grabbed the wheel and turned it. "There's a ledge down there, a narrow gap. We're going through it now."

"Has anyone with a boat like yours scraped it on a ledge and sunk?" I asked.

He hesitated. "Anyone who's got a boat would be lying if they said they'd never sunk a boat round here," he said.

So reassured, we moved on. I sat back and we passed the Daymark lighthouse on St Martin's, and we left St Martin's sandy beaches and entered the many Eastern Islands, some of which were mere rocks.

"Seals," he called above the chugging of the engine.

Three grey seals basked on a rock, and slid into the water as we approached.

"More seals there," he called.

Each seal looked at us mournfully. One stretched and raised its flippered tail and looked pleadingly with soft, lovable eyes that delighted Pippa, who took its photograph.

"The wind's from the south," he said. "The birds and the seals always go for the sheltered side, they're on the north side of the rocks. They know where the wind is. They've a mechanism for assessing the wind. There's more in the animal kingdom than humans have discovered."

We saw many sea-birds – cormorants, shags, fulmars which followed our wake and a flock of tiny....

"Dunlins," he said, looking through his binoculars. "Curved beaks, whitish. Dozens of them on that rock."

We passed several more basking seals and then saw three oyster-catchers with orange beaks, black backs and red legs.

"That's Great Ganilly with St Martin's behind it."

I stood with my back to the wheel and looked out at the wake we made which charted our way forward among hundreds of groups of rocks and tiny islands. I felt the sun warm on my cheeks. It seemed we were among a thousand islands, and in the clear brilliant autumn sunshine among the flocks of black cormorants with white face-patches, dark grey shags, fulmars and gulls on the rocks and basking seals which knew the direction the wind blew I felt a quiet joy and I was sure that all those tiny islands and the five or six main ones were connected under the water – were one – just as I was sure the Scillies were once connected to Land's End, that the sea mirrored the sky and the sun the inner light that shone through my being. I had spent the spring and summer of my life voyaging between my thousand stories and I felt that they too were all connected at a deep level beneath the surface sparkle that seemed to divide them. In the brilliant autumn sunshine I knew that the universe was a unity, and was an interconnectedness rather than a separateness.

We continued, and he pointed out Great Arthur with St Mary's behind it: a green mound, at one end of which there was a lot of seaweed in the water, indicating submerged rocks. According to Scillonian lore, King Arthur had been buried there, having fallen at the battle of Camlann in AD 537, having left Appletree Beach on Tresco, which may then have been covered in apple trees, and crossed to this Isle of Avalon. "Avalon" comes from the old Cornish "Avallen", meaning apple tree. In Arthur's day, I had read in a book as I had told the captain, the islands were all connected and the continent they formed was called Ennor. According to Scillonian lore, this was the Isle of Avalon, "that mystical island of apples called fortunate, presided over by Morgan le Fay and her eight sisters all skilled in the healing arts" (Geoffrey of Monmouth wrote). There were other Avalons elsewhere in Britain, for example in Glastonbury, but Tennyson had stayed at Tresco Abbey in 1860 and I could see the barge in his 'Passing of Arthur' put out across the lake that separated Tresco and Ennor. In my mystical Oneness I was sure that Arthur had come here.

We passed the north coast of St Mary's, and the south coast of Tresco.

"The Abbey looks splendid," Pippa said, eyeing the distant grey building through field glasses. "No wonder Prince Charles stays there every Whitsun."

I had read in a book that a successor of Augustus Smith had sold it to the Duchy of Cornwall and had leased it back for a rent of one daffodil a year; so Prince Charles visited as landlord and took an interest in the Abbey Gardens, which were filled with exotic frondy shrubs from all round the world.

We approached Samson and the captain called out, "That's Bryher through there. You see those houses? That's where I live. I'm on Watch Hill. I've got four sons. Two are in boats with me, one's got a boarding house in St Mary's, and one's an engineer. He's a roll-his-sleeves-up-and-do-it engineer, he services lawnmowers, like the lawnmowers of Hell Bay Hotel which isn't even in Hell Bay. I hope he'll leave and join my business in boats."

"The grass must need cutting all the time," I said. "You don't have much snow here?"

"Haven't had snow for eighteen years. If snow comes, we wake the children so they can see it, because it won't be there the next day."

I smiled.

"And you have cars on Bryher?"

"Yes. Sometimes people from outside say we should be like Tresco and not have them. I say, 'I go to the supermarket and bring my shopping over on the ferry. *You* carry my shopping up to Watch Hill and *I'll* forego my car. *You* carry it.'

"One of the ladies who told me I shouldn't have a car was a lady who came to see my 'pantiles'. We've got a farm building, and this lady came and said, 'Those pantiles have got to be reproduced in exactly the same style. You can't patch them as you're doing now.' I said, 'They're not pantiles, they're rusty galvanised iron.' I hate people who come to Bryher and try to tell us what to do."

We peered at Samson and saw the ruined houses on top, including one where Sir Walter Besant created *Amorel of Lyonesse*. We passed the Norrard Rocks and Gweal and then hugged the coast of north-west Bryher and reached Hell Bay, where there was suddenly a swell and for the first time the boat was thrown about. We rounded the promontory and, back in calm water, retraced our passage between Bryher and Tresco. We chugged in the blinding sunshine and the captain called across to a young man with blond hair and a ruddy face who was piloting a small boat in the opposite direction.

"Son number one," he said, and he took up a rope tied to his dinghy, freeing it from its mooring, and jumped down into it and edged alongside our boat to where Pippa sat.

"Right, my dear," he said to Pippa, "put your hand on my shoulder and ease yourself down."

Pippa had arthritis in one knee and had difficulty in clambering down. I swung my legs over the side and eased myself down into the small dinghy carefully so that I would not capsize it and send us all sprawling into the water. We were among a lot of moored boats and launches.

Pippa asked, "Where are those boats from?"

"All over, that one's from Brest in France. That one's from Ipswich. That one's from Italy. They don't winter here, that's good. They come in the summer and then go."

Standing up and steering towards the quay as the dinghy sputtered along, Dick told another story.

"We bring our dinghies down by trailer. There's a special dinghy trailer. One of the boat-owners wanted to get his dinghy down. There's a trolley for loading dinghies and launching them that all can use, but ours is better. This boat-owner wanted to use ours. I said, 'You can't, it's private.' But he said he was going to anyway. The cheek of it! I mean, if you went to buy paving-stones from a garden shop and you said, 'I'm taking your wheelbarrow to take them away in', there'd soon be a blue light at the end of your road wouldn't there? But he didn't see that.

"I hate the boat-owners. They come and mess us locals about, like the ladies who tell us what to do because of prehistoric stones they claim to have found. I said to him, 'You go that way and keep going. Or if you want, you go that way and keep going. And if you want to complain about me for saying it, my name's Dick Jameson.'"

We laughed. He was a local, he hated all experts who came in and messed his life about. He was as contemptuous of outsiders who told him he was doing wrong as provincials in Roman times had been of Romans who had come out and told them to change their ways.

We beached with a gentle rasp on the sand. Pippa climbed out and I followed.

"How much do I owe you?" I asked.

"Seventy. Just seventy."

I gave him eighty pounds and thanked him.

"Thank you very much," he said. "I've got an hour to have my lunch and then I'm on again for another client."

And I realised that we had not seen St Agnes and Western Rocks because of the tides, but because he had booked himself out with someone else after lunch.

I watched him go. He was an angry, put-upon islander, happiest when left alone and not told what to do by interfering historians, boat-owners or boat-tripping sightseers like me. He doubted academics and books and took the practical, commonsense view that the past was done with and gone. He focused on the present.

But to the imagination the past is like a sea that cries out for the mind to make a boat trip. And I was a solitary quester, happiest when imagining and recreating in my mind, and therefore understanding, the awesome events of the past – the sinkings of land masses and the burials of Dark-Age pre-Saxon kings; and happiest when I could confirm the unity between heaven, earth, sea and man, the One, the *Tao*.

I was as set in my mystical ways as he was in his sceptical ways, but I had a profound conviction (which if he'd known it he would have disputed) that although I was Charles to his Cromwell – although in terms of the world his scepticism had defeated my imaginative enquiring – ultimately my imaginative and mystical vision was right.

27
Walking on From the Harbour

Harry Good had been a farmer all his life and had driven the lime-lorries for the china clay company. He kept the guest-house for years and was a well-known water-polo player. He had felt unwell that Easter. He felt energyless and was losing weight. His GP dismissed his ailment, so he and his wife paid for a private consultation. By May cancer had been diagnosed and he was waiting to start his treatment.

"When can I have chemotherapy?" he asked his doctor.

"When you can walk round the harbour," his doctor replied.

Harry was in his sixties, thickset and bald with numerous grand-children, one of the lynch-pins of village life. The days passed and became weeks, and he did not walk round the harbour.

I was down in Cornwall a few days before the end of July. I heard from our neighbour Geoffrey.

"Harry has been given two days to live. It's cancer of the oesophagus, the upper part. Very painful. They've stopped his medication. He came to see me a fortnight ago. His wife had to drive him, he couldn't walk here, what sixty yards."

The news haunted me, and I could not help focusing on his house. I went out late that night as usual for my midnight walk. It was hot. The upstairs windows, which were set back some twenty yards from the front gate, were open from sash to sash, and there was a light on in the back room. I could see pictures on the wall. Perhaps they were keeping the light on all night in his room. The front gate was covered by a notice about the Regatta Week's raft races in a week's time.

The next morning I ran into his wife.

"He's not good," she said. "He's sleeping a lot. He's in pain when he's awake. He's not good."

His son was putting a table and five chairs out by the front door for visitors to sit at without being indoors.

That afternoon it was the first day of the Regatta: a cream tea above the inner harbour with a band. My wife and I wandered along at four on a scorching afternoon and bought two cream teas and carried them to the mackerel-smokery's garden, where we sat and ate them and listened to the shirt-sleeved band, who were sitting on chairs on a grassed island almost outside Harry's front gate.

My attention was distracted. A succession of women descended on us and sold us raffle tickets, a quiz sheet and lucky numbers – all in the good cause of the village.

The band were playing very softly. I became aware of what they were playing. I could scarcely believe what I was hearing. The band had just begun 'You'll Never Walk Alone'. They played it very very softly. I said the words to myself in the appropriate places: "Walk on, walk on, with hope in your heart and you'll never walk alone, you'll never walk alone."

"Perhaps someone in the house requested it," my wife said.

"I hope so," I said.

For if they hadn't it was an appalling *faux pas*, bearing in mind who might be listening through the open sash windows above where the band was playing. He had not been able to walk round the harbour and begin chemotherapy, yet was being enjoined to "walk on". But if it had been asked for….

"It's very poignant," I said.

And I felt a rush of emotion. Somewhere, a cricket pitch or so away, a man who had lived here all his life was dying, was in the last twenty-four hours of his life, and the local band were giving him a send-off, softly encouraging him to die. I hoped he would now walk on with hope in his heart and not feel alone as death's night closed round him and left him in dark so pitch he would not be able to see at all. At least he would not be in any more pain.

He had lived here all his life, and now his three-score years and ten had boiled down to one last sweltering afternoon, and the entire village was carrying on outside his gate as though nothing exceptional was happening, selling raffle tickets, quizzes, lucky numbers. The band now stood to be applauded. I stood up.

Tears misted my eyes as we left the tea-garden.

Later his two daughters-in-law stopped where Geoffrey was sitting on a seat outside his house.

One said: "It won't be long now, he's drifting in and out of sleep. He's comfortable, he's not in pain. The McMillan nurses have made sure of that. He mentioned your name a couple of times. He's organizing water-polo and a clay-pigeon shoot as he used to years ago. He's back in the past, it's on his mind."

Geoffrey said, "He was in the county water-polo team. He was well-known in the county. And he had the guest-house."

"We thought the band music was lovely. Usually they play rousing music but it was all soft and quiet. We think someone on the committee must have said. It was lovely music."

That evening I went for my usual night walk round the harbour. The evening star, Venus, was glowing a bright yellow near the headland. As I advanced towards the harbour bar by the outer mole it slid behind the headland and disappeared into night.

Next morning I walked past Harry's house on my way to pick up the papers. The front bedroom windows were still open sash to sash, but one room had drawn beige curtains.

That evening I walked to the post office to post a letter. Both curtains were drawn and I knew it had happened. I later heard that the transition took place before the male-voiced choir sang in the harbour. From a distance I heard 'Hey, Jude'. There was apparently an announcement over the microphone which I did not hear. Two of Harry's grandchildren were walking round the harbour. They heard it and were upset as they did not know he had died.

The hearse came after the singing. Geoffrey was in tears, and my wife sat with him and his relatives until quite late. I joined them. Venus, the evening star, shone brightly near the moon.

I walked with one of Geoffrey's relatives to the mole.

He said, "The light on the water there he knew and grew up with."

The dark headland was between me and the evening star. As I

moved to have a better view of the light on the water, the evening star suddenly came into view. It was rising in the night sky. A star that had slid into dark was rising towards the moon.

28
A Sallow Octogenarian and a Slow Ambulance

I found Ellie, Geoffrey's cousin, on our doorstep. Geoffrey was feeling poorly, she said, and so she'd called an ambulance. Pippa went and sat with Geoffrey and when I'd extricated myself from showing a new gardener what to do, I went round. I walked into the low-beamed room. I came out of the sun and it took me a few seconds to acclimatize in the gloom. John, the elderly fellow from next door, was sitting in a chair, and – I was shocked – Geoffrey, half-sitting, half-lying to his right, thick bifocal spectacles giving him a piercing look, grey-haired and eighty-five, one leg crossed over the other showing brown ankle-length boots, and looking so sallow, so yellow. He looked very jaundiced.

"Is it the ambulanceman?" Geoffrey said in a thin voice one tenth of its usual strength.

"No, it's Philip."

"Oh, Philip," he said in surprise, as if to say 'I must be ill to warrant a visit from Philip'.

"How are you feeling, Geoffrey?" I asked.

"All right so long as I don't move," Geoffrey said. "I can't keep my food down. I've brought my breakfast up. And my drink."

"The ambulance response time's set at two hours," Ellie said. "I'm to ring the surgery after one and a half hours, at twelve-fifteen."

"Did you faint?" John asked.

"Of course I fainted. I'm not like this for nothing," Geoffrey said.

"But you didn't hit your head?" I asked.

"No," Ellie said, "he didn't."

We talked about hospitals and waiting-lists and matrons in the old days as we all waited for the ambulance.

"It'll be a bit like a bus," Pippa said. "It's doing a round, it'll be like getting on a bus."

"But you won't have a conductor saying, 'Any more fares please?'" I said. "Or clicking one of those silver machines they wore round their necks with a strap in the bad old days when the response time was two minutes." John laughed. Geoffrey laughed wanly.

"It might be a fishermen's van in the end," Pippa said, trying to keep his spirits up.

"But it won't be the binmen," I said, and everyone laughed, including Geoffrey.

We talked about delays in hospitals and how we'd been to Fowey the day before, and eventually I talked about the remedial work being done on the dock.

"Reg told me it's not what's really needed," I said. "I went down to watch the boats come in, and he said, 'I hope our night work's not kept you awake,' and I said, 'Oh no, I slept through it.' They really needed an eighty-ton crane, but last time they used one a few years ago one of its feet sank into the dockside. The harbour has to be strengthened before there can be a crane of that size. They were supposed to remove the bridge, but with the neap tides they couldn't do the repair they wanted so they've just done the bearing. The cement round it was like sand, Reg said. They had to improvise to find something that would hold the new bearing in place. They've not done a fundamental repair but a bodge."

"That's right," said Geoffrey, warming to my theme. "I said that's what it would be when they started. Them's not interested in sorting it out properly."

"I'm concerned about when they do it next time," John began.

"You mustn't be pessimistic," Geoffrey said. "Listen, you might not be around when they do that. Be optimistic."

And we all fell silent, for Geoffrey had let on that he felt he might not be returning from hospital.

"Hospital will sort you out," I said, to fill the silence.

"They'd better," Geoffrey said thinly. "Otherwise...."

"They'll sort Geoffrey's problem out," I said to everybody, "but not Geoffrey. He's too strong a character."

Everyone laughed and I had to leave as a workman wanted to ask me a question about a paving-stone he was cementing.

When I returned, Pippa was standing on the grass outside.

"He's wet himself, and he's out at the back changing his trousers," Pippa said. "He's not well. It's not like him. We've all left him to let Ellie cope with it."

Then the ambulance arrived. Most of us went back in to Geoffrey's front room. The ambulanceman unfolded a wheelchair, bent and gave Geoffrey instructions. He raised Geoffrey, swivelled him and lowered him gently on the wheelchair. Then he strapped him up. Geoffrey had webbing round his chest and elbows.

"That's so you don't fall off," I said.

"I'm going to tilt you," the ambulanceman said.

He wheeled Geoffrey to the ambulance.

"Good luck, Geoffrey," I said quietly, touching his sallow elbow as he passed.

The driver got out and together they lifted Geoffrey in and transferred him to a wide bed where he sat up with his head on a pillow and looked down at us in the road below.

"Now I'm taking your pulse," the ambulanceman said, putting a blue ring on a lead on Geoffrey's thumb. He also unwound tubing for a drip.

"Comfortable?"

"Yes."

Geoffrey put both thumbs up. I put both my thumbs up and waved both hands.

The ambulanceman closed the rear door. We could not see Geoffrey now. We waved him off as the ambulance pulled away, aware that he could see us through the dark back although we could not see him.

"What else could we do?" Ellie said. "We come down an hour a day, but when he's like that an hour a day's no good. It's got to be full time."

"You did right," I said quietly.

I walked back towards the sea. The sun danced and sparkled on the waves. It was the height of the summer and life was good. And I had a deep sense that Geoffrey had gone away and would not return. He had a blockage in his bowel which might be cancerous. He could not eat. If the hospital treated him on a maintenance basis, he would weaken and slowly die. He might require an operation to make a fundamental change.

The truth was, I thought, we are all waiting for an ambulance. Some of us have longer to wait than others, but our time will surely come. There is a slow ambulance heading for each one of us. Its response time may be several years, but it will surely arrive one day.

29
Bluebells Between Souls

We drove down a muddy lane by a square-towered church. At the end was a low weatherboarded house and beyond it a field with two horses. We left the car and walked to the front door, which was partly obscured by honeysuckle. We entered the kitchen where washers-up nodded, walked through to the next room and greeted Sidney's father, who was eighty-two. Someone said, "Go through," and we went through to the tiny, cosy sitting-room and, ducking under low beams, I sat on a sofa. Then Sidney's mother came in, an active eighty-eight, and announced, "He was a lovely boy. I never thought I'd live to see this day." We exchanged glances in silence.

Amy appeared. She looked white-faced and drawn. I hugged her and she whispered, "Thank you for coming."

She left the low-ceilinged room, and, wary of the beams round my head, I sat back on the sofa and beneath the desultory conversation I thought how Sidney had settled down to watch a video the previous Saturday evening. I noticed the television by the log-burner and wondered where he had been sitting when he had his brain haemorrhage: not the sofa under the window, which was on top of the television.... Where I was sitting! With a shock I realised I was sitting in the death seat. I leapt up and stood, my head touching the beams, until we were ready to set off.

Amy returned holding half-a-dozen bluebells she had just picked. She looked a bit like a distressed Ophelia.

"We went riding last weekend," she said to everybody. "We passed the wood and he said, 'Oh look, the bluebells may be out next weekend.' He loved bluebells."

We set off, half-a-dozen of us, and walked up the muddy lane in our suits. A fellow in a white shirt and black tie said, "I was a colleague of his. I played golf with him every Sunday for twenty years. I was at the hospital when they turned the life-support machine off on Sunday morning."

The Tudor church was packed. All the men wore white shirts and black ties. There must have been a hundred from his work. I was shown to a pew near the front.

Four undertakers carried the coffin down the aisle and lowered it onto two trestles. It had a white lilied wreath on top. Close family followed, including Amy, who walked to the front and laid her bluebells on the coffin by the wreath, affectionately running her right hand down the end of the coffin as she turned.

The vicar was balding and hesitant. He seemed overcome by emotion and in a muddle. He welcomed everyone falteringly: "We don't have proper rules here. I don't tell you when to stand or sit, but you just do what you feel like. But I suggest you sit during the address."

There was a hymn, which included the line "Perverse and foolish oft I strayed", and a prayer which included the lines, "And whatsoever sins ye may have committed… we beseech thee to do away with" – Sidney had not been a churchgoer – and then his boss gave the address. He stood at the front, bearded in his mourning clothes, and read from typed sheets of A4. He spoke for nearly a quarter of an hour, telling of Sidney's hard work, how he would encounter Sidney returning to the office at six in the evening after a hard day to work until midnight.

Sidney had been a workaholic and had not been home much. As his boss spoke about his efficient filing system and legendary reports for the Council, I wondered at how little he must have seen of Amy. He seemed to have worked six eighteen-hour days a week and played golf every Sunday morning with a colleague. Did they talk work on the golf course? "Many men," Sidney's boss said, "tell their wives they're working when they're playing golf. Sidney was one of the few who could have said he was playing golf when he was working."

I thought, 'You should have told him to go home at six in the evening. He died from overwork, you killed him before he could enjoy any retirement, the turn-out from work indicates a guilty conscience.'

The service ended with a hauntingly plaintive playing of Albinoni's Adagio in G minor. I was startled, for I had told Sidney and Amy about it when they came to dinner. I described how we'd heard it in Venice, and they had gone to Venice and attended the same concert hall a year later.

We filed outside. Amy stood in tears and greeted each mourner individually with a hug or a handshake while the coffin was replaced in the hearse to be taken away until the private cremation after the weekend. This service had been arranged on a Saturday so his work colleagues from the Council could attend without missing work on a weekday.

I stood well back in the churchyard, and the vicar ambled over and stood awkwardly beside me.

"Lovely spot," I said, "and a lovely church."

"Yes. It was derelict when I came thirty years ago. I spent a long time restoring it. I'm retiring later this year, but I'm staying in the neighbourhood so I can be near the church."

"I like the view," I said, looking across fields to the River Orwell.

"Yes. The light is magnificent. You don't get light like that anywhere else in East Anglia. It comes off the silver river. I love it." The queue seemed to have ended. Amy turned and joined us.

"The bluebells were a lovely touch," the vicar said. "It was stilted and formal until then, and you brought it all to life with that touch."

"I was letting him know that the bluebells were out," Amy said.

"You've done very well," the vicar said. "Remember what I told you. These people have come for you as much as for him."

"I went to see him yesterday," Amy said, "but I took one look at him and turned round and walked out. I said, 'That's not Sidney.' He wasn't there. He'd gone."

"Remember what I told you. Souls are *between* people. If you're looking for his soul, look in your mirror."

I had last heard that idea from a Cartesian philosopher. He claimed it was also Coleridge's theory of perception. "When you look at a flower," he had told me, "your soul is between you and the flower."

I wanted to say, 'That's wrong,' but I bit my tongue.

Amy nodded doubtfully, and we all set off for the local pub, walking down a country lane with hedges on either side.

In the function room there were plates of sausage rolls and assorted sandwiches, and a girl walked round pouring coffee in white cups. Many people were crowded together.

I saw Amy standing by herself and went over.

"Many traditions say that something survives death," I said. "They give different lengths of time. The Tibetan tradition says that the soul is attached to the body by a kind of umbilical cord for three-and-a-half days before the cord is severed and it goes on its way. Other traditions say longer. He may have been there and heard his funeral service from up in the rafters and seen all of us – and understood your message about the bluebells."

"That's what I believe," she said.

"When the vicar says 'Go forth', that may be when the soul goes on its way," I said. "But although it's elsewhere, the soul doesn't lose contact with us down here. It can be reached through a medium."

"That's what I want to do – find a medium."

"Souls are within the mind," I said. "On death they leave and linger round their dead body before going on elsewhere. Sometimes they're in shock, they don't realise they've died, they're bewildered."

"Yes, I wondered about that."

"It's necessary to tell them they've died. Then they know they have to go on to the next stage of their being. Materialists don't believe what I've just said."

"But I do," she said. "I believe it. I shall talk to him tonight."

I moved away and looked back at her. She had more people round her. She looked very thin and pale beneath groomed hair. She had sat at home in her tiny sitting-room in front of her log-burner while he'd spent his life at work and had somehow forgotten to make his will. She had snatched times when they'd be together, riding past the woods, and she was still in dialogue with him about the bluebells.

Her view of the continuation of his immaterial being was right. The vicar had renovated the ruined church but his view of the soul was a social one: that it was left behind in the faces of loved ones. He spoke of natural rather than supernatural light. She had received his wrong advice about souls but had demonstrated her continuing relationship with Sidney's soul by laying bluebells on his coffin. Her bluebells were between continuing souls. She, more than the vicar, had given the packed church a lesson in metaphysics.

30
New-Mown Grass

I spent a wretched night tossing and turning in that Georgian Welsh town. I could not turn off the central heating and opened a window and was kept awake by the rumble of traffic. I had a slight headache and eye ache over breakfast. There was time to kill before the funeral so we drove to the road where the Reverend George Hokham lived, and I gazed at the tiny modern, glassy bungalow where he had passed the days since his retirement, handicapped by Parkinson's disease, looking across to the distant Black Mountains, living in humility and quiet readiness.

We arrived at the Cathedral very early and I walked round it in an open-necked shirt. It was deserted, we were the only two in the building. In the aisle between the choir-stalls I encountered, with a shock, a banner-draped coffin under a lit candle in a tall candle-holder. It contained the Reverend George Hokham, I was sure of it. I stood and contemplated the coffin, and thought how strange it was that I had been an eight-year-old eye-witness of the first service he had held as chaplain in the New Hall at my old school, and that he had been an eye-witness of my last cricket innings, when I scored sixty-three not out for the Headmaster's XI against the school nearly forty years ago.

I went out to the car park, fished my black tie from the boot of our car, tied it, put on a blazer, and as I finished I saw a grey-haired man standing without a stick, wearing a suit and a black tie.

"I'm going to speak to him," I said to Pippa. "He was my Headmaster. He's ninety-one."

"He's not even sixty-one," Pippa said, studying his almost boyish straight, groomed grey hair. "You can't go and speak to him, you've got the wrong person, he's younger than you."

"No, he's ninety-one," I said, and I walked a few paces over to him and said hello and identified myself.

"Oh yes," he said, gazing into the distance. "I remember you very well."

We fell in with him and his wife and walked back to the Cathedral together. A small congregation had gathered. I sat next to him in a pew, half-way back.

I can't remember much about the service, but I recall that there was no eulogy. The vicar announced that this was at the Reverend George Hokham's request. He had lived by Christian humility – sometimes with a fierceness that seemed decidedly unchristian – and he did not want any praise about his life.

The coffin was carried to the Cathedral door and we all wandered after it. His two sons were lined up outside with his widow. The coffin was now in the open back of a black Estate car.

"We're getting rid of him as quickly as we can and then we're off to Egypt," one of his sons told me. In other words, there was no reception. His widow thanked us for coming.

I wandered on to the car park and fell in with the Headmaster, who was making his way slightly stiffly but without a stick, though ninety-one.

"He was my first appointment," he said. "I came in January 1947, and he came in May 1947."

I said, "It was an inspired choice."

"Yes," he said, smiling to himself. "When I arrived there was snow on the ground, and there was a fuse. I didn't know where the fuses were. That seems a long time ago now. Now I do the *Times* crossword each day – it's getting harder." He looked into the distance. "I shall be next."

I said, "Oh no, you'll live to be a hundred. You'll put your bat up to acknowledge the applause for your century."

"I've never scored a century," he said. "No, this is my penultimate."

I did not know at the time that he would die in less than four years' time, and that he was being insufficiently optimistic. I did not know he would be taken to hospital and would catch an infection – MRSA? – that would kill him, and that he too would direct that there should be no eulogy at his funeral. He was driven by the same Christian humility that had driven the Reverend George Hokham.

I said goodbye to my old Head, for the last time as it turned out, and went back to the souvenir shop for a guidebook. Nearby there was a push-button waist-high machine, and a small notice said "Push me". Pippa obliged.

Suddenly a familiar voice rasped: "I am George Hokham. I was ordained in this Cathedral in 1937. I've always loved the Black Mountains…."

It was uncanny, indeed eerie. We had just followed his coffin out of the lych-door, and now he was speaking to us as if from another world. A few connected with the school were nearby and I rounded them up – fewer than half a dozen – and Pippa said, "Listen to this." The school party listened in amazement. When the voice reached its end they pressed the button and heard it all over again.

I walked away, and we took a long route back to the car park. We passed a tea room. A fellow in a T-shirt and shorts was mowing a lawn.

I was aware of the smell of new-mown grass. Suddenly everything blended. The coffin and the disembodied voice that defied it, the Headmaster saying he would be next, the blades of new-mown grass lying on the lawn, the sound of the hand-propelled lawnmower. The dead and dying were like blades of mown grass, but I felt overjoyed at the smell of new-mown grass. It suggested growth and the drowsiness of summer, it was intoxicating and brought me close to the earth and Nature, within life. It suggested all that was good about life which my former teacher would miss, if he could come back like his voice and savour it now.

31
Fortitude Like a Navy Pullover

That morning Sarah rang to say, "Today's a good day, do come and see Les if you can."

His bungalow was approached from an alley at the back, and we went down steps and into the large entrance where a dog yapped at my ankles. Sarah led us through, greying white hair in a bun and spectacled, and I saw a thin Les stand in the window to greet us, wearing a navy pullover. He grinned, and as we shook hands I looked into his mirthful eyes above his grizzled, trimmed beard and realised he had lost a lot of weight.

I sat beside him, a table between us. The two women sat away from us so I could talk with him on my own.

I commented on the view of shrubs, a bowling-green, the sea.

"Oh yes, it's a lovely view."

We smiled at each other.

He said, "How are you keeping?"

"Fine," I said. "You've had a wretched time, going to the doctor and being told not to fuss. It must have been a relief when someone took you seriously."

"Oh yes, but there's nothing you can do."

"You're doing brilliantly. Sarah said you're managing your doses."

"Yes. I keep taking the painkillers, and I wonder if I need them. But I daren't not take them."

"They probably make you feel floaty. Most painkillers do."

"Yes, I'm not as sharp as I could be."

Sarah had said the cancer masqueraded as the type caused by asbestosis. It had wrapped itself round his lungs and had begun to affect his neck. I sensed his vulnerability and transience.

I talked about other things: the sport that was going to be on television, the Ashes series and golf he'd be able to watch, and gossip from the village, how a pipe had been leaking into the harbour for more than fifteen years at the rate of three gallons per minute and how it was under a neighbour's conservatory floor.

He chuckled, "Will you be getting a bill for three gallons a minute for fifteen years?"

I talked about how I'd been for a walk on the harbour the previous evening.

"I said to Sarah, it's not as good as it used to be when I used to run into you and we'd look at the stars. I go out and the stars are immense, but I haven't got your knowledge to advise me."

He smiled.

I looked at my watch. Sarah had said we should not stay more than ten minutes.

"We'll see you in July," I said. "If we may."

"Oh yes. I'll look forward to it."

"It'll be round the middle of July," I said. "Today's June the second, so it'll be in five or six weeks' time."

"Yes, see you then."

I stood up. We shook hands and both avoided the unspoken question.

As I left I turned back and had a last glimpse of him standing in his V-necked pullover, thin and gaunt, but smiling.

Sarah walked with us to the car. We kissed her and she walked back and suddenly Cornwall was very quiet. Everything banally went on. In the car I thought how nobly he had borne – worn – his lung cancer. He was uncomplaining, in the Roman Stoic tradition. In the Roman time there were no antibiotics, and you had to get on with disease and pain, and so endurance was deemed a virtue by the philosophers.

He had pulled on an uncomplaining endurance and fortitude like a navy pullover. He had a proud, noble bearing which made light of the fact that he was terminally ill, and now I understood why he had left the hospice and chosen to spend his last few weeks or days at home. Death would befall us all one day, and his one day was nearer than my own, that was the distance between our situations. And so, there but for the grace of God went I.

32
Fireworks and the One

I sat in my window and watched the peaceful silver sea stretch to the horizon and the pink sky of sunset and twilight slowly blend with the glistening dark. I thought of the interactions between sea and sky, how a breeze, a wind, could stir the still surface into choppy, dipping, curling waves. Before me, from twenty yards away to many miles out towards France, sea and sky blended as reflected silver-pink passed indiscernibly into pink and showed the One pared down, simplified to water and air, beyond the earth below my window and beneath the fire of the setting sun.

Through my other window from the quay blared a live band, and a singer shouted, "What shall we do with the drunken sailor/Earlie in the morning?" Song after song beat out with an electronic thud magnified a hundredfold on the PA system. A crowd sat, leaned, lolled or stood, waiting for the fireworks, guzzling from cans, munching hot dogs, babbling among themselves, talking to each other, interacting, seemingly unaware of the way parts of Nature merged into each other and the way Nature so beautifully and simply revealed the elusive One which cradled it. And I thought as the light faded: man is both a knower and a forgetter of the universe, he can live between the sea and the sky like the Taoist "Heaven, earth and man", or he can live in a blur of chatter to other people or self-absorption and be unaware of the universe which is his context. Awareness is the problem.

The band thudded out, 'Is this the way to Amarillo?' Thousands filled the normally deserted harbour on both sides of the bridge. It was like a football crowd waiting for the teams to run out. And then, with a countdown over the PA system, the fireworks display began over the hill at the back of the harbour houses. We went out to our back garden in the dark and sat on chairs on our decking and watched as a computer-synchronised firing began to music, which was at first 'Star Wars'. Hundreds of fireworks filled the night sky, sometimes a dozen at the same time. Round globes like sunbursts exploded in all directions. There were ovals like the Milky Way. The music became more classical, and in an explosive finale many glittering bangs formed a palm tree that faded as the final applause swelled round the harbour. It later transpired that the finale set the cliff brake on fire, causing the attendance an hour later of several fire-engines.

We went back indoors and looked out of a window at the front. The crowd were on the move now, talking animatedly. Some still stood or sat. Floodlights from the other side of the harbour dazzled, and music thumped out again.

I thought: for twenty minutes their attention was held by sparkle, glitter and bangs, by man-made images of round globes that lit up the sky and then were no more. And now they were back talking among themselves.

I returned to the back garden and sat again on a chair on the decking. The Plough was above me, like a soup-ladle or a question mark on its side. I could see the W of Cassiopeia. Then it struck me, it was the dog days, a day when there were meteorite showers that burnt up in the atmosphere. There should be shooting stars. As I looked I saw one dart. It was gone as soon as I saw it. Then another skittered like a firefly.

Now the universe was putting on its own firework display. It was not as tinselly as the man-made one we had just seen, but somehow it was more authentic. The meteors had come from space to our atmosphere and were dying in fiery glory that was real, natural, part of the process of the universal whirl through space. Somewhere from far away the One that pervades the universe and permeates Nature was sending fiery messages from space to our sky, from its heaven to our earth.

The music had stopped now and I could hear the hubbub of the departing crowd which was blind to, and therefore ignorant of, the universe's spectacle, lost in its own small world. I sat on, content to wait and watch the universe vie for our attention with little fiery messages as if the One tugged at our sleeves when we were looking elsewhere.

33
A Shell House and Plunging Gorges

We stayed at Endsleigh, an 1810 house built by Georgiana, Duchess to the 6th Duke of Bedford, above the River Tamar in a wild setting as a sporting retreat. The idea was that the Duke and his family would leave Woburn Abbey and interact with the ravines and gorges on the estate in true Romantic manner.

From our room on the first floor we descended a steep, narrow staircase to the hall where a log fire warmed and made our way through several rooms to the library, where we sat until we were called to dinner. Out of the window in the dark the sloping herbaceous border was lit at either end by *flambeaux,* the red flames of which leapt in the dark. After dinner we sat in an outdoor arbour for liqueurs and watched a flying beetle settle on our table before the dimly-lit sundial.

The next morning after breakfast we went for a walk in the garden. It had been designed by Humphrey Repton, the successor to Capability Brown, and in the Regency manner he had devised a Picturesque landscape house – the commission for which was given to Sir Jeffry Wyatville whose ideas were more grand than Repton's – that interacted with its garden. He had been influenced by the Picturesque movement which admired wild landscapes, and he had advocated a gradual transition between house and grounds by means of terraces, balustrades and steps. The house was given the illusion of being several houses, and flowers and plants featured in conservatories and up verandah columns.

We wandered along the yew walk which was terraced into the slope with a rose tunnel and grass terrace below. Soon we were by the upper and lower Georgy (named after Georgiana, but punning on gorges) and looking across at the wooded ravine through which the Tamar flowed over a couple of weirs that echoed a distant plash of running water. We made out several wooded hills beyond.

We descended some old steps and found a grotto with three arched entrances or exits, and the adjoining Shell House which had been designed by Wyatville, a hexagonal stone summer-house with internal walls covered with every kind of shell, including large conches and corals, and three marble seats.

A notice explained that grottos were fashionable in the Romantic time and were places where the treasures of the natural world could be displayed, such as fossils, minerals and shells. A grotto had to be deep in woods yet command a view, and there should be cascades. It was like bringing Aira Force, the Lake-District waterfall, into one's own garden.

Inside the Shell House I sat on a marble seat and admired the detail. There were six bays, and on the floor two interconnected triangles giving six points, and six outer triangles. There were six spider-web windows near the roof, which was conical, rising to an apex. The door was intricately made of strips of wood. And all round me, every kind of shell. It was a house that said, "Look at the wonders of Nature."

I had entered into the Romantic spirit and was already all soul. My soul was attuned to Nature. We walked back along the grass terrace through the children's *parterre* which hid a spider's web of paths and a grottoed fountain on the outside of the surrounding wall. We walked on, climbed some steps and found ourselves in the rock garden. There was a pool of lilies in the centre and steps led in several directions. There must have been twenty flights of steps. We took one of the flights and looked across the gorge, down the steep-sided dingle to the dell. I descended more steps and saw a cascade from a subterranean, hidden grotto below the rock garden, and a crag.

I stood in the wooded hollow and felt the power of Nature, magically enhanced by Capability Brown's successor's skilful work. He had tried to bring the universe here – mountains, valleys, waterfalls, trees, rocks, ravines, gorges and the treasures of geology – and connect different levels on the slope to the Tamar with flights of steps. He had tried to blend all together into a whole that pleased and obeyed carefully balanced aesthetic principles of beauty, scenes that feasted the senses – sound, sight and smell – and drew the curved arches of the house's conservatory and long border into a Picturesque whole that suggested the One.

I stood in the world of Wordsworth, Coleridge, Keats and Shelley and savoured their sense of beauty. The leaflet in my hand showed old pictures of the prospect without the enclosing trees. Four of the hills had no trees at all, merely grass. I wondered if it were not now a bit forbidding, remote and austere, all these plunging deeps and distant wooded caverns and flowerless rocks. Were not these views a bit contrived, did they not strive to impress a little? Was that not Repton's wish?

I preferred the lush sensuality of teeming plants in a simple cottage garden or the formal balance and elegance of a plain knot- and herb-garden, which could just as easily take one to the One. The Shell House by itself conveyed a hint of the One. The vast landscaping of steepness, abruptness and moving water – was it not to impress? As Pope wrote in his 'Epistle to Boyle', "At Timon's villa let us pass a day, /Where all cry out, 'What sums are thrown away!'/So proud, so grand…."

The Romantic sensibility communed with Nature and felt the unity of creation, and once, perhaps, this scene had done that. But since then the woods had taken over, and the Picturesque was now harder to relate to the One. Times had moved on and we no longer looked for beauty in steepness, precipitous rocks and rapid water, but in sloping panoramic width, distant sea or woods and a sweep of sky down to the horizon. Now a natural landscape of lawns, woods and sky took us to the One more directly than Picturesque landscaping.

34
Daubenton's Bats and the One

We gathered for the bat walk at Connaught Water on a fine night in the second half of August. I took an echolocator Pippa had given me. "*They* look batty people," Pippa said, and we joined a group of casually dressed men, women and children. Our leader was the Head Forest Keeper and, having introduced his assistant, a youngish fellow, he gave us a talk beside his Corporation of London van which had an orange beacon on top.

Speaking in a loud deep voice that suited his rugged dark looks and massive bare arms, clad in a cap, jerkin and boots, he said: "The bats are late in coming out on clear, still nights like tonight. It's been dry and hot and there aren't many insects so they spread about, go round forest glades. Cloud's better for seeing bats, there may not be many tonight. There are seventeen species of bats in the UK. Very little was known about them until recently. The Victorian naturalists used to shoot bats and spread them out and pin their wings and identify different species that way. They had no echolocators, it's only recently we've been able to work out how bats communicate. Our echolocators take the sound bats emit and bring it down so we can hear it. They have their own language, it can be aggressive or they make social calls and mating calls. The male calls to the female like an electronic pulse – it can go on for three hours non-stop. The males of all bat species are very independent. They'll roost alone in roof space. Just one by itself. The females tend to be in colonies, the males keep themselves to themselves.

"People with acute hearing can hear their calls. Children can often hear them. The pipistrelle can be heard on an echolocator at forty-four to fifty-five kilohertz. (One kilohertz is a thousand cycles per second.)

The sound they make is hard to describe. It's like a clap or… a song. I want to show you a pipistrelle."

He opened a small box and showed it round. Lying inside, completely still, was a little furry bat with its wings closed.

"They only need a seven-millimetre opening to get into your roof space," he said. "The noctule is the largest bat and its chip-chop cry can be heard from twenty-five to thirty kilohertz. Bats have the best brain of any mammal, they throw out a sound which bounces back and they hear the bounce-back on every upbeat of their wings. A bat's brain contains more knowledge than any computer we have built. In Mexico sixty-four thousand bats emerged from a smallish opening in a cave at the same time – in one second – and not one collided. Each one took sixty-four thousand instantaneous readings from each of them, every second.

"One pipistrelle eats three thousand biting midges a night, one colony eats thirty-seven tons of midges per night. They go where there are insects at night, gardens where there are night scents such as honeysuckle which attract insects, or ponds. Wherever there are insects they go. They have to hibernate in the winter for four months because of the shortage of food. Bats are our friends. They eat insects that harm us and they pollinate for us and disperse seeds and keep Nature going. Bats are like us, they have five fingers. They're not mice with wings."

We walked round the water as the light slowly faded and listened on our echolocators, but there were no pipistrelles or noctules. We walked farther on and the Forest Keeper called: "Daubenton's. Look. Daubenton's, named after the eighteenth-century French natural historian who first identified them as a species."

They were flitting low over the water like birds. I could see them against a lighter patch of water in the deep dusk.

"You can hear them about thirty-five kilohertz," he said. "You can hear them at forty-five as well."

I pointed my echolocator and heard the rat-a-tat machine-gun-like clicks of flying Daubenton's bats. It was now dark and the Forest Keeper shone a very powerful torch whose beam picked up bats flying round in an arc.

"They don't like the light," he said, "but they do like midges and mayflies. They fly a few centimetres over the water surface like hovercraft and catch their midges and eat them on the wing. Sometimes they take prey from the water surface itself, using their large feet as a gaff or their tail membrane as a scoop. Ten days ago there were thousands of midges over the water here. If I'd shone this torch, within ten seconds they'd have surrounded me and bitten me. Now they're all gone, and so the bats have gone except for Daubenton's, and they're here because they can still find midges and mayflies low down. Look, there's one there and one there, they're flying about fifteen miles per hour."

In the early dark his torch was like a torchlight.

"We're both passionate about bats," he said. "We come out at two or three in the morning, and sometimes we're here at dawn. They're fascinating creatures. Pipistrelles bite – never handle one if you find it on the ground, because you need rabies shots before you do that. We've both had them. But they're not hostile to us, in fact they're friendly to us. They eat three thousand midges a night and do us a favour. What I still can't get over is that there are creatures out there that are flying around and helping us, eating midges that would bite us if they were not eaten, and no one knows they're doing it."

And suddenly I saw deep into the workings of the orderly One. It was an elaborate system with checks and balances, and things that were bad for humans were kept down by creatures such as bats, which ate biting midges, and by herbs, which provided antidotes to diseases. The One worked as a whole, and for whatever was harmful there was a suppressant. Every creature had its place in the workings of Nature, and humans were to a large extent blind to the help they received from creatures such as bats and ignorant of all the assistance they gave.

I resolved to make a list of every creature – bees, wasps, flies, insects, grubs, caterpillars, grasshoppers, butterflies, moths, crows, jackals – and list the good things they did in keeping Nature's System running. Crows and jackals stripped dead creatures back to their bones and performed a service. My eye had been opened to one aspect to the workings of the One.

I had been trying to live like a Nature hermit up to a point, communing with the natural world in part of my time. I had glimpsed the One at work. I had put myself in a state of readiness to approach the

One by joining the bat walk, and the One had revealed itself to me in a glimpse by showing me, through the Forest Keeper, what bats do for the Whole.

35
A Study Like a Bittern-Hide

One Sunday morning in mid-February we drove to Fisher's Green where various bird societies were holding a two-day convention. We parked in a field with long grass and walked to two marquees. There were many stalls promoting all aspects of bird-watching. We joined a guided tour to the bittern-hide.

We walked in a group of about twenty along a path to the sixty-eight acre lake in extreme cold and stopped to identify various uncommon ducks on the reed-surrounded water. Through my binoculars I saw a golden eye and pochards.

We reached a curved bridge over the River Lea and assembled in the middle on a hump. On a nearby field we saw a flock of lapwings, and in nearby trees on the other side of the water a flock of siskins, yellow-green birds very clearly visible through binoculars, sitting on the branches of tall elms, perhaps forty feet up. On the river itself there were several interesting birds, and I saw a pair of great-crested grebes, red and black, one with a very distinctive crest.

Our guide talked about the habitats and habits of the birds we identified. Some of our group were manically peering through binoculars in all directions and ticking birds off on small printed lists they held in the palm of one hand in the freezing cold. In the Arctic wind I felt a thrill at seeing a siskin, a grebe. It was like glimpsing an image within.

We walked back on ourselves and continued to the bittern-hide, a rectangular hut with viewing apertures on the lake side above benches at which we could sit in the cold and hope that a bittern would appear, a wading bird of the heron family with a booming call. We joined half a dozen red-faced stalwarts who had braved the cold all morning, scanning the empty water through binoculars with great single-mindedness. One told me a bittern had been seen several times the previous morning, emerging from the nearby reeds, but that no bittern had been glimpsed today. The bitterns were hiding in the reeds where they had built their nests. We sat for a quarter of an hour, but there was no indication that there would be a bittern and we slipped away, leaving the hardy fanatics to keep themselves warm for the rest of the day.

We trudged back to the marquees and warmed up with coffee which we held in our hands in a semi-outdoor tent, and I thought of the bittern-watchers whose purpose for the whole of that Sunday morning had been to scan the Arctic lake for a bird that had not appeared, and I wondered at how we give our life meaning through self-imposed tasks.

I was not unlike them. I sat in my study, my own version of a bittern-hide, and gazed at grass and trees, my version of a lake, hiding from Nature, trying to glimpse the unity of the universe, to catch the One unaware, and waited for an image of the One that I could shape into a poem or story but which sometimes did not appear. Like the bitterns, my images sometimes hid from me, but pursuing them gave me a task to complete and a purpose for the day.

36
Shadow and Sun

I scooped fish-food pellets from a large tub into a plastic box and opened the back door. A yellow wagtail was bobbing on the terrace and a heron was standing motionless on the lawn, grey and white. It took off when it saw me approach, and with slowly beating wings gained height and sailed away over the forest.

I walked in the warm sun down to the pond hidden behind shrubs. More than a hundred goldfish and a few large *koi* saw me and rose to the surface, wriggling and writhing in one group soul's anticipatory urge. I waited while they frothed in the water. I then slung handfuls of tiny round grey pellets so they rained all round the heaving red-yellow mass. They all broke away at the same time, dispersed into individuals and swam excitedly to and fro. Each seized a pellet and, flicking its tail, turned and dived and headed excitedly away.

I walked back with my shadow. Once my shadow had been my future self, calling me to fulfil a lifetime's achievement. Now I had become that future self and my achievement was behind me – and my shadow had become my other lifelong companion, Death. What was I but a skeleton with a bulging food-sack in my midriff? I walked with Death – but also with the sun that casts all shadows, a material copy of the spiritual sun, the Light. And, walking between my shadow and the sun I thought, to my own surprise: I accept death. What used to fill me with horror was now as natural as seeing a shadow. I had travelled from horror to acceptance. Readiness was really a profound, instinctive acceptance.

In a sense, everything I could see – the green trees, grass under my feet, herbs and flowers – was a shadow cast by an invisible sun, I thought, an illusion in relation to its reality. I did not need to look at it any more than I squinted up at the sun, instinctively avoiding looking at it directly. It was enough that I walked in warm sunlight and rejoiced in the world around me, this part of Nature and the universe, and smiled at the shadows of each phenomenal form – each tree, shrub and flower.

I stood near herbs, pinched rosemary and chive and smelt my scented fingers. I wandered round different plants, inspecting each one. They all seemed happy, smiled back at the smiling universe on this late summer's day. I thought of how herbs provided medicines and antidotes to the Celtic hermits and medieval monks: agrimony for stomach-ache, sweet marjoram for indigestion, cowslip for coughs, dandelion for rashes, dock for nettle stings, perforate St John's wort for wounds and 300 others whose uses were known to witches and are now applied by homeopaths. Some herbs were made into watery drinks for stomach or bronchial complaints, and some were made into poultices for lesioned skin.

The Celtic hermits who built stone cells on the Tintagel cliffs in Cornwall high above Merlin's cave lived on green turf and flowers and communed with the sparkling sea, the horizon and the vast sky. The medieval monks who woke early in their remote monasteries modelled on Iona for prayers and devotions, and structured their day round the divine office or canonical hours – Prime in the morning, Lauds, Terce, Sext, None and Vespers and Compline at night – slipped out into the garden during silent time and like pharmacists picked leaves as remedies to keep their community healthy. From the length and breadth of the land, hermits interacted with Nature.

I travelled in their footsteps. The Ancient Mariner proclaimed, "This Hermit good lives in that wood." I lived in a forest, at one and the same time like an anchorite (who lived near a populous centre) and a hermit (who retired to the wilderness such as the desert at Scetis), but also like Wordsworth's solitary, a recluse interactive with Nature. I left my cell – a palace in relation to the cells of the Celtic saints and medieval monks – and observed tiny, crawling, flying creatures and burgeoning plants, feeling each in a two-way emotional engagement, not as an alienated spectator, and then going back to sit alone and sometimes look within for the Light. Like monks, hermits discover and emancipate the true self from the clutching ego's illusory pleasures.

I recalled my first glimpse of the Light in the East, a glow like the reflection of dawn in the polished floor of the Zen centre where I was meditating. And I recalled experiencing it as an explosion one morning before breakfast at a conference in Winchester. And the many times the Light had appeared behind my closed eyes like a brilliant moon in a night sky, turning into a sun at midnight.

I returned to my study and sat quietly in a window like a latter-day hermit, and closed my eyes. The dark cloud of my night sky, slowly, broke light, like a star, then like a moon appearing from behind cloud bathing my interior in moonlight and now a dazzling sun that made me gasp.... I sat on tranquil with acceptance and readiness.

The sun poured through my window and cast my shadow behind me on the carpeted floor and I loved the outlines of the phenomena round me – the shape of my desk and the two little Charles-II tables – and the silhouette of the two oak trees outside and of the smiling, laughing universe that was happy and mocked the unhappiness of insufficiently-aware, imperfect humankind.

37
A Bat Like a Soul

There were bat droppings in the tall, spacious, L-shaped loft, again.

The last time that happened a pest-control man found them while looking for evidence of rodents. He said, studying the droppings, "You've got a horseshoe bat." But the Head Forest Keeper later told me that horseshoe bats had not been found in our part of the country for decades, they were confined to the West Country and Wales. He had told me that male bats roost alone whereas females roost in colonies. Now when I turned out the loft light I could see daylight showing through at least three holes in our roof, through which rain could lash and freezing cold, wasps and bees, bats and even birds and a host of flying creatures could gain entrance – and through which a bat had squeezed and scattered its droppings over our storage boxes.

Arthur, our ginger-haired all-purpose builder, came and foamed-in the holes, and he began hoovering up the droppings. He came and found me and said, "I've found a bat."

We went back to the loft and took the central well-lit walkway on either side of which were boxes containing rolls of wallpaper and carpet and framed pictures under dust-sheets. The roof sloped down to the floor to left and right. We turned at right angles and half-way along, in the unlit part beyond where the walkway stopped, in the part of the loft obstructed by diagonal rafters, as he shone his torch I could see the bat hanging where three roof rafters joined.

"It can't get out now I've blocked the holes. I need a net," Arthur said, so I went out to the fish-pond and brought back the fishnet. He had found a cardboard box and a broom. Holding the broom upside down, with the handle he nudged the bat so it dropped into the net, which he flipped over to its side so the bat could not escape. He brought the net back to the box under the strip light and we crouched and examined the bat. It looked quite small and had long ears that bent forward, too long for a pipistrelle, I thought. Its claws gripped the mesh of the net.

We held it over the box and tried to dislodge it but it crawled round the mesh. The net was round and the box square, leaving a gap in the corner of the box nearest to it, and as I gently pushed the bat downwards, somehow it crawled round to the gap and flew out over my shoulder.

"Oh no," I exclaimed.

It was above us, flapping by the light like a bird with an enormous wing-span that nearly touched the sides of the sloping roof. It fluttered away from the light into the dark part of the roof and lodged in the rafters beyond the walkway, gripping the canvas apex of the sloping roof.

Arthur followed it with his torch, net and broom, ducking under and clambering over diagonal rafters, and tried to scoop it back into the net with the broom handle. But it fluttered away back towards me under the light, turned and returned to the dark end and lodged beyond Arthur, who clambered after it, treading carefully from joist to joist across strips of lagging.

Six times it defeated Arthur's attempts to net it. Six times it fluttered down to me, turned round my head, hovering like a bird with its great wing-span showing the pointed barbs (its thumbs or first fingers) on the edges of its wings and its long ears, and fluttered back towards Arthur.

The seventh time Arthur gently dislodged it with the broom handle into the net and returned to the box with the bat crawling inside the mesh, and this time we made no mistake. I gave the bat a gentle prod with my finger, and it dropped onto the bottom of the box and lay with its wings outspread for a couple of seconds before righting itself and folding them.

We quickly closed the flaps on top of the box and sealed them with parcel tape, leaving an air hole, and Arthur put the box in the back of his car and later let it out in the woods behind his house 30 miles away. And I went back into the loft to tidy up.

Standing in the light part of the loft on the walkway and looking down towards the dark part beyond the walkway and the diagonal rafters that Arthur had ducked under or clambered over, I thought of the mind within the brain. It was not unlike this light-dark place. It too had things stored to left and right and there was a dark, inaccessible part where the soul roosted, occasionally fluttering out into the bright light but preferring to hang alone like a male and leave through a hole in the roof to catch insects on the wing, flitting at twilight.

I believed in boxing the ego that hunts socially to leave the true self in charge, but it was as if I had somehow caught the soul that lived in the dark and whose presence could only be detected from the droppings it left after its meal and which could not be controlled. Most of the time the soul dwelt in darkness but occasionally it flitted and darted and swooped through evenings of clear beauty at dusk, and I was sad that we had removed an image of how it operated. I thought it might try to find its way back to its roost by using its superb navigating system. I was glad that I believed in the existence of this mostly unseen winged creature in my mind. I did not regard the mind as an empty place for storage among the sloping rafters of the attic-like brain.

Standing in the loft, I thought of these stories. Each was like a snapshot, a painting to enshrine a moment for ever, take it out of the clutches of time and make it eternal. Was I not like this bat? I – my soul – roosted in dark and flitted out and fed on thousands of insect-like impressions and midge-like perceptions on the wing and digested them and left evidence – my stories – like droppings for all to see. (*Guano*, the accumulated excrement of birds, bats and seals, is valued as a fertilizer, and bats' *guano* is collected from caves.) Was not my finishing of my thousand stories like a bat being removed in a box, leaving its traces behind?

I lived in a parallel universe to the one that contained the events I described, in which things were different, like standing between two mirrors and looking in on another world from this one. I, Philip Rawley, told of events that allegedly happened to me, which I could change, exaggerate, distort into events that did not happen but which a reader would take on trust. I came, caught my midges, left my evidence and went like a bat removed in a box or a bat that had died, and the universe I described and created was similar to, but different from, the universe through which I flitted, darted and swooped.

38
Kingfishers, Crassula and the One

We went to Rye Meads and joined a walk to some of the hides by the wetlands. We walked in a group to the first hide beside a lagoon and sat on a wooden bench and through binoculars spotted coots, moorhens, Canada geese, a greylag goose, snipe with long curved beaks, shovelers with bright orange legs, teal with a flash of green in their wings, little grebes and tufted ducks that dived, and, loveliest of ducks, several gadwells, each with a white *speculum* on its wings. There were no green sandpipers visible. There were a couple of swans.

Our leader, a strapping young woman with a loud voice, said, "Look at that teal preening. They preen to take care of their feathers so they can fly efficiently. And that swan has a long neck because all the birds feed at different levels. If they all fed at the same level there wouldn't be enough food to go round. All the birds eat different food. Teals, gadwells and shovelers up-end, grebes and tufted ducks dive. So there's enough food for all birds."

And her words reverberated, tore aside a veil and revealed a glimpse of a plan, the workings of the Whole. All birds were catered for in the Whole.

"Whether out of competitiveness," she was saying, "or because it is in their genes, all birds instinctively feed at different levels."

They fed at different levels so that the Whole worked. It seemed as if they were competing, but each instinctively knew what to do. Fish, too, fed at different levels. The same law was at work in birds and fish.

We walked to another hide. Before us was a lagoon edged with reeds. There were fewer birds on the water.

"Shh," our guide said. "On that stick, that forked stick just beyond the reeds below us, look, a kingfisher. It's a male, it's got a black beak."

I had always wanted to see a kingfisher perched in the wild. Excited, we sat on the bench and trained our binoculars. I saw him very clearly for a long while: a pale blue back, pale orange front and a black beak. He was sitting on his perch above the water waiting to dive for fish with an open beak and closed eyes, I knew kingfishers catch their fish blind. I studied the colours of its wings. Its brightest blue ran down its back to the tip of its tail, its wings and head were a darker blue. Its colour was created by iridescence – reflection and refraction of light within its feathers so it gained colour according to its position – rather than pigment. It changed colour with the light, and was now quite dull. It had a chestnut orange front, a white throat, an orange and white patch behind its eyes and red legs. It looked around and then suddenly flew away, a flash of blue and orange above the reedbed immediately before us.

Our guide said, "Most female birds are brownish, like female blackbirds, for example. It's because they sit on their nests and have to blend in, be camouflaged. So in most species the male bird is more brightly coloured to display and the female is duller. But the male and female kingfishers are both blue and orange because they nest in a bank, they excavate a burrow and lay their eggs within it on sandy soil, and so the female doesn't need camouflage."

Again I thought: every eventuality is taken care of. There was a plan within Nature, and the colourings for the females were matched to the requirements of their nesting habits. They all knew instinctively what to do, and again I sensed the workings of the Whole.

We went on to another hide. Before us was a very large lagoon, more like a lake. There were two herons standing, one with black plumage below and more grey, a juvenile. There were cormorants, pochards with brown rather than red heads because of the approach of winter, and some black-headed gulls which had lost the chocolate-brown colouring on their heads as winter was approaching and merely had a chocolate-brown patch behind their eyes. Another hide nearby looked out on another two herons and more cormorants and shovelers.

As we walked back I asked the guide, "Do trees, shrubs and plants drive roots to different levels so there is enough moisture for each? Is the same principle at work as with the birds?

She said, "They compete for water I think. It's the survival of the fittest. If they can't get water near the surface they go further down in search of it."

I thought: competition, survival of the fittest – she's a Darwinian. She did not see a plan, merely individual trees, shrubs, plants and birds struggling to survive and developing long roots or necks that would help them survive.

I tried again: "You said all birds feed at different levels so the food goes round. All the food they eat is there for a reason, to feed the birds. What in all you can see here at Rye Meads – in the way of trees, shrubs, plants, birds and fish – is *not* of use to something else?"

She reflected and then said, "I can think of plants that have invaded from abroad. For example, crassula. It's run wild here. It covered acres to a height of two or three inches. It's of no use to birds, fish, anything. We're clearing it here but it's been a big problem. We've got duckweed sorted out, but not crassula."

She shrugged, and we parted. I returned home and looked up *crassulaceae,* and found it is the stonecrop or orpine family of the flowering plant order *saxifragale*s, which contains 28 families and over 3,000 species of perennial herbs or low shrubs native to dry regions and suitable for rock gardens. There are several well-known members of the *crassulaceae* family, including crassula. Some of *crassulaceae*'s 1,500 species produce medicinal balms, a few produce edible fruits and some capture and utilise the bodies of insects as a source of nitrogen. Crassula does have its uses in the Grand Plan.

I sat and looked out of my window as rain clouds hung over the dull green forest at dusk and pondered a plan, the Whole, that included birds, fish and plants, kingfishers and crassula. Each phenomenal form was not a Darwinian individual struggling to survive in competition with the rest but a stitch in the tapestry of a vast floral and faunal pattern and design which included all creatures and growing things, in which all living creatures were born with an instinctive knowledge of their place in the grand scheme of things and of the need to perform accordingly. That included human beings, who chose varied careers and therefore enabled the earth's resources to go round for everybody.

I sat enfolded in a vision of gigantic meaning. The lady guide had articulated the principal law of Nature without realising it as her Darwinian training had blinded her to the mysterious workings of the One.

39
A Fountain of Light

First thing that day a heron stood in the fountain looking for fish in the weed, until magpies chased it off, fluttering bravely at it in little jumps. I worked hard all morning on America's Founding Fathers and then stopped and looked through the newspapers. In the obituaries I saw that a college friend had died of "the return of his illness, bravely borne". Donations could be made to a hospice. I had sat next to him at a reunion and I could imagine his tall barrister's presence in court.

Outside there was a cloudless blue sky. I went out into the brilliant autumn sunshine of an Indian summer and felt the sun warm on my cheeks. I wandered down to the field. In the distance the Brazilian was driving the ride-on mower. He waved. There was a smell of new-mown grass. Immediately before me on the cut field there was a circle of heron feathers. The fox must have caught the heron.

I thought of the opposites under the blue dome of the One, the opposites of heron and fish, fox and heron. I thought of more-philosophical opposites, of reason and revelation. I thought of how America's Founding Fathers, being Deists, approached the One through their reason and had a social view of Nature. I, on the other hand, approached the One through revelation, a pouring into the soul of the One's Light.

The sun-lounger was out on the terrace. I took off my top, lay on the padded foam in the autumn sunshine by the bust of Apollo at the foot of the spiral staircase, and felt the sun, centre of our solar system, warm my face, chest and legs. I sank into a kind of trance way below my reason and soaked in the One, breathing shallowly on my back, blending with the universe. I was like the fountain not far from my feet, a still bowl with a spurt of light from within that trickled over my brim and splashed out into the world.

I lay in a physical torpor for at least an hour, then sat up, put my top on and returned inside, drank some water and sat at my desk in my study, feeling the air cooler cool my back. My limbs were heavy from my deep relaxing, my breaths were slow and shallow and my eyelids drooped. Behind my closed eyes I looked for the midnight sun in a night sky, the spiritual Light of which the physical sun is a copy. There were glimmerings, but it was hidden behind cloud. I had to keep watching.

I lay down on my sofa and held a cushion over my eyes to black out daylight, and behind my closed lids my third eye opened, the eye of my soul, and on the blackness within there was a faint light seen through black branches, like looking out and up through a decorated tracery church window. Beyond the tracery there was a word in medieval script of about eight letters I could not decipher. And then I was through some of the tracery and I was looking up within a magnificent tree hung with green leaves and apples against the blue sky. The whiteness returned in scrivenings of Light, and then I was heavy behind my throat and there was a blueness and at its heart a wonderful white glowing diamond, and then a many-faced crystal, then a white chrysanthemum appeared in pale light. There was a fountain, just like the one the heron had stood in, and I confronted strange forms that had meaning and significance, and I felt cleansed within, washed through with a stream of image-bearing Light and all grime and clogging matter had been swept away. My slowly-breathing chest, throat and head were like a pipe through which these images spurted up like water and splashed down round my watching soul, which, like a heron, was very still.

I returned to my desk and looked out at the clouds in the rosy sky. I felt tranquil, utterly peaceful and between the distant clouds and the depth of my being there was a bond. Outside there was Being, and I was Being. And what had seemed to be opposites were all aspects of Being, reason and revelation included. But no one could know the One without sinking into a sleep-like trance and *becoming* the fountain of Being which welled up from far below the surface reason.

40
Paralysed Bodies and the One

I went to the gym and walked, cycled, treadmilled, pushed chest-weights and pulled arm-weights and did sit-ups on a large ball. When

I returned home I sat in my window and thought of the body and of all I knew whose lives had been handicapped in some way.

I thought of Paul Strickland, a banker I had met once each year at the bank dinners. He had a very disabled daughter and had spent years of his life looking after her until, having looked at many places, he placed her in a care-home that suited her, where she was happy in activities with other children. He led a life of self-sacrifice, giving up his Arsenal season ticket to tend to her at weekends.

I thought of Chris White, a film producer with four daughters, who had a stroke. It left him unable to walk properly and affected his speech. When I met him out with his wife he grinned and smiled and nodded and, not saying a word, touched my hand warmly, and said, "Yes." That was the only word he was able to speak: "Yes." His wife attended to all his needs, working from home with him, setting up an equipment company and doing all the paperwork for him so they could be together. And despite his affliction he had the lovely smile of a Yea-sayer.

I thought of Ted Darley, who had had the chance to retire when he reached sixty but carried on working. He was fit and active, he played golf and did not smoke. Then he had a stroke which disabled him down one side and left him barely able to speak. He was bedridden for months, and when his grandson was taken to see him, the little boy, not understanding as he was only four, said, "Get up, lazybones." He slowly improved and eventually went home. He lived on his own and carers came in, paid for out of his savings, but he could not operate the television remote and was bored and bitter, and swore in the presence of anyone who went to see him. It was part of his condition. He was no longer able to censure his words, and as a result few wanted to go a second time.

I thought of the heroism of these three people and their families, and of the suffering, paralyses and strokes that had disabled people younger than me. The body is the temple of the soul, I reflected, and carries it through its threescore years and ten. So why were some paralysed earlier than that? The world was full of invalids who, like me, had wanted to keep their bodies healthy, look after them, feed their souls, complete their work – their tasks – while healthy and live in readiness – and who had been struck down for no understandable reason.

Then I thought that the One cares for paralysed bodies as much as the well ones. And I wondered if disabilities were left over from former lives, karmic residues? How did we not know that the One is teaching certain qualities through the strokes it inflicted – Paul Strickland's daughter enthusiastic involvement in activities; Chris White a lovely transparent smile and trusting innocence; and Ted Darley a resigned and stoical acceptance of his lot?

Why was there paralysis in the universe if it was not to teach souls certain qualities that they would not otherwise develop? I had not met a single disabled person through whose face a remarkable quality did not shine. Was that a coincidence? Or had they been stroked tenderly by divine Providence to shine out transparent goodness? If so, it could be expected that Ted Darley would soon be greeting his visitors with a radiant smile.

41
A Dance of Death and the Dance of Life

In Spain, forty-eight years ago, I put my sleeping-bag down and slept wherever I was – on a hillside, on a beach, on a roundabout even on one occasion – and I spent one night on open, flat duneland not far from the sea. There were wispy reeds and clumps of grass here and there, and in places thicker vegetation.

Around dawn I was woken by a rustle of grass and I sat up. A figure clad in black from head to toe, showing only his face and wearing a short cape, was making exaggeratedly large, slow, stealing strides past me, holding the hand of a man who looked like a medieval pope who held the hand of a man wearing a crown, who held the hand of a little girl who held the hand of a monk who held the hand of a poorly-clad, barefoot man. There were six of them in a line, all wearing costumes, all holding hands, and the last five followed the black-clad figure in silence, stealing across the dunes in a mannered, sideways, striding dance.

I thought of a film directed by Ingmar Bergman – *The Seventh Seal* – in which Death heads a line of half a dozen people holding hands across the skyline on top of a hill. I said out loud, "It's a Dance of Death – a *Totentanz*." They turned a corner and disappeared, and I lay down and went back to sleep.

The Dance of Death haunted me and I came to realise how it came into being. In Europe one third of the population died from the Black Death between 1347 and 1351, and death became a familiar everyday occurrence to people at that time and for the next hundred years, which were dominated by The Hundred Years' War that lasted until 1453. Art reflected this familiarity and skeletal figures soon surfaced in paintings in France and were present in North-European painting for a long while. Between 1523 and 1526 Hans Holbein the Younger produced a Dance-of-Death series of woodcuts in which Death surprises victims in the midst of daily life.

Critics speak of the psychological morbidness in the art between 1350 and the 1530s. But to an existentialist, the skeletal figure is not morbid but a call to real living, and the Dance of Death is exhilarating as the dance is enjoyed despite the ubiquitousness of death. In my consciousness there was a polar opposition between the Dance and Death.

I warmed to the *danse macabre* which began in France, the medieval allegorical treatment of the all-conquering, impartial and equalizing power of Death. This mime dance represented typical figures from society being led to the grave in order of rank: pope, emperor, child, clerk, hermit – spiritual and worldly power, innocent, learned and holy alike. Death attacks his victims in their daily life without warning, and is inevitable and imminent, but the dance defies Death.

Over the years I have warmed to Greek dancing, as when Zorba the Greek dances on the beach in the film. When in Greece I have joined in and danced and seen the brightening eyes and the way the dancers lose themselves in the dance and the performance and give out sheer joy. I have also warmed to Siva, Lord of the Dance, who embodied dance as a creative principle. In my lifetime Death has stalked everywhere with his scythe: in Europe, the Middle East, the Balkans, Africa and Asia.

But there are other ways of defying Death than by dancing. The principal way is going to the Light and communing with the One which is above death. Life plus death equals Great Nothing or Zero, the One. Death is only one aspect of the One, one half of the equation. I came to see that in its highest meaning life, by embracing Nature and the One, enables us to grasp the order within the universe and sense a meaning and purpose which triumphs over Death.

42
A Thousand Selves and the One

In Japan I was invited to tour Kyoto and Nara by a bank I worked for. I went by the new Tokaido train to Kyoto and was met by a bank representative, who accompanied me to an inn. The next morning he called for me and took me in the bank's car to Nara to see the Big Buddha and the deer.

In the afternoon we visited Sanjusangendo, a Tendai temple founded in 1164 by an emperor who was a devotee of Kannon Bodhisattva. Kannon stood for peace and saved people from the miseries of human existence. In 1249 the Hall was burned down, and it was rebuilt and completed about ten years later. The principal image of Kannon, 3.3 metres tall, was carved in 1254 and by 1266 a further thousand standing images of Kannon, each 1.7 metres tall, had been completed.

I entered the Hall and was confronted by a thousand life-size images in five or six tiers, each made of wood and japanned (varnished black) and plated with gold leaves. They stood with spoked suns behind their heads, silent like a football crowd in a grandstand, and I felt discomfort at being in their presence as if being studied by a thousand people, and I hurried out, then looked back. The central image was a thousand-handed Kannon in a sitting position, making a thousand and one Kannons in all.

In a flash of intuition I saw a thousand selves, all replicas of the central Self, all spoked with Light, all lit from the Light that illumined the central Self. Collectively they were an image for the fragmentation of the personality, the same self in a thousand different situations, and for the need to become one central Self at peace like the Kannon who had a hand for each, but also to escape the thousand attachments that made us miserable.

Now that I am nearing the end of my thousand stories, I see that those images held a special message for me: to write a thousand stories in which I would superficially be the same but in fact different in each as each showed a different situation, though each would reflect the One at the centre. There would be a thousand reflections of the One. And so in a sense all these stories are one story.

Looking back from now I see one self in a thousand different situations, experiencing or hearing about a thousand different experiences – all of which are reflections of the One, all of which are unreal in relation to the reality they reflect but real to the illusion we live in until we are shocked out of it when confronted by reality; as I was that hot afternoon in Japan forty-one years ago. Chiliad living is realising that we are a thousand fragments, all of which reflect the one person that we should all become.

43
The Secret of the Desert

We went into Sinai from Sharm el-Sheikh, which is on the Red Sea. With a guide sitting beside the driver in the front, we headed out into the desert. We crossed a bleak landscape of volcanic rock that had been captured by Israel in 1967 and held for a while, and we passed Bedouin settlements. One group were standing by a camel. The Bedouin roamed the barren sands of the desert at will and lived close to Nature.

We stopped at a roadside Bedouin market. Beads, stones and fossils were spread along the top of a low wall, behind which stretched an arid, dusty plain between mountains. Clear-skinned, handsome children implored us to buy. We bought crystals and fossils and two halves of a stone that had been split by fire, with beautiful crystals inside.

A dignified old man of about eighty told our guide that the Bedouin search for these stones in the dusty plain and at the foot of the mountains, and split them by putting them in a fire. He told our guide in Arabic, "We call it 'The Secret of the Desert'."

I asked him how many generations he could remember and he said, "Five." He must have meant that he could remember his grandparents, parents, brothers and sisters, children and grandchildren – no different from me.

We drove on and reached the checkpoint for St Catherine's Monastery, beyond which only taxis were allowed. We parked and took a taxi across rough desert ground, climbing to the sixth-century fortified monastery walls. Mountains towered all round, including the mountain from which Moses brought down the tablets of stone. It rose sheer behind the monastery.

We got out and were approached by Bedouin. One spoke English. He told me his tribe looked after the monastery, that his tribe was descended from two hundred Roman soldiers recruited locally in Justinian's time. He said, "They are Romany" – Romans, but perhaps also cousins of our Romany gypsies.

The Bedouin's world was the desert, the volcanic mountains (*jebel*) and the blue sky. Their kingdom was of the sands, and in death they belonged to the sand: nearby a cairn of stones on the desert ground marked the place of a Bedouin's grave.

We entered the fortified wall of the monastery. Christianity came to Egypt at the end of the first century or beginning of the second century. Helena, wife of Constantine, the founder of the Byzantine empire, built a chapel round what was deemed to be the Burning Bush in 337. Justinian visited it in 530 and ordered that the monastery should be expanded. Helena's chapel was to continue to house the Burning Bush.

In the ninth century monks allegedly found the remains of St Catherine, the daughter of the Roman governor of Alexandria. She had converted to Christianity and had been tortured and beheaded in a public square in Alexandria on the orders of Emperor Maximinus, and the monastery displayed what was claimed to be part of her skull, her chest bones and her arm bones.

Once inside the walls we walked to where "the Burning Bush", more a tree than a shrub, like a head of straight hair with trailing strands that never flower, stood, outside Helena's chapel now.

The sixth-century church was festooned with hanging chandeliers, censers and late icons. Catherine's wrist-bone was in a glass case, displayed as a genuine relic. We passed through the Chapel of the Transfiguration and saw the sixth-century half-dome and curved mosaic of Christ, which must have been constructed about 530 on Justinian's instructions. We went on to the Chapel of the Burning Bush and saw the elaborate fourth-century doorway, but the interior was roped off. There was no explanation as to how the Burning Bush used to be inside it – Helena had built her chapel round it – but was now outside it.

We looked in on the museum and bought a ticket from a monk dressed in black with a Greek Orthodox hat. He sported a beard and wore spectacles. We saw the famous icon of Christ Pantocrator which had been painted in the first half of the sixth century. There was a Heavenly Ladder of the twelfth century. Monks endeavoured to climb to Heaven along its gentle upward slope, but some were shown falling off.

We went on to the charnel-house. I peered through the barred entrance and saw a robed skeleton in a glass case. It was the skeleton of the sixth-century architect of the expanded church, Stephanos. Behind were the piled bones of all the monks since then, all heaped together in an ossuary. When a monk died he was buried for two years and then exhumed when no flesh clung to his bones, which were then placed here. On my right were the remains of archbishops in niches. On my left was a mound of two or three hundred skulls – all the monks, one on top of another, together in death. The Greek Orthodox monk with a long black hat, beard and spectacles who sold me our museum tickets would join them and take his place on top of the heaped tradition – in the present part on top, for the past was at the bottom, the present on top.

The monks, I saw, were different from the Bedouin. The Bedouin had no books. They had blood-knowledge about their Romany ancestors, the Jebeliya tribe of Sinai Bedouin, which they knew was recorded in the chronicle of Eutychios, patriarch of Alexandria in the ninth century. They had not read the chronicle. They had no books, only hearsay. They were uncluttered by the thirst for knowledge that troubled the monks and me. They were happy so long as they could guide visitors up Mount Sinai. Bedouin cannot read or write, so only a heap of stones –

and the Bedouin memories – commemorates their lives.

On the way back we stopped near some roadside Bedouin. A young fellow spoke to our guide. He said he was twenty-one and that his name was Suleiman. He wore a *jellaba* and his head was covered. His "cousin" came, winding her black veil round her head, with her two children who were aged five and four, she said. He brought us tea with *shih* in it, a plant or herb that is good for flu or colds. They find it in the mountains of Sinai, where it rains and snows and plants grow. (St Catherine's is the only place in Egypt where it snows.) He said they use *hahak*, which was like mint, for stomach upsets, and *handol*, an oil for pain in the bones or rheumatism.

I asked him if he knew the old man of about eighty the other side of the mountain. He told our guide in Arabic, "Yes, he's called Sheikh Hamid. He lives in the plain the other side of the mountain. He's eighty. We Bedouin don't get ill. We have little, few possessions, but the sand, the mountains and the sky are ours."

We bought some beads and stones, and they waved us off, having done business via the tea. And as we returned to the Red Sea I thought of the Bedouin roaming their kingdom of sand, under the mountains and the sky. They lived in the physical world, the here-and-now. And I thought of the monks who sought a heavenly kingdom on a ladder they might fall off. But both ended up as skulls, in a charnel-house or under a heap of stones.

I reflected that the Bedouin had nothing, like the monks, and were content with a close family life. They were calm, inwardly at peace, strictly religious and praying at set hours – like monks. They knew the secret of happiness: not to be too attached to possessions, to treasure the universe. In that, they were like monks. They found stones they call "the Secret of the Desert", but they also knew that the secret of the desert is happiness through non-attachment. They lived by tradition – the legend that they were Romany or "Romans" – as did the monks who were waiting for their skulls to be added to the heap of skulls in the charnel-house.

The monks also lived simply with nothing, but they were trying to escape the here-and-now for a heavenly kingdom within their souls, whereas the Bedouin were at one with the desert, the mountains and the sky, and they lived in the One in the here-and-now and waited for their skulls to be added to the desert under a cairn of stones.

Both lived in readiness until they became skulls. It was what one should do when one has reached a certain stage in life – live in readiness until one becomes a skull.

The secret of the desert was to embrace the here-and-now and to live in the One in the hot desert sunshine.

Epilogue

Two views from c.2600BC

In *A New Philosophy of Literature* Nicholas Hagger traced the fundamental theme of world literature back to c.2600BC, when *The Epic of Gilgamesh* was written. The two stories, or parables, that follow, written in 1963 and 2005 respectively and until now unpublished, purport to predate the fundamental theme in c.2600BC, when the Great Pyramid was built. They report the bafflement of an official who has worked at Giza for 29 years and sees the Great Pyramid as an empty tomb, a secular folly; and then his breakthrough into seeing it as a means for all to become an *akh*, a spiritual soul or Shining One. The official finds himself mirroring Reality after what amounts to a metaphysical quest.

Both accounts from Giza are included here as they present the secular and metaphysical aspects of the fundamental theme of *A New Philosophy of Literature* reflected in his *Selected Poems* and this volume, *Selected Stories*, in terms of their source in c.2600BC, before the beginning of world literature, the literary tradition and its fundamental theme.

Historical note: Khufu ordained his Great Pyramid near the beginning of the Fourth Dynasty (c.2600 or 2540BC). Khufu is thought to have lived from c.2620 to 2566BC. According to one view he reigned for 46 years. According to another view he reigned for 23 years, which are variously given as 2604–2581BC; 2589–2566BC; or 2551–2528BC. The Great Pyramid is thought to have been finished c.2560BC.

The Riddle of the Great Pyramid

"'Riddle', 'a question or statement testing ingenuity in divining its answer or meaning, a puzzling fact'" (*Concise Oxford Dictionary*)

I

I have been an official here at Giza for twenty-nine years. Since I have witnessed the whole operation from the first scratch on the sand, I may have some justification for regarding myself as something of an authority on the matter.

The manner in which the Great Pyramid has been constructed is as follows. As soon as Khufu succeeded as Pharaoh on the death of his father Snefru, work began to prepare the site. The vizier and building manager Prince Hemiunu and his chief architect Mirabu[1] (neither of whom I have ever seen) were heavily involved in the drawings. The builders first drew a line in the sand directed at true north. They then laid out a square with precise right-angles. To strengthen and stabilise the structure a mass of bedrock was incorporated within the square, which prevented the builders from checking the square's accuracy by measuring the diagonals, yet by mathematical calculations they still managed to achieve an unsurpassed degree of precision. As soon as the surveyors had finished marking out the site news came through that Khufu was anxious to begin work. Accordingly Recruitment Offices were opened in each of the twenty-two provinces (*sepat*s) in our land to attract workers with high wages and tax exemptions. Once the workers had been transported here to Giza their first task was to build the stone compounds. Tented camps were considered and rejected in view of the anticipated length of the project. And so workers were shipped across the Nile to the east bank and under my direction (I am Superintendent and Controller of Compounds) they hewed limestone blocks from the quarries, levered them on to rollers, dragged them to the river, floated them across on rafts and dragged them to the sites appointed by the surveyors.

This process continued for three years before any start was made on the actual project. In due course the compounds will be demolished. Once a suitable number of workers were housed, work began on the levelling of the plateau and on the laying out of the base of the Great Pyramid with knotted ropes. At the same time more workers made a road to the high-water mark of the Nile. Altogether this took a further ten years, and during this time reinforcements were constantly arriving and building more stone compounds round the plateau. Only when all this had been done did work begin on the Great Pyramid.

The plan, as conceived by the architects, was simple. Workers were to achieve the shape that Khufu wanted by laying blocks all over the square base and then by piling on further layers until they tapered to one block at the top. They were to get the blocks into position by building ramps of wet sand, mud-bricks and stones which were to be lengthened and mounded up as each new layer was reached so that the gradients remained constant, and by using rollers and levers when dragging the blocks up the ramps. The sides of the Great Pyramid beneath the ramps would therefore be a series of small steps. When the top was reached, triangular casing blocks were to be fitted into position to give a sloping effect. Thus, four casing blocks would meet in a point at the top, and thereafter there would be enough to fill in all the steps. And as the casing was to be built downwards, so the ramps would be dismantled downwards. And this is the position today, sixteen years after the first block of the Great Pyramid was laid into place: we have just begun the casing.

For the last sixteen years the organisation of labour has been based on the principle of four annual shifts of three months each. Although, therefore, a total of 400,000 unskilled workers work on the Great Pyramid during one year, at any one time there are only 100,000, and for their shift, they are paid what elsewhere would be six months' wages and exempted from one year's taxes. By this means enthusiasm and morale are maintained all the year round and only a minimum of compounds are required. The 100,000 workers are apportioned equally on the east and west sides of the Nile. On the east side 20,000 mine the quarries, and 30,000 haul the blocks to the river, float them across, and deliver them to the masons. On the west side 30,000 haul the blocks from the masons to the ramps, and 20,000 work on the ramps and lend a hand with the gruelling work of dragging the blocks up the ramps. Yet so delicate is the organisation that each block is staggered in relation to the others so as to avoid congestion on the ramps.

This staggering is achieved by the "Hundred Gang System", whereby the miners, the haulers, the masons and the ramp-workers are each composed of 100 gangs, and gang 1 of each handles the same block throughout, as do gangs 2, 3, and 4, and so on up to 100.

Consider the complications of this system. On the east side, for example, there are two conditions of labour: that the miners should produce 100 blocks a week, and that the haulers should take no more than one week (168 hours) in dragging each block to the river, in floating it across and in delivering it to the masons, although each block weighs some two and a half tons. Now the miners work in gangs of 100, and two gangs to a block, gangs 1A and 1B – one on, one off. And the haulers work in gangs of 150, and two gangs to a block, gangs 1A and 1B – one on, one off. Nevertheless, somehow there is a gap of one hour between the time that miners 1A and 1B hand over their block to haulers 1A and 1B, and the time that miners 2A and 2B hand over their block to haulers 2A and 2B. And what is more, each gap is seen in relation to the state of the Nile in about 160 hours' time. And moreover, this gap is maintained throughout the year in spite of the end of annual shifts and the beginning of new ones, and in spite of the fact that each block, although roughly cut, must be of the correct measurement, for miners 1A and 1B are acting on the conveyed instructions of gang 1 of the masons, and so on.

Indeed, the slightest delay could destroy the whole co-ordination. For consider with regard to the masons: each casing block must arrive at the masons' yard in the order in which it is expected, just as, another 168 hours later, it must leave the masons' yard in the order in which it arrived. This co-ordination is effected in this way. There are 1,000 masons, and they work in 100 gangs, ten to a block. The block mined by miners gangs 1A and 1B, and hauled by haulers gangs 1A and 1B, goes to masons gang 1, and the second block to masons gang 2, and so on. Thus, one hour after gang 100 has completed its (previous week's) block, gang 1 discharges the first block of the new week. But if the block for gang 2 arrives before the block for gang 1 owing to the delay of haulers 1A and 1B, for example, then gangs 2–100 will be delayed while gang 1 waits, for gang 1's casing block must be keyed into the Great Pyramid before gang 2's casing block.

It is to this end that gang 1 has already conferred with the mathematicians and determined the exact measurements and angles of the particular block that is expected, making allowances for any slight discrepancy there may be in one of the blocks on which it will rest. And it is to this end that gang 1 has likewise conferred with the architects and engineers. The masons are craftsmen – each block is to them a masterpiece, they scorn mass-production – and their task is much more complex than merely smoothing the surfaces and marking the blocks with red ink to indicate their place in the structure of the Great Pyramid to the engineers. In view of such care and accuracy there can be no delay. And never yet has there been one error, not in sixteen years.

Consider the scale of the project. I have been told that in all there are 2.3 million stone blocks, which rise to a height of 146.6m.[2] The bottom one weighs 6.18 tons, the top one 2.5 tons. The blocks over the Upper Chamber weigh 50–80 tons yet the greatest difference in length between the four 230m sides of the Great Pyramid is only 4cms (2ins). Thousands of craftsmen have been involved in this astonishing project, which has built the world's highest building.[3]

Who is responsible for so elaborate an organisation? Certainly credit for maintaining the flow of blocks in their correct order must go to the officials, to the Directors and Inspectors of Mathematics, Engineering, Architecture and Stonemasonry in the beginning, and, under their expert direction, to the Directors and Inspectors of Production and Design, to the Directors of Haulage, to the Directors of Navigation, and to the Directors and Inspectors of Ramps. Nor must the contribution of the foremen be overlooked. But it must be remembered that there could have been no flow of blocks at all in the first place without the initial plan, and that the officials (very completely, to be sure) are merely following the instructions of the Pyramid Committee, as are all of us who are engaged in this operation.

Little is known about the Pyramid Committee. Its messages and commands come through remote and devious channels, and were it not for the evidence of the complexity of the organisation of this project it might even be possible to doubt its existence. For some years, ever since the levelling of the plateau, in fact, there has been some speculation as to its location, and rumour has it variously that the Pyramid Committee resides on the forbidden western side of the Great Pyramid, or in a large palace near Memphis. (It is of course well known that the west is associated with death and the east with life, so it is only natural and appropriate that the western side should be forbidden to workers.) By now the rumours have become legends, and the legends conflict, and all that can be said with certainty is that somewhere, doubtless surrounded by all the most modern equipment, it bears the incessant responsibility of the highest command, together with the foreknowledge of the horrible consequences of so much as one error or oversight. For it is well known that the Pyramid Committee is directly responsible to none other than Khufu himself, the most powerful god-man the world has ever seen or will ever be likely to see.

II

But the organisation is far from being entirely economic. For every official engaged in the production and distribution of blocks there is another official engaged in the direction of the workers' welfare. Here on the south side of the Great Pyramid reside the Directors and Inspectors of Food, Clothing, and Working Conditions, the Directors of Public Health and Free-Time Education, and the Directors of Letters and River Transport – not to mention the Directors of Admissions and Departures, the Director of Roll Calls and the Director of Personnel Problems. Furthermore, each official has a clerical staff of the magnitude of any government office in any of the provinces, and whole armies of scribes often work far into the night to keep abreast of the work.

Consider the Directorate of Accounts, for example. The Pyramid Committee wisely foresaw that if workers were paid at Giza there would be robberies. On completion of their annual three-month shift, therefore, the workers return to their provinces and collect their wages from their local Recruitment Office, and the pay-days are staggered to avoid congestion. Four times a year, therefore, the Directorate of Accounts must complete the necessary forms for 100,000 men (taking account of any absences without leave) and ensure that each form reaches the correct Recruitment Office in the correct province. And what is more, each form must be accompanied by a Certificate of Tax Exemption, which must be signed by the Director of Accounts himself. And furthermore the returns to the Pyramid Committee must be accurate to the last scratch on a tablet.

The social conditions of the workers, then, are good. They live 50 to a compound, so there are 1,000 compounds by the quarries on the east side of the Nile and 1,000 compounds on the north side of the Great

Pyramid on the west side of the Nile. They work a ten-hour day and a five-and-a-half-day week, and during the hot months they are permitted a siesta and make up the time in the comparative cool of the evenings. At the end of the day's stint the haulers return to their compounds, no matter how near the river or the ramps they may be, and there they are fed with lentils, leeks, radishes, onions, garlic and bread, and if for some reason one compound is to hold a celebration, then wine is provided free of charge.

And it is likewise with the miners, the masons and the ramp-workers. If during the day any worker has suffered what he considers to be an injustice at the hands of an official, then he can go to one of the Workers' Brotherhoods – there is one on either side of the river – for the workers have their own organisation for redressing grievances and ensuring the best conditions.

As regards recreation, the workers have opportunities to play games or hold horse-races, and some attend Free-Time education, though this is not so popular. Otherwise they can walk by the Nile or watch the professional entertainers. It should be added that behind the compounds there are some specially guarded rest-houses, in which visiting wives can stay for a maximum of one week a month, although most workers reconcile themselves to three months' celibacy in the year in return for the rewards they will enjoy with their wages during the remaining nine months.

There is therefore great justice in the organisation, and social reformers have no cause to protest against the foresight and humanitarianism of the Pyramid Committee. Every worker is free – there are no slaves or foreign captives, as there were under Snefru – and there seems to be little to substantiate the rumours which assert that criminals are treated inhumanely on the forbidden western side of the Great Pyramid. Moreover no worker is paid less than the official clerks.

There are admittedly class distinctions: the officials here on the south side of the Great Pyramid and their clerical staff will have little to do socially with the workers on the north side of the Great Pyramid, just as the Pyramid Committee (which is rumoured to have been drawn from the aristocracy) will have nothing to do socially with the officials. But in my experience as Superintendent and Controller of Compounds, this does not unduly worry the workers, who are anyway apt to feel a trifle awkward in the presence of their "social betters". They are content to work for their subsistence and to enjoy their leisure. And they can always console themselves with the thought that, no matter what class distinction there may be, all men engaged on this operation are, without exception, enslaved to the Great Pyramid, and have their lives dominated by it. And that is true from the meanest labourer to the highest authority, Khufu himself.

III

In view of all this it must be admitted that the Pyramid Committee has left nothing to chance. In that case, so much organisation and endeavour must surely be justified by the purpose and value of work? So I thought before the first block of the Great Pyramid was laid, and so I have thought every day for the last sixteen years. Every day I have seen hosts of men in loin-cloths bent double, the ropes chaffing their naked bodies in the hot sun, and every day I have looked up at the Great Pyramid and asked myself 'Why? What's it all for? Surely it has some purpose, some meaning?' For sixteen years I have been reluctant to admit that my question is unanswerable – every day for sixteen years I have duly conducted my own private speculations, and I regret to have to report that even now my conclusion is far from firm.

Consider. The most obvious solution seems to be the religious one, that through the Great Pyramid Khufu's body and *ka* (his double body) will, on his death, allow his *ba* (soul) and *akh* (shining spirit) to find their way to the spirit world in the West, perhaps sailing to Ra (in whom Khufu does not believe) in his solar wooden boat which is to be buried on the southern side of his pyramid, where they will assume the form of Osiris and judge the dead and dwell with Ra in Eternal Sunshine. It is rumoured that one of the Queens' pyramids contains the unmarked tomb of Khufu's mother, Queen Hetepheres, who had her internal organs stored in four compartments of a square alabaster jar, including her lungs. Of course her heart and kidneys were not removed – her heart was of course left in her mummy so it could be weighed in the scales against a feather by Osiris in the Last Judgement. Her body was bound in 100 double arm's lengths (i.e. 100 yards) of linen. If such elaborate mummification practices took place on Khufu's mother, how could they not have taken place on Khufu? We all know that Khufu is now the main god, that there is a local divine cult of Khufu at Giza, that he belongs to the horizon, is *akhty* (a Shining One) and has taken the place of Ra. Traditionally Khepri is the rising morning sun in the east, the scarab pushing the sun like a dung-beetle rolling a ball of dung; Ra is the sun at midday; and Atum is the setting evening sun. Perhaps this pyramid is to reflect one or all of these with its shining casing stones, when they are in place – even though Khufu has not taken the name of, and therefore does not believe in, Ra. It is dangerous – seditious – to confess this, but I personally do not believe in the spirit world in the West, or in the *ka*, or in the resurrection of the body after this life, or, indeed, in any of the Horus-Osiris or Ra/Sun-god legends which pass as our national religion, but I of course believe that Khufu is a god and if Khufu believes in them, then at least the Great Pyramid makes sense. On the other hand, even if Khufu does believe in them, why the necessity to build a Pyramid? Why not merely an ordinary burial chamber, a *mastaba* – a luxurious *mastaba* of course, but a *mastaba* of the conventional shape?

According to the priests the conditions for attaining the spirit world are relatively simple. Neither *ka* nor body will survive unless they are incarcerated in a tomb. If the body is to survive there must, in addition, be mummification, and to guard against the possibility that mummification may fail to preserve the body, there should be a statue of the body to stand in the body's stead should the need arise. And in addition, if the *ka* is to survive, offerings must be brought to the tomb.

Nowhere do the priests assert that the Pyramid form is a condition for attaining the spirit world. Nowhere do they assert that the Pyramid is shaped like rays from the sun bursting through cloud, up which Khufu will travel to reach Eternal Sunshine. Nor is there any evidence to suggest that the Pyramid form is astronomical in its origins, or that the fact that the entrance is on the north face is to be associated with the imperishable Pole Star or circumpolar stars. Nor indeed is there any evidence to suggest that Khufu himself is to be associated with the imperishable Pole Star. If, as is rumoured, there is an alignment with particular stars this is unbeknown to us, the builders of the Great

Pyramid. It is rumoured that there will be more pyramids to replicate three stars close together,[4] but we dismiss this as fanciful. There is no precedent or evidence for such a view. In the past we believed that the circumpolar stars are eternal as they never dip below the horizon, but the change from worship of the lunar night sky to sun-worship happened two hundred years ago with Pharaohs of the second dynasty – for example Nebra and Neferkara – who took the name Ra long before Khufu's reign.

Perhaps then the Pyramid form is to protect the burial chamber against thieves? But will it afford any protection at all? For the Pyramid has a door, like any burial chamber, and the door cannot be permanently sealed because of the offerings which must be laid in the chamber. Moreover, the two air-channels for the Upper Chamber – one to the north and one to the south – are not for a *ka*, which does not need air to survive. There may theoretically be a link between the air-holes on the north side and Khufu's journey to the northern stars, but there has never been a tradition linking Khufu's *ba* or *akh* to the southern stars. Nor could they have been left for Sokar, god of the underworld, for it is well known that gods do not breathe or need air. In fact, the air-holes are not really air-holes at all. Strangely, though the mouths of these two air-holes in the Upper Chamber are open (as I have seen with my own eyes), the passages bend and are blocked – I am told on excellent authority – by stones a finger long (i.e. 8cms), so the air-flow stops at them and does not reach the Pyramid's outer casing which, I am reliably informed, was always going to cover the outer walls where the "air-holes" might have come out. The work to achieve these two "air-holes", and the two in the Lower Chamber, has been very complicated – a builder's nightmare – and yet no one knows why this complication has been necessary.

Consider again, if Khufu were so eager to preserve his *ka* and his body, why did he close the temples and forbid the priests to make sacrifices or make statues of him? And why did he place himself above the high priest and our religion and declare himself a god, "*Khut*", "Glory"? The official explanation is that the poor in our land have been harassed by burdensome temple dues (and of that there is no doubt), and that Khufu, although of course believing in our national religion, is a realist

– a humanitarian, not a tyrant. But however commendable his action may be to an atheist or a progressive reformer, there is no denying the fact that Khufu has made enemies of the very priests who will sacrifice and make offerings to his *ka* when he lies within the Great Pyramid. For unless the priests make sacrifices they cannot live.

It would seem, then, that – in spite of the official explanation – Khufu does not in fact believe in the spirit world. In any event, there is certainly no religious reason for the size of the Great Pyramid, and none that I can see for its shape. And its purpose is a mystery in religious terms, for there is no certainty that when finished it will actually be used as a tomb.

Surely, therefore, there are secular reasons for the function and form of the Great Pyramid?

Does history throw any light on the matter? So far as the form is concerned, our historians see the Great Pyramid as the culmination of a tradition that began with Zoser's stepped pyramid at Saqqara and continued with Snefru's half-stepped, half-smooth pyramid and the first to have any form of casing, his Red Pyramid, which were both at Medum. (Snefru, Khufu's father, did not take the name Ra, and Khufu followed him in this. Did the pyramid form have something to do with his not being a follower of Ra?) According to one of our leading architects, the Pyramid Committee issued instructions to the effect that the form of the pyramid at Medum was to be pushed to its logical conclusion. But why? Merely to follow an architectural tradition?

Unfortunately, in all my research – and research is treated with suspicion here and discouraged, for it may be seen as questioning and deemed seditious – I have been unable to discover what led Zoser and Snefru to chance upon the forms they did. And so long as this crucial question remains in obscurity, it would appear that the problem of the form is insoluble.

So far as the function is concerned, the Great Pyramid does not fit into this historical tradition. In fact Khufu has confused this historical tradition. For everyone knows that, for all their tyranny, both Zoser and Snefru were deeply religious men who even went so far as to increase the temple dues. Their tombs, if not the pyramids which enclose them, were built for eschatological reasons, unlike (as it would seem) the burial chamber in the Great Pyramid. Nor does the Great Pyramid fit into the tradition that began with Zoser's pyramid and Snefru's second pyramid at Dahshur. For it is well known that the pyramids at Medum and Dahshur are cenotaphs. It may seem that there is good reason for believing that the Great Pyramid is also a cenotaph as the sarcophagus in the Upper Chamber is too wide to pass through the entrance to the chamber and was dragged up the ramp and placed in position while the stones round it were being raised and was then enclosed from above. I saw this with my own eyes. As tradition dictates that the Pharaoh should be dragged to his burial chamber in his sarcophagus, there was clearly never any intention to use the Upper Chamber as a burial chamber. The same may be true of the two lower chambers. No one knows why there are three in all – one underground and two above ground. Did Khufu plan to be buried in the subterranean lower chamber, then change his mind and introduce a second chamber with two air-holes above it, and then change his mind again and build the Upper Chamber with two air-holes? It is seditious to believe that Khufu, who is a god, could change his mind, and it is inconceivable that in all this meticulous planning and precision of execution the project should turn out to be so haphazard that one, let alone two, changes of mind could take place. And so, it may be thought, the Great Pyramid must be a cenotaph.

Nevertheless, the Great Pyramid cannot be a cenotaph, for a cenotaph is, by definition, an empty tomb and, say what you will, the Great Pyramid contains a burial chamber which no one doubts Khufu himself will one day occupy although there has never been any confirmation of this and there are actually good reasons for believing otherwise. Why make not just one but three burial chambers if there was no intention of using them for burial and if they are to remain empty tombs? Why all this gigantic labour to produce an empty tomb? Why, his mother Queen Hetepheres was buried in a tomb on the eastern side of the Great Pyramid, suggesting that Khufu *will* one day be laid to rest in one of the three burial chambers here.

Furthermore, it is traditional for the Pharaoh to have 23 statues of himself in his mortuary temple near his pyramid, one for each of the 22 provinces of Upper Egypt which themselves reflect the 22 parts of

Osiris's body when it was torn to pieces, before Isis collected them and reassembled them, and one for himself. Will Khufu not follow the tradition? He is, after all, King of Upper and Lower Egypt, and a symbol of all the provinces.

Could it not be, then, that the Great Pyramid bears no functional relation to any historical tradition, and is to be regarded as a secular memorial, an enduring monument by which Khufu's people will remember him after he is dead? A cartouche in the wall of the highest of the five tiered chambers above the Upper Chamber says (according to a workman who has seen it and informed me): "Wonderful is the White Crown of Khufu" (meaning the crown of Upper Egypt). It is common knowledge that Khufu refers to the Great Pyramid as *"Khut"* or "Glory" – could not this "Glory" be an expression of his temporal power, and does it not tower to a height of 480 feet over the desert solely to subjugate all visible nature from the east to west?

For ten years, I must admit, I thought this interpretation to be the most likely. There was one main objection, of course. No matter what the priests say – and they have an axe to grind – Khufu cannot be a tyrant. He is a god, after all, and all his speculations are therefore divine. And would a man as progressive as he evidently is spend twenty-nine years in subjecting so many of his people to so egoistic a task? Would a man whose concern for social justice is to be seen everywhere yield so totally to the pomps and vanities of temporal power? I did not think so. And, as subsequent events have shown, I am sure I have been proved right.

Perhaps, then, there are economic reasons? Perhaps Khufu conceived of the operation as a convenient means of ensuring full employment while at the same time completing the necessary task of building what he would regard as his secular tomb? As evidence for this there is the convention, which has been consistently upheld throughout the last sixteen years, that the annual shift of three months which coincides with the inundation of the Nile should be devoted exclusively to the peasants, who would otherwise be idle.

But if so, are there not more constructive ways of obtaining full employment than by building a Great Pyramid merely for the sake of building it? Throughout the twenty-two provinces in our land one could devise dozens of projects which would not only absorb all our labour, both skilled and unskilled, but which would furthermore benefit all sections of our people materially, and raise their standard of living. And if so, why the necessity for so vast and delicate an organisation based on the principle of saving time?

The whole organisation of this project suggests that it has a purpose. Yet an economic interpretation of this project suggests that it has no purpose. And furthermore, if the Great Pyramid is purely economic in its conception, then Khufu himself cannot believe it has a purpose. And who can believe in a purpose if Khufu, the highest authority, who we all know is a god, does not believe in one?

But there is another possibility. Perhaps Khufu believed in the spirit world and the *ka* when he began this project, before he became the god that all now worship. There is some doubt as to the exact year in which he first closed the temples, but most agree that it was some time after the first block of the Great Pyramid was laid. If so, then perhaps he intended the Great Pyramid to have a religious purpose when he began this project, and has subsequently lost interest.

There is some evidence for this. First, although he is officially supposed to make frequent tours of inspection throughout our land, no one I know has ever seen him. He is reputed to remain remote from us in the capital, Memphis, and, surrounded by his scribes, to direct this project from the seclusion of his palace there. Everyone quakes at the mere mention of his name and hastens to praise his glory, yet no one has had the slightest confirmation that he is remotely interested in our work. Indeed, were it not blasphemous and seditious to suggest it openly, one might reasonably suppose that he does not exist, that he is an invention on the part of the Pyramid Committee. I personally am inclined to believe in his existence, for the Pharaoh-tradition has now, so our historians tell us, reached the Fourth Dynasty since King Aha (Menes) united Upper and Lower Egypt, and in view of the weight of the past, no matter how clandestine the Pyramid Committee might be, our land could not change suddenly from a Kingdom into a Republic without anyone among the middle and lower classes knowing anything about it.

The fact remains, however: if he does exist, no one I know has seen him. Somewhere he bears the responsibility of the highest command, but where? On the forbidden western side of the Great Pyramid? In Memphis? No one I know knows for sure. And just because no one seems to have seen him, he would not, it might be argued, attract attention when he makes his visits of inspection. But is this likely? Would not such a visit of inspection be regarded as a State occasion – would he not be accompanied by his Pyramid Committee and follow the proud fingers of the Committee members as they explain the minute detail with which they have carried out his instructions?

In any event there has been no such occasion. Word would soon get round if there had. And this in itself suggests that he has lost interest. Moreover it has been rumoured that the chief architect, Mirabu, has died, and that his replacement has become rather slapdash of late. I myself have seen no visible evidence of the blocks failing to fit – it is not my job to watch the keying in – and I have heard no rumours to that effect, but half a millimetre would be sufficient proof. And half a millimetre cannot be detected with the naked eye, and the mathematicians are not sociable men. The enthusiasm of the masons and the engineers, of the mathematicians and the architects has not changed, but the crucial question is, have their measurements changed?

There is, however, one major objection to this interpretation. If Khufu exists, and if he has in fact lost interest in the Great Pyramid, why has the organisation and the labour been allowed to continue unchecked as regards its timing? Is it not inconceivable that a man as just as Khufu actually consents to our being merely the anachronism of his will?

Then there is the matter of the huge human-faced lion[5] that has recently gone up out of blocks left over from the Great Pyramid and existing rock. No one knows what this means. A huge face looking to the east must be the Sun-god. But Khufu did not take the name of Ra and opposed the priests of the Sun-god. I have never seen Khufu but I have seen the small statue shown to me in Abydos, which is minute – less than a little finger's length. It is impossible to say whether the rock-face bears Khufu's features but it is possible that it does. Does it show Khufu as Sun-god? Does it show Khufu saying "I am the Sun-god" and asserting his own divinity while watching the rising of Ra? I am now getting into difficult, seditious terrain. Suffice it to say that there has been a lot of speculation among the pyramid-workers as to what the rock-face means and all agree that it actually compounds the mystery at Giza rather than solves it.

In all these suppositions I have failed to mention one vital consideration. What if Khufu should die before the Great Pyramid is finished? Has he bargained for this possible eventuality which would deprive the Great Pyramid of any significance it may have as a tomb? For if he were to die tomorrow, he would probably have to be buried in an ordinary *mastaba* – no one of Khufu's rank can be laid to rest in an incomplete tomb – and, shape and all, the Great Pyramid would have to be abandoned to the elements, unless Khufu's successor were to decide to take over the project for himself.

And so I conclude that the Great Pyramid defies all purpose and meanings. Does this mean that it has no purpose or meaning? All that can be said with certainty is that all this daily organisation and endeavour does not appear to be justified by the purpose and value of the work. But I would go further than that. In fact I would go so far as to maintain that the Great Pyramid would appear to be futile. We are all enslaved to it, yet no one seems to know why, except for Khufu, if he exists, and I doubt whether even he knows, now.

IV

I had my suspicions very early on in this project, but I was unwilling to acknowledge this conclusion. Those were early days, and I assumed there must be some cryptic purpose behind the operation which I did not fully comprehend. I told myself that all this would become clear when the Great Pyramid was finished, and I used to speculate, over my evening drink, as to how the final revelation would come. Would it come in a blinding flash that would leave me thrillingly aglow, or would it come quietly and calmly, perhaps making me a little angry at my stupidity and blindness in not perceiving the answer sooner? But the years dragged by, and the Great Pyramid showed few signs of being finished, and I became impatient.

Then, ten years ago, I determined to find out what it was all for. Someone must know, I argued. I could not expect an audience with

Khufu himself – that would be hoping for too much – but there was a chance that the Pyramid Committee might know. And if they did not know they might be able to find out, they might be able to approach Khufu. So I determined to contact the Pyramid Committee, and that meant going to the Directorate of Publicity, for everyone knows that the only contact with the Pyramid Committee is through Publicity.

Of course I told no one of the action I proposed to take. I flattered myself that I knew my colleagues, my fellow-officials, too well for that. They did not seem to be given to speculation, as I was, and being veritable pillars of society their replies would have been all too predictable. Without exception, they would have been shocked. "Don't interfere," some would have said. "Khufu knows best." Or else: "Worry about your compounds and leave Khufu to worry about the rest." Or: "You mustn't criticise the Committee – the Committee knows what it's doing." But behind their discouragement there would have been a fear: "If you're not careful, Publicity will report you to the Committee." For although Khufu is just, it is well known that he shows no mercy to "rebels who seek to undermine our society". They can be imprisoned for sedition or blasphemy, and what could be more anti-social than to question the whole basis of society here at Giza, the purpose of the Great Pyramid? I was aware of all this, but I had to know. I must confess that I went to Publicity in some trepidation.

The Director of Publicity is of course as much in the dark as the rest of us, and because of his position he is not unnaturally especially sensitive to the question of sedition. Not unnaturally he tried to discourage me. He even went to great lengths to show me all the official slogans in the hopes that my communication would not be necessary. "There is no authority but Khufu." I already knew that. "There is brotherhood before the Great Pyramid." That was of no assistance. "There has been no war since Perabsen." With all due respect, I could not understand how that might be relevant. And so on. At length, however, he reluctantly accepted my short memorandum and agreed to send it through the normal channels to the Pyramid Committee.

For the next few weeks I waited in hope, though I was half afraid that my action might be deemed seditious. Nothing happened. The weeks became months, and a year passed. But still nothing happened.

There was nothing I could do to expedite the matter. That would have been most unwise in view of the gravity of my inquiry. So I waited in patience and continued to speculate over my evening drink, and another year passed, and then another, and another.

Eventually I gave up hope of obtaining an answer. My memorandum has been lost, I would tell myself, or else it is waiting in some in-tray beneath a huge stack of papers relating to more immediate problems, the organisation of this project for example. Or perhaps the Pyramid Committee had read my inquiry and deliberately decided that it should receive no answer. Anyhow, as time went on I almost forgot that I had inquired in the first place. In fact I waited ten years.

Then, this morning, quite out of the blue, a servant knocked on my office door and announced that he had been sent by the Director of Publicity. Would I go to Publicity straight away. Even as I stood up, wondering at the urgency of this request, I thought with a sudden hope: 'Perhaps my answer has come.' I hurried excitedly to Publicity, and the Director gravely handed me a large heavy envelope which read: TO THE SUPERINTENDENT AND CONTROLLER OF COMPOUNDS FROM THE PYRAMID COMMITTEE. It was a direct personal communication, and judging by the bulk the Pyramid Committee had replied at some length. This was worth waiting for. Shaking and trembling I tore out the thick papyrus parchment paper and read eagerly: MAN NEEDS THE GREAT PYRAMID. That was all.

The Director of Publicity had done his job. He had other business that required his attention, and he was not going to compromise himself by engaging in a discussion of the riddle. He merely shrugged and said, "The Pyramid Committee always act for the best."

And so I returned to my office bitterly disappointed, and sat down and tried to puzzle the riddle out. Was it a joke – perhaps an official rebuke for my impertinence in asking – or was it a serious reply? The more I pondered, the more I began to suspect that it was in fact a serious reply. I did not think that the Pyramid Committee would jest about a matter of such importance both to them and to Khufu, not to me as a government official. That in itself would be seditious. In that case, what did it mean?

And so I proceeded to reinterpret the interpretations I had tentatively put forward, acting on the assumption that the tone of the missive was serious. I could rule out the religious interpretation for a start. And of the secular interpretations, I could no longer regard the Great Pyramid as a monument to Khufu's worldly power. What was left? The economic interpretation.

To my horror, I began to realise that the economic interpretation might fit the riddle. Why does man need the Great Pyramid? I asked. Evidently because he cannot do without it. Why can't he do without it? The answers began to present themselves. Because the wages are high and he has to subsist. Because work averts boredom. Because his life would be empty without it. Perhaps because all that the Great Pyramid represents has become a habit.

And then I began to have a glimpse of what the Pyramid Committee might mean. "There has been no war since Perabsen" – there is certainly no need to conscript us for military service by using the work here as a form of physical discipline or preparation for fighting battles. Was the Great Pyramid, then, merely a means of channelling off man's peace-time energies? In that case the senselessness of the project was appalling, and neither of my original objections had been answered: why so unconstructive a way of ensuring full employment, and why so time-conscious an organisation?

Nevertheless, there seemed no escaping the conclusion that there was no specific purpose in the construction of the Great Pyramid, save for the incidental purpose that it (allegedly) contained a tomb; the only purpose was to consume man's economic effort.

I was sure of this solution now, as far as one can ever be sure, assuming that the riddle was not intended as a joke, and I immediately began to protest to myself. Man does not need the Great Pyramid, not if he has educated himself to use his leisure profitably. In which case the Great Pyramid is nothing more than a necessary nuisance. Man is not primarily an economic unit in a system. Working for money so debilitates a man that he is too tired to use his leisure profitably. Man ought not to need the Great Pyramid, and Khufu and the Pyramid Committee have based their project on a false view of man. Are Khufu and the Pyramid Committee so out of touch with realities?

And so, after twenty-nine years I have become a rebel. Since this morning I have become so disillusioned with this whole project that I do not think I can ever bear to face the Pyramid-centred conventions of our society again. For one thing, the chief topic of conversation here is the progress of the work, and introductions at social gatherings are invariably accompanied by the question, "What job are you doing on the Great Pyramid?" For another thing, it is the accepted code at social gatherings to invoke Horus, Osiris and Ra, for in spite of the predicament of the priests it is still considered blasphemous to say a word against our national religion, and most of the officials and workers here at Giza still believe that the Great Pyramid has a religious meaning. But I know better, now.

What should I do? Should I tender my resignation to the Director of Departures tomorrow? It would do me no good. I would merely be replaced. One of Publicity's slogans says, "Here no one is indispensable save Khufu", and there are plenty of capable men waiting to be promoted to my position. And then I would have to apply for another job, and I would not be paid one half of what I am earning now, and there would be no tax exemptions. Furthermore, in view of my long service on the Great Pyramid I should have to state the reasons for my resignation in a memorandum, and everyone knows that all memoranda addressed to the Directorate of Departures find their way to the Pyramid Committee through Publicity. And whereas it took the Pyramid Committee ten years to reply to an official inquiry, it might take them only ten minutes to associate my unofficial inquiry with my official resignation, and they might reasonably prefer a charge of sedition against me.

But even though my resignation would do me no good, I would still resign as a protest against the pointlessness of this project if I thought that my act might influence others in our society. However, I am all too aware that my act might have no influence whatsoever. The others are very much on their guard against rebels – in twenty-nine years I have failed to find one kindred spirit – and their attitude is, "If you don't like it, get out of it."

So I shall not resign. Moreover, I do not think I could bring myself to resign, not because I need the Great Pyramid, but because the conundrum it poses has fascinated me for so long that it is now, as it were, part of me. And even though I now feel I am groping towards a certainty, following the communication I received this morning from the Pyramid Committee, I am not absolutely certain why it was intended that man should need the Great Pyramid. Perhaps my interpretation was wrong and man has a non-economic need for the Great Pyramid? One that I have not seen or understood? For all my disillusion, I shall endure to see it completed in the hope that every side of its futile riddle will become clear.

But although the only sane conclusion about the Great Pyramid is a pessimistic one, I do not regard myself as a pessimist. Though I have no religious belief – national religions come and go just as prophets come and go – there are experiences beyond the economic experiences that I enjoy every day. Round the Great Pyramid men laugh and hope for love and choose their futures – men develop their talents and strive and give themselves to the texture of the hard, clear evening sun on the palms by the river. And one can at least be certain of those moments – admiring the universe (as I often do) one can almost forget the primordial symbol of the tomb that (reputedly) towers above all. And perhaps in future times, perhaps in five thousand years from now, men who know the answers will gaze at the finished work and will see it as a monument to our senseless hope and baffled wonderings.

8 June 1963;[6] revised Feb 2005

Editor's notes and footnotes:

"Rainer Stadelmann, in his study of the reigns of the early pyramid builders, concludes that, like his father Sneferu (i.e. Snefru), Khufu reigned longer than the 23 years given him in the Turin Papyrus, compiled some 1,400 years later. Even with a reign of 30 to 32 years, the estimated combined mass of 2,700,000cu.m (95,350,000cu.ft) for his pyramid, causeway, two temples, satellite pyramid, three queens' pyramids and officials' *mastaba*s, means that Khufu's builders had to set in place a staggering 230cu.m (8,122cu.ft) of stone per day, a rate of one average size block every two or three minutes in a ten-hour day."

Mark Lehner, *The Complete Pyramids*, p.108.

Between 2011 and 2015 a French team of archaeologists found evidence that the 2.3 million stone blocks used in the Great Pyramid were quarried at Tur on the east coast of the Gulf of Suez (where submerged boulders that formed an anchorage have been found) and shipped from Sinai downriver to a port at Wadi al-Jarf on the west coast of the Gulf of Suez (where papyri fragments detailing the operation and stone anchors have been discovered), and then transported across the desert to Giza as described in paragraph 2 of the official's account. There was a report on this corroborating evidence in *The Times*, 23 May 2015, 'Pyramid stones that took a Nile cruise'.

Herodotus wrote that 100,000 men worked on the Great Pyramid three months at a time for 20 years. Archaeologists such as Petrie found this convincing. (It has recently been conjectured that there were only 25,000–30,000 workers in all, but this is speculation.)

Ancient Egyptians measured length in terms of cubits, i.e. arm lengths (from elbow to thumb-tip), handbreadths (measured on the back across the knuckles) or *setjat*s (100 cubits square, approximately two-thirds of an acre). Weight was measured in *deben*s (a standard weight of 93.3 grams though some weights from the Old and Middle Kingdoms appear to have been in units of 12 to 14 grams and sometimes 27 grams). In modern equivalents one metric ton – the Continental tonne – is 1m grams and 1,000 kilos; the English ton is 907,184.7 grams and 907.1847 kilos. All Egyptian measurements have been translated into modern equivalents.

1. Mirabu is mentioned in *Khufu's Wisdom*, a historically researched novel by Egypt's Nobel prizewinner Naguib Mahfouz.
2. Now 138.75m as the capstone is missing.
3. The highest until the Empire State Building completed in New York in 1931.
4. Orion's belt.
5. The Sphinx.
6. Nicholas Hagger, *Awakening to the Light*, p.36, 8 June 1963: "I wrote *The Great Pyramid* first version quickly because a lodger was coming

to take over my room at 6. I wrote it between 4.30 and 6. Then the lodger decided not to come. Now for the second version at 7.30."

The Meaning and Purpose of the Great Pyramid

I

I can hardly contain my excitement. I have just had the most thrilling news. I have actually met someone from the Pyramid Committee who personally read my questions about the mystery of the Great Pyramid which I submitted nearly eleven years ago. I met him by accident, of course, for such an important meeting could not happen by design.

I had just finished work for the day and I looked in on a reception to mark thirty years' service on the part of one of the building managers. I had half wondered if Prince Hemiunu would be there, but he wasn't. As I entered, an attendant took me to one side and said, "You may like to meet our guest of honour, who's from the Pyramid Committee. He's in that room. Follow me."

I couldn't believe my luck. Quivering with excitement I followed the attendant through to a cool room where a distinguished-looking man with a noble face and upright bearing stood, holding a drink in a pottery wine-cup. He looked like an official, he had great presence, and immediately put me at my ease. "I saw your name on the guest list when I arrived. You wrote to the Pyramid Committee some while back?"

I nodded, a bit tongue-tied before such an important man and noting that he had identified me and presumably asked the attendant to introduce me to him as soon as I arrived.

"I remember your papyrus letter. The reply was delegated to one of our scribes, but I particularly remember your main question. It's one that I've often asked myself, what the purpose of this vast building is. But as you have yourself done such excellent service on the Great Pyramid, I can let you into a secret." He lowered his voice and looked around to make sure he was not being overheard. "I'm sorry to be the bearer of bad tidings, but I can tell you, in confidence, that Khufu is dead."

"Dead?" I gasped.

He nodded. "Exactly when he died I don't know, but I believe he's been dead some while. News of his death was hushed up so that the transfer of power could happen smoothly. The pyramid-workers do not know, but as you are an official with an important position I feel I owe it to you to tell you. At one time his successor was supposed to have been his oldest son Kawab, but as all know, he was unfortunately killed in tragic circumstances. It's his son Djedef who's succeeded him. He has taken the name of Ra and will subordinate himself to Ra. He will build his pyramid away from Giza, I'm not sure where."

I was still reeling at the momentous news of Khufu's demise.

"So where has Khufu been buried?" I eventually asked.

"I don't know. No one on the Pyramid Committee knows. Not here. Perhaps in a *mastaba*, near his mortuary temple," he conjectured. "He could not be buried in the Upper Chamber of the Great Pyramid."

I had suspected as much as his sarcophagus is standing empty in the Upper Chamber. Ever since I climbed the ramp between the high corbelled walls of the great gallery of the Great Pyramid under guise of looking for one of my workers, and saw the red-granite sarcophagus being dragged in place and the walls and ceiling being built round it, I suspected this. For first the sarcophagus is wider than the entrance to the chamber, and all I have asked have denied that the entrance was subsequently made smaller. Secondly, Khufu's body must be dragged in the sarcophagus through wailing crowds to its final resting-place. But the red-granite sarcophagus could not possibly have been dragged up the steep incline to its final place – even if the entrance had been wide enough to take it; it could only have been placed there in the course of the building. And there are three chambers – one leading downwards underground and two above ground, one of which (the Upper Chamber) has five rooms above it. I myself have seen the inscription on the wall of the highest room: "Wonderful is the White Crown of Khufu", referring of course to the Upper Kingdom and not the Lower Kingdom, which is represented by a Red Crown.

"Even in Khufu's lifetime the decision was taken not to use the Great Pyramid as a tomb," the noble official told me. "One day there was a dreadful ear-splitting groan from the massive ceiling blocks of the

Upper Chamber, each weighing between 3.5m and 6.6m *debens*,[1] and a great crack appeared. The noise was heard by many of the construction workers, who rushed in to see what had happened. It was felt that the Pyramid might be unsafe – that it might come crashing down – and the decision was taken within twenty-four hours by the Pyramid Committee that Khufu, whose face will stare from the great lion-shape[2] at the eastern horizon for ever, should not be interred in a monument that could collapse, leaving it open prey for tomb-robbers."

I was staggered. After so much planning and care, it was inconceivable that the Great Pyramid could have cracked up and that it had to be abandoned. There must have been dreadful consequences for such an obvious error.

"What happened to those whose calculations did not anticipate this cracking?" I asked. "Who was accountable? Were officials blamed? What happened to them? Were there executions?"

"Oh no," he said. "This work defies the forces of nature, it's the biggest project the world has ever known. The miracle is that such size and grandeur is possible, not that cracks appear in it. Besides, the calculations were approved – not done, mark you, but approved – by none other than the vizier Prince Hemiunu and his chief architect Mirabu, and they – although I have never seen them, you understand – are in Khufu's court. No, nothing happened to anybody. That is not to say that errors were not noticed and noted, and have not been written by scribes on their records. Promotions may well be blocked as a result of that episode. I am not saying blame was not allocated. Only time will tell as the consequences slowly unfold. For round the Great Pyramid, as you well know, there is a culture of precision, meticulousness, accuracy, and nothing untoward can happen without grave consequences at a future date. And I can tell you…." He dropped his voice confidentially. "Despite what I have just said – which, you understand, is the official line – some officials were rounded up and incarcerated on the forbidden western side of the Great Pyramid where even you are not allowed to go, and they are…. Not mistreated, for they have deserved their treatment. Punished, that is the word. They are punished every minute of every hour of every day, in ways which are too dreadful even to bring to mind. But if you are asked, you now know the official line."

So it's astonishing. All this planning and organising and building for twenty-nine years and putting-on of the casing blocks so the whole Pyramid shines in the morning sun of Khepri, the midday sun of Ra and the evening sun of Atum – and the project has been so badly bungled that the Pyramid can no longer be used for the purpose for which it was built. And no one knows where Khufu's mummified body rests. Perhaps this is on security grounds, to keep it safe from tomb-robbers.

"So that's why the subterranean burial chamber is unfinished," I said.

"Yes, the two upper chambers had been more or less finished. Work stopped straightaway, nothing more was done in the subterranean chamber. The idea that Khufu would be buried in the Great Pyramid was abandoned, but the Great Pyramid had to be completed because Khufu wanted it. In fact, there was a problem because of the cracking. It was hard to persuade some of the working teams to continue. I can tell you now he's dead, but his daughter visited each member of the Pyramid Committee to plead with us to push the work on and compel the gangs to get it finished. She actually – seriously – prostituted herself among some members of the Pyramid Committee – not me, of course – to persuade them to continue the work. She offered her 'services' to anyone who would take the decision to push the work along. Khufu was still alive, and her prostituting herself was apparently done with his knowledge and blessing. Some members took her up on her offer with great enthusiasm and complied with her wishes. Of course, they paid lip service to the religious gloss put on her actions, that she was embodying the divine god and spreading his gift of immortality to the Pyramid Committee. But that is how the Great Pyramid is so near completion."

The news about Khufu's daughter was immensely shocking and incredible. I still can't believe it. That she should have offered herself to members of the Pyramid Committee with Khufu's knowledge.... I am dumbfounded. The great Khufu's daughter – Pharaoh's daughter, the daughter of a god – a prostitute! It is too dreadful to contemplate.

I did not know what to say. My mind was reeling. In all my calculations I had never dared to think that the great Khufu could be so self-serving and ruthless towards his own daughter, so corrupt.

"So why," I asked at length, "if the decision had already been taken to abandon this Great Pyramid as a tomb, did Khufu set such importance on completing the work, subjecting his daughter to such humiliation?"

"Because he was a god," my informant said simply, clutching his clay wine-flagon. "Here in Giza there was a local divine cult of Khufu, as we all know. Khufu did not take the name Ra because he had replaced Ra. It wasn't Ra who illumined Khufu's *akh* (his spiritual soul so he was a Shining One). Khufu himself received the power that illumined him, he was the *akh* that illumined our *akh*s. That's why that stone lion's been built...."

I thought of the massive stone lion that had gone up in recent times out of superfluous blocks that were not needed now the Great Pyramid was nearing completion. I had often wondered what it represented.

"The lion has Khufu's face looking calmly at the eastern rising of Khepri, the morning sun, and also Ra at midday and Atum, the evening sun. The lion is associated with mountains and the rising of the Sun-god. Khufu, '*Khut*', 'Glory', is looking towards the east, and even the rising sun Khepri and the midday sun Ra acknowledge his glory as being above theirs. The stone lion represents the deification of Khufu. Khufu is the *akh*, and our *akh*s shine from his."

Again I was reeling. So the stone lion's face *is* Khufu's. No one was sure of that. Khufu forbad statues of himself, and there are no images of him except illegal ones, like one only a finger's height[3] and wearing the crown of Lower Egypt which was shown to me when I visited the Temple at Abydos.[4]

"And the Great Pyramid?" I asked. "How does that fit in with Khufu's deification?"

"The Great Pyramid is covered in polished limestone casing stones to symbolise the *akh*. The whole thing is a temple to the *akh*, and living people wearing masks can go into the chambers and act out scenes about becoming an *akh*. That is the secret the priests keep, the re-enactment of rituals involving becoming an *akh* which guarantees eternity and an immortal life in the Eternal Sunshine."

I tried to make sense of what he had told me. "The answer I had from the Pyramid Committee was: 'Man needs the Great Pyramid.'"

"The answer you received was of course the interpretation of one particular scribe and has the status of one man's opinion. It was not the view of the Pyramid Committee, who were naturally informed of the reply. For nothing goes out from their offices without all members of the Pyramid Committee being apprised of every word that is being said. Nevertheless, the scribe was right. Man needs guidance to become an *akh* so he can follow Khufu into the Eternal Sunshine. Khufu has been saying, 'Work for me, build my pyramid, and you can be with me in the after-life.'"

I was stunned. So ever since the cracking of the stone in the Upper Chamber, the Great Pyramid had been a cenotaph, an empty tomb – and a temple for rituals about becoming an *akh*. That is what I had spent nearly thirty years of my life pondering.

"How did you learn that?" I asked. "Who was your source? Khufu himself?"

"Oh no. No one on the Pyramid Committee has ever seen, let alone spoken to Khufu. We don't live in Memphis. I'm not at liberty to say where we live but like you we receive our instructions from a higher authority."

That in itself was a stunning new idea, that the Pyramid Committee is itself under another authority in the chain of command.

"No, this came from one of the Pyramid Committee who asked Khufu's daughter why it was so important to finish the building of the Great Pyramid. That is what she is reported to have replied. I believe the story, but I do agree, it's not a very good source."

"How many of you are there on the Pyramid Committee?" I asked. "I've heard some say, nine."

"It's more than that," he smiled.

"Three hundred? I've heard some say three hundred. As many as that?"

"Oh, I'm afraid I'm not allowed to disclose that. It's privileged information."

"Can I become a member of the Pyramid Committee?"

At that moment the attendant returned and said, before my informant could answer, that the construction workers awaited him, and now I stood back and bowed to allow him to be led to the reception.

I followed holding my clay flagon of wine and stood at the back of a crowded room, and I did not manage to speak to my informant again. I listened to his few words of faint praise for the worker being honoured – my informant clearly did not know him – and turned to speak to another worker who approached me with a question about his compound; and when I looked back the member of the Pyramid Committee, my informant, had completely vanished. I could not find anyone who even knew his name.

II

So now my mind is racing. After nearly thirty years, do I at last have all the answers?

First of all, do I believe what I have been told? Was my Pyramid Committee member a reliable source? And was his source, Khufu's daughter, reliable? And had any member of the Pyramid Committee actually met Khufu's daughter, as he had said? And why had he volunteered so much information about the meaning and purpose of the Great Pyramid when he wouldn't tell me the number of the Pyramid Committee, which to me was far less important than the State secrets he revealed about Khufu's death, Djedef's succession, Khufu's daughter's prostituting herself on Khufu's instructions – I still cannot get my head round that idea – and the function of the Great Pyramid, that it is an empty *akh*, a blaze of Light. Now it has casing blocks on most of it, which reflects the sun, I can see the logic of what he told me.

In all my searches for a rational explanation over nearly thirty years, I overlooked the possibility that the Great Pyramid was an *akh* for ritual re-enactments by priests wearing masks of gods. So why the blocked air-channels? To absorb some of the candle-smoke – torch-light – these rituals might generate? Are they lighting aids, with deep vents so that those taking part in the rituals do not suffocate? And yet surely the channels, which are blocked with stops of a little finger's length[5] – as I've been told by one of the construction workers – cannot help the ventilation or flow of air for the living in the Upper Chamber with the red-granite sarcophagus?

I keep thinking again and again, man needs the Great Pyramid to become an *akh* and join Khufu in the Eternal Sunshine. I know that the true Ra is supposed to be an inner power all can find behind their closed eyes, although this is supposed to be given by the high priest of Ra as an intermediary and cannot be known directly without the hierarchy. Khufu himself is the Shining Ra, and his Great Pyramid, now it's encased, shines in the morning sun to his glory as the casing reflects the sun's rays. It is aglow in the morning and every sunset; on whatever side the sun is, it reflects and shines.

Yet when Khufu set out to build the Great Pyramid he did not have it in his mind that it would be an *akh*. Had the ceiling of the Upper Chamber not cracked, that room might have been his tomb – that is the implication of what the member of the Pyramid Committee told me. Or would Khufu have been buried in the unfinished underground chamber and not above ground? I think again, why does man need the Great Pyramid?

Furthermore, when he decided not to be buried in the Great Pyramid, we are asked to believe, Khufu offered all men a chance to share his immortality. But until the ceiling cracked there was no plan to share it. He would have been buried there, I repeat, and the entrance to his tomb would have been sealed. So of how much value is a ritual that was a kind of after-thought, after the chance and arbitrary cracking of the Upper Chamber ceiling, not – never – a part of the meticulous plan for this operation?

The more I have thought about my meeting with my informant, the more I have begun to wonder if it was a blind. The attendant showed me into a private room. The member of the Pyramid Committee had seen my name on the guest list. Perhaps the whole story was an elaborate concoction to put me off the scent, following my letter? Perhaps Khufu is not dead, perhaps Djedef is not the present Pharaoh. And – I think this is quite likely as it is so shocking and unbelievable – perhaps the news of Khufu's daughter prostituting herself is a complete fabrication, a plant to lure me into repeating it so I can be arrested for sedition. Why, if Khufu is still alive and the Great Pyramid is his tomb, the story that it's an empty *akh* is itself seditious. Perhaps the approach to me was an instance of sinister Pyramid-Committee misinformation? Perhaps it is planned that I should be exiled for my question? Can my informant be relied on?

I now think I will be well advised not to repeat what he told me, for my own safety. On reflection, I think I will be well advised to forget everything I was told as it is too dangerous to share the news, given the organisation that has gone into producing a society round the Great Pyramid whose beliefs are so different from what the member of the Pyramid Committee told me.

And so now my excitement has cooled and I am aware that I am at odds with all those I have worked with for nearly thirty years. I know more than is good for me. And yet what I know is essentially without evidence or proof; it is at the level of a leak from the Pyramid Committee, which is extremely difficult to verify. If I were rash enough to ask any of my fellow workers on this project, "Is it true Khufu has died?" I would be reported immediately for questioning the basis of our long presence here – which is that we are doing Khufu's will and serving him, which is an honour seeing that he is a god.

Privately I have always doubted that Khufu was a god. If I were to say to one of my colleagues, "Khufu's dead and so we don't have to pretend to believe he was a god any more," and if it turned out that Khufu is still alive, I might disappear for ever.

So if I keep quiet about the revelation I received today, what do I privately think of it? I am being asked to believe that Khufu believed that the purpose of life is to become an *akh*, a Shining One, that can dwell with him in the Eternal Sunshine. If the purpose of life is to become an *akh*, I can see when you are *not* an *akh* the Great Pyramid may seem to have no purpose; whereas when you *are* an *akh*, the Great Pyramid may seem to have a purpose. The purpose of the Great Pyramid depends on one's perception. I can see that one's perception may reflect the level of truth one is at. And so, before one becomes an *akh*, the Great Pyramid may appear futile. But after one has become an *akh*, the Great Pyramid may seem to be a House of Eternity.

But I must stress, all this is theoretical. For I am not sure that I have been told the truth and I exercise some private scepticism about what I should believe. Should I be a fan of the Great Pyramid and an enthusiastic supporter of Khufu? Have the Pyramid Committee all become *akh*s, are they illumined Shining Ones? Is everyone on the Pyramid

Committee illuminated? And when an official becomes an *akh*, does he still manipulate those below him? Is *akh*-hood a measure of inner saintliness or a kind of club which the Pyramid Committee join, which allows exclusive access to secret knowledge and which they use to outmanoeuvre or even destroy those slaves below them who do their bidding for nearly thirty years?

And so now I am even more confused than before. I have been told the answer to the question that has haunted me for nearly thirty years, but only a part of myself believes the answer. The rest of me – the majority of me – is incredulous, even sceptical. I need to consult a priest; preferably a high priest. Yet the very act of discussing what I have been told with a religious official could – if he reported me (as priests and high priests are known to do) – land me with a charge of sedition.

And so I have decided that I am neither going to believe nor disbelieve what the member of the Pyramid Committee told me. I will act quietly on the assumption that it is true, and will try to progress my becoming an *akh*, just in case what I was told is right. But I will not attach any great significance to my progress to *akh*-hood in case I have been told wrong, so I can avoid a trap that might have been set for me. In short, I shall continue as if I had not been told the answer to the question I asked nearly eleven years ago.

And in the evening, as I look up at the towering Great Pyramid that glints in the evening sun and throws its shadow towards the massive stone lion with Khufu's face, I shall think, as I take my evening drink, that it may be a tomb that towers over all and that it may also be a hollow sham; that it may be a temple for rituals about *akh*-hood and that it may also be an abandoned consequence of a bungle; that it may be a gateway – the gateway – to immortal life thanks to Khufu's questing knowledge and profound humanitarian feelings for his subjects, and that it may also be a botched job with ceiling stones that have cracked under the massive weight they bear, excused with tales of religious significance that may be no more than public-relations spin. I shall at one and the same time admire the meticulous calculations of the mathematicians which have raised this monument, the highest in the world, and deride the failure which omitted to take account of the weight the ceiling stones bear, which got wrong the durability of load-bearing stones.

And then I shall look above it at the vast sky which is also a tomb over all of us who are alive such a short while, and down at the sand that will cover us. I shall look up at the sun which warms my cheeks and burns my back, and I shall imagine I am an *akh* of Light in Eternal Sunshine which is always temperate, balmy and pleasant, and that all my uncertainties and doubts and rational questionings have been put aside as surely as if I had spread a cloth on the hot sand and laid myself out, closed my eyes and given myself to the warm, life-giving sun. I used to think that the sky, like the Great Pyramid, had no meaning or purpose in itself, but only what humans invested in it. But now I shall look at the sky and the temporal sun and invest them with a possible meaning and purpose – that they are scenery for my growth to an *akh* which will take me from this copy of a temporal sun to a greater reality, Eternal Sunshine; a meaning and purpose I have not been aware of until my chance meeting today. And I shall think this without reference to Khufu. And although everyone continues to praise Khufu's humane qualities, I shall think, privately, that he was in fact a tyrant who was in effect saying to us, "Work for me and be with me in Paradise" – and I shall say quietly, to myself: "I prefer the Paradise I consider when I am alone, after I have finished work and wander off and perceive through my *akh* and become one with the desert sand and sky and with sunshine that is both temporal and eternal."

8, 16, 20 February 2005[6]

Editor's notes and footnotes:

Diodorus Siculus maintained that Khufu was not buried in the Great Pyramid. Herodotus tells the story of Khufu's daughter prostituting herself to get the building of the Great Pyramid finished. Prince Hemiunu, the vizier, was Snefru's grandson and the building manager entrusted by Khufu with the building of the Great Pyramid.

1. In fact, 50–80m tonnes. During the Old Kingdom 1 *deben* was 12 to 14 grams. At 12 grams per *deben* 50 tonnes, i.e. 50m grams, equals

4,166,666.60 *debens*; at 14 grams per *deben* 50 tonnes, i.e. 50m grams, equals 3,571,428.5 *debens*. At 12 grams per *deben* 80 tonnes, i.e. 80m grams, equals 6,666,666.60 *debens*; at 14 grams per *deben* 80 tonnes, i.e. 80m grams, equals 5,714,285.70 *debens*.

2. The Sphinx.
3. "A finger's height", i.e. 7.5 cms.
4. Abydos had a temple from Khufu's time. Now it is occupied by a later temple which contains *bas*-reliefs carved in the reign of Seti I.
5. "A little finger's length", i.e. 7 cms or less.
6. Nicholas Hagger, *Diaries*, 8 February 2005: "In the *café* area [of Cairo airport] in front of Gate 3, extreme left front table, facing the gate, I scribbled the first two pages of 'The Solution to the Mystery of the Great Pyramid', the sequel (42 years later) to 'The Riddle of the Great Pyramid'.... A good flight and a long flying around over Heathrow (1 hour) – which allowed me to complete my revisions of 'The Riddle of the Great Pyramid'." *Diaries*, 16 February 2005: "By 6 began the sequel to 'The Riddle of the Great Pyramid' and finished it by 8.30 when I was called for supper."

Follies and Vices, and Quest Themes

List of Follies and Vices in Part One of *Selected Stories*
(F indicates folly)

from *A Spade Fresh with Mud*

1 Neck out to Sea: gluttony (abuse of alcohol), hypocrisy, infidelity, inconstancy, drunkenness, prodigality
2 Angels in a Golden Light: idealisation, betrayal, treachery; lack of good sense (F)
3 People Like Masks: egotism, confidence tricks, vanity, roguery, pursuit of wealth, obstinacy; lack of good sense (F)
4 The Need to Smash: aggressiveness, know-all superiority, self-righteousness, pretension, hubristic contentment, enmity, meanness, pedantry, shrewishness; foolish behaviour (F)
5 Rainbow Trout: self-deceit (F), self-deception (F), naïve beliefs (F)
6 *Fils* Under the Palms: pride, self-conceit, hubristic contentment, arrogance
7 A Kingdom and a Tear: manipulativeness, interference
8 A Cuckoo in Casa Pupos: envy, usurpation, snobbishness, covetousness, know-all superiority, jealousy, shrewishness, social climbing
9 Lumps Under Snow: tyrannical ruthlessness, injury, war, murder
10 Jewels of a Ruling Class: theft, revenge, acquisitiveness, burglary, corrupting worldly power, corruption, duplicity, greed, rebelliousness
11 A Villa on Cap Ferrat: extortion, fortune-hunting, money-seeking, insincerity, unscrupulousness, hedonism, hubristic contentment
12 A Liar in Paris: deception, deceit, mendacity, boastfulness, bravado, confidence tricks, lying, lust, unscrupulousness, self-interestedness, seduction, infatuation, desertion, egotistical sensuality, dishonesty, insincerity; self-deception (F), self-deceit (F), credulousness (F)
13 A Screw-Manufacturer in Business: infidelity, exploitation, corruptibility (F)
14 Yawns Under a Sepulchral Sky: lust, boredom, infatuation,

seduction, self-centredness, sloth, debauchery, nihilism, lies, discontent, excessive mourning; lack of good sense (F)

15 Pipe-Clay Breeches and Geese: posing, bravado, capriciousness; naïve beliefs (F), foolish act (F)

16 Skewered Pheasants Under a Scarlet Knife: cruelty, brutality, war, corrupting worldly power

from *A Smell of Leaves and Summer*

17 Capitalism and Mr Bluett: servitude, bullying, being domineering, strictness

18 The Director is an Idiot: self-love, self-importance, pomposity, ambition

19 An Imperial Egoist and a Car Wallah: egoism, being domineering, imperiousness, mistreatment, self-centredness, self-interestedness, shrewishness; lack of good sense (F)

from *Wheeling Bats and a Harvest Moon*

20 Angry Old Man: anger, murder, cynicism

21 A Tie in his Tea: false jokiness, trying to impress; foolish act (F)

22 The Bride and a Forgotten Joint: nun's worldliness, rebelliousness; absent-mindedness (F)

from *The Warm Glow of the Monastery Courtyard*

23 Feet on the Ground: stinginess, confidence tricks, alcoholism, exploitation, vanity, trickery, egotism, fantasies, troublemaking, swindling, hero-worship, phoniness, money-seeking

24 Aladdin's Cave and a Disgruntled Look: greed, acquisitiveness, burglary, villainy, bullying, dictatorial behaviour, threatening behaviour, troublemaking, bitterness, shadiness, self-centredness, money-seeking, thieving/stealing, robbery, swindling, miserliness, murder

25 A Chunk of Rock with a Fossil in it: childishness, egocentricity, acquisitiveness, shadiness; naïve beliefs (F), foolish behaviour (F)

26 Bacon, Eggs, Sausage and Tomato: peremptoriness, exploitation; foolish behaviour (F)

27 A Browning in Belsen: revenge, cruelty, war, persecution

28 Ry-bald Comments and a Lost Cheque: corrupting worldly power, infidelity, lust for power
29 An Important Star and a Fossil-Lady: self-importance, peremptoriness, arrogance
30 Twenty-Five Years Like a Banquet: long-windedness; absent-mindedness (F), foolish behaviour (F)
31 Past for the Best: villainy, bribery; gullibility (F)

from *In the Brilliant Autumn Sunshine*
32 A Russian Girl and a Credit Card: vanity, self-love, misjudgement, denial of principles, obstinacy, voluptuousness; lack of good sense (F), gullibility (F), eagerness to marry (F), credulousness (F), self-deception
33 A Dead Pipistrelle and Blown-Up Skyscrapers: terrorism, moral blindness, warmongering, massacres, inhumanity, hatred
34 A Spectre at the Old Boys' Feast: boastfulness, hubristic contentment; foolish behaviour (F), illusions (F)
35 A Sombre Cherry Tree and Sunflowers: rivalry, fantasies; illusions (F), self-deception (F), self-deceit (F)
36 A Tyrant and a Lie: intolerance, ruthlessness, lack of truthfulness, dictatorial behaviour, mendacity, hypocrisy, inhumanity, massacres, tyranny
37 A Coffin and a Ladybird: overbearingness, dictatorial behaviour, mistreatment; overreaching (F)
38 A Shrill "Shut Up" and Shambles: imperiousness, asperity, petulance, pretension; being domineering (F)
39 Horror After the Rave: gluttony (drug addiction), abandonment, dishonesty, lack of truthfulness
40 An Awesome Queen and Umbrella-ed Flunkeys: phoniness, self-importance, snobbishness; foolish behaviour (F)
41 Notice and a Wheel: lack of truthfulness, mercenary motives, money-seeking, greed, ruthlessness, pursuit of wealth, neglect
42 Exhausted: suicide, alcoholism, abandonment, concealment, destructiveness, prodigality, neglect
43 Fossilised Chivalry and Unknightly Yobbery: yobbishness, self-centredness, impudence

List of Quest Themes in Part Two of *Selected Stories*

(V indicates vice)

from *A Spade Fresh with Mud*

1 A Spade Fresh with Mud: confronting death in an atheistic cemetery in relation to the One (earth, rain, mud), truthfulness; bigotry (V)
2 A Crown of Thorns: loss of faith, discovery of meaning and purpose through suffering; nihilism (V), suicide (V)
3 A Gun-Runner in Danger: intense experience of the One (waves, lightning, storm), exultation; rebelliousness (V), usurpation (V)
4 A Thousand Feet and a Cage: intense experience of the One (sun, cloud, cliff, rock)
5 A Crag and Bursting Stars: experience of the One (shooting stars, universe alive); pride (V)
6 Mosquitoes in a Bamboo-Grove: enlightenment despite mosquitoes, knowing reality "for ten seconds – ten minutes"
7 A Scarlet-Robed Bedouin and a Colossus: oneness with the universe (sea, sand and sky), Colossus and meaning
8 The Portmellon Water Splash: awareness of unity (water surging across road), meaning, images of reality
9 Freedom Over the Canal: awareness of freedom
10 Chinese Flies on a Mountain: unity between man and mountain, the present dwarfed within the process of time
11 *Saké* and the Meaning of Life: opposites reconciled within unity, meaning of life

from *A Smell of Leaves and Summer*

12 A Smell of Leaves and Summer: experience of oneness of universe (blue sky, sun, green leaves) after experience of death
13 A Ladder and Quarrels at Church: loss of social meaning, and the One
14 The Clear, Shining Sunlight of Eternity: a life out of harmony with the universe, a few years in relation to the sunlight of eternity; defiance (V), anger (V)
15 Frothy Weirs and a Rising Sun: experience of Reality, the Light;

concealment (V), falsely claiming knowledge (V)

from *Wheeling Bats and a Harvest Moon*

16 Wheeling Bats and a Harvest Moon: image of direction and the One, messengers of death

17 The Sweet, Fresh Mountain Air: oneness of Nature (stream, trout, worms, sky), in harmony with Nature

18 Coughing and an Accepted Calvary: death of a good organiser, acceptance of suffering, soul and the One

from *The Warm Glow of the Monastery Courtyard*

19 The Warm Glow of the Monastery Courtyard: death and the One, image of mortality; credulousness (V), confidence tricks (V)

20 A Gardener Goes into the Fire: being confronted with death before the One; idleness (V)

21 A Lion and Clacking Sticks: death contrasted with life, oneness of history (Harold II)

22 A Headless Statue in Nettles: time has ruined an Elizabethan Hall, oneness of history (Elizabethan time)

23 Love Like a Cheek-Warming Log-Burner: image of the One warming the soul with love

24 A Soul Like Ripe Grain: death of ripe soul before the One

25 Morphine and Tears: death, soul facing reality before the One; not facing reality (V)

from *In the Brilliant Autumn Sunshine*

26 In the Brilliant Autumn Sunshine, Among a Thousand Islands: unity of the universe, a thousand islands/a thousand stories all interconnected, a quester like a boat on a sea, confirming the One; interference (V)

27 Walking on From the Harbour: death, passing into the One

28 A Sallow Octogenarian and a Slow Ambulance: confronting death, soul passing into the One; asperity (V)

29 Bluebells Between Souls: death, continuing souls and the One; exploitation (V), ambition (V)

30 New-Mown Grass: death, the soul's humility and the One

31 Fortitude Like a Navy Pullover: facing death, enduring soul before the oneness of Nature (grass, earth), the One
32 Fireworks and the One: universe alive, Nature revealing the One that permeates it; frivolity (V), blindness (V)
33 A Shell House and Plunging Gorges: soul attuned to Nature, the power of Nature (mountains, valleys, waterfalls, trees, rocks, ravines, gorges), panoramic Nature (sea, woods, sky) and hint of the One
34 Daubenton's Bats and the One: awareness of the workings of the orderly One, suppressants of what is harmful, revelation of the One; blindness (V)
35 A Study Like a Bittern-Hide: unity of the universe (grass, trees, lake) giving life a meaning, trying to glimpse the One, waiting for images
36 Shadow and Sun: unity of the universe, Death as a companion (my shadow), union of shadowy phenomena of Nature and the sun, interaction with Nature, image of the One
37 A Bat Like a Soul: the workings of the soul within the One
38 Kingfishers, Crassula and the One: oneness of Nature, all creatures catered for, a plan within Nature, the workings of the Whole, the One
39 A Fountain of Light: approaching the One through revelation, the fountain of Being which unites reason and revelation, image of the One (field, fountain, sky)
40 Paralysed Bodies and the One: the One cares for paralysed bodies, and develops their souls; bitterness (V)
41 A Dance of Death and the Dance of Life: life and death are reconciled by, and united in, the One
42 A Thousand Selves and the One: a thousand reflections of the One in stories, a thousand fragments of one person
43 The Secret of the Desert: living in the One (at oneness with desert, sand, mountains, sky), happiness through non-attachment in the here-and-now

Footnote and final thought. The reader may like to assess and list the follies and vices in the Epilogue of *Selected Stories*, bearing in mind that the two accounts from Giza are set at the beginning of the tradition of follies and vices in c.2600BC. What to one reader is shrewdness may be gullibility to another.

INDEX OF TITLES

BOOKS

O is a symbol of the world, of oneness and unity; this eye represents knowledge and insight. We publish titles on general spirituality and living a spiritual life. We aim to inform and help you on your own journey in this life.

Visit our website: http://www.o-books.com

Find us on Facebook:
https://www.facebook.com/OBooks

Follow us on Twitter: @obooks